SALLY GRATZ GARCIA

MERCY MARKOS
AND THE
BLADES OF BETRAYAL

REALM OF ARA'JA

BOOK ONE

Black Rose Writing | Texas

The author grants the final approval for this literary material.

Second printing

This is a work of fiction. Names, characters, businesses, places, events, and incidents are either the products of the author's imagination or used in a fictitious manner. Any resemblance to actual persons, living or dead, or actual events is purely coincidental.

ISBN: 978-1-68513-179-1
PUBLISHED BY BLACK ROSE WRITING
www.blackrosewriting.com

Printed in the United States of America
Suggested Retail Price (SRP) $22.95

Mercy Markos and the Blades of Betrayal is printed in Adobe Garamond Pro

*As a planet-friendly publisher, Black Rose Writing does its best to eliminate unnecessary waste to reduce paper usage and energy costs, while never compromising the reading experience. As a result, the final word count vs. page count may not meet common expectations.

This book is dedicated to my sons, Nick and Matt, and to my grandchildren, Anjelica (Jelli), Alex, Addy, and Jaycie who learned very early that their Gigi was a book pusher, and who were my first inspiration for writing this novel. And a special dedication in memory of my granddaughter, Raina. I'd like to believe she would be proud of me.

Thank you to my extensive network of family, friends, and co-workers for their support and encouragement; particularly my sister Wendy, who never stopped aggressively, and I do mean aggressively, believing in me.

Also, a huge shout-out to Kathie Giorgio, Carrie Newberry, and the workshop students at All Writers' Workplace & Workshop. I would never have finished without you.

MERCY MARKOS
AND THE
BLADES OF BETRAYAL

TITUS SERVES PIE

1945

"It is 1:00, and all is as it should be."

High Elder Jonathan Broomfield glanced at the mother-of-pearl visage of the crystal Situation Clock hovering near his desk. He was compelled to verify every announcement of time and current state of affairs made by the clock. The bothersome ching-chimey tone the clockmakers opted to use for the design annoyed him. Time and time again, he wished to chuck a shoe at the impertinent wanna-be town crier. In fact, he often took his shoe off and raised it up to take aim at the little pest. The clock realized he didn't have the heart to hurt it. Mindful of the High Elder's compassionate nature, it would glide around the large circular room in a clear taunt for him to try.

Due in part to technological and industrial progresses in the human society, many changes transpired over the course of Broomfield's 153-year tenure as High Elder of the Ara'Jaeon Ecclesia—the longest term anyone served as High Elder for the previous 1,200 years. Fatigue swept through his body and mind, and he felt every bit of his 326 years of age. Considerable trouble loomed over the earth. If he accurately interpreted the Book of Prophecies, Broomfield doubted he would live to witness the outcome. He considered himself ready to pass through the Gates of Vatek, where the mortal Ara'Jaeons crossed into immortality. However, he first needed to attend to unfinished business. It was an unfortunate business which saddened him to include the imminent appointment he arranged for that very afternoon.

The High Elder sat at his desk, empty except for a knife and a jamun fruit pie brought in by his personal assistant, Solomon Caudel, as a gift from his wife. His gaze traveled around the white office, devoid of most color except for the large marble sculpture he had commissioned years earlier. The sculpture represented the four elements. The pastel marble pieces were fitted together to form an abstract illustration of a tree blowing in the wind, as water and fire lapped at opposite sides of the trunk. The monument exemplified the entirety of not only himself, but all Ara'Jaeons—Earth, Wind, Fire, and Water.

The Mediterranean sun dazzled off the white buildings outside the window by his desk, catching his attention. Broomfield loved Nikonea City, the coastal capital of Ara'Ja. The spectacular views from the Assembly Building still enamored him. Built on a peninsula on the north coast of the island Realm of Ara'Ja, Nikonea City was flanked on the west by Thyella Bay and the Gulf of Achanés on the east. The Mediterranean Sea bordered the north. His window faced the western Thyella Bay, where a clearing in the high forested hills across the bay drew his attention. On the hilltop stood the Tray, the youth center for the children of the elite Ecclesia. The Book of Prophecies, which only the High Elder held permission to open, alerted Broomfield to events still to come. And greatness would come to the Tray. But those occurrences were decades away.

Broomfield stroked his long, white beard. His hair and beard were once bright, coppery red. He lost his hair to time and experience a century earlier. And the beard, his most prized personal attribute, became a stark and brilliant white. He left his desk and paced the room to examine his favorite marble collectibles and statues he purchased from over three centuries of discreet trips to Greece, located north of Ara'Ja. An intense energy pulsated with each step he took. A luminescence flowed from his spotless robes, undulating in harmony alongside his vigorous strides. He paused at the sculpture and studied the symbolism of the four elements.

His mind wandered to when he had commissioned the piece, but he put aside his fond memories to return his concern to the task at hand.

He selected one white plate, one fork, and one napkin from his credenza and set them on his desk next to the pie. He closed his eyes to ready himself for the confrontation ahead. The clang of the bell placed next to the office door interrupted his thoughts. Broomfield wondered why Solomon did not announce his visitor. Solomon sat at a desk out in the hall and kept excellent care of the High Elder's affairs. Broomfield swept his hand through the air. A rush of strong wind blew from an unknown source, causing the heavy door to slide open with ease. His favorite apprentice peeked in. The regrettable appointment was about to begin. The younger man bore a grin, amiable and familiar to the old Ara'Jaeon leader. Broomfield noticed the man wore a new hairstyle. Typically, the long blond hair was tied in the back, but the High Elder spotted a drastic change of a cut and several short, messy snake-like coils which dangled from his student's entire head.

"Did you ask to see me, High Elder?" His apprentice did not greet him with the standard Ara'Jaeon greeting. Broomfield considered the absence of convention odd and revealing of the young man's new lack of respect.

"Harmony and balance. Yes, I did." Broomfield suffered the weight of his heavy heart and grieved within himself. "Come on in. Have a seat and make yourself comfortable."

He waved his hand again. Another gust of air simultaneously closed the door and moved a simple, yet elegant, wing-tip chair across the room to a place in front of his desk. He addressed his visitor. "I notice you've had a type of... er... hairstyle change over the past few days."

His guest brought his hand up to his hair and smoothed down a few messy locks. "Yes, sir. They're called dreadlocks. Many of our Brother Ara'Jaeons stationed in the Caribbean wear them long. This shorter style is the rage amongst the younger adults here in Nikonea City."

"Dreadlocks, eh?" Broomfield alleged they appeared dreadful but did not speak his views of the abominable Medusa-inspired fad, which appeared to mismatch the three-piece tweed suit the apprentice wore. He sat down and cut a generous piece of pie. "Here. Have some pie. I won't be able to eat the entire thing by myself." He handed the slice to his student, who scarfed down the pastry, as many young men were inclined to do. Broomfield cut another piece of pie and returned the plate to his student. He leaned back in his chair, clasping his hands together. "I'm sure you are aware the Metalicons have not been exactly quiet about their intention to amass and activate the four element orbs. Now, I don't need to tell you absolute power over the elements would cause tremendous destruction and chaos, both here and in human society. Not to mention this would also uncloak the Realm of Ara'Ja and the rest of our Regional Agencies located around the world. Under no circumstances should humankind know of our existence and our duty. We cannot allow the Metalicons to come into possession of those orbs."

"Yes, indeed. That would be catastrophic, High Elder, sir."

"My friend, I have even more unsettling news." The High Elder leaned forward toward his apprentice, as though he expected to divulge a secret. "A conspirator in the ranks of Ecclesia is scheming with the Metalicons against us. I am most distressed about it. We have great faith in the Ecclesia. Applicants are intensely scrutinized, and the idea of disloyalty has never been considered."

The young man grimaced, nodding in apparent understanding.

Broomfield sat upright in his chair, ran his fingers through his beard, and peered deep under the surface of his student's obligatory agreement. "If my memory has not failed, I recall you are a member of the Ecclesia, yes?"

"Ye... yes, sir. I applied and was accepted last year, but I haven't been called to active service yet."

"Quite noble of you. Guardianship of the elements is a critical task. The exact purpose for our existence as Ara'Jaeons." The High Elder surveyed the young man as he finished the last bite of pie and wiped a smear of the black plum fruit from his mouth. Broomfield's gaze darted to the empty plate. "Did you enjoy the pie?"

"Oh yes, sir. It was quite tasty."

Broomfield leaned back with his elbows on the arms of his chair and clasped his hands. He paused a moment before he continued. "Did you know the human playwright, known as Shakespeare, penned a story about a general in the Roman Army? I believe his name was Titus Andronicus."

"Yes, sir. I seem to recall there was a play, although I remember little about it."

"Titus served a pie to the queen of his enemy. A pie made from the flesh of her two sons. Gruesome, is it not?"

"Ummm… yes, High Elder, it is," said the apprentice, who pushed his plate away and visibly stifled a dry heave. He loosened his necktie.

Broomfield smiled, quite aware his friendliness did not reflect in his eyes. The purple eyes of an Ara'Jaeon. His were dark violet. So dark, they resembled the deep color of the fruit in the pie he just served. "As luck would have it, you do not have sons. And as you can tell, this is clearly a fruit pie and does not contain meat."

The young intern gave a nervous laugh and squirmed, grabbing onto the arms of his chair. "Sir, I admit you had me alarmed and thought to treat me as your enemy."

"You *should* be alarmed," replied the High Elder.

"Pardon?"

Deep sorrow filled Broomfield's soul as he stared at the youth, who, until then, held the unofficial title of favorite apprentice. The betrayal he found there validated his suspicions. "Brother, your treachery has been brought to light."

The apprentice tightened his grip on the chair arms. "Sir, I—"

"But all is not lost," Broomfield said. "Your place here at the Assembly and in the Ecclesia are forfeited, but if you can come to recognize the error of your actions, I will not relinquish you to the Regulators."

Regulators, dispatched by the High Elder or the Assembly to keep and restore order within the Ara'Jaeon community, were large, dark, and ominous figures made of shadow and voids with eyes full of fire. Nothing else. No countenance. No clothing. Only a black, hazy abyss which looked large enough to swallow a person whole. Regulators defied logic, because although they contained no physical mass, they were still bound by the natural laws of physics. They possessed no ability to walk through walls, or materialize and disappear at will, and they could grasp hold of tangible items. They dwelled in the hollow of enormous tree trunks when not on duty. No one fully understood the origins of the Regulators or how they came to be in service to the Assembly. And no one rose above the commitments the Regulators held for law and order, not even an apprentice to the High Elder.

The young man's nostrils flared. He stared at the High Elder momentarily before he jumped to his feet, knocking over his chair. His purple eyes flashed bright. "The orbs are rightly ours. The Metalicons and I will be victorious. I swear Azrael will arise!"

Broomfield rose from his own chair in anger. His fury heightened his six-and-a-half foot stature, short for an adult Ara'Jaeon. He pounded his fist on his desk and the thunderous sound echoed throughout the room. The overhead lights buzzed, and the Situation Clock squealed and flew around the perimeter of the office, dodging in and out of every orifice as if searching for a corner within the round chamber to hide. Situation Clocks were not well known for their bravery, and the High Elder's clock proved to be no exception.

"Best not to swear victory for what is already defeated," Broomfield roared, moving to stand behind his chair. "A champion is coming. One who holds more power than you or I might ever presume to aim for." He set his hands on the back of his wooden chair and leaned toward his guest, softening his voice. "Son, I implore you. I, and I alone, am aware of your duplicity. Do not throw everything away that you've—"

The apprentice snapped his fingers and Broomfield's chair dissolved into sawdust, leaving the High Elder minus a support for his weight.

Broomfield caught himself before he fell. "Please. Rethink your position."

The young man threw up both hands, his fingers splayed and taut. A ribbon of fire shot toward Broomfield, but the High Elder was ready. He waved his arms and created an armor of wind, deflecting the flame onto his desk. The glass top continued to hang intact in midair, but the wooden base caught fire and broke apart.

Broomfield fixated on the blazes of the kindling which once formed a source of comfort to him. He extended his hand. A puddle of water gurgled up from the floor, drowning out the fire. He redirected his focus to the younger man.

"Solomon!" Broomfield bellowed for his assistant.

The apprentice threw his head back in laughter. "Solomon is no longer of any use to you. Or to anyone, really. I took care of him, right outside your own door, and you were unaware."

The High Elder's spirit fell upon the discovery of the loss of his assistant. He did not know how far the disloyalty would go. He reached for the Assembly Book of Conduct on the credenza behind him. "Young man, you swore an oath to not use your powers against our people. I will give you one more chance to—"

The High Elder's apprentice did not start the day intending to cause harm. His goal was not yet accomplished, and he harbored no reason to expose his secret. However, when Broomfield summoned him to his office, he reckoned his activities were uncovered by the High Elder.

Broomfield held a widespread reputation for his generosity and grants of second chances without the consultation of others. And since none of the young man's contacts or cohorts possessed knowledge of any rumors on the subject, he hoped he might silence Broomfield before the High Elder made his discoveries public. Poor Solomon Caudel positioned himself in the wrong place at the wrong time, plain and simple.

Except for a little repulsive reference to human meat pie, the appointment with Broomfield proceeded as the apprentice expected. He carried no pre-meditated plan on how he would end the High Elder's life, but when the older gentleman turned away to retrieve a book, the apprentice grabbed his opportunity. He noticed one brief flicker of an ember in the ashes of what remained of Broomfield's desk. His gaze seized control of the not quite dead cinder. In a frenzied fanaticism, he spun the ash into a ring of sparks and electricity. He flipped his hand and a dozen electrically charged metal daggers formed within the loop. He pointed to the High Elder. The knives hurled across the room and the sharp blades struck their target deep in the spine. The High Elder collapsed to the floor.

As Jonathan Broomfield, the longest-reigning High Elder of the Realm of Ara'Ja in the past 1,200 years, lay dying, an expression of shock and disbelief appeared on his face. He uttered, "You have Metal."

The apprentice pulled out a peppermint from his pocket and threw the candy into his mouth to calm his agitated stomach. He kneeled beside his mentor and scrutinized the blades in the older man's back. He found the small mark he hoped to see, the uncontrolled result of the attack's significance. He considered it just a legend, but it excited him to discover the myth was real. It was unfortunate he could not share his discovery. He observed as the smoldering essence of the High Elder's mortal life drifted away to the Gates of Vatek. A pool of blood—in the most incredible shade of red—spread over the pristine white floor. He leaned in and whispered into Broomfield's unhearing ear. "Yes, sir. I have Metal."

He stood and made his way toward the door, but he came to an ironic realization and spun around to mock the lifeless room. "Even Shakespeare's great general Titus was killed in the end." As he turned to leave, he caught his reflection in a mirror on the opposite wall. Returning his gaze, the shocked eyes in the mirror were not his own, but those of an innocent child. Disturbed by the image, he staggered backward, stumbling over the chair he knocked over earlier. But his rehearsals of composure allowed him to snap out of his momentary panic. He pushed the button to trigger the door, keeping his eyes averted from the mirror.

A tinkle of breaking glass startled him and he twisted his head in alarm. Near the High Elder's body, the faithful Situation Clock lay shattered on the floor. Its feeble voice proclaimed the time and state of affairs in its last moments of lucidity. "It is 3:00, and all is as it has never been."

CHAPTER 1

UTTER DARKNESS

Present Day

"But Mom." Twelve-year-old Mercy Markos flung herself down on the edge of the extra thick mattress of her huge double bed. The bounce disrupted her favorite possessions placed at the foot of the mattress, ready to be packed.

Mercy's mother, Emzlie, picked up a pair of pants from the floor and re-folded them. She pushed the side-swept bangs of her strawberry blonde cropped hair out of her face. It was a classic, but edgy, textured style and well suited for her. "No buts, Mercy," she said in the perfect and polished British accent of where she spent her childhood. "This is non-negotiable. We knew this day would come, eventually."

"But shouldn't I at least have a choice where I go?" Mercy asked. "Why can't I stay with Grandma Yvonne instead? You didn't have to attend the Tray when you were my age."

That was not the first time Mercy used her mother's non-attendance at the Tray argument since her parents received a call to service by the Ecclesia a few days earlier. As one of the most exclusive groups of Ara'Jaeons, the Ecclesia held the ultimate responsibility to keep the earth elements in balance. Although membership in the Ecclesia was for life, each term of active service was a mere five years. A pittance compared to the lifespan of an Ara'Jaeon. An Ecclesiastic could serve multiple active terms over a lifetime, but each term included several opportunities to take time off for family visits or vacations.

"My mother was home to care for me." Mercy's mother's pale, almost colorless, lavender eyes sparkled, and her slight grin showed she was not upset. "You know you're not allowed off the island until your thirteenth birthday. You have several months to go."

"That's just about the stupidest rule I've ever heard."

"Stupid or not, we follow the rules in this house." Mercy's mother sat next to her and took her hand. "Listen Mercy, I understand why you would prefer to stay with your grandmother in Crete instead of the youth center. I honestly do. But children born on Ara'Ja are ill prepared to cope in the human world, and the Tray really is the best place for you while your father and I are away on assignment." She stood and sifted through Mercy's belongings. "Look, you can either continue to fight a battle you will not win and live the next few years with anger and bitterness eating away at you, or you can accept the situation with grace and dignity and be open to new and exciting possibilities. The choice is yours, my dear."

"I know, I know. As the wise old owl, Emzlie Markos, always says, 'Choose your battles' and 'Live to fight another day.'" Mercy wagged her forefinger in fake mockery. Her long, unruly, dark poppy red curls bounced right along. She often believed they embraced a life of their own.

Her mother tweaked Mercy's nose before she left the room. "Right on the money. Get those belongings packed up. We need to leave in an hour. And I'm not old, I'm only forty-three… still young. But your father, he's fifty. He's ancient. True story."

Mercy laughed at the joke. Her parents were not old. They were not even middle-aged yet. The lifespan of Ara'Jaeons was over two hundred years. In her heart, Mercy understood her mother was correct about letting inconsequential matters go, but knowing it didn't make Mercy any more receptive to her immediate future. She pulled out her journal to make one last entry before her exile. She loved vocabulary, and she yearned to be a novelist when she grew up. When her grandmother discovered Mercy's love of writing earlier in the year, she gave Mercy a journal made of handcrafted paper and bound in supple leather. The card attached said to use the gift to hone her writing skills and to keep a record for future writing ideas. Mercy contemplated long and hard before she wrote.

To suddenly be thrown into the unknown can be a terrifying experience for anyone. But to a child, abandoned by her parents, and stranded away from the entirety of what she knows and holds dear, this incident can be irreversibly destructive.

"Wow. This sounds pretentious," Mercy muttered to herself and erased the entry. Instead, she wrote, *Getting cast into utter darkness today.* Mercy's definition of utter darkness was better known as the Tray—officially and formally christened, Training and Residence for Ara'Jaeon Youth Center, although most people used the nickname derived by its acronym. Constructed with a series of large round buildings connected by tunnels, halls, and over-passes, the Tray was located high on a hill in an unpopulated area on the most northwestern tip of the island, Ara'Ja. The school opened to the minor children of the Ecclesia while their parents worked on assignment, the precise reason for Mercy's pending residence at the center. A few days earlier, her parents received an order to report to SARA in three days. SARA, the Southern Atlantic Regional Agency, was on the cloaked Brazilian island, Belleza del Mar. The couple first met and fell in love there fourteen years earlier. The directive was the first call to active service for her parents since Mercy was a toddler. Thus, the summons threw the family into a bit of a tailspin. Preparations and packing began right away, but the top priority was to enroll Mercy at the Tray, where she would live on campus and study general education and element training. Mercy could not force herself to be happy about her move to the Tray. She felt too distressed over the requirement to leave her school and her friends in her hometown of Athlenan just a few weeks into the school year. To make matters worse, she could not stay with her grandmother—her human grandmother—on Crete. Mercy opted to go for midpoint between happy and upset. She tolerated the situation, but remained resentful. She arrived at the Tray in a state of mind.

———————◆———————

Mercy trudged ahead of her parents and through the red revolving door, which opened into the lobby of the Tray. The cool air inside the building hit her in the face when she entered, making her grateful for the cardigan she wore. Every step she took in her sweet, burgundy suede ankle boots clicked on the gray slate floors. Her footsteps echoed through the silence of the room, amplifying the perception of loneliness. She alleged the Tray would offer her hours and hours of boredom, and she would suffer a long and tedious death before her parents returned from their assignment.

Hoping to avoid announcing her presence with her awkward boot clicks, Mercy tiptoed further into the entrance hall and scrutinized her surroundings. The lobby was a circular room, several stories tall. The stairway to the second floor ran up along one side of the curved wall. She looked up at the top. The stairways and hallways of every level, except one, were open and overlooked the lobby from every angle. They created a corkscrew effect in the room, which, when viewed as a whole, gave the impression of better days abandoned long ago. Etchings of the ancient Ara'Jaeon symbols, created to represent the four elements, covered much of the faded wall. Bright patches of color splotches implied the room was once a brilliant amber. A soft whoosh caught her attention. Startled, she spun around. An antique Situation Clock, covered in elaborate scrollwork, slithered through the room and came straight at her.

"Don't you even consider it." Mercy scowled at the clock, in no mood to have her business announced to the entire world.

The clock stopped mid-air at her command for a mere second, then appeared to regain its insolence and continued toward her. The nuisance buzzed about her, dangling close to her. It squawked, "It is 2:45, and all hidden things shall be revealed."

Mercy groaned and stuck a finger in her ear. She never understood the often cryptic messages of Situation Clocks and wondered why, after centuries, no one adjusted the awful screechy voice incorporated into them. The clock skittered away, and she continued to sulk. If she didn't, the chances were high she would succumb to her desire to weep, and she refused to snivel like a baby.

The red door spun around and her parents stepped in. Mercy's dad scanned the room. His gray and black plaid pea coat hung open, revealing an ivory turtleneck sweater and a light green knitted scarf. He looked good for an old guy. And cool, as always.

"Wow, not much has changed since I stayed here forty years ago," he said. "A fresh coat of paint would do wonders."

Mercy's mother put her hand on her husband's arm. "Now, Orion. I'm sure they're using their budget as best as they can."

"Let's have a quick look around. Perhaps we can find someone in charge," he said. "Mercy, hold down the fort, and don't let any—" He lowered his voice to a whisper for just a single word. "*Metalicons* in. We won't be long." He winked and walked away with her mother.

"Yes, sir." Mercy fingered the aquamarine crystal in her pocket. She snatched it from the decorative bowl of crystals and other minerals her mother kept in their living room. She didn't know why, perhaps to keep her mother close to her at the Tray. Mercy stepped on a tiny water spill, and in an iconic moment, not unlike many others in her short life, her foot slipped out from under her. She let out a shrill shriek which pierced the silence as she plummeted to the floor and landed on her back. The flowers in the lobby bouquets retreated into their leaves and covered their delicate petals. Many of the peonies, tinted in the palest of pink, threw themselves onto the floor and thrashed about in agony, while serene lotus blossoms, well known for their fondness of tranquility, escaped to the bottom of the huge indoor water garden. Her screams resonated throughout the lobby and up the stairway. They rose through every floor, one excruciating level at a time, creating a new tormented echo upon arrival at each landing, until, at last, they culminated at the top in a chorus of agonizing sorrow. From her sprawled-out position, she watched as floor by floor, the amused faces of the youth center residents burst into view over the guard rails. They whispered amongst themselves while Mercy, mortified beyond belief, rose to her feet. Her cheeks burned, and she sensed several hundred pairs of eyes, in every shade of purple, staring down at her. She looked down to hide under the long hair which spilled out from under her favorite oversized newsboy hat adorned with rustic handmade fabric flowers and imitation pearls. She perceived a movement and peeked through her bangs. Two identical platinum haired children poked their heads out of the arched doorway by the base of the stairs, then bobbed out of sight again.

Her parents returned to the lobby, and she directed her attention to them with the singular purpose of demanding to go home. But echoes of her screams still permeated throughout the upper levels of the school, keeping her thoughts scattered and disordered.

"Mercy, what happened here?" Mercy's mother rushed to her side. Dressed in a mint-green chiffon two-piece outfit with delicate white scalloped lace trim, Mercy's mother was flawless. Mercy's maternal grandmother, Yvonne, was human, and as much as Mercy adored her, most Ara'Jaeons believed the attractiveness of humans simply didn't hold up to the beauty of Ara'Jaeons. But that belief didn't pertain to Mercy's half-human mother.

Mercy's father winked at her. "No worries. Your handsome and awe-inspiring dad will take care of this awful noise." Mercy's father *was* handsome *and* awe-inspiring. His shoulder-length, wavy red hair was partially tied back with a thin ribbon and his beard, although full, was kept neat and trimmed. He closed his eyes and moved his mouth in silence until a gentle breeze circled around and embraced the family. Flowers emerged from behind leaves as the room became peaceful.

Mercy witnessed him do the same ritual on several previous occasions. It was his preferred method to summon a calming wind. Without doubt, they were beautiful, her parents. Inside and out. Kind, smart, funny. They embodied everything about a perfect couple. Not for the first time, she wished she inherited some of their magnificence, but destiny gave her a simple freckled face, wild red hair, and eyes of the most common and unexciting shade of purple. She feared she must have been born with more human genes than Ara'Jaeon.

The sound of delicate footsteps on the stairs pulled Mercy to the present. A tall, chic woman approached them. Mercy's parents were quite tall themselves—close to seven feet tall, as was common for adult Ara'Jaeons—but this woman towered over them by a foot or more, even though she wore flat shoes. She wore a simple crisp white top and buttoned high-waisted, wide legged navy trousers. The silver highlights in her long, white hair shimmered as she moved.

"Harmony and balance. You must be the Markos family," the lady said. "I'm Carmen DeLuca, the headmistress. Most people call me Miss Carmen." The faces of the blooms followed her as she passed by them. After a graceful sweep of her hand, the flowers which earlier jumped to the floor when Mercy screeched, arose and returned to where they belonged. Another gesture of her hand triggered the water in the water garden to resume its gentle ripple, raising the lotus blossoms to the surface. A bud on a stem of white orchids extended toward her and she reached out to caress it. "There, there, my darlings. All is well. Rest now and know you are loved."

Mercy raised her brows and stifled a giggle, and as usual, instead produced a not-so-subtle snort. Her father elbowed her and cleared his throat before he stepped forward to shake Miss Carmen's hand.

"Harmony and balance, Miss Carmen. I'm Orion Markos. This is my wife, Emzlie, and our daughter, Mercy. We are grateful for the last-minute accommodations." He beamed at the headmistress.

Mercy knew he shared her amusement at the way Miss Carmen addressed her flowers. She loved his sense of humor, and although, many times, he aimed his jests at her, she loved him all the more for them. His smiles, always amicable and genuine, won over those who met him.

Miss Carmen was no exception and her stylish conduct made a sharp U-turn. She giggled like a giddy young girl, experiencing her first crush. "Oh. Ha-ha. There is no problem at all. We frequently get urgent requests from the Ecclesia. We're delighted to have you here. Er... I mean, your daughter. We're delighted to have your daughter here. Her room is prepared, and her Academy attire and belongings await her up on the residential floor. Vesuvius, Tambora! Please come out from your hideaway and join us."

A silhouette of a hand pushed a petite girl, around Mercy's age, through the doorway where the two peeping Toms stole a look at her a few minutes earlier. The girl, whose hair color matched the gauzy ivory tunic and cropped pants she wore, stumbled into the lobby. In a comedy of physical errors, she stepped on the loose orange shoelace of one of her hot pink sneakers, squealed in the most delicate and ladylike way, and toppled forward, landing face down onto the floor. A boy with matching hair and dressed in an identical outfit with long pants, followed too closely behind her and tripped over her sprawled-out body.

"Oof," the boy groaned.

"Ow! Vesu. Off. Now!" The girl moaned and tried to crawl out from under him.

Distracted, Mercy forgot about her own woes and watched the dynamic production. The two children's struggle to get to their feet, and their repeated trips over themselves, and each other, enthralled her.

"Vesu, I said get off me, you klutzomaniac."

"I'm trying, but you keep moving and getting in my way."

"I keep moving because you keep stepping on me."

Miss Carmen stepped in to separate the two and beamed at Mercy's father. "I believe the legendary St. Clair grace and dignity have skipped a generation." She helped the children up from the floor and spoke to the students, who still peered out from the higher levels. "The show is over. Please report back to your classrooms." She turned to address the clumsy duo. "Vesuvius, Tambora, this is Mercy Markos, our new student. As long as you two considered it necessary to dodge your Spontaneous Combustion class today, please make yourselves useful and show her to her quarters. She's in Miss Oliver's room."

"Yes, Miss Carmen," the siblings replied in unison.

"And Tambora?"

"Yes, ma'am?" Tambora swept her hair off her face and smoothed her disheveled side-parted bob.

"Tie your shoes before you trip again and create more havoc."

"Yes, ma'am." Tambora bent down and tied her shoelaces. When finished, she introduced herself to Mercy. "Harmony and balance. I'm Tambora and this is my twin brother, Vesuvius."

"Like the volcanoes?" Mercy asked.

"We're named after volcanoes because we're pure blood Fires. It was our parents' feeble attempt at humor," said Tambora.

"Hey, hey. You can call me Vesu." Vesuvius extended his hand to Mercy. To her horror, smoke seeped out from his palm. She gasped in shock and recoiled before she could stop herself.

"Uh, sorry about that." Vesuvius withdrew his hand and patted it against his leg to dispel the smolders.

"Let's go on upstairs." Tambora ignored her brother. "The student areas for our age and younger are on the sixth and seventh floors. The older kids are housed in the upper south wing. We aren't allowed to go there, but maybe I can sneak you over later on."

"Tambora," said Miss Carmen, "there will be no sneaking."

"Yes, ma'am." Tambora proceeded toward the stairs, turned back toward Mercy, and rolled her eyes from behind Miss Carmen.

Mercy hesitated to follow them. She feared her parents would take off while she unpacked her belongings. Her mother bent to whisper in her ear. "Go ahead. We need to finish our arrangements with Miss Carmen. We'll be up before we leave."

Mercy nodded.

"Mr. and Mrs. Markos, if you would come this way, we can get the paperwork in order," Miss Carmen said.

She purred like a cat. Women purred around Mercy's father a lot. She caught his attention and nodded in Miss Carmen's direction. He winked at Mercy and followed his wife and Miss Carmen.

Mercy studied the multiple levels above her. "Isn't there a portal?" she asked.

The twins exchanged glances and burst out in laughter. Tambora stepped up onto the first stair of the long climb to the top. "Portals are forbidden at the Tray except for the library and the training rooms. The library portals lead to larger rooms than what would fit here at the school, and the training rooms have portals because—well, because they're for training."

"It's to keep the students from bugging out of here without permission, but climbing's not so terrible once you get used to it," Vesuvius added.

When they arrived at the top of the first set of stairs, Tambora said, "Obviously, there are many wings and offshoots to the main building. Most of them are used for staff quarters or are assigned to the upper grades and for training rooms. They're off limits to us unless we're in training. The library, dining room, and guest lounge are on the first floor." Tambora continued on to describe the classrooms and staff offices on the massive second, third, and fourth floors. "And last, but most definitely not least, the basement has the kitchen, storage facilities, communications room, and game room." Tambora was an enthusiastic chatterbox, and she mentioned the location of every area of significance, including the fact their age group's student lounge occupied the entire seventh floor. The outer walls were made of thick glass and provided incredible 360-degree unobstructed views. Because the Tray was situated atop a hill surrounded by ancient, overgrown and gnarled olive tree forests, Tambora explained you could look over the treetops and watch the sunrise over Nikonea City across from Thyella Bay from the eastern side of the building, and if you walked around to the opposite side of the room that evening, you could view the sunset over the Mediterranean Sea, which Mercy thought was pretty amazing.

Mercy suspected Tambora loved to play tour guide. Mercy nodded in the charade that her mind kept up as she tried to soak in the abundance of information. By the time they passed through the fourth floor, Mercy realized Tambora neglected to mention details of the fifth floor in her speech. Dark, dank, and creepy were the first words which came to Mercy's mind when she first stepped foot onto the fifth floor. The lights were out and the doors along the hallway were closed. Instead of opening to the foyer below, as the other floors did, large sheets of plywood covered the open space above the railings. What little natural light they had filtered through the cracks between the boards and cast an eerie glow over the entire level. If that bit of light faded away, they would be in utter darkness. Ironic, Mercy thought. She didn't realize she would be in literal utter darkness at the Tray. "Why aren't the lights on?"

"Um… the electricity doesn't work here, so we don't use this area except to pass through." Vesuvius looked down and away from Mercy.

The dark ambiance made Mercy uneasy and goosebumps formed on her arms. She fumbled around in her pocket and fingered the aquamarine. It provided comfort, as though her mother's presence surrounded her. She peered through a crack between two boards, but only bright open space and the boards of the opposite side of the fifth floor were visible. "Why do they have everything boarded up? Wouldn't it be a big light source for this floor?"

Tambora closed her eyes and cupped her hands together in front of her. "It would seem so, but common sense doesn't always show up here."

"What are you doing?" Mercy bit her lip, aware of the habit that revealed her nervousness.

Tambora opened one eyelid and explained in a soft voice, "I'm making a glow bubble. Lights haven't worked on this level for years. They've tried many ways to fix them. Normally, there are Regulators posted on this floor to make sure everything is okay, but I don't see them right now. They must be off doing other duties."

"Re... Regulators?" Mercy sputtered. Her heart rate increased and her breath was shallow. The Regulators were supposed to be the good guys, but everyone knew they were ruthless when necessary. Kids at her last school gossiped about how the Regulators could not discern middle ground. For them, the line between right and wrong was absolute, so a display of best behavior was imperative when in their presence. When Regulators were on duty, they were most likely seen standing at attention, their heavy legs apart, one hand behind their back, and the other holding a pole planted firmly on the floor.

"Don't worry. They don't mess with us kids at all unless there's a problem. They're only here because there's no light on this floor, and it gets pretty dark, even using a flashlight." Tambora closed her opened eye, then unclenched her hands to reveal an orange radiant ball. "Here we go." She showed the bubble to Mercy. "We're not supposed to use our abilities outside of training classes, but Miss Carmen gave the students permission to use a light source on this floor."

"That's so cool," Mercy said, happy for a distraction.

"We both have Fire." Vesuvius conjured up his own little ball of light. "We're direct descendants of Canicus, the first Fire Eater."

"Eventually, we'll have the chance to be Fire Eaters too, since we have pure bloodlines through our ancestry back to the beginning," said Tambora. "What are your abilities?"

If Tambora's intention was to impress Mercy, she succeeded. Without a doubt, those kids knew who they were and where they came from, unlike Mercy, whose own family came from a mix of various elements. "I don't know yet," said Mercy. "But I probably won't be any kind of special. My parents told me there's a little of each element in our ancestry. We're a hodgepodge of a family, so I might end up with anything. And my mother's half human, too. There was even a Metalicon in my family back during the dark ages."

Vesuvius stopped in his tracks. "Metal? You're kidding me. And you're part human? That is way amazing. You're the first person I've known with Metal abilities."

"Well. I don't have it." Mercy denounced personal association with Metal without hesitation and kicked herself for the reference to a Metalicon ancestor. Metalicons were bad. Evil. Anyone who dared talk about them said so, and Mercy wanted no part in any suggestion of a link to them. "It was just one person in my family, a couple of hundred years ago, but my dream is to have Wind and, eventually, be a Wind Rider. I want to fly." Mercy bit her lip, surprised by her admission. She never spoke those words aloud before. Not even her grandmother, whom she cherished, knew of her secret desire to become a Wind Rider. She held the yearning sacred to her heart.

Vesuvius smirked. "Mate, Wind Riders don't fly. They might hover for a bit, but not fly."

"But I assumed they rode the wind." Disappointed, Mercy averted her gaze, embarrassed at her obvious misinterpretation. She realized the small school in her hometown must lack in the basic Ara'Jaeon knowledge area.

Vesuvius stood a little taller and rattled off the fruits of his education. "No. They don't literally ride the wind, like the Fire Eaters don't eat fire, the Water Dancers don't dance on water, and Earth Watchers don't spend their days standing about, staring at the ground. Anyway, you can't be a Wind Rider if you don't have a pure bloodline to the first Wind Riders."

Mercy's heart dropped. Her biggest dream in the entire world, other than writing, burst from its cocoon as a common moth instead of a butterfly. She spun away from the twins. She didn't want them to witness her deep disappointment and her developing tears.

"Don't worry, Mercy," said Tambora. "You're pretty special as you are. We barely know you and already, I can tell." A draft of cold air swept over them and Tambora shivered. "Let's leave. I don't like this place."

The group quickened their pace to the next flight of stairs. Mercy noticed a padlock on every door. Many of the doors were also boarded or sealed shut. "Why are those rooms closed off?"

"Shh—" Tambora lowered her voice. "We probably should be quiet. We try not to talk here. It's best not to make disturbances. Just to be safe."

Mercy grabbed Tambora's arm. "Disturbances? What is there to disturb?" She rubbed the aquamarine in her pocket for comfort.

The twins exchanged a quick glance.

Mercy's eyes widened. "What? What was that look about? What exactly is wrong here?"

Tambora spoke first, still in hushed tones. "It's nothing. Just silly superstitions. Don't worry, we're fine. This floor is unsettling though, and we prefer to go quickly without bothering the Regulators."

"This floor is supposed to be haunted," Vesuvius said, his eyes large and round.

"Vesu. Stop it." Tambora elbowed him.

A wave of apprehension ran through Mercy. "Haun… HAUNTED?"

"Yeah," Vesuvius said. "Super bad stuff happened here to the students in the old days. They found—"

Tambora glared at her brother. "Uh… they didn't find anything. The haunting is only a rumor," she interrupted, although her shaky voice didn't quite convince Mercy.

"What kind of stuff?" Mercy asked.

"A student became stuck in a haunted room and disappeared," Vesuvius said.

Mercy's cup of tentative confidence in the Tray developed a major crack. Her eyes grew larger and her goosebumps returned.

"Don't worry, Mercy. That's not true." Tambora kicked her brother. "The doors are bolted shut. No one could get in."

"They could be stuck in a haunted room," Vesuvius insisted. "If it's truly haunted, any ghost worthy of haunting could get through a measly lock and take a hostage."

"I don't wish to hear any more ghost stories." Mercy held her hands on her abdomen and tried to remain calm.

"Vesu, can't you see you're scaring Mercy? Stop creeping her out," said Tambora.

"Mercy, I promise, I'm not trying to scare you," he said. "My friend, Phin, walked through one night. A lot of rattling came from a bolted-up room."

Mercy took a moment, her gaze flitted back and forth between the twins, who both returned her stare, anxiety spilled out of their expressions. The talk about hauntings made her scared. Mercy didn't habitually believe in superstitions, but the sole spotlight in her mind right then, shone on the imaginary Metalicon who lived under her bed and terrorized her as a child. He seemed real enough.

They walked to the next staircase in eerie silence. Mercy's focus on observing her surroundings kept her from getting too nervous about the dark. Still, she breathed a sigh of relief when they reached the stairwell to the sixth floor. The steps between floors were without doors, and a beam of light from above shone down on them. The twins let go of their light globes. Instead of falling to the ground, they floated into the air high above them. Astonished at the sight, Mercy watched the lights dissipate into thousands of sparkly sprinkles and collapse into nothingness. She never experienced such wonders before. "That's amazing," she said. She tucked her hand into her pocket and rummaged around for her mother's gemstone, but her pocket was empty.

CHAPTER 2

A DANCE WITH MADNESS

Mercy panicked. The aquamarine was her mother's favorite. She would have a lot of explaining to do if she didn't put it back when she returned home the following summer before her mother discovered it missing. "Hey, guys. I lost my mom's aquamarine that was in my pocket. I need to backtrack and find it."

"When did you have it last?" Tambora asked.

"I felt it in my pocket about halfway through the fifth floor," Mercy said. "I need to find it." She didn't experience the bravado she flaunted and the contents of her stomach were inching dangerously close to her throat. She took a deep breath to calm herself and turned toward the darkness.

Vesuvius called out. "Wait. You can't go alone. We need to stick together. Weird stuff happens on this floor and you need our light."

Mercy realized he was right and stopped to wait for them.

"We *have* no light," Tambora said. "You know our abilities aren't strong enough to use them again right away."

"Oh. Right. What can we do then?" Vesuvius plopped down on the steps, sporting an expression about as gloomy as the dark hallway they exited a minute earlier.

"We'll go in the dark. I have to find it. It's my mother's," Mercy whispered. She took off her hat to see better and tried to ignore the sick, heavy feeling in the pit of her tummy.

The fifth-floor air was colder on their return than their first pass through. Even in the darkness, Mercy's breath shimmered and the warm mist spiraled around in a gentle whirl before the vapor drifted away.

A creaky noise came from ahead. Mercy paused. Vesuvius must not have realized she stopped, and he rammed into her back, knocking her forward into something solid. Something that moved.

"Eek!" Mercy shrieked.

"Ouch." A voice came from the shadows. "Watch where you're going."

"Phin?" Tambora screeched.

"Phin!" Vesuvius cried out. "My man."

"Phineas Jaymes," Tambora said, "we heard you weren't returning for another two weeks."

"Yeah, well. Something major is happening and my parents received an early call to duty. So here I am," said Phin. "What are you guys doing in the dark?"

"We used all of our Fire energy on the way up. What are *you* doing in the dark?" Tambora said.

"I have a flashlight but the battery fizzled out. It was strange. Suddenly, it flickered and went kaput."

Mercy could not distinguish much of Phin's appearance, but when he faced the trace of light, she glimpsed his bright, reflective eyes.

"Hey, Phin. This is Mercy, she's new here," said Vesuvius. "Mercy, this is my best pal, Phin."

"Hey," Phin said.

"Hi," Mercy said, eager to recover her mother's gemstone.

She was about to go alone, letting the others continue their reunion when a loud zap sounded from the door closest to them. Flickering lights shone from under the door. Before they reacted, buzzing noises resonated behind each barricaded door along the hall. The doors shuddered as though someone tried to get out.

"Argh!" Vesuvius yelped.

The girls screamed, and the foursome bolted down the hall, Vesuvius leading the way. He zig-zagged in front of them, and they followed his dark shape. But in their panicky and unexpected game of follow-the-leader, he led them past the line of bolted doors and through a door into an even darker area. Vesuvius stopped, and the others skidded to a halt behind him. "Whoa. I don't know where we are."

"This is spooky. There isn't a room here." Phin's voice called out from somewhere in the black void. "Let's go back."

They retraced their steps to the main corridor, making their way toward the faint light, glimmering through the open door. They were mere steps from their destination when a creak sounded and the door began a slow swing.

"It's closing!" Mercy shouted.

They scrambled to get out before the door slammed shut, leaving them on the wrong side and extinguishing all light from the outside.

Tambora pulled at the door handle. "It won't budge."

The children crowded the door, trying to push and pull, failing at every attempt.

"It appears we're stuck here. I don't like this," said Phin.

Mercy felt around for the walls. "We aren't in a room. This is a hall. Hey. There's a faint light coming from that direction."

Tambora said, "What direction? Where are you looking? I can't see a thing. Not even you."

"I can't see it either," said Phin and Vesuvius agreed with him.

"Let's all hold hands." Mercy reached out for Tambora's hand. "I'll guide us along."

"I'm not holding Phin's hand," Vesuvius said, his voice shaky.

"Well. I'm not holding yours either, dearie. And stop blubbering," said Phin.

"I'm not blubbering," Vesuvius said. "I'm just… tense."

"All right, all right," Mercy groaned. "Vesu, you hold my hand and Tambora's. Phin can take Tambora's other hand. Come this way. Stay close to the wall."

Hand-in-hand-in-hand-in-hand, they sidestepped down the hallway with their backs against the wall, except Vesuvius, who faced the wall. He said in the dark, it made no difference what direction he faced. He made a fair point, Mercy reasoned, and forgave his nonconformity. The corridor went on much farther than Mercy expected. The light grew brighter, and she noticed it was not constant gleam, but a fast, sporadic sparking. "We're getting close," she whispered. "Do you see the light now? It's coming from around the corner up ahead."

"I don't see what you're talking about," Tambora said. "All I see is pitch black."

"Me too," said Vesuvius.

"And me," Phin said.

"Shh. Everyone be quiet for a second. Can you guys hear a zapping noise?" Mercy tightened her grip on Vesu's hand. "I think this is causing the shaking around here. It sounds like electricity."

"You're hearing things," Tambora said. "Besides, the electricity doesn't work on this floor. We have to go back. This is too weird."

"Not yet," Mercy insisted.

"I reckon Mercy's mad," said Vesuvius. "Maybe we should be afraid of Mad Mercy."

"Mercy, did your parents dropped you off at the right institution?" Phin chuckled.

Mercy elbowed Vesuvius because he was the only one next to her. "I'm not imagining this. It's there. Aren't you guys curious to figure this out?"

"Ow. How can I be curious about something I don't think exists?" Vesuvius said. "Besides, curiosity killed the muskrat, and I'm not willing to die over fantasy lights and sounds."

"Cat." Tambora's voice sounded from the dark.

"Cat, what?" asked her brother.

"It's cat. Curiosity killed the cat," Tambora said. "Mercy, we don't know what's down there. We should probably stop here."

"I know, but we're already headed that way, and we can't leave the way we came in. What other choice do we have? Listen, I know we're in a scary situation, but I'm going to find out what is causing this. You guys can stay here. I'm going on. I might locate a way to break out of here while I'm there. I'll be back in a few minutes."

She tiptoed alone toward the light show only she detected. From behind her, she overheard Vesuvius say, "That girl has maxie."

Phin asked, "What's maxie? Is it anything like chutzpah?"

Mercy rolled her eyes. Being a word connoisseur, she knew Vesuvius meant moxie. She was also familiar with the Jewish word chutzpah, which held a similar, yet subtly different, definition. She wondered how Phin would know such an expression. Perhaps he enjoyed words too. A brief spark jolted inside her at the idea of a potential vocab buddy. She continued to slink alone down the hall. The zapping and light surges grew stronger as she proceeded. "This is definitely electrical," Mercy muttered to herself when she neared what she sensed to be the corridor's end.

A glint of light on the floor caught Mercy's attention, and she bent over to investigate, discovering her mother's aquamarine. She wondered how it ended up there and tried to pick it up, but on its own volition, the stone rolled away from her and toward the flashing blue light which radiated into the hallway from a few feet ahead. Mercy followed the crystal, trying multiple times to pick it up, but each time, it tumbled away from her grasp until it rounded the corner and through the doorway to where the light came from. Perplexed, she took a few steps to try again to grab it, but the crystal flew across a large, plain room with no furnishings, no decor, or floor treatments. Just a single shelf and an enormous crystal slab which hung from the middle of the high ceiling. It almost grazed the floor. The gemstone was in the irregular shape of a magnificent geode slice. The front and back were polished and made even more brilliant by the huge bolts of electricity, emanating from the walls and into the stone. The texture and pale aqua color matched her mother's. Mercy knew the crystal was an aquamarine.

At that point, she realized what she walked into. Alarmed, she covered her mouth to stifle a gasp. Three people, facing away from Mercy, conversed in low tones. She recognized Cockney accents. She caught the words Fire orb, but little else. She took another sharp intake of air and backed up toward the door. Her boots scuffled across the floor and the trio whirled about. Her presence was revealed. Mercy's mouth hung open and her instinct was to take another step back. Although they were the first of their kind that she saw in person, there was no doubt in her mind the raven-haired woman and her two male companions were, in fact, Metalicons. The fifth unsanctioned element class of the Ara'Jaeons, whose sole element ability, as far as she knew, was to manipulate metals. Dressed in dark apparel and makeup, and adorned with piercings and tattoos, they embodied every punk, gothic stereotype Mercy ever heard used to describe Metalicons. Although she sensed a sinister vibe, she connected to their British accents and mysterious fashion. Mercy knew little about Metalicons. No one talked about them except in hushed voices. But all the same, most Ara'Jaeon children grew up with a Metalicon as their personal boogeyman, hiding under their bed or in their closet. The stuff of nightmares. Mercy's nightmare was named Azrael. Once, she looked up the name up in a book of baby names and learned it meant Angel of Death. Eventually, she outgrew her belief that he lived in her room at night. When she finally told him to leave with an air of conviction and confidence, he did. And he stayed gone.

One man raised his brows and appeared surprised, but judging by his expression, he soon lost interest and returned to his work on a metal case connected to the crystal. His short spiky, stark white hair gleamed in the room's glow, in absolute contrast to that of his companions.

The other male, his long black dreadlocks partially tied up in a loose ponytail, took a step toward a terrified Mercy. She froze, unable to pull back. He taunted, "Well. What do we have 'ere? A sweet little lady out for a walk?" His dark eyes, the color of eggplant, narrowed, and he circled around her. He hung his thumbs from the belt loops of his tight black pants. His short leather jacket fell open, revealing several chains and knives inside. Long black fur tails of various lengths hung from his shoulders. He reminded Mercy of a stalking panther, and she was its prey.

The woman cocked her head sideways. "We must be misplaced," she said, her voice sickeningly sweet. Although a wire half-mask, created of open scrollwork and black beads, covered much of the left side of her face, the empty, dazed expression in her eyes was not hidden. The woman's dark hair was pinned up and teased into long loose strands going in all directions, similar to a peacock. A goth peacock. Mercy wondered if all Metalicons resembled animals.

The female stared at Mercy, her eyes vacant and glassy. She sported a cold, frightening, and feral grin. "Are we lost, little one? Did our mum misplace us?" The woman beckoned Mercy to come closer. Despite her fear, the lady in the black petticoat mesmerized Mercy, who found herself unable to stop from taking a single step toward the fascinating, peculiar creature.

"That's it, sweetheart, come to Patina." The lady bared her teeth and her tone changed to a soft hiss. "You shall be my little dove."

Mercy stiffened, afraid to get closer. She regained her bearings and twirled around to flee. Instead, she found the dreadlocked man between her and the door, blocking her path. He laughed at her. "And where might you be going, little girl? This party is just getting started." He bowed, one hand over his abdomen and the other extended to his side.

Patina jumped up and down, clapping her hands. "Oh! A party! We do so love a party. Shall we dance?" She held out her hand again to Mercy. A large bolt of electricity made a deafening zap, startling Mercy. She yelped and jumped right into Patina's clutch. Patina squealed. "We will have a SHOCK-ingly fun time!" She pulled and clawed at Mercy's arm. Patina's long pointed fingernails poked through the cardigan Mercy wore and scratched her. She winced at the sting. "Do… let's dance," Patina said. She hummed an unfamiliar tune and waltzed around, dragging Mercy along.

The icy-haired man closed his box and disconnected the cables from the crystal. The light in the room grew dim. He glanced at Patina and panther-man and snipped, "Let her be, you two. She's naught to us. We're finished for today. Let's go." He tossed a silver rock, muttered something about a cave, and created an opening in mid-air, filled with what appeared to be pulsating liquid metal. The swirling mass fluctuated from silver to gold to bronze to copper.

"A portal," Mercy croaked as she was forced to spin around in Patina's dance. It surprised her to find a portal of any type in a forbidden area, and although portals were common in Ara'Ja, portals of Metal origin were not used. Mercy regained her voice and cried out, "You can't have that in here. Portals aren't allowed at the Tray."

The dreadlocked panther-man mocked her. "You can't have that 'ere. It's not allowed."

Patina released Mercy from her hold. "Will we tattle, my little dove?" she asked in a musical tone. She grabbed Mercy again, twirled around, and sang, "It's a tattle-tale world, where no one sleeps. They snoop around, like little creeps. The little dove tries to cause great strife, but the big one knows how to steal her—" Patina stopped dancing and caressed Mercy's chin. "—life."

Mercy shivered from the chill that ran through her.

"Patina, luv, come on. Let her go." The white-haired man's voice was quieter than his companions. "Pip, let's be off."

Mercy recognized his accent. He spoke a bit more mainstream British than cockney. The same as her mother and great uncle. Her grandpa and his family were from the outpost off the coast of England. Her mother lived there with her parents for the first years of her life, before they transferred to Ara'Ja permanently when she was young.

"Telys, you're simply no fun anymore." Patina pouted sweetly, but she did as Telys requested, and she and the scary panther-man, who Mercy just discovered was called Pip, jumped through the portal one at a time, disappearing into the swirling mass.

Telys stared at Mercy for a moment. She returned his stare. She considered him handsome, and she was enthralled, not afraid. She dared to give him a slight, shy smile. He half-way smiled and nodded toward her as he buttoned up his long black trench coat, murmuring, "Farewell for now, Miss Mercy Markos." And then he was gone. The portal vanished moments before Vesuvius, Tambora, and Phin burst into the emptiness, where darkness again made a home.

"How did he know my name?" Mercy was baffled. "Don't tell me you didn't see that."

"No. We think you're bonkers," said Vesuvius.

A fading, residual light shone on the floor under the space where the large crystal hung, and Mercy spotted her aquamarine. The gemstone did not move again, allowing Mercy to reclaim her mother's possession and slip it into her pocket. She headed toward her friends who stood at the door.

"Mercy." A calm voice called from the darkness.

Mercy turned in a panic, afraid the Metalicons returned. Instead, a glow radiated from a smoky figure, hovering in mid-air. The delicate graceful robes whirled about, like a movie scene playing in slow motion.

"Mercy, what are you doing?" Tambora asked.

The gentle figure spoke again. "Mercy, do not fear me."

Mercy knew her new classmates whispered behind her, but she paid them no attention. The haziness cleared and what replaced the fog took her breath away. Before her lingered a glorious individual made of pure light. Bright, but not so much that it blinded her.

Goosebumps sprung up on Mercy's arms and she could only stare at the ethereal manifestation. "Who are you?"

"Who is who?" Phin said. "She's spaced out again."

"I am the whisper in the wind, the ripple on the water, the crackle of the fire, the abundance of the earth." The entity's brightness fluctuated as it spoke. "Mercy, your senses are enhanced. Thus, you can perceive much more than the others. Do not reveal what you have witnessed. Sinister plans set in motion decades ago are swiftly coming together. In preparation to counter this attack, key components are set in place for the inevitable battle. Revealing any part of this encounter, will jeopardize these efforts and several lives would be in peril."

"I don't understand." So strong was the heavy weight of bewilderment on Mercy, she was surprised the words made their way out of her mouth.

"Trust you are a part of destiny." The being faded out of focus.

"Wait. Exactly what is my destiny?" Mercy's inquiry came too late. The glowing form vanished, and she addressed an empty room.

"Your destiny is most likely the looney bin, if you keep this up," Vesuvius said.

"Mercy, you *are* talking a bit nonsensically." Phin used a big word again. Correctly, Mercy noted, but she was not in a mental place to figure him out.

"Guys, can't you tell she's upset?" Tambora said. "Mercy, are you okay? You're trembling the way my mom does after she's consumed her sixth cup of coffee in the morning."

"I'm fine," said Mercy. "Just shaken." She rubbed her arm where Patina scratched her. The Tray was weird. Too weird for her comfort. She decided she would make one last effort of appeal to her parents before they departed.

Tambora put her arm around Mercy's shoulder. They followed the boys through the darkness the way they came in. The door, which slammed behind them earlier, stood open, and whatever force which kept them imprisoned released its grasp, allowing them to escape safe and sound into the main fifth floor corridor. The door slammed shut again behind them, causing the children to jump.

Mercy flinched. "Can you please show me to my room?"

"Of course," Tambora said in a most adult voice. "Phin, Vesu, why don't you go save a table for dinner. We'll be down soon."

"Will do," Vesuvius said. "Hope you can regroup soon, Mercy. The food here is always delicious, but they put out their best meals when we welcome new students."

"I'll be there," Mercy promised.

Vesuvius and Phin moved toward the lower levels, their voices trailing behind them.

"Dude." Vesuvius snickered. "Are you wearing a skirt?"

"Aw, shucks," Phin said. "I forgot to change. It's a kilt. My dad wanted me to try it on for my cousin's wedding at the British outpost."

Mercy and Tambora exchanged an appalled look and burst out laughing.

Vesuvius said, "I thought you were from the South Atlantic near the Ivory Coast."

"That's my mom. My dad's family is from Scotland."

Tambora patted Mercy's arm. "Come, let's get you settled. I can make a small light, at least to get us through the dark." Tambora repeated her process to create the ball of light and was rewarded with a less vibrant, miniature version of the one she made earlier. "Whew. Just enough for what we need."

Mercy followed Tambora to the dorms on the next floor. Several times, she observed Tambora glance at her. She figured Tambora hoped to learn more about Mercy's adventure, but Mercy kept quiet. Convinced Tambora already considered her strange, she did not want to add any credibility to that sort of thinking.

"Here's your room," Tambora said when they reached the girls' side of the residential floor. "You'll be sharing with CJ Oliver. She's a couple of years older than us and hangs out with girls her age. She's nice, but pretentious. You'll be all right with her. I wish we could room together, but Angela Juneau has already been assigned as my roomie."

Mercy replied, "I'm sure CJ and I will get along okay."

The tidy dorm room lacked décor, and a dreary, dated pinky-tan color covered the walls. Two beds were placed on bunks over a desk area. Mercy's antique trunk and other belongings were on the floor by a desk. The quirky, vintage charm of her personal effects added some character to the otherwise drab room.

"You're allowed to jazz up your side," Tambora said. "Put up posters, hang curtains to hide your desk, whatever you want to do as long as you don't cause any damage."

"I suppose this bed is mine." Mercy climbed up to the bed above her possessions, sat down, and gave the mattress a little bounce. The bouncing jolted her arm, and she winced at the pain. She glanced down and discovered a rip in her sweater and several scratches on her arm in the same spot where Patina grabbed her. The scratches were already in the early stages of accelerated healing the Ara'Jaeons were blessed to possess.

"Wow, Mercy." Tambora touched Mercy's arm. "I didn't notice this before. What happened?"

Mercy blinked and inspected her wounds. "This is what happens when madness wants to dance with you."

"What do you mean?" A light rap on the door interrupted Tambora.

Emzlie Markos peeked into the room before she stepped in, her husband close behind her. "Mercy? Where've you been? We waited here for you but when you didn't show up, we walked around and your father showed me his old hangouts."

"Oh. Um… Tambora gave me a brief tour. I'm sorry, it took longer than expected."

"I'm glad to see you're making a friend so soon." Her mother put on her stylish white gloves. "Your father and I are getting ready to leave. We came up to tell our little girl goodbye."

Something about being referred to as their little girl knocked down the new student defensive wall Mercy built up earlier in the day, and she became exactly what her mother called her. A little girl. She jumped down from her bed and ran to her mother who opened her arms to receive her only child. Mercy flung herself into her mother's embrace. Her shoulders trembled as she released her repressed sobs.

"I'll wait in the hallway." Tambora stepped out, closing the door behind her.

Orion kneeled down and turned Mercy toward him. "Mercy, what is it? What's wrong?"

"Nothing. I just—I don't want you to go. I don't like it here."

Her father took her into his arms. "Mercy, I hoped you understood it's not our wish to leave you. But it's our sacred duty. It's a responsibility much greater than our desires."

"I understand. But I'm going to miss you terribly." Mercy's heart broke at the idea of not being around them for several months.

"We're going to miss you too, darling," her mom said. "We'll be in the field and won't always be available for calls. But the school knows how to get emergency messages to us. We'll call you when we can and we'll visit before long. Miss Carmen said there's a Parents' Day in a few months. We should be able to attend." She rubbed Mercy's arm. "Mercy, did you realize you have a snag in your cardigan?"

Mercy pretended to scrutinize the tear. "Oh. It must've caught on something."

Mercy's mother straightened Mercy's flyaway curls. "No matter. It's easily fixed. Just set it aside until later. You'll have so much fun, you won't notice time go by."

Mercy nodded. "I'll be fine. I'm just tired. I'm sure I'll be better once I've eaten."

"I've heard extraordinary stories about the cooking here," her father said. "The food must've improved since I came here as a boy. When I attended the Tray, dinner was usually raw frog legs and bat stew. I could tell you horror stories." Mercy wiped her tears and giggled as her father continued. "I wish I could stay for a do-over. But your mother wouldn't allow it. I suppose you'll have to eat my portion too, then I can bounce you home like a roly-poly ball when this is over." He rubbed the top of her head. "Okay, kiddo. It's time your mom, and I got going. Harmony and balance, Mercy."

Mercy smoothed down the frizz left behind where her dad rubbed her hair. "Harmony and balance, Dad."

"Harmony and balance, my daughter," her mother said.

"Harmony and balance, Mom." She hugged and kissed her parents. Guilt struck her conscience as she followed them into the hall, where Tambora waited. "Mom?"

"Yes, dear?"

Mercy held out the aquamarine. "I'm sorry. I took this from home to remind me of you while you're gone. You should take this. I nearly lost it."

Her mother folded Mercy's hand around the stone and covered it with her own. "You keep this. I can get more."

Mercy fought the urge to throw herself at her parents' feet and grab ahold of them until they agreed to let her leave with them. But she held off too long and missed her opportunity, and soon they were gone. Mercy groaned, reentered her room, and took a seat on her trunk.

"Hey." Tambora sat next to Mercy. "Don't be too sad. I'm here. Vesu and Phin are here, too. I've been the only girl in the group for far too long. You balance us out. We're going to have fantastic adventures together. Just wait."

"Yes. I believe you. We're going to be great friends and make enormous discoveries, but not today. Let's have dinner before we tackle any more escapades." Mercy nudged her new friend with her shoulder, surprised to realize she may, eventually, mean it.

CHAPTER 3

AN ANCIENT VOICE

Tambora escorted Mercy to the large dining hall, which was a perfect complement to the shabby, but clean, condition of the lobby. In awe, Mercy looked around her. Antiquated elegance was a valid description. Round, dark wooden tables of all sizes filled the room and a crystal-beaded chandelier hung over each one. Many of the light blue crystal drops were broken or missing, but the fixtures were glamorous. The embroidered white linen placemats and runners on the tables were classic, but thin from decades of use. Faded teal wallpaper, gilded in golden peacocks, clung to the walls, refusing to submit to the inevitable peeling which already scarred the corners. Chaos ruled the room. Several paper airplanes flew about, but with over 400 uniformed students gathered into one place, there were no expectations for the dining hall to be anything else.

Vesuvius and Phin waved at Mercy and Tambora from a table for four. In the light, Mercy caught a better look at Phin. He *is* cute, she thought. She saw his eyes were more vivid than imaginable, of course they were purple as were all Ara'Jaeon's eyes, including Metalicons, but Phin's were on the edge of blue. Close, but not quite. Periwinkle, perhaps. But neon, for sure. The color was exotic against his light golden, brown skin, and his shoulder-length burgundy dreadlocks added a hint of bad boy. The type of boy who appealed to Mercy since she first noticed boys the previous year. She bit her lip to get rid of those thoughts. Although intrigued by so-called bad boys, Mercy knew they were trouble. An older sister of one of her classmates in Athlenan regularly dated them, and she was always in a conflict with her parents because of her boyfriends.

Tambora and Mercy wormed their way through the maze of tables, bumping into students and apologizing along the way.

"Hi, Mercy. Are you feeling better?" Phin pulled out the chair next to him for her.

Mercy sat down and scooted the chair closer to the table. "Thanks. I'm much better. I only needed a minute to pull myself together."

"That's good," Vesuvius said. "We'd hate for you to have a nervous breakdown on your first day."

Tambora stood by the last empty chair. "Mercy will be fine. We'll make sure of it." She continued to stand, her gaze flicking back and forth between her brother and the empty chair beside her. "Vesu. Wasn't it super nice of Phin to pull out the seat for Mercy?"

"Did he? I didn't notice," Vesuvius said.

Mercy covered her mouth to hide her amusement.

After an uncomfortable minute, Tambora sighed, pulled out her own chair, and sat down. "Thanks for the help, Vesu."

Vesuvius raised his brows. "I didn't—"

Tambora interrupted him. "Never mind." Her flared nostrils gave away her irritation.

Soon, a large royal blue enamel platter, adorned by a gold rim, flew past their table and dozens more sailed through the room, delivering dinner to the students. They sported all shapes and sizes, but their color was the same. Delicate golden filigree wings carried them on their flights in and out of the kitchen. So delicate were the wings, that Mercy wondered how they bore the burden of their load. Puzzled, Mercy asked Tambora to explain. "What are those? They're lovely."

"They are marvelous little inventions called Petit Serveurs," Tambora said. "They were trendy ages and ages ago. They were gifted to the most important families. When the novelty wore off, no one wanted them anymore."

Phin leaned forward, his arms crossed on the table. "Their origin is a mystery, and since no one knew where they came from, someone suggested sending them to the Tray to use until they can't be fixed anymore."

"That's why you don't find them anywhere else," Vesuvius said.

"Wow," Mercy said. "Are there any more surprises around here?"

"You can probably count on that." Tambora smiled wide, showing her perfect pearly white teeth.

The serveur which assisted their table bore a little chip on the edge of its enamel, further evidence of a past finer than the present. Their serveur set down the dinner plates filled with a fragrant fig and lamb stew over orange and lemon infused rice. Mercy smelled the deliciousness long before food was placed in front of her. "Thank you," she told the serveur. The serveur adjusted itself into an upright position facing Mercy, placing one wing on its center, throwing the other to the side, and taking a bow before it flew toward the kitchen. Mercy clapped her hands, delighted at the gesture. "Well. That was unexpected," she said.

Tambora cranked her neck around to watch the serveur fly away. "It's actually quite interesting, because no one usually pays attention to them. I never considered they might have any awareness outside of service."

As Tambora finished speaking, a dozen serveurs rushed in, keeping low to the floor, the one with the chipped edge in the lead. They looped under and around the other tables and chairs, so discreet, no one, except Mercy and her friends, noticed. Or perhaps, no one cared enough to notice. With a fluttering wing, the chipped serveur pointed to Mercy. One by one, the Petit Serveurs confronted her, made a dipping movement, and returned the way it came. She watched her tablemates in uncertainty and they returned her gaze in the same manner. But before they voiced their surprise, a hush fell over the room. Their attention moved to where Miss Carmen and several other adults sat at a long table. Miss Carmen stood and asked for the Creator's blessing over the meal, then took her seat. Once more, the quieted room became a lively blend of chatter and laughter as the students, Mercy included, gobbled down their dinner and enjoyed their friends.

"The stew was wonderful. Do they always cook like this?" asked Mercy.

"Pretty much," said Vesuvius. "Of course, you are new today, and I heard they're putting out a special dessert in your honor."

"They're making fried diples covered in honey and cinnamon," Phin said.

"I've never had diples before. What are they?" Mercy said.

"They're thin dough rolled into logs and fried," said Tambora. "Then they're drizzled with honey or dipped in sugar. They're messy. We don't get them often, but they're so, so yummy. Hey, Mercy." Tambora pointed to a group of girls who appeared to be a year or two older than them. "The girl over there with the long hair is your roommate, CJ. Those highlights? They're natural."

The rose gold strands in CJ's beach blonde hair dazzled even under the soft warm glow of the chandeliers. She and her friends twittered, as teenage girls do, and took pictures of themselves, using their messaging and translation devices. Mercy begged her parents for one of those gadgets before they left, but they told her she must wait until she turned thirteen.

"I've never seen highlights like that before. They're incredible," Mercy said, envious of both the lustrous hair and of the communication equipment, and mortified that she endlessly seemed to say 'I've never, insert action here, before' since she arrived earlier that day.

The adults at the head table stood while dessert was served. Miss Carmen towered over them all. "Students, may I have your attention, please. I'd like for us all to welcome a new pupil to the Tray. Mercy Markos, will you stand please?"

Mercy felt her cheeks burn, but she stood as commanded. The room erupted in applause and whistles. She plopped down, eager to escape the limelight.

"Mercy, I want to introduce you to a few of our faculty and staff. To my left are Magister Pappas, Mr. and Mrs. Kishan, and the housemother for the mid-level students, Miss Birgitta Callaghan, who prefers to be called Miss Birdie. On my right, we have Mademoiselle Manigot and Miss Petula Lefevre, who is the housemother for the upper-level students."

The staff members nodded in Mercy's direction, then sat after they were acknowledged. Mercy examined the staff at the head table. Many appeared as though they came from regions outside of the island. She found the diverseness stimulating and was excited at the possibility of learning more about the Ara'Jaeons from outlying posts. Her perusal stopped at Magister Pappas when she noticed he watched her. His arm rested on the table and he drummed the surface with his fingers. His brows furrowed, as if he studied a puzzle with too many pieces. Her eyes met his, and they locked, and for the second time since her arrival, she felt powerless to move.

"The prophecy of the Council declares the ranks of Kadius and Marokos shall become one to produce a daughter. But beware, she shall reinstate the Iron Crown and bring forth death."

The voice sounded distant, like an ancient echo traveling across ages. But the declaration seemed personal, critical, and quite disturbing. Mercy blinked hard to break the invisible connection she shared with the magister and shook herself to reality. She glanced around to discover if anyone else heard, but everyone focused their attention on Miss Carmen. All except Mrs. Kishan, who regarded her with concern plastered on her face. She had paled to a shade considerably lighter than when she was first introduced. Mercy concentrated on Miss Carmen and attempted to forget the teachers and the strange voice in her head.

"There are many other staff members who could not be here tonight, but I'm sure the self-proclaimed Fire Twins will fill you in." Miss Carmen gestured toward Vesuvius and Tambora.

Whispers and snickers filled the room. Tambora reddened. Embarrassed for Tambora, Mercy thought it best to pretend not to notice. However, her concern was short-lived, because Vesuvius, ever the clown, stood and mimicked a royal wave, effectively diverting attention away from his sister.

Mercy dug into her dessert, excited to taste the diples. They were messy and gooey, but the thoughtful kitchen staff provided a pack of hand wipes to each table. Just as she finished cleaning the stickiness from her hands, a voice behind her called her name. Mercy turned toward the speaker, shocked to find CJ there. The shiny rose gold highlights in CJ's hair captivated Mercy. She could scarce drag her attention away from them while CJ spoke.

"Hi, I'm CJ. Miss Carmen told me we're roommates. We like your wild, curly hair." CJ smirked and glanced toward her friends. One pointed toward Mercy and covered her mouth as she whispered to the others. They burst into school girl giggles. "I just wanted to say hi. I'll see you later in the room."

Mercy's cheeks grew hot. "Nice to meet you," she said, but CJ was already headed to her table.

"Don't mind them," Tambora said. "They stick to their clique. We can have our own." After dinner, Tambora accompanied Mercy to help light the fifth floor. "You can get a flashlight from the commissary. It's closed right now, but I can show you where it is tomorrow. I'm sure your parents have set up an account for you there. Miss Carmen asks all the parents to do it."

As they neared the fifth floor, Mercy became fearful of another Metalicon visit, but when they stepped off of the fourth-floor steps, she detected the dark silhouettes of the Regulators standing guard deep in the shadows. She gasped. Her gut reaction was to back away.

Tambora grabbed her hand and dragged her forward. "They won't bother us if we go through quietly."

Mercy was frightened to see the Regulators in person, but she realized there would most likely be no Metalicons dropping in while they were on duty, offering a smidgeon of comfort. Up in the dorms, Mercy reached for her door, but it opened before she made contact and CJ emerged, accompanied by two of her friends.

"Oh. Hi, CJ," Mercy stammered. "Hey. I want to apologize if I'm intruding on your space. You were probably happy having a room of your own."

"Well, yeah," CJ said. "But no worries. Miss Carmen warned me a few weeks ago that many of the Ecclesia were getting called to service, and I would probably have to get a roommate, so I expected it."

"Okay. Will I see you later?" Mercy asked.

"Maybe." CJ winked at her friends, and they twittered amongst themselves as they walked away.

Mercy didn't hold out a lot of hope she and CJ would become very chummy. She thanked Tambora for her help and bid her goodnight, even though there were another three hours before lights out. She was tired and needed time alone. Still dressed, Mercy climbed up onto her bunk, lay on her back, and stared at the ceiling, recalling the voice she heard during dinner and the mention of Kadius and Marokos. They sounded remarkably like Kadarius and Markos, her family names. She supposed there must be a connection. Thoughts of her family names took her mind to a time when both sets of her grandparents were around. She thought about her paternal grandparents, Grandmother and Grandfather Markos. She last saw them the previous year. They were important members of the Ecclesia and also of the Assembly, resulting in many extended absences while they were on tours and assignments. Mercy loved them with all her soul, but they were a serious and austere couple, and she often felt uncomfortable around them. She could not imagine how her warm, humorous, and charming father came from such a somber upbringing. However, her mother's parents, Grandma and Grampa Kadarius, were the complete opposite. Her heart skipped a beat at the thought of them. Nurturing, loving, and warm. And they were devoted to each other. Theirs was an epic love story between an Ara'Jaeon and a human. She never grew tired of her grandma telling the tale, and if she remained quiet and still enough, Mercy was able hear her grandmother's voice describe their first encounter. They met in the United States when she came across him injured from a covert mission and on the verge of unconsciousness. The risk was high for their chance meeting to cause major problems and setbacks, but Grandma Yvonne proved to be trustworthy and hid him while she nursed him back to health. After he recovered enough to go home, he continued to visit her in secret until they fell in love and married.

As Mercy lay there, she remembered her grandma's embrace. She was saddened by the fact she could not be in her grandmother's company as often as she desired. Not long after her grandfather passed away four years earlier, her grandma left Ara'Ja and returned to human society, moving to the nearby island of Crete. Mercy could not visit her grandma because Ara'Jaeon children did not leave the island until they reached thirteen years of age. And because she was human, her grandma could not enter Ara'Ja without the escort of an adult Ara'Jaeon, which meant she only visited a few times a year, when her mother or father could accompany her in. With them called out to service, it looked like it would be a very long time before she could see her grandmother again. Mercy rolled onto her side and propped up her cheek on her fist. She looked over at CJ's empty bunk, glad CJ was still out. Mercy wanted to be alone, as her experiences that day drained her. Soon her eyes crossed and became heavy. She didn't want to fall asleep, because then she would be awake during the night. But her weighty eyelids won the battle, and she closed them to give them a brief rest.

———————◆———————

Mercy crept alone down the thin, dark hall and headed toward the pulsating blue light. The beam sparked and crackled. The brilliance was both fearful and beautiful to behold. She worried for her safety and resisted going farther, but an invisible tether tugged at her. A light touch at first, like the gentle persuasion of a fragrant flower in a midnight garden. She drew near the hall's end. Her heart pounded and her breathing was ragged. She struggled against the pull but was overcome with an uncontrollable compulsion. Each time she fought the urge, the lure became fiercer, stronger, and relentless, until she no longer held custody of her own body.

She rounded the corner at the end of the corridor and stepped into a room where Pip and Patina stood, their backs to her. They held large, heavy poles in both hands and pounded them up and down on the floor. They stopped their incessant clanking and turned toward her. To her horror, their faces melted away to reveal the empty orifice of the Regulators. They shuffled toward her and resumed to hammer the poles on the floor.

She screamed.

Mercy bolted upright, unsure of her whereabouts. The persistent knock at the door brought her to reality.

"Hold on," she yelled and rubbed her eyes with her shaky hands.

"Mercy, it's me, Tambora," said a voice from the other side of the door. "Are you okay? I heard you scream."

"You can come in," Mercy called out. "I fell asleep and had a creepy dream, but I'm fine."

Tambora stepped into the room. "Oof. I hate those. Then you feel weirded out when you wake up. Are you all weirded out?"

"A bit," Mercy admitted and jumped down from her bunk. "What's going on?"

"Miss Carmen asked me to deliver your class schedule and to walk you through it tonight before lights out. Do you have time?"

"Absolutely. Let me wash up first. Um… where's the restroom?"

Tambora chuckled. "Have you been holding it in all day?"

Mercy wrinkled her nose. "Well. Pretty much."

"Come with me, it's down the hall by the rear stairwell. Every floor has them in the same spot, so they'll be easy for you to find." Tambora ushered Mercy to the bathroom, and on the way, chatted about topics too inconsequential for Mercy to recollect later.

Mercy felt much better after she splashed cool water on her face. She supposed Tambora and she would end up being good friends. She might have been wrong about the Tray, and although she was not ready to concede, she detected a dash of excitement for what might come.

CHAPTER 4

THE BEST FRIEND CODE

Mercy settled in nicely during her first two months at the Tray. She and CJ were friendly, but not chummy, and despite CJ's claim to the contrary, Mercy felt like an intruder in CJ's room and CJ didn't make Mercy feel welcomed. Mercy didn't mind too much. She became close companions with the St. Clair twins and Phin. Time with them filled most of her days outside of classes. She didn't expect to enjoy her new home as much as she did. Her earlier encounter with the Metalicons seemed like a dream, but she woke up each morning, wondering if that would be the day they might reappear. Many questions ran through her mind and it was difficult to put her attention to other matters. She threw herself into her studies to direct her thoughts away from her obsession. Mercy convinced the others to not talk to anyone else about the mysterious door and her supposed delusions when they first met. She asked them to trust her. Although she was a virtual stranger to them, and with little reason to do so, they agreed to keep quiet and continue to investigate on their own. But the fact was, their entire group experienced the appearance and disappearance of the mysterious door, which Mercy believed played a part in their ability to trust in her word. They snuck past the Regulators several times to search the fifth floor for the door they encountered. They unearthed nothing except the other barricaded doors which lined the hall.

Mercy was placed in Early Secondary School and her class schedule kept her busy during weekdays. Besides normal school subjects, such as math and literature, her classes included Etiquette: Conscientious and Appropriate Application of Your Abilities, Ara'Jaeon History I, and General Abilities, which focused on understanding the various elemental abilities and determining one's own talents. School at the Tray demanded a lot more than her previous classes in Athlenan, but she was up for the challenge.

On that particular Saturday morning, Mercy sat in the student lounge, her Ara'Jaeon History book open on her lap and her General Abilities textbook at her side. The oversized, overstuffed sofa was her favorite spot. She often went there to curl up, wrapped in her beloved patchwork quilt, her most prized possession. Her grandmother made the quilt for Mercy's fifth birthday. Hundreds of petite diamonds cut out of bright colorful fabrics were sewn together, grouping similar colors in a manner which created a wavy design distinguishable only when viewed from a distance. Each diamond was a unique, vibrant patterned cloth, and she found a different one every time she studied the craftmanship. She could spend hours cuddled up in her quilt, thinking about her grandma, and peering out of the windowed walls and glass ceiling of the top floor lounge.

The entire outer wall of the student lounge, as well as the inner wall overlooking the lobby seven stories below, was made of thick, clear, unbreakable glass. The glass allowed a panoramic view to the outside from any vantage point in the lounge. The Tray sat high on a hill on the northwestern peninsula of the island. The sea was visible in all directions from the high viewpoint of the lounge. On clear, bright mornings, when the sun was in the perfect position, you could make out the faint, white skyline of Nikonea City across the bay waters toward the east. It was an enchanting sight reminiscent of a glittering fairy castle. That day, a cloud cluster hid the sun. The bright rays caused a gleam of hot white gold to rim the edge of its cotton candy sanctuary, a perfect fall day in early October. The vista was spectacular. A myriad of trees dotted the landscape beyond the olive tree forest, yielding a colorful array of bright gold, orange, fire red, burgundy, and lime green leaves.

Ara'Ja was hidden from the world with a cloaking spell, cast by the four elementals—Earth, Wind, Fire, and Water—when they created the first Ara'Jaeons to become keepers of Earth's elements. Mercy's grandmother was one of few humans who knew about the Ara'Jaeons and their home of Ara'Ja, an island of diverse geography. Stately mountains arose on the east, high forested hills on the west. Nikonea City was built on a peninsula between them with white sandy beaches and fertile valleys all along the coastline. The island's tranquility and beauty were surrounded by majestic seas, whose colors, on a good day, vacillated between brilliant sapphire and dazzling turquoise, depending on its mood.

Mercy finished her studies and flipped ahead through the pages in her history book. She knew the basics of Ara'Jaeon history, but she hoped to find something more interesting to read than the already familiar Ara'Jaeon Purpose, which every Ara'Jaeon child learned during their first five years of life. She could recite the mantra word for word.

> *Born of Wind and Water*
> *Bred of Earth and Fire*
> *This Sacred Vow we utter*
> *No vow could be made higher*
> *We give of every talent*
> *And pledge we will provide*
> *The Harmony and Balance*
> *That keep the earth alive*

Mercy skimmed past God's creation of the four elementals and past the creation of the first Ara'Jaeons by the elements. She happened across an index of names, illustrations, and presumed biographies of the Firsts, the original four Ara'Jaeons—Canicus the Fire Eater, Kenwei the Water Dancer, Nayavu the Earth Watcher, and Zephyrine the Wind Rider. "This book doesn't tell me anything," Mercy muttered to herself and dashed down to the library to search for more information about Wind Riders. Mercy gathered her belongings and was about to leave when the sky caught her eye.

A storm was predicted for the afternoon and evening, and Mercy spotted dark clouds forming in the distance. She reasoned she should get outdoors while the weather was still nice, find Tambora and the boys, and then go to the library later. Mercy dropped her books off at her room and raced to the lobby. As she arrived, a drenched Phin and Tambora ran in and stood under the warm air propellants suspended from the ceiling inside the door. The propellants blew warm air on rainy days. Students and staff alike were grateful to not have to walk through the entire building while rain-soaked.

Disappointed, Mercy peered outside and saw the deluge. "Wow. I just looked out the window upstairs and the rain clouds were far away, so I thought I had time to get out a bit before the weather turned nasty."

"You almost made it, but the storm blew in a lot faster than expected. You didn't miss much, though." Phin stepped out from under the air blower, fully dry. "Vesuvius kicked the garden gate and knocked it off its hinges."

Tambora puckered her lips in a fake pout. "We wasted all of our time, struggling to fix the thing. Luckily, there isn't lightning yet, because Vesu is still out there, finishing up."

"Well. I'm going to the library to research. Do you wanna come with?" Mercy asked.

"I will," Tambora said. "I need to get a book to read if I have to stay inside for the rest of the weekend."

"Not me." Phin ran up a few steps and yelled down, "I'm going to hunt for a photo of Magister Pappas and throw darts." He winked at Mercy, who bit a corner of her lower lip, hoping she would not respond in childish overreaction at the flirtation. Phin resumed his ascent up the steps, taking two at a time, nearly colliding with the magister who was on his way down.

"You can find an exceptional image on page forty-two of last year's memory book." Magister Pappas cocked his brow. "But your aim must be accurate or you will skewer poor Mr. Kishan instead." He nodded to the girls as he continued on his way. "Ladies."

Phin grimaced down at the girls before he continued up the stairs, and they giggled until they reached the library. The main library room was shadowy and quiet. Mercy looked out the large picture window. The sky was as dark as the unlit library. Gray clouds, bursting with bolts of lightning, illuminated the room with each flash.

"I hope Vesu made it inside okay," said Mercy.

"I'm sure he did. He was practically finished when Phin and I came in." Tambora reached for the light switch and twisted the dial. "Way better. Have you used the new automated checkout yet?"

"I have, although it's awkward, knowing there's a camera pointed directly at the checkout counter. I hate feeling as though I'm being watched."

The girls walked past the front desk to the four Earth portals. The library itself was a mid-sized room, but the Tray held such an extensive collection of books, portals were necessary to access the remotely located vast rooms required to contain all the fiction, non-fiction, and reference books. The fourth portal led to another chamber full of private reading rooms. The library portals were the only portals in the Tray the students could use without restrictions. They were on a permanent setting to lead only between library areas, and there could be no temptation to use them to leave the premises.

"I need to go to Ara'Jaeon history," Mercy said. "I want to find out if there is anything about the first Wind Rider, Zephyrine. We'll be studying Wind Riders in the next few weeks, and I want to get a head start."

"I'll be in fiction. There's a new author who writes adventure stories about a group of kids who go on quests and solve mysteries. Catch me there if you finish before me."

"Okay. See you soon."

Two girls stepped out of the fiction room portal and snickered when Mercy smiled at them. She recognized them as friends of CJ. When they walked away, Mercy overheard one say before their voices drifted off, "CJ said she…" Mercy furrowed her brows, wondering what CJ said and hoped the conversation was not about her.

Mercy and Tambora walked through the portals to their separate destinations. Each portal was filled with nature's confetti, thousands of red and gold grapevine leaves, blowing around. A few weeks earlier, Mercy learned the library portals changed with every season. She was charmed by many such simple details at the Tray. She located the history section toward the rear of the room and browsed through the titles of the books. She took her time to amble down each row, running her fingers over the book spines. The caress of each embossed letter thrilled her. The library contained hundreds of books which began in the letter A, *Ara'Ja: Beginnings, Ara'Jaeon Combat and Warfare, Ara'Jaeon Holidays* to name a few. None of the titles jumped out at her until she got to the N section and came across an old, thick, ragged book titled, *Navigate the Wind: A Beginner's Guide to the Early Wind Riders.* With much care, Mercy removed the relic from the appointed position on the shelf and sat on the floor, placing the book on her lap. Her fingers left telltale marks in the heavy layer of dust on the book cover. The edges of the pages were worn and yellowed. She wished she possessed Wind capabilities so she could flip the pages without using her hands on the delicate paper. She did her best to blow the dust off the cover and used the utmost of caution to open it to the Table of Contents.

Mercy scarcely turned the page when footsteps resonated from the main aisle. Startled, she held her breath as they moved closer. Fearful a Metalicon entered the library, she set the book down and stood, ready for flight. She glimpsed a shadow at the end of her aisle and a figure rounded the corner. Mercy shrieked. The figure jumped and screamed in return. They both squealed until they burst into a fit of laughter.

"Where did you come from?" Mercy asked Tambora, who held a paperback novel in her hand.

"I located the book I wanted right away and was coming to get you."

"I thought you were another Metalic—" Mercy slapped her hand over her mouth and gave herself a silent lecture on how to keep secrets. "Sorry. Nothing. Forget it," she murmured through her self-imposed muzzle and dropped to the floor, shifting her hand from her lips to cover her racing heart.

"Don't *nothing* me." Tambora parked herself on the floor. "Spill."

"I'm not supposed to talk about it." Mercy sat down, crossing her legs.

"Ummm. Yeah. Let me explain this to you. We're best friends now and there is a code that needs to be followed."

"What kind of code?"

"It basically states best friends are exempt from secrecy vows," said Tambora. Earnestness filled her eyes and Mercy believed her.

"Really? I've never actually had a best friend before. I hung around a group of kids at my last school, but no one person in particular. I didn't know there were codes."

"Oh yes. There are plenty of codes. I'll tell you about them later, as we need them. But for now, I seriously must know what's going on with you."

Mercy confided the details about her Metalicon encounter and the being made of light, who Mercy dubbed the Emissary.

Tambora leaned back, resting her elbows on the floor by her sides. She didn't take her eyes off of her friend until Mercy finished. "You understand how this sounds, right?" Tambora sat up.

Mercy nodded.

Tambora sighed. "I'm torn. On one hand, this sounds too implausible. I mean, the boys and I were right there, and we didn't see or hear it."

"But the Emissary, I mean, the light figure, said my senses were enhanced and I could see and hear what others couldn't."

"This is true, but how do you know it wasn't lying?"

"Do you even understand the implications of what you just said?"

"What do you mean?"

"It means you believe me. Why would you say something that didn't happen might tell me a lie, or even the truth? If it wasn't real, how would this creature tell me anything?"

Tambora smirked. "Good point. Which brings me to my other hand. It sounds so fantastical that you clearly couldn't make it up. My head tells me not to believe, but my gut says you're not insane. Oh my golly, Mercy. What will you do? It sounds as if those Metalicons were stealing electricity from the Tray. No wonder nothing works there. Tell someone."

"Ummm, that's a big fat no. Maybe you believe me, maybe even the boys would believe me, but everyone else would say I was certifiable." Mercy stood and moved toward the next aisle. "Hey. While we're here, I want to search for a book about Metalicons. I know little about them, except they are wicked."

"I don't know much either. The topic is taboo at my house. Actually, I never hear *anyone* talk about them except in whispers."

"It's the same in my family. You would think if they are so dangerous, we should know about them."

The girls walked up and down and back and forth several times in search of books which might give them the slightest information on the forbidden subject, but success eluded them.

"No surprise. I can't find anything," Mercy said. "The next time the librarian comes, we'll have to ask her where she keeps the books about Metalicons, if they even have them at all, since it's obvious no one wants us to know anything about them." Mercy rounded the corner to the last aisle. "Hey. We missed a section here. Let's check it out." She stopped. "Whoa!"

"What?" Tambora asked, running to catch up to Mercy.

"The medallion on the wall, isn't it exquisite?"

"It is," Tambora agreed and examined the books on the rack closest to where they stood.

Mercy reached out her hand to the medallion. Rings, covered in etchings of symbols, surrounded the central design inlaid with turquoise and copper. "This isn't just a decoration. See how the symbols don't match? They must mean something." Mercy's fingers traced over the shapes of the marks. At her touch, the rings on the medallion slowly spun around, each ring in a different speed and in the opposite direction of the surrounding bands, until they spun out of control. Mercy jumped. Tambora came up behind her and peered over her shoulder. The spinning subsided bit by bit and came to a stop. A bright golden light from inside the medallion lit up and glowed through several of the etchings.

"What is *that*?" Tambora asked.

"I don't know. But I'm sure these symbols mean something. Quick, do you have a pencil and paper?"

"I saw a stack on the table a few aisles over. I'll run and get them."

"Hurry, before the lights go out." Mercy examined the lit symbols while Tambora retrieved the writing supplies. She decided not to risk touching the object again. She didn't want to chance any disruption to the settings.

"Here you go." Tambora handed Mercy a pad of paper and a pencil.

Mercy thanked her. She sketched a small circle surrounded by several circles until she completed a replica of the medallion. She then mapped out each lighted symbol on the drawing.

"There. I'm finished." Mercy smiled at her accomplishment. "It's a pretty fair rendering, if I say so myself."

"It looks identical," Tambora said. "Do you think this has something to do with what you saw on your first day here?"

"I don't know, could be."

As suddenly as the medallion first spun, the rings rotated to their original position, and the light went out.

"Wow," Tambora whispered. "It's like it waited for you to finish."

"I know, weird, huh?" Mercy studied the paper. "We need these symbol meanings. I have an idea." Mercy glanced up. "I know who we can ask. My great-uncle Atticus knows about this stuff. He studied ancient Ara'Jaeon history."

"Should we set up a visual with him?"

"No. Then we'd have to get an adult involved. I'd rather it only be us."

"Where is he, and how do you plan on getting there without an adult?"

"He's in Nikonea City, and I don't know yet. But between us, we're bound to get some ideas. We might find a stray portal hidden on the grounds and sneak out." Mercy folded the paper and tucked the note into her pocket as they walked back to the portal.

They stepped into the library and the overhead lights flickered off and on.

"There's the last call for lunch," Tambora said.

"Then let's hurry." Mercy made a deliberate point to smile at the camera as she checked out her books.

CHAPTER 5

A CURT DISMISSAL

Mercy struggled to stay awake the following Monday. She slept little since she and Tambora came across the medallion in the library two days earlier. She hoped in vain for another message from the Emissary, who failed to fulfill its promise to revisit.

Her first class of the day, General Abilities, was in session for only a few minutes and Mercy's head already bobbed with heaviness. Mercy loved General Abilities. She learned a great deal about the many uses of the various abilities, and she lived for the day when she and her classmates would discover their talent aptitudes. She would love the class even more if the students didn't have to walk on eggshells every day. The teacher, Magister Pelagius Pappas, was brilliant, but also rude and condescending, staring at his students through emotionless, heavily lined eyes. To make matters worse, he wore his long, shocking red hair in a ponytail. The severe hairstyle did little to hide the hideous contrast of the bright red against his pallid skin and thin lips and brows. Each time he entered her line of sight, her thoughts centered on how he unnerved her when he stared at her during her first dinner at the Tray, when the ancient voice told her about a daughter.

Mercy's chin dropped to her chest and her body jerked awake.

"Psst. Mercy." Tambora sat in the desk behind Mercy and kicked Mercy's chair. "You better wake up or Pappas will make you an example to the class. You need to stop staying up at night, waiting for that emissary creature."

"I know." Mercy turned around in her seat to whisper to Tambora. "I'll do better, I promise."

"Mercy Markos, do you wish to share what you feel is of more importance than my lesson?" Magister Pappas touched the end of his pointer stick on her desk.

Mercy spun around to face Pappas, shook her head, and scooted down in her seat, hoping he would not rap on her knuckles.

The magister sniffed and pulled a lace-edged hanky from the pocket of his long Victorian dinner jacket. On that day, he wore one in dark green velvet. Mercy concluded he owned twenty-two. When she first realized he must possess a massive collection, she counted them until he started over. Although she disliked the magister, she admitted he dressed in a style of his own, and she respected it. She favored his black and gold brocade. She yearned for one for herself to wear over her black mini dress. Her black studded combat boots would provide the perfect accessory.

"I suggest you control your urges to listen to your own articulations and pay attention to mine if you want to pass this class. Am I understood?" he said as he walked back to the head of the class and wrote *Elemental Aptitudes* on the blackboard.

Mercy nodded and slunk even further in her chair, mortified at being singled out. The electric blue enameled Situation Clock, which seemed to have made itself at home in the classroom, spun mid-air in front of her desk and chimed, "It is 8:37, and time to pay attention." Mercy picked up her textbook and swung at the clock, but just as she moved to swat, the timepiece flew to hide behind Magister Pappas. It peeked over the magister's shoulder to tease Mercy. The flapping wings on both sides of the clock resembled the hands of a child with his thumbs in his ears, wiggling his fingers in the "neener neener" position. The students giggled, and the magister shooed it off to hover in the corner. Perturbed at how the clock treated her, Mercy stared down at her notebook and wrote her thoughts for a story about a young girl who challenged a Situation Clock to a duel.

"All right, students. Pay attention. Today, we will determine your elemental aptitudes," the magister said. "A few of you have already gone through this assessment and, for the sake of this class, will repeat the process. But for most of you, this will be a fresh experience."

Mercy jolted to attention at the announcement she had expected for the past several weeks—the opportunity to feed her fantasy of becoming a Wind Rider someday, even if she needed to fudge her family history to the elements themselves. Excited, she hoped she would be one of the first tested.

"Those of you who possess a pure bloodline from a First could someday become a master of your skill set. You might become a Fire Eater, a Wind Rider, an Earth Watcher, or a Water Dancer. But—and this is a significant but—it is rare for anyone to attain the titles carried by the first Ara'Jaeons, even for those who boast an untainted bloodline to a First. Not only must one master multiple skill levels of their particular element, one must also pass a series of unannounced challenges to assess skill, problem-solving, leadership, and whatever else the Assembly, or possibly even the elements, decide to throw into the mix. But worry not. Many years will pass by before you are qualified enough for the challenge." Pappas raised an eyebrow and directed his attention toward Mercy. "The rest of you will have to be satisfied with lesser goals. And don't consider trying to pretend you're eligible. The elements know."

Mercy suspected he knew how to delve straight into her soul and uncover her deepest desires with the singular intent to ridicule what he unearthed. Disappointed, she opened her notebook and wrote more ideas for her story. She added a snooty professor as the second to the clock in the duel. But writing her ideas didn't stop the disheartening she suffered, knowing she could never attain the highest level of any element. Her bloodline was impure. Her ancestry was a general mix of elements, not to mention her mother's family was tainted by human blood *and* Metalicon ancestry.

"Your results in today's assessment do not indicate you will develop skills for a specific element, but rather your aptitude, your potential to cultivate skills in those areas. Should you fail to exercise your abilities, you will fail to develop them. The burden to advance yourself is on you and only you." Magister Pappas walked around the room and tapped the end of his pointer in his hand. "Today, the majority of you will succeed in demonstrating an aptitude for one or two elements. A scant few of you may even show potential in three elements. None of you will exhibit all four, but do not obsess too much over your inferiority. Only two Ara'Jaeons in the entire history of Ara'Ja have developed skills in all four elements, and both of them lacked the natural inclination for most of them. They achieved this distinction only after a century or two of arduous training."

Vesuvius raised his hand, and the magister called on him. "Who are they?"

"The first was Leonidas the Defier in 1178 BC. The other was High Elder Jonathan Broomfield, who was killed in office in 1945. Both men have passed through the Gates of Vatek."

Vesuvius raised his hand again and Pappas aimed his pointer at him. "Yes, Vesuvius."

"What did Leonidas the Defier defy?"

A snort came from the direction of Phin's desk. Mercy tightened her lips to keep from joining in.

The magister stared blankly at his student. Mercy visualized the gears spinning in his mind to generate a response. "Well. Um," the magister said. "He defied logic. He defied everyone who said he could not accomplish what he set out to do."

The answer seemed to satisfied Vesuvius, as he nodded and said, "Excellent."

Pappas cocked an eyebrow at Vesuvius, nodded once, and turned his attention to a table next to him. "On this table, you will notice many items which represent various elemental qualities. A tree branch, candles, a glass of water, a thermometer, a wind spinner, and many others. I will call each of you up individually. Simply focus on the objects. When you feel ready, you will close your eyes, stretch out your hands over the table, and concentrate on the individual elements. Adele Grayson, please come forward."

Adele, a pretty blonde with hair almost as curly as Mercy's, but less unruly, took slow, deliberate steps and made her way from the rear of the room to the front, clearly intimidated to be the first one called.

"In my lifetime, Adele," Magister Pappas mocked, and she hurried her pace to reach the front. "Carefully regard the objects on the table before you, and when you are confident you have thoroughly scrutinized them, close your eyes."

Adele stood still for a moment. Mercy sat forward in her seat, excited to witness the event.

"Are you ready?" the magister asked. Adele nodded. "Concentrate. Envision the elements and stretch your hands out over the table," he instructed.

Adele reached toward the table, her hands outstretched. The stance reminded Mercy of Frankenstein. She suppressed a grin and held her breath while she waited to learn what would happen next. She waited. The class waited. Nothing happened. Not a single thing. Mercy let out a puff of air and sat back in her seat, disappointed.

"Adele, study the items again," Pappas said, "then close your eyes and visualize the effects of Wind. Visualize Earth. Visualize Water. Fire. View them in motion. Observe as they conceive and birth the exquisiteness of their art."

Mercy, along with most of her fellow students, leaned forward.

Adele extended her somewhat shaky hands. The class gave a collective gasp when the water in the glass spouted up similar to a fountain, a bowl of ice spit out ice shavings and created a miniature snow pile on the table, and steam escaped from a kettle spout to form the shape of a swan. Every water object on the table shifted or was altered.

"Nicely done, Adele. You most likely will have strong water abilities, if you can keep yourself from drowning in your own sea of insecurity. You may return to your seat. Who will be next?"

Xander Jacobs, who sat next to Mercy, jumped up, ran to the front and yelled, "ME! I want to go next."

"All right, Xander, since you are already up here, you will be next. And do try to restrain your eagerness. Tapping into one's abilities should be executed using self-control and concentration. We do not need to trigger a perilous incident, such as an epic flood or a major earthquake. Do you remember the instructions?"

Xander nodded. "Yes, sir."

"Then you may proceed."

Xander examined the articles and stretched his arms over the table. In an instant, the tree branch cracked, several stones bobbled about on the tabletop, and the candle wick briefly lit up and sizzled out.

"Well done, Xander. You have minor capabilities for Earth and Fire, but you caught on quickly, therefore, with hard work and perseverance, you should be able to change that mediocrity to something of more significance."

Red-faced, Xander took his seat and Magister Pappas tested the students one by one. Phin evaluated well for Wind and Water capabilities, and Mercy clapped for him as he bounded to his desk, sporting an immense grin. He rewarded her with a thumb's up. Tambora and Vesuvius both tested for superior skills in the Fire element. The results did not surprise them, or anyone, actually. They both began Fire skill training at a very young age and openly discussed their prestigious heritage.

Mercy scrutinized each performance, impatient for her own opportunity. At last, after the other students tested, Mercy's chance arrived. She readied herself for the pay-off. She would soon learn the first part of her destiny. Pappas called her name, and she walked toward him, careful to not go too fast or too slow to lower the risk of being on the receiving end of the magister's snarky remarks.

"Mercy, by now, you should know the drill. Please proceed, unless you need for me to, yet again, go over the instructions."

"No. I understand." Mercy took a breath and studied the objects. She squeezed her eyes shut and held her hands out over the table. She concentrated hard on the wind objects and neglected the others. She imagined herself floating on air as she performed multiple Wind tricks. Satisfied she accomplished what she set out to do, she opened her eyes before the magister even commanded it. She looked to him, expecting an accolade. Instead, he treated her to a stern glare and arms folded over his chest.

"Mercy, either you are playing games or you have no element potential. I highly doubt the latter, so I can only deduce it to be the former. So, tell me. Are you playing games, Miss Markos?"

"No." Mercy's lips trembled and she bit the bottom corner to steady them as she noticed no changes to the objects on the table.

"Then let us begin again."

Mercy nodded and started over, at which time, she gave all the elements her attention. She visualized each of the elements as they blew, consumed, flowed, and quaked. She envisioned the effects and the sounds they would produce while in motion, until finally, she became one with them.

She smelled pine and checked her surroundings. In doing so, she realized she no longer existed as the timid, self-conscious Mercy, standing at the front of her classroom, but as an unconstrained, confident entity on a narrow lane in the middle of a forest. Surprised at first, because no other student commented on getting transported during their testing, she discovered herself gliding a few inches above the pine needle-covered ground. She knew she had never been there before, but it seemed like home. The transcendental sensation rendered her incapable of knowing if she dwelled in her body or observed from the outside. She realized she didn't care. She almost flew, as she always desired, and she continued to enjoy the path and its surroundings.

Mercy lowered herself to walk on the ground. Pine cones and twigs covered the earth beneath her bare feet and crackled and snapped when she stepped. She danced, filled with childlike joy until soothing sounds of a nearby waterfall grabbed her attention. The gentle splashes sang to her in quiet, still voices. Lured by the lullaby, she left the trail to find the source. She followed the song until she came to a cascade that flowed down among a cluster of jagged boulders, pouring into a creek at the bottom. Water nipped at her feet, beckoning her to follow. But before she could pursue the water's call, a velvety white feather drifted down from the sky. The downy plume kissed her cheek and floated away into a nearby shrub which reached out and ensnared it. The trapped feather fluttered about, as if struggling to be freed, but the branch held fast onto its catch. Angered, Mercy rescued the prisoner from captivity. She moved to dip her toes back in the water and kindly set the feather down on the swollen brook where it whirled lightly on the water's surface. Water accepted the plume and formed a low wave to carry it downstream and out of sight.

Contented, she took a short hike alongside the stream until she came to a peaceful, sunlit meadow, surrounded by high, snow-peaked mountains, towering against the brilliant blue sky. A breeze, giving off the faint taste of salt, flowed down from the mountaintops and Mercy supposed the ocean must be beyond the summit. She gloried in the experience, again wondering why no other student mentioned similar incidents.

The sun grew warmer, boosting her serenity. Mercy lifted her chin to the sky, held out her arms, and pirouetted. A playful wind gust pushed her long curls into her face as she twirled. No sooner would she brush the strands away, when Wind blew them back again. She gathered her hair into her hand and spied a dandelion at her feet, white and fluffy with seeds. She wished to assist destiny and plucked the aging weed from the ground. She raised the maestro of future dandelions to her mouth and blew until the stem was bare and spent. Wind acknowledged her gift and flung the tiny white parachutes higher and higher until they scattered to unknown places to take root.

Mercy spotted a bed of vibrant flowers across the creek. Sweet perfume stretched its long fingers to invite her in. She savored the fragrance, yearning to rest among the blooms. She jumped over the water and hurried to get there. The splendor overwhelmed her, and she dropped to her knees and wept. Her hot tears fell to the ground and Earth received them. The irrigated flowers grew tall and distorted. What once appeared as a gracious garden, mutated into a grove of pine trees, leaving Mercy in the forest where she began. She experienced no sorrow upon her separation from the beauty of the garden, but looked forward to the next chapter in the wondrous experience. She breathed in, expecting to take in the earthy pine scent. Instead, she choked on acrid smoke. Flames approached her from both sides with the tumultuous fury of an unquenchable hunger. The heat intensified, and she grew faint. She dared not delay her departure.

Wind teased Fire into a further frenzy until Fire consumed all in its path and closed in around Mercy. Her labored breathing and pounding heartbeat pulsated throughout her body. She knew she must find her way to the classroom. In a panic, she scanned for a way of escape, whirling this way and that, but came across only one way to run, a narrow passage which opened before her amid the fiery trees. Adrenaline kicked in and she made a mad dash through the opening, fleeing the flames which chased her. She kept focused on the trail, detecting a glimmering rock in the dirt a short distance ahead. She ran forward and stooped to investigate. The stone fit in her palm, and ribbons and chunks of raw gold ran throughout. In her distraction, she lost the lead in her race against Fire, and the blazing inferno encircled and trapped her. Without forethought, she threw the rock into the flames.

"May this precious metal be an offering of peace between us," she yelled.

The sacrifice appeased Fire, and the flames collapsed into a pile of smoking ash around her. A shiny gold nugget rested amid the soot, returned from Fire as an acceptance of her goodwill. She bent down for a closer view, reaching out to touch the gold. Although fresh from the flames, the silky, smooth gold nugget felt cool to the touch, purified by Fire. She placed it in her pocket and stood up.

When she arose, she no longer lingered in the burned forest, but was transported to the center of the grassy meadow where she stood moments earlier. Just when she supposed her journey ended, the essence of the elements surrounded her. Their tall, smoky spirits danced to the poignant melodies created by their earthly manifestations. Wispy impressions trailed behind their movements and clamored to keep up with the tempo. They reminded Mercy of the colorful artist renderings of gaseous pillars and nebulas in space. One by one, the spirits faded away. Drained, but yet enchanted, she mourned when their time together ended.

Screams, from somewhere in the far distance, made their way toward her and the magister called her name. But the voice morphed into a softer and unforeseen utterance.

"Mercy. Mercy—"

A slight gust of wind blew from across the meadow and stopped before her, and she came face to face with the specter of the Emissary.

"Mercy, you have done well. You have passed your first test and have created harmony in the company of the elements. Much will be required of you, for you have been trusted with much. You will wield the authority of the elements, but remember to respect their power. This strength can do marvelous things. Miraculous things. But strength can also destroy and devastate. You must practice fervently. Practice relentlessly. The day will come when you will be called on to defend honor. But be cautious, for honor may not reside in the most honorable of places."

The voice faded out and a different voice arose, a deeper voice.

"Mercy. Mercy, are you okay?" a frantic voice demanded. "Open your eyes. Now!"

Mercy blinked, recovering her wits. She returned to a hushed classroom and a mess in front of her. To her surprise, the contents of the table were destroyed. Most of the nails which held the table together popped out and embedded themselves in the brick wall behind it, leaving the table on the verge of collapse. She realized the screams she heard before her conversation with the Emissary came from the students, many of whom moved to the rear of the class. She must have done something terrible to cause the disaster before her. Pappas stared at Mercy, his features changed in a split second from one of shock and awe to hardened annoyance.

"Students," he purred, using perfect diction. "What you have witnessed here is what we will call a showboating."

A snicker or two came from the students behind her. She fumbled around, trying to pick up whatever fell to the floor to put them back on the table, but merely caused the table's ultimate demise. It crashed to the floor at her feet and she jumped. Brutal laughter erupted from her classmates.

"I'm sorry, sir. About all of this." Mercy spread her arms out. "I didn't know what I was doing."

The magister's lips twisted into something resembling a smile. "Of course. You didn't know what you were doing." He practically spat on Mercy with his hyper pronunciation.

Mercy stood still, her hands clasped behind her, as Magister Pappas addressed the class. "It seems we have a prodigy among us." He emphasized the word prodigy, and not politely. He tapped his pointer in his hand. "Mercy, here, has put each of you to shame and has shown the rare potential for all four elements."

Mercy's classmates talked among themselves, not even bothering to whisper. Some students, like Beaumont Chamberlain and his best friend Conrad Montague, poked fun at her predicament, while others professed curiosity or awe at her newfound abilities. She knew she should be excited about her test results, but the magister's attitude embarrassed her.

Xander raised his hand.

"Quiet, students. Xander, you may speak," the magister said.

"What about the nails? Why did they fly?"

The magister's nostrils flared and his mouth tightened. Without a word, he turned from his students and erased his writings from the blackboard. When he swung back around toward the class, he abruptly announced, "No more questions. Class is dismissed for today."

It took all the control Mercy could muster not to run out the door from where she stood. But she kept a modicum of dignity and made her way to her desk, ignoring Vesuvius and Phin, who both watched her with their mouths hung open. Tambora waited for her, her brows knit together in compassion. She opened her mouth to speak, but Mercy interrupted her.

"Not here," Mercy said as she picked up her belongings. She sensed the magister's hard gaze burning into her back, but she chose not to give him the satisfaction of knowing how much he rattled her. She lifted her chin high as she clutched her books in one arm and put her other hand in her pocket. A surprise awaited her there. She struggled to contain her excitement as she fingered the cool, smooth object tucked into the corner of her pocket.

CHAPTER 6

AN ACCIDENTAL SQUALL

Mercy exited the classroom, plastered on a smile, and pretended everything was normal.

"Hey, Mercy. Wait for me," Tambora yelled. She wormed her way through the throng of students, rushing to get to their next class. She fell in step beside Mercy. "Are you okay?"

"Yeah," Mercy answered. "I'm a little embarrassed, but I'm fine."

"What happened? In my test, I saw fire and electricity."

"I saw them all. All the elements. It was surreal. I could tell I wasn't flesh and blood. And I wasn't in the classroom. At first, I stood in a pine forest, then I spotted a brook with a waterfall and a flower garden in a field. And fire. Hot fire. It was if the elements and I communicated to each other through nature."

"That's amazing. When I did it, I didn't envision myself in a specific place. Fire was simply there. Like it was a part of me," said Tambora. "But what happened with you? What made the items on the table go bonkers?"

"I don't know. One minute, I danced alongside the elements in the meadow, and the next, the Emissary showed up and told me I passed the test. Basically, it said I'm going to do great things, but I have to be careful because of someone or something dishonorable. The whole incident was dreamlike, and I'm still a little disoriented. I can't remember exactly what it said." Mercy's gaze dropped. "The other kids think I'm a freak."

Tambora stepped to the side of the hall and yanked Mercy's arm to follow. "They don't. They're just surprised. It's unexpected and unfamiliar and amusement is an easier coping method. Actually, it *was* a little frightening when you destroyed the entire table. We'll chuckle about this in the future. I promise."

Mercy shrugged. "I suppose you're right."

"Well. Here's my next class. You have Ara'Jaeon History, right?"

"Yeah, I should probably get going, too," Mercy said.

"We'll talk more later?"

"Sure. Wait. I forgot to show you something." Mercy paused and glanced around to make sure no one watched them. "When I was surrounded by the fire, I came across a piece of raw gold and I threw it into the flames. When the fire died down, a gold nugget lay in the ashes, completely polished up. I put it in my pocket and guess what?" Mercy's hand went to her pocket. "Guess what I found when I came back to reality?" She pulled out the gold and showed it to Tambora, keeping her other hand over it to hide it from the other students who walked past them.

Tambora touched her hand to her heart. "No way. Are you joshing me?"

"No. Not at all. It literally returned with me."

"It's beautiful. You need to keep it somewhere safe. The school has a lockbox for our valuables, you should keep it there."

"And have them interrogate me about where it came from? No, thank you. They would never believe the truth."

"Well. Think of somewhere safe, then."

Mrs. Kishan, her history instructor, stood in the classroom door down the hall and signaled to her. "I will," Mercy said. "Gotta go. We'll get together later and we can talk then."

"Okay. But don't forget to be marvelous. You're a rising star now. Pappas so much as said so. Just imagine. My best friend. A prodigy."

"You goof. I'm no such thing. I'm the same as I was this morning." Mercy brushed off the compliment, but Tambora's declaration energized her. She mingled into the moving crowd headed to her next class. "Hi, Mrs. Kishan," Mercy said.

"Harmony and balance, Mercy. I've been told you've had quite a start to the day," Mrs. Kishan said in her clipped Indian accent.

Mercy grinned at her teacher. "Already?"

"News spreads fast around here."

Dressed in an exotic pink and gold sari and a red bindi dot on her forehead, Mrs. Kishan completed her ensemble with matching flowers tucked into the auburn hair she wore in a traditional low bun. Selena Kishan and her husband, Nedim, the Skill Trainer for the lower-level students, came from the little Ara'Jaeon island outpost, Nanghi, near Sri Lanka. After centuries of being spread out across the Earth, Ara'Jaeon outpost communities grew and adapted to embrace the customs, manners, and language of the surrounding areas. Subsequently, although the Kishans were genetically Ara'Jaeon and shared much of their physical attributes with their fellow Ara'Jaeons—tall, purple eyes, and shades of red or blond hair—their skin possessed the deep brown, amber tones of the South Asian region. "Come in quickly now," Mrs. Kishan said. "Class is about to start."

Mercy sat next to Phin in the mid-section of the classroom. As usual, she preferred to be in the most inconspicuous area.

Phin leaned across the aisle. "So, what happened back there?"

"I interacted with the elements. I mean, I didn't simply see it. I experienced it."

"Interesting. I don't think anyone else did that. Why do you believe it happened with you?"

Mercy shrugged. "No clue. But it was pretty cool."

"Students, take your seats, please," Mrs. Kishan said. "Today, we will discuss the High Eldership of Ara'Ja. Can any of you give me the name of an Ara'Jaeon High Elders?"

Angela Juneau, Tambora's bunk mate, raised her hand and waved frantically.

"Yes, Angela."

"High Elder Atticus Kadarius."

Mercy scooted down, hunching her shoulders to make herself smaller. High Elder Kadarius was her great-uncle, and she didn't want her classmates to find out. In the past, whenever kids learned of her relationship to the High Elder, they would either fake-friend her or think she was treated with privilege.

"Absolutely correct. High Elder Kadarius is our current High Elder. He's been in office for about four years," Mrs. Kishan said. She glanced at Mercy, who lowered her gaze.

"Only because Caudel disappeared in disgrace after everyone figured out he murdered Broomfield and his assistant all those years ago." Beau snickered, reaching across the aisle to give Conrad a fist bump.

"First, let me remind you to raise your hands and not to speak out of turn," Mrs. Kishan said. "Second, this story hasn't been proven, nor has there been even one official accusation that High Elder Caudel was involved in High Elder Broomfield's death or the death of his assistant. It is hearsay and gossip. And he didn't leave in disgrace, he was killed in a Metalicon attack, alongside several other high-standing members of the Assembly."

A collective murmur in the classroom arose as the students realized the tragedy occurred only a few years earlier. Mercy's chin dropped, and she dabbed at sudden tears. Her grandfather, Augustus Kadarius, was among those who were killed in the attack that catapulted her Uncle Atticus to the High Elder's office.

Mrs. Kishan continued. "But since we've brought up the past three High Elders, we shall begin our lesson by discussing High Elder Broomfield. Jonathan Broomfield was the most distinguished High Elders ever to rule Ara'Ja. He mastered talents in each of the four elements. He began as a teenager and it took him close to 200 years to accomplish. His tenure as High Elder lasted for one hundred and fifty-three years. Longer than any other High Elder in the previous twelve centuries. His time in office was unexpectedly ended in 1945 by his murder, which, by no means, has been solved. We will not speculate in this class on the many theories of his murder, as we do not perpetuate rumor at this facility."

Beaumont raised his hand and made a show of waving wildly in the air. "Me, oh, me. Pick me!" he cried out. Angela, the target of his jest, flushed and picked at her fingernails.

"Yes, Beaumont?" Mrs. Kishan said.

"What exactly DO we perpetuate at this facility?"

The entire classroom snickered and even Mercy could not stifle a little giggle.

Mrs. Kishan strolled to where Beau sat and grabbed both sides of his desk. She bent over until her face hovered mere inches from his and glared down at him. She said, "We perpetuate we are *Born of Wind and Water, Bred of Earth and Fire, This Sacred Vow we utter, No vow could be made higher, We give of every talent, And pledge we will provide, The Harmony and Balance, That keep the earth alive.* Nothing more, nothing less. Now, students, let's get back to the lesson."

The class erupted in applause and Beau slumped down, his hands clenched and fisted in his lap. Mercy figured even bullies, such as Beaumont Chamberlain, knew better than to mock the Ara'Jaeon Purpose, and the idea made her happy.

———————

The prospects for a quiet evening were slim when Mercy arrived at the entrance of the student lounge for her routine study time after that night's dinner. On most evenings, there were perhaps only a half a dozen children there. That night, a throng of students crowded around the entrance to the full room, blocking her. She caught her name getting tossed around by several students. Mercy despised the idea of being the topic of conversation—good or bad. She didn't want to discuss her experiences in front of passive friends and decided not to stay. She walked away before anyone spotted her.

"Mercy," Tambora called out. "Hold up."

"Shh," Mercy said. "I'm trying to leave before anyone realizes I'm here."

"Where are you going?"

"Down to the library to study." Mercy tried to avoid eye contact with other students.

"I don't think so."

"What?"

"I mean, let's go down there, but you're not studying. We're going to a reading room, where we can be alone and talk about what happened today. Come on, before we're followed."

Vesuvius and Phin stepped out of the crowd. "Not without us, you don't," Vesuvius said. "You can't go all renegade and leave the men out. It's the four of us."

Mercy lamented internally. She hoped for time alone, but deep down, she was grateful for the support of her friends, and so she agreed.

They made it down to the second floor without interference, when they encountered the arrogant Beaumont and his tyrant-in-training, Conrad.

"Well. Lookie what we have here." Beau sneered at the group. He circled around Mercy and rubbed his chin. "Sorry. I'm just not impressed. I mean, shouldn't you be sparkly or glittery with all that power running through your veins?"

Conrad snickered. "Yeah. Then she wouldn't be so dull."

Mercy grimaced at the lame attempt of a joke. If they were going to insult her, they should at least make it legitimately humorous.

"Guys, cut it out," Tambora bellowed. "Get yourselves a couple of muzzles and put them on like the dogs you are."

"Woo hoo! What's the matter, Mercy? You can't speak for yourself? You need your little spitfire of a pet to defend you?" Beaumont then directed his attention to the much tinier Tambora and shoved her shoulder.

"Hey. Stop it." Vesuvius pushed Beaumont away from his sister and restrained her when she struggled to get around him to fight her own battle. "Why don't you pick on a brute of your own size? Or are you chicken?"

"Hey, Beau." Conrad chuckled loudly. "They can't even tell if you're a dog or a chicken."

Mercy scowled and clenched her hands into fists. She stepped in to separate the boys, who were on the verge of a rumble. When she brought her hands up to grab onto them, a burst of wind emerged from her palms. The gust twisted into a mini tornado and wrapped around all six of the children. They were lifted off the ground, several feet into the air, and spun around.

"Argh!!!" they yelped in unison.

The funnel carried them down the hall and spit out the disheveled and disoriented group in the most unfortunate of places—at the door of Magister Pappas's office. The door opened, and the magister himself stepped out into the corridor. "What is this ruckus about?" He swept his hand in front of him and shooed away the squall. He crossed his arms and rested his side on the wall. "My, my. What happened here?" He squinted at Mercy. "Oh. Do let me guess. One of you ignored the *no use of power* rules."

Perplexed and stunned, Mercy said, "I. Uh. I didn't mean to do it. I don't know what happened, honest." She was as surprised as anyone by what came out of her hands.

"What happened is you lost control," Pappas said.

Tambora protested. "But it wasn't her fault."

Phin pointed to their tormentors. "Beau and Conrad were harassing us, and Mercy tried to stop them."

Beaumont propped himself against the wall, mimicking the magister's stance. He seemed bored by the whole scenario. Conrad made a show of snickering, but exposed his true spinelessness when he moved to cower behind Beaumont.

Pappas frowned. "Beaumont, Conrad. Leave us. But I want both of you in my office tomorrow after classes are finished for the day."

Beaumont's lip curled. "See you later, losers." He swaggered away, bumping Phin's arm as he passed by. Conrad followed close behind, also knocking into Phin's arm.

Pappas tapped Mercy's shoulder. "You, come with me. The rest of you can go."

Mercy slumped as she addressed her friends. "I'll catch up with you guys tomorrow." She let out an enormous sigh and followed the magister into his office.

The office décor was as she suspected. Dark, heavy, and ornate. The furnishings were old, and the drapes were made of gold and green brocade. Mercy gasped. Her mouth hung open as she took in the stunning sight, her gaze swept from the floor up to the high ceiling. A built-in bookcase ran across an entire wall. The shelves were filled with statues and books that looked so ancient, she figured they were possibly original editions.

Pappas directed Mercy to have a seat in a nearby chair and he sat on the edge of his leather desk, his hands clasped in front of him.

"Magister, I've never done this before." Mercy used every bit of her resolve to hold in her tears. "I don't even know *what* I can do, let alone know how to control it."

"I am aware of this, Mercy. What you experienced in class earlier today appears to have triggered your powers into manifesting much earlier and more rapidly than usual. Normally, they develop gradually through age or practice, but since you have neither, you have not acquired the time necessary for your natural tendencies and instincts to adjust to accommodate them. Are you familiar with the term restraining?"

Mercy nodded, fearful of the question's implications. "Yes. I've overheard my parents talk of performing them on rogue Ara'Jaeons." Her heartbeat raced. Restraining was what they did to criminals. Would they do that to her?

"This is not an approach we take lightly. In your case, what we will do is sanction a temporary restraint on you until you become more comfortable with your talents. This means we would bind your abilities in such a manner that we can remove the restraint and put it back on you as necessary. Of course, you will be required to begin your training classes immediately and the restraint will be off during those periods. Once you have proven you can control your elemental abilities through a series of small tests, we will perform a complete reversal of the restraining. I will contact your parents tomorrow to fill them in on this development and to obtain their permission. In the meantime, please be careful. Actually, perhaps you should stay away from anyone or anything upsetting." The magister's mouth twisted into a replica of a smile.

For the first time since she arrived at the Tray, Pappas behaved more or less kind to her. After her overwhelming day, the glimpse of humanity proved too much for Mercy and the tears which threatened to spill earlier made good on their promise. The instant the first tear fell, the nearly kind Pappas disappeared, and in his place stood the rude man Mercy knew him to be. He cleared his throat and abruptly stood up. "You may go."

Mercy stiffened and silently departed the room.

———————◆———————

Mercy lay under her bedcovers in the dark room that night, holding a flashlight and her journal. She wrote about how horrific it felt to be the center of attention and the exhilaration of learning she was not ordinary. She wrote about the shame she experienced when Pappas abruptly dismissed her and how refreshing it was for Tambora to check on her afterwards. The door swung open and the light in the room came on. Startled, Mercy tossed her blanket aside and sat up.

"Oh. I didn't know you were here." CJ took off her shoes and tossed them under her loft bed.

"I decided to turn in early tonight."

"Is it because everyone's talking about you?" CJ pulled her nightgown out from her drawer and changed for bed.

"Everyone's talking about me?"

"Come on, you honestly believe anyone could do what you did today and no one would talk about it?"

"What are they saying?"

"Most kids were pretty impressed by your show, but there are some who say you only pulled off a few tricks to make yourself appear better than the rest of them. That it wasn't real. It was a set up."

"How would you know? You didn't see it. You're not even in that class." Mercy lashed out.

"Cool down, I didn't say it was a set-up. I'm saying that's what some kids are saying." CJ flipped off the light switch and climbed the ladder to get into bed.

"You believe me then? You believe it was real?" Mercy aimed her flashlight at CJ.

CJ stopped at the top rung, rested her arms on the bed frame, and fixed her eyes on Mercy. "I don't know. I didn't see it. I'm not even in that class." CJ threw Mercy's words back at her.

Mercy flung herself backwards on her bed and pulled the covers over her head. "Ugh."

CJ got into bed. "Whatever you did to Beau Chamberlain and Conrad Fairchild gets my approval. Those boys are obnoxious."

Mercy threw the blanket off, turning out the flashlight. "I don't know what I did. It was an accident."

"Accident or not, they deserved whatever they got."

Mercy hesitated before she spoke, unsure of how to respond. "Thank you?"

"Yup," CJ said.

"Good night." Mercy turned to face the wall. She was self-conscious earlier because she stood out from the crowd, not because she suspected the other students would accuse her of cheating. She fell asleep and tossed and turned throughout the night, dreaming she woke up too ill the next morning to attend class.

CHAPTER 7

FAREWELL, DEAR QUIET LIFE

Mercy took each anguished step as though she were a dead girl walking. Earlier that morning, she climbed out of bed on legs made of lead, heavy to lift and difficult to maneuver. But she forged through the day as best she could. She heard a few whispers behind her back, but several students who never spoke to her before greeted her as they passed in the hall. She arrived at her classes right as the bell rung and left as soon as they let out, allowing no opportunity for unwanted conversations.

As Pappas said the night before, he contacted Mercy's parents and received their permission but they asked to speak to her prior to the restraining. He arranged for Mercy to call them when classes ended for the day. She had no reason to fear her parents, they were always supportive of her, but she dreaded the conversation. She preferred a quiet life, having nothing to report to them. She favored invisibility. She certainly didn't want to be an anomaly. She followed Miss Birdie, the house mother, to the Visual Communications Room in the basement where she would make an image call to her parents. Trailing behind Miss Birdie, her mind conjured up illustrations of her following a red-haired dumpling on legs. Her analogy was not meant to be unkind. It was simply a product of her overactive imagination. She was fond of Miss Birdie, who wore a white apron each day and a matching kerchief in her short, curly hair. Her fashion sense bordered on dowdy, but Mercy supposed the intent was to provide a relaxed and homey presence for the students. She didn't seem to have any element gifts, which was uncharacteristic for an Ara'Jaeon adult, and she was short, which was also an oddity. She was only a few inches taller than Mercy, about the height of an average teenager. In normal circumstances, Ara'Jaeon children developed the same as human children until they were approximately sixteen years old. At that point, they grew one or two inches each year up into their mid-twenties, when they reached their full height of six-and-a-half to possibly seven-and-a-half feet tall or taller. Then, their growth tapered off and their aging process slowed down. Mercy wondered if there were any stories about Miss Birdie, about why she didn't grow. She would ask Tambora, who always kept on top of the gossip which ran rampant at the Tray.

"Come on, girl, quit dawdling. Your parents are waiting for your call. Honestly, you kids these days have no drive. I should just retire and—" Miss Birdie's tired Irish lilt trailed off as she progressed farther ahead, turning down another hall.

Mercy was accustomed to the harmless mutterings of Miss Birdie. She assumed Miss Birdie's gripes were more akin to the groanings of a weary, elderly lady rather than cantankerous remarks. She was actually a caring and giving person, and Mercy yearned to know her story. She quickened her steps to catch up. When she rounded the corner, Miss Birdie stood at the locked door to the Communications Room, sifting through dozens of vintage skeleton keys on her large keyring. They sang when they clanked against one another, sounding like a bell choir. Mercy loved the musicality and didn't much mind the extra time it took for the correct key to be located. "Here we are, sweetie. Come inside now."

Mercy didn't know what to expect inside the room, but what she didn't expect was a modest, dim circular area. Three partitions jutted out from the center to create three separate pie-shaped units. Mercy peeked into them and discovered they were identical. Each contained a large thin monitor on one wall, a circle on the floor in front of it, and a spotlight on the ceiling over the circle. Miss Birdie explained the circle was a sensor to trigger the system. Speakers, a camera, and a microphone were all located inside the monitors. All one needed to do was stand on the sensor and speak the name and location of the recipient of the call. Since three calls could happen at one time, heavy curtains hung over the tops of the partitions to create privacy. A simple set-up for a modern mechanism. Miss Birdie exited the room so Mercy could be alone with her parents. Mercy stood on the sensor and waited for the red light on the monitor to change to green. Her spotlight came on and she wiped her sweaty palms on her uniform pants.

"Good afternoon, Mercy." A nearly realistic computerized voice spoke in surround sound and the image of a synthesized man, presenting an exceptional lifelike appearance, materialized on the monitor screen. "Whom are you contacting today?"

Mercy was astonished the entity was aware of her name, but many happenings surprised her those days. "Emzlie and Orion Markos. Belleza del Mar," Mercy said. Earlier in the day, Miss Carmen said her parents expected her call and waited on the other end. She hoped it was true. She got confused about what was expected of her when situations didn't play out as projected.

"Dialing," the virtual operator said.

Mercy rocked in place while she waited.

After a few seconds, he vanished from the screen, replaced by her parents. She sighed in relief. She would not be left in limbo, after all. Her parents stood in front of a large picture window with a view of the South Atlantic. It was six hours earlier at SARA, and the rosy morning sun kissed the turquoise waters, diffusing into a mixed array of brilliant warm and cool colors. Seeing them, she suffered a stir of homesickness for her parents. She wished she could be with them in Brazil, in part because she longed to travel the world.

"Harmony and balance." She didn't know where the camera was and was not sure where to look. She ended up smiling straight into the monitor.

"Harmony and balance, dear," Emzlie said.

Orion grinned wide and gave a little wave.

"Hey, Dad. How are things at SARA?"

"Doing well, Mercy. We're making progress with our assignment," he said. "Well enough that we'll probably be able to attend your Parents' Day next month."

Mercy perked up at the news.

"Mercy," Emzlie said, "Magister Pappas contacted us earlier about the restraining. He explained what happened yesterday. We agree with him. It's a suitable solution, at least for the time being."

Mercy dropped her shoulders and frowned. "I don't understand. Isn't being able to do all four elements a good thing? Restraining is what you do to prisoners. Why am I being punished?" Her throat tightened as she resisted the urge to cry.

"No. No, sweetheart." Her mother leaned in closer to the camera. "You've done nothing wrong, what's transpiring with you is actually pretty amazing, but it's going to require special attention. Magister Pappas is the perfect person to oversee your needs."

"But I'm nervous about what's going to happen. I wish you could be here."

"Oh, Mercy." Orion's soothing voice cut through her nerves. "We asked to talk with you to reassure you. There is no need to worry or be anxious about the restraining. It's a relatively simple procedure. Actually, not even much of a procedure, more of a ceremony. They'll simply put bands on your wrists, comparable to wide bracelets, then add a few charms. Completion will only take a minute or two. But we want to discuss what happened yesterday when we visit you next month."

A voice from off camera called her father's name. He turned away and nodded at whoever was there. "Honey," her mother said. "We're being asked to report for our shift a few minutes early. There's a rare hurricane brewing in the South Atlantic, so we have to sign off for now. If you feel you need to talk to us after the ceremony, tell the magister and he can arrange it."

"Okay." Mercy was reluctant to agree, but believed she held no other option. At least her fear of a painful restraining was eased. She could deal with the rest of it.

"We love you, Mercy," Orion said. "We can't wait to visit you."

"Me too, Dad."

"Mercy, we must go now," Emzlie said. "We love you, and please, have no fears for the restraining."

"Love you too, Mom."

"Harmony and balance."

"Bye," Mercy replied, but they were already gone.

The synth male reappeared on the screen. "Call terminated. Have a good evening, Mercy."

"Thank you," she said and realized she spoke to an already darkened screen. She stared at the floor and let out a huge breath. Mercy blamed the Ecclesia for taking her parents away from her just when she needed them, but she admitted fate used the Ecclesia and Mercy's great uncle, Atticus Kadarius, to bring the two of them together. Atticus was a junior elder to High Elder Caudel, and if not for him, the great love story between Emzlie Kadarius and Orion Markos might not have happened. Emzlie was half-human and as a general rule, ineligible to join the Ecclesia. But she displayed high skills in handling her gifts and received permission to join only after Atticus persuaded the Assembly to make an exception for his niece. She met Orion when she was stationed at SARA, and they fell in love.

Mercy left the room lonelier than when she entered. Miss Birdie waited outside the door, but Mercy walked past her.

Miss Birdie locked the door behind Mercy and caught up to her. "Did you get everything squared away with your folks?"

"Yes."

"Miss Carmen and a few other staff members are waiting for you in Training Room 3. Do you want me to take you there?"

"No, thank you. I can find it myself. Tambora showed me how to get there."

"Are you okay? You seem blue. You know, you shouldn't worry about this. It's performed more often than people realize. A few minutes is all it takes. Are you sure you don't want me to walk you over?"

"I'm sure." Mercy put on a cheerful demeanor, but inside her mouth, her teeth were clenched.

"All right, but if you need anything at all, you know where to find me."

Mercy nodded and proceeded to the staircase at the rear of the school. It led to a second story overpass, connecting the primary structure to another building. She located Training Room 3 and stood timidly inside the door. She examined the room, curious about what she might find there. The walls were obscured by a puffy, silvery material, resembling the shiny, crispy mylar used to make helium balloons, and a spongy athletic mat covered the floor. She wondered how often kids were injured when training. Except for a few chairs and a large cabinet against a wall, the room was empty of any furnishings. Miss Carmen, Mr. and Mrs. Kishan, and Mr. Romani—the swarthy dreamboat Abilities Trainer for the upper-level students—conversed in the center of the room. Overwhelmed, Mercy became short of breath. Regardless of the staff and her parents' insistence there was no reason to fear, she was full of trepidation of the unknown. Her stomach rebelled, and she feared she might become ill. She moved to back out of the room, but Pappas burst in behind her.

"I apologize for being late, I was obliged to meet with a couple of students," he said.

Despite her queasiness, she needed to tighten her lips to suppress a smirk. She knew who those students were and why Pappas needed to meet them. She wondered what was said, but realized she would probably never know.

Pappas took hold of Mercy's elbow and led her into the room. "Now, Mercy, this will not hurt. There is no pomp and only a small formality involved. The others are here primarily because our policy requires witnesses, not because of any danger. As you know, we have been in contact with your parents, and they have given their approval for the restraining. The restraining itself is as simple as putting on a piece of jewelry. We are using a training room today as they have padded fire retardant walls in case of unforeseen occurrences, although, this is merely a precautionary measure. Complications are highly unlikely. I have never witnessed an incident during a restraining. Are we okay to proceed?"

Mercy hesitated. All accounts suggested the experience was easy and painless. Those declarations meant one of two things. One—it really *didn't* hurt, and no one wanted her to worry, or two—it really *did* hurt but no one wanted her to worry. Despite her doubts and fears, her only conclusion reasoned the restraining was the right course to take. Even her parents agreed and they never steered her wrong. "I'm ready," she told Pappas.

"All right, we will begin," Pappas said. "Miss DeLuca, are you set with the cuffs? Mrs. Kishan, do you have the talismans?"

Miss Carmen and Mrs. Kishan said they were prepared.

"Mercy," Pappas said, "when we are finished, you will not be able to take off the cuffs or the charms. The talismans we are using are specific to the elemental abilities being restrained, in your case, all four. The restraints will be relaxed during the times you are in training class, which I believe is to kick off tomorrow, am I correct, Nedim?"

"That is correct, Pelagius," Mr. Kishan said in a brisk, concise accent identical to his wife's.

"The element charms specific to your lessons will be deactivated by a disengagement device Mr. Kishan will use before your class, and he will reactivate them when the class is over. This will allow you to access your abilities while training. These will not require special care on a day-to-day basis. They can get wet. Therefore, you can bathe and swim in your normal routine." He beckoned to Miss Carmen, who stepped forward, holding the cuffs. To Mercy's relief, they resembled leather bracelets more than handcuffs, taking an enormous load off her shoulders. Since she was first told about the cuffs, all she pictured was herself existing all day, every day, resembling a criminal. But the actual cuffs suited the boho and vintage fashions she wore when not in school uniform.

The magister asked Mercy to hold out her hands, and he buckled the cuffs to her wrists and locked them in place with a miniature metal key. Mr. Kishan looked upward and chanted in what Mercy assumed was his native language, and Mr. Romani patted his thighs to create a rhythmic drum accompaniment. Her surprise must have shown because Pappas stopped his task and said, "Pay them no mind, they are petitioning a blessing on your behalf."

"Okay," Mercy said. The chanting beguiled and calmed her and she hoped it might go on throughout the ceremony.

Pappas returned his attention to the cuffs. "Mrs. Kishan, the talismans, please."

Mrs. Kishan gave two of the charms to the magister and declared, "Water."

Pappas attached a Water talisman to both wristbands. "Mercy Markos, I restrain the gift of Water." A small green light came on in the center of each charm as Pappas put them on.

"Fire." Mrs. Kishan handed another set of charms to Pappas.

"Mercy Markos, I restrain the gift of Fire."

They repeated the procedure twice more for Earth and Wind, and a little light glowed on every charm. When Pappas fastened the last charm, Mr. Kishan ceased his chants, and the women relaxed and chatted together. Astonished, Mercy realized there was absolutely no reason for her to have been worried. The restraining was a breeze. Nothing to it. And the cuffs were no heavier than a normal charm bracelet.

"Wait—" Pappas said. "We are not finished. There is one more matter."

Uh, oh, Mercy thought. Maybe she relaxed too soon.

The other staff members appeared to not understand. Mercy glanced from teacher to teacher and waited to be told what to do. The magister turned and whispered to the others. They nodded, and a few opened their mouths in a large, silent *Oh*.

"Yes, right." Mrs. Kishan unlocked a wall cabinet and fished out an item. From her viewpoint, Mercy could not distinguish what it was, but they appeared to be another set of charms. Mrs. Kishan relocked the cabinet and handed the items over to Pappas. "Met—"

Pappas cleared his throat and interrupted her. "That will not be necessary, Selena. These are added precautions." He fastened the extra talismans to each of Mercy's cuffs. He moved his mouth in silent dialogue, but no sound escaped from him.

Mercy pointed to the last set of charms. "What are these symbols?" she asked when the magister finished. She didn't recognize the symbol, although it resembled a crude depiction of a circle.

"They are only safe guards, my dear," Miss Carmen said.

"Safeguards? Against what?" Mercy asked, unsure if her question was appropriately addressed. But no sooner did she speak when the lights went out. A loud buzz emitted from the cuffs and they spewed out colorful neon beams into the room. Alarmed, Mercy screeched, but was not injured. The teachers jumped. Miss Carmen ran to Mercy, her arms outstretched. But she was stopped by a barricade of impenetrable lights woven around the girl. Shafts of bright light in every color flew in all directions, disappearing whenever they struck a floor or a wall. After Mercy's initial shock wore off, she enjoyed the chaos, dazzled by the beams of colors surrounding her. It ended too soon.

"Well. We did not expect the spectacular light show, but as far as side effects, it was unexpected, but harmless," Pappas said.

"What happened? What were those lights? Why couldn't anyone get past them?" Mercy asked.

"Let me recheck your charms," said Pappas. He took Mercy's hands and examined the cuffs. "There seems to be nothing amiss here. Mercy, you are an anomaly. The first we know of to carry the natural tendency for the four elements. Remember, the others who possessed all four gifts worked relentlessly to get them. Naturally, we should expect there will be occurrences we cannot explain. But the staff here at the Tray is committed to shield you from harm and ensure your training progresses smoothly."

Again, Mercy was not sure her questions were answered, but she was hopeful the staff would take care of her.

Mr. Kishan said, "Mercy, we are finished here. Dinner is about to be served. You may take your leave."

"Yes, sir." Relieved by the conclusion of the ritual, Mercy made a dash for the door. But when the teachers murmured to each other behind her, she slowed down to catch their conversation. Although she didn't make out most of the words, she worked out part of what Miss Carmen said. "We've never had... student before... suppose it will work?"

Mercy fumed the entire way to the main building. What did Miss Carmen mean when she wondered if it would work? It irritated her to think she must endure the public humiliation of a restraint just for there to be a possibility it might not even work. She wanted to sit down. She needed to sit down. She hoped the others were already in the dining room, holding a table. Once there, she stood on her tiptoes to look around and found them at their usual spot. Adele sat in the seat Mercy typically used, her attention on Phin. Mercy clenched her jaw and wondered if she should try to join them and force Adele from her chair or simply find another table.

But Vesuvius saved her from the need to make a choice. He stood and waved at her. "Come on over. We saved you a seat," he called out. He elbowed Adele, who glanced over at Mercy and, to Mercy's horror, Adele checked her out from head to toe, then stood, touched her fingers to Phin's shoulder, and went to the table where her own friends sat.

"Hi, guys." Mercy plopped down. She noticed the boys watched Tambora who narrowed her eyes at them, and no one mentioned the cuffs. Tambora always had her back. Mercy's choice was to ignore the topic as well. "What are we having?"

"Moussaka," Phin said, looking everywhere but at her.

"And halva for dessert," Vesuvius added. Less sensitive than the others, he openly stared at her wrists, although he didn't comment on them.

"Sounds wonderful." Mercy cheered up and played along. She made it a game to observe how each of them reacted. She could always count on her friends and food to put her in a better mood. Her friends and moussaka, the delicious sliced eggplant or potato casserole layered with a thick meaty mixture and covered in crusted béchamel sauce. But her favorite was the sweet semolina confection called halva. She was most fond of the ones topped with pistachios.

"So. What's the word about what happened when Pappas met with Beau and Conrad?" Mercy kept her tone light and carefree, grateful for a diversion from the obvious. She searched the room for the offenders, and found them, returning her gaze with contempt plastered on their faces.

"Apparently, Pappas railed on them for quite a while and warned if they caused more trouble, they would be expelled," Tambora said.

"A student in my Spontaneous Combustion class told me when they came out of the magister's office, Beau's face was red and puffy and all Conrad did was giggle like a little girl." Vesuvius reached for his glass of water.

Phin glanced at Mercy's hands, then quickly averted his gaze.

Miss Birdie entered the room and Mercy remembered she wanted to ask about her. "Tambora, are there any stories going around about Miss Birdie?"

"What do you mean?"

"Well. She's not tall like the other adults and she doesn't appear to have element powers. I was curious about why."

"I don't know the details, but I remember hearing she was friends with someone who took advantage of her powers when she was a teenager."

"She lost her powers," Vesuvius said. "And ever since, she stopped growing." He sat motionless as he spoke, a spoon in one hand and a fork in the other, and eye-stalked the food platter as it made its way around the table.

Mercy rubbed her wrists to ease the mild chafing she already experienced from the cuffs. "How awful for her." It horrified her to discover one's powers could be taken away permanently. It was hard enough to know it might happen temporarily, as was her own situation.

Tambora sat in silence across from Mercy, watching her in apparent concern. "Are you okay, Mercy?"

"I'm fine." Mercy acknowledged the elephant sitting at their table. "See my new jewelry?" She air-quoted *jewelry* then held out her arms.

Tambora took Mercy's hand and inspected the cuff she sported. "These are actually kind of cool. Did you notice the symbols match the element symbols on the walls in the lobby?"

"No. I haven't been able to study them yet. I came straight here, but it makes sense they would."

"What's this one?" Tambora pointed to the extra charm Pappas was adamant to include.

"I don't know. Miss Carmen said it was for additional precautions."

"Precautions against what?" Tambora said.

"That's exactly what I asked," said Mercy. "But I didn't find out. There was an incident before I received an answer. Lights came out of the cuffs and zapped around. They weren't electrical, just colorful lights. But they created a barricade around me and Miss Carmen couldn't get through them. It was remarkable. No one knew it was going to happen."

"Weren't you scared?" Tambora said.

"No. Surprised, at first, but not afraid. It was too fun to be frightening."

With the taboo of mentioning Mercy's new accessories broken, Phin entered the conversation. "This last charm reminds me of a crown." he said.

The mention of a crown reminded Mercy of the symbols from the medallion and she recalled the prophecy she heard referenced a crown. The hair on her arms stood up.

"Oooo, it really does," Tambora said.

Vesuvius widened his eyes. "Hey. Maybe you're a princess."

"Ara'Jaeons don't have a royal family, silly," Tambora said. "We can probably find it in the library. It might be a fun secret mission."

"What a great idea. Perhaps the medallion will give us a hint." Mercy pushed aside her thoughts of the crown. "That reminds me." She quit talking when their Petit Serveur showed up and put an enormous platter of moussaka on the table. She thanked the serveur. It bounced a few times in what Mercy interpreted to be a bow, then sped off and Mercy continued. "Tambora, somehow, we need to get to Nikonea City to visit my uncle, and I figured out when might be a convenient time to go. Parents' Day is in a few weeks on Saturday. On Friday, the day before, there are no classes."

"We're going to Nikonea City?" Vesuvius reached across Phin's plate to grab a large slice of moussaka.

"Shh." Tambora hushed her brother. "We're trying to keep this quiet."

"I guess we can fill them in on it though," Mercy said. "It's not as though they won't find out, anyway."

Phin put a fork full of food in his mouth and asked, "What's going on?"

"Geez." Tambora wrinkled her nose. "Could you maybe put a little more food in your mouth the next time you talk?"

Phin's eyes sparkled as he gave her a wicked smirk. "That—" He took several more big bites of food. "—will not be a problem."

"I would expect this from Vesu, but not from you." Tambora wagged her finger at Phin.

"Listen, guys, I want to keep this just between us." Mercy lowered her voice and leaned in to tell the boys the complete story about what happened when she met the Metalicons.

Vesuvius and Phin didn't make a sound, transfixed on every word. Mercy rather enjoyed the power her words held over them, giving her more confidence in her choice of writing as a vocation.

"There's a medallion in the library with some type of symbols on it. Several of the symbols lit up when I touched it, and Tambora and I think it gave me a message. We copied them down, but we need to go to the Assembly and show them to my Uncle Atticus."

"Wait. The Assembly? Uncle Atticus? *The* Atticus? Your uncle is High Elder Atticus Kadarius?" Phin asked. "Why didn't you say something in class yesterday when we learned about the High Eldership?"

Mercy shrugged, giving the impression her high-ranking uncle was no big deal, when in fact, she desperately wished to show off to her best friends. "I don't always go around and talk about everyone I'm related to. Do you? But yes, he's actually my great-uncle. He and my grandfather were brothers. Uncle Atticus is an expert on ancient Ara'Jaeon artifacts and hieroglyphics. I'm sure he can help us."

Tambora said, "We obviously need to talk to someone about this and who better than the High Elder?"

"So why are we waiting?" asked Vesuvius.

"Because of the preparations for the festival, they've canceled classes that day. It would be an opportunity to sneak away without getting caught. But I haven't figured out how we're going to get there."

"At least we have time to plan this out," Tambora said.

"Planning how to get there isn't necessary," Phin said.

"How so?" Mercy asked.

"Every semester, my parents give me a few portal crystals to use for emergencies. I've never used any. I've been saving them up. I have dozens in my room."

"Dude. Impressive," Vesuvius said.

They continued to discuss their little upcoming adventure until the Petit Serveur reappeared, carrying a variety of halva. It set three pieces of pistachio onto Mercy's plate and placed the rest of the sweets on the table. Mercy grinned at the serveur and asked, "How did you know pistachio is my favorite?"

The Petit Serveur plopped down in front of Mercy. It simply sat there, facing her. But she was certain the serveur stared straight into her soul, and the same peace and calmness she experienced whenever she was around her grandmother, surrounded her. One of its wings took Mercy's hand, and it patted her restraint with its other wing. It put down her hand, jumped into the air, and sped off after a hasty little bow.

"What do you suppose that was about?" Vesuvius asked.

"I have no clue." Mercy picked up a piece of halva. "But I was comforted, like I am when I'm around my Grandma Kadarius." She popped the sweet into her mouth.

"That's truly charming, Mercy," Tambora said.

Mercy finished chewing the food in her mouth before she spoke. "Guys, I need to get going. I need to study for the math test tomorrow. Not my favorite subject."

"Oh, right," Phin said. "Me too."

"Us too," said Tambora.

"We should study together," said Vesuvius.

"You guys can." Mercy stood and wrapped her remaining halva in a napkin. "I need to study alone. I would get too distracted by all of you and we would chit-chat. See you in the morning."

"Goodnight," said Tambora.

"Night, Mercy." Phin and Vesu spoke in unison, then gave each other a high five.

Alone in her room, Mercy inspected her restraining cuffs. It was her first alone-time since she got them. She liked them. They actually looked boho groovy and hip, She still scrutinized them when CJ entered the room.

"What are you doing?" CJ asked. "Are those the restraints?"

"Yes. I'm just checking them over. I like them." Mercy put her hands down and reached for her math book.

"Yeah, I suppose they are a little trendy, if you're into that sort of style," CJ said. "Do you have to wear them all the time?"

Mercy nodded. "Until further notice." She opened her math book and notepad.

"Well. I guess there's always a trade-off for being the best."

"What did you say?" Mercy's head jerked up to find CJ sported a wide grin. Mercy jumped up and pulled a pillow from her bunk. "So that's how it's going to be. You take that back." Mercy laughed and threw the pillow at CJ.

CJ shrieked and ducked. She grabbed her own pillow and slung it at Mercy, who retrieved her pillow and hit CJ in the face. Back and forth, they squealed and tossed their pillows until a loud knock sounded at their door. CJ stood closest and answered it.

Miss Birdie peered in. "Girls, it's past lights out. You're disturbing the other students. Now quickly get this room in order and go to bed."

"Yes, ma'am." Mercy said.

"Goodnight," Miss Birdie said and closed the door.

"Lights out?" Mercy said. "How long were we playing around?"

CJ glanced around the room. "By the looks of things, it must've been hours."

"I guess we'd better get busy then," Mercy said.

After they cleared the disarray in the room, the two girls changed, turned out the light, and climbed into their beds. Mercy giggled, pleased to hear a soft snicker from the other bunk.

"Goodnight, Mercy," CJ said.

"Goodnight, CJ." Mercy closed her eyes and drifted off to sleep, happy that her relationship with CJ seemed headed in a more positive direction. But worried she didn't get the chance to study for her math test.

CHAPTER 8

IT STARTS AS A RIPPLE

Mercy spent the next day on an emotional teeter-totter. On one end, thoughts about her first training weighed her down. The idea of possessing as much power as she suspected she might have, intimidated her. But her excitement to put her skills into practice played against the burden of her nervousness. She longed to experience more equality with Tambora and Vesuvius. The twins were small when their parents first put them in Fire training classes. They were already accomplished in several minor techniques. They also took early intermediary Fire lessons from Mr. Kishan as part of their daily classroom schedules.

Mercy reported to the training room when her classes were finished. Mr. Kishan awaited her. He said they would kick off with some small water exercises. He pulled a miniature ratchet out from the cabinet, saying the tool was the only mechanism capable of taking the restrictions off of her restraints. He used the device on the water charms, leaving the others alone. The little lights went out as he adjusted them which showed inactive restraints. Mercy followed him to where two buckets sat side by side on a tarp. Water filled one pail. The other was empty. He instructed her to stand five feet away from them.

"Your first task is to create a ripple in the water." He took a step back. "Go ahead."

"But I don't know how," Mercy answered.

"Just see what you can do."

Pessimism washed over Mercy like the water ripples she needed to create. She doubted she would accomplish much, but to appease Mr. Kishan, she bugged out her eyes and stared hard at the bucket. She waited to no avail. She waved her hands. Still nothing happened. Next, she attempted her interpretation of a Native American water dance from a Pow Wow she once saw on a video. She endeavored to imitate it by hopping sideways, back and forth between each leg, while she circled around the buckets. She felt a little ridiculous when she noticed Mr. Kishan cover his mouth. Although the dance seemed silly out of context, it was fun, and she was disappointed that method failed. Discouraged, her face fell.

Mr. Kishan patted her shoulder. "Magnificent efforts. How did you feel when I asked you to execute this task?"

"I couldn't believe you asked me to perform something you knew I didn't know how to do. I knew I couldn't do it, and I was right."

"And that is precisely why you weren't able to complete the assignment. Accomplishing the goal has little to do with your actions or how hard you try, but everything to do with your attitude. You didn't believe. Therefore, you were unsuccessful. Let's build up your confidence. Until you develop your own techniques, I will guide you with step-by-step instructions."

Mercy clapped her hands, thrilled to know she would create and design her own methods to use her skills. "Yes. Thank you."

Mr. Kishan said, "Now close your eyes and imagine rippling water inside the bucket. Let me know when you have achieved this."

Mercy imagined the bucket, but in her mind, the water remained motionless. She tried with all her might to make it ripple, but without reward. She opened her eyes. "I can't make it move in my thoughts. The water just stays still."

"You are trying too hard. Try again."

Mercy shook herself to release the tension in her body and gave it another go. She imagined the bucket of water and studied it. "Move, move, please move," she whispered. In her mind's conception, the water remained still. She shrugged. "It's not working."

Mr. Kishan said, "Simply relax and don't get frustrated. Frustration will merely hinder you. Let's try again. And this time, with your eyes still closed, I want you to only watch the bucket of water. Have no expectations. Simply observe. Keep watching and listen to my voice. Rain is falling, a few drops here, a few drops there. Can you feel it? It's refreshing, yes?"

Mercy felt light and carefree. "It is."

"The raindrops are falling into the bucket, causing the water to ripple out from each drop. You see it, don't you? When you're ready, reach out to the water, thrust out your hands as though you are pushing something toward the bucket, and keep your arms extended."

Mercy saw it all as Mr. Kishan described and reacted as instructed.

"Now, open your eyes and stay steady," he said.

Mercy's gaze fell on the pail of water. She spotted rings on the water surface, rippling out from the imagined raindrops. Satisfaction and euphoria came over her, knowing she held the power to manipulate a situation to her will. Mercy thought she might be invincible.

"You're doing well. It's good, yes? Eventually, you'll be able to manifest Wind and Water simultaneously to achieve your vision. But small steps for now. Let's try another approach. This time, I want your eyes open. When you're ready, hold out your hand and picture a small fountain in the middle of the bucket, then slightly raise your hand."

Mercy engaged the water in a stare-down. High on her victory, she determined she would be the winner for the next round of the Water versus Mercy battle. She fixated on the bucket, reached out, and held her hand over the water. She held her breath as the water rose higher and higher. She squealed and her mind did a happy little dance. But instead of stopping at a delicate fountain, the water transformed into a miniature tidal wave, splashing out all over the tarp. She moaned and bowed her head, one hand on her hip. Her fleeting moment of jubilation gone.

"Not to worry, this is your first day, you can't expect to be an expert yet. You're doing great. Keep steady in your concentration, don't get too excited," Mr. Kishan said. "Mercy, it's all in the focus and visualization. They work in tandem with your body and hands. If you lose concentration or your mind becomes overwhelmed with emotions or thoughts, your hands will create mayhem." He wiggled his hands all around his head. "You already experienced this during your run-in with other students a few nights ago. It's essential to keep your mind and your body in balance. It's a complicated process, requiring a lot of patience and practice. But I'm convinced your abilities will eventually go even beyond my own, so let's try this again. Take your time and concentrate."

He retrieved another pail of water from the line-up of ten placed by the wall. Mercy wondered how many more she would spill. Her attention went to the water on the floor. "Do I have to clean this up?" she asked.

Mr. Kishan chuckled. "No. We have a special crew to clean the training rooms. You may witness them in action someday. It's quite amazing. Mrs. Kishan has been after me for some time to sneak them into our cottage at the far edge of the property. Since our children began attending school at the Nanghi outpost, they haven't been around to help with the day-to-day duties." His eyes were dewy, and he appeared lost in thought.

"Mr. Kishan? Are you alright?" asked Mercy.

He blinked several times. "Yes. I'm fine. It's all fine."

"Why don't they attend the Tray?"

"They did, but the children didn't acclimate well to Ara'Ja. Mrs. Kishan and I thought they would do better at home. They are staying with family and seem very content to be rid of the two of us."

"Don't you miss them?"

"More than you know, but we visit every couple of weeks. Are you ready to continue?"

Mercy nodded. She concentrated on the bucket of water and imagined a charming little fountain springing up from inside the bucket. She pictured what she wanted. She raised her hand and gave a small flick. When a delicate spout of water appeared, she tried extra hard to not be over-exuberant; although on the inside, she made a calm declaration of personal victory. She kept her focus, and the fountain continued to spout, looking like the perfect spray of an animated whale. When she glanced away, the water stilled.

"Wonderful. Do it again," Mr. Kishan said.

Mercy went through the motions and caused another fountain to spring up.

"Again," Mr. Kishan said, his tone grew harsh and his accent more pronounced.

Mercy did.

"And again," he demanded.

"But why? I've already successfully done it three times."

"Because I'm telling you to do it another time."

Mercy huffed and clenched her lips together. She did not appreciate being treated as a child, just when she adulted so perfectly. But she did as he insisted, without the payoff of a triumph. She glared at her teacher. She did not understand why he acted overly and uncharacteristically mean. "It won't work," she said.

"What's changed?" he asked.

"Nothing, I'm doing the same as before."

"No. There has been a change. Again, please."

"I won't."

"I can tell you're angry with me."

Mercy crossed her arms. "I am, and apparently, I can't do it when I'm mad, so why even try?"

"Do it again. If you fail, we will stay all evening until you get it right." He dragged a chair close to where Mercy stood, sat down, folded his hands, and crossed his legs. "There is nowhere else I need to be, what about you?"

Mercy clenched her teeth. Her entire body rigid by annoyance, she tried again and again without results.

"Deal with your anger, Mercy, or we'll remain here all night."

Mercy's nostrils flared. She gave Mr. Kishan the worst stink eye she could muster and refocused on the bucket. She did not want to be there all evening. She took a breath and focused inward. In her mind, she pictured herself shaking her arms and body until all of negative thoughts and emotions flew off. She fixed her gaze onto the bucket. A tiny notion crept in of how mean Mr. Kishan acted, but she banished the thought.

She regained her composure and repeated her hand gesture. A perfect fountain rewarded her.

"Congratulations, Mercy, you have passed my first test."

"You mean—" Mercy's spirits lifted at the epiphany. "Ohhhh. You did that on purpose."

"There will be times of great stress or emotion when you need to call on your abilities. Circumstances may arise which may mean life or death and you won't have time to try again and again."

"Okay. I get it now," she said.

Mr. Kishan touched Mercy's shoulder. "There is great satisfaction in a job well done, yes? Remember, you have been given your abilities as gifts. They are not generated by you. You are merely the custodian and operator. You have been entrusted to use your talents with responsibility and wisdom. And to paraphrase St. Luke, the physician and traveling companion of St. Paul, 'To whom much is given, much shall be required.' You've been given more than most. You're going to have to work incredibly hard."

Mercy nodded. The Emissary told her the same thing. "I understand." They worked for almost another hour on transferring water from the full bucket to the empty one. She tried several times to get the water flow to arc at the correct angle, and she spilled a lot. On the seventh try, Mercy got most of the water to flow from one pail to the other.

"You've done astonishingly well for your first time," Mr. Kishan said. "I'm sorry we went over a bit, but you've learned valuable information tonight that you'll use for the rest of your life. I'll reset those charms for you and you can be off." He reactivated the charms and patted Mercy's hand. "There you go. We'll meet again tomorrow, yes?"

"I'll be here," Mercy said. She skipped to the door, hopeful for excellent outcomes on all of her training sessions.

CHAPTER 9

———————◆———————

THE MAKING OF MURPHY VESTAM

Mercy put all her mind and might into her water training over the next few weeks. Repeating the same exercises lost all appeal early on and she grew bored. Mr. Kishan told her she would soon be ready to try new tasks. Although she asked him almost every day, he did not mention any specifics. Her days and nights ran one into the other. Classes during the day, then training and dinner. She devoted the rest of her evenings to homework and studies. Too busy to contemplate the prophecy or the Metalicons, the topics remained shelved.

"The only time I see you outside of class and meals is when we're practicing our parts for the Parents' Day program," Tambora complained one Saturday at breakfast. "We haven't even been to the library to look for an explanation for the crown charm on your bracelet."

"I know. I miss you guys, too," Mercy said. "I've been crazy busy. Mr. Kishan told me I need to be responsible and work doubly hard."

"I don't think he meant for you to only study and train," Tambora said. "You need to balance out all the serious stuff and have a bit of fun."

"Yeah," Vesuvius said. "Have some fun, or we'll have to change your name to Merryless Markos." Vesuvius flinched, and Mercy suspected he received a hard kick under the table, compliments of his sister.

"Oh. But we *will* have fun," said Mercy. "We're still going to Nikonea City next Friday, right? To ask him about the symbols from the medallion?"

"Right. Parents' Day is next weekend," Phin said. "Don't forget, Mr. Romani is having choir rehearsal Monday night. Mercy, how is your solo coming along?"

"It's going well. I'm going to surprise my parents," Mercy said.

"And I get to give a speech before the presentation," Tambora said. "Mercy and I have been practicing our pieces for each other. We've got them down pretty good."

Mercy nodded in agreement.

"And I get to witness the three of you make clowns out of yourselves," said Vesuvius.

Phin made a play at grabbing Vesuvius by the hair. "Just for that, you're going to sing in the choir, even if we have to drag you by the white ragged mop of a haircut you think is trendy."

"Phineas Jaymes." Miss Carmen hovered over them. They were startled as no one saw her approach their table.

"I'm sorry, we were only playing around." Phin quickly let go of Vesuvius.

"Understood. See to it this doesn't happen again," said Miss Carmen, and she moved to investigate another catastrophe a few tables over.

Mercy snickered and elbowed Phin. He responded by elbowing her in return, and her heart skipped a beat.

"Okay. Let's continue planning our mission to Nikonea City," said Tambora.

"What's our code name?" Vesuvius asked. "We must have a code name if this is a legitimate mission."

"What a fun idea," Mercy said. "Any thoughts?"

"What about Symbol Search? Or Quest of the Medallion?" Tambora pulled out a sheet of paper and a pencil and wrote all their suggestions as they poured out—Answer Seekers, Operation Clueless, Translation Station, amongst many others.

"Guys, these names are great and all, but don't you think they're too complicated? Why don't we just use a name?" Mercy said.

"You mean like Jane or Tarzan?" asked Phin.

"Sort of. But something unique to us." Mercy scoped the almost emptied room. With breakfast finished, they could speak with a little more freedom.

"I know," Tambora said. "Why don't we make up a name using our initials?"

"I love that idea," Mercy said. "T-V-P-M. But, no matter how we arrange the letters, it won't make sense. What about including the initials of our last names?"

"That won't work either, there are no vowels," said Phin.

"What about the first two or three letters of all of our first names, there are vowels there," Vesuvius said.

"Good idea, Vesu. Tambora, why don't you write them down and we can try to arrange them." Mercy leaned toward Tambora, who wrote Phi-Ves-Mer-Tam, then Tam-Mer-Ves-Phi.

"Hey. Try this." Mercy reached over to Tambora's paper and wrote Mer-Phi-Ves-Tam. Merphivestam. Merphi Vestam. Murphy Vestam. "That's it! Murphy Vestam. It might even be a real name."

"I'm loving it," said Tambora.

Both boys agreed. And Murphy Vestam was born.

The following days passed in slow motion for Mercy and the others. More excited for the secret trip than for the actual purpose, they were unfocused and preoccupied. If Mercy did not attend training each evening, her week would have been a complete waste of time. On Friday, the day of the big adventure, classes were canceled to free the staff to prepare for Saturday's festivities. As the appointed departure time drew near, Mercy took a few minutes to gather her thoughts. She stood at the big window in the lounge, viewing the grounds. Many experts were there, pooling their various talents and working together to create an invisible barrier over the

Tray lawns, in case of rain. Over the course of the past several days, they employed their powers to weave an intricate structure from thick vines to use as a frame for ultra-thin, flexible glass. The glass arrived in huge rolls from the industrial district in the valley near the Matacaeton Mountains. The region was set up for element specialists to manufacture and produce several items to export to humans. *Made in Germany* tags branded the products to conceal the existence of Ara'Ja. In human society, Germany held an esteemed reputation for exporting quality goods, due, in part, to the high standards of Ara'Jaeon merchandise masquerading as German. Deutschland, happy to take the credit, never questioned the true origins of the commodities. Mercy watched the workers unload the rolls of glass from the delivery trucks and place them over the framework to fashion a delicate canopy. Thin ribbons of gold, incorporated into the glass during the manufacturing process, reached out toward the sky and grasped the sun's rays, casting a sprinkling of reflections onto the lush green lawn below.

Mercy returned her attention to the task at hand, remembering she needed to stop by her dorm. She ran to her room and sifted through the drawers of her wooden apothecary where she kept her trinkets. The hand-painted ceramic drawers tossed a splash of vibrant color into the room. She inherited it from her Grandfather Kadarius when he died. The little cabinet became one of Mercy's most treasured possessions. She located the paper of symbols she copied from the medallion and the duplicate she made in case she lost the original. When she took one out, she noticed the gold nugget she got during her element aptitude test and realized she never searched for a hiding place. She wrapped the duplicate paper around the gold and returned them to the drawer for safe-keeping until she came up with a better plan.

Tambora peeked in through the open door. "Are you ready for Murphy Vestam? The guys are downstairs, waiting with the portal crystals. One to go and one to get back."

"Yes. I need to get my hat and I'm all set." Mercy put her paper into her crocheted bag, another handmade gift from her grandmother. She pulled a felted beret from her closet and tilted the cap to one side when she put it on. "I'm ready."

They met Vesuvius and Phin in the lobby. The plan was to get into the hedge maze without being noticed, where they would use Phin's portal crystal to go to the city.

"Murphy Vestam." Phin stretched out his arm for a huddle salute.

"Murphy Vestam," repeated the others, joining their hands one on top of another.

"Don't draw attention to yourselves," Phin said as they stepped through the revolving red door.

They continued toward the maze in a straight line, trying to appear inconspicuous. Phin took the lead, his face to the sky and his hands in his pockets, while he whistled a non-melodic tune. Vesuvius tiptoed a few yards behind in large, stealthy, cartoonish steps, his arms bent at the elbows and hands curved in a claw-like manner. Tambora followed her brother. She skipped and sang a made-up song with senseless lyrics. Mercy witnessed the extreme acts of the others from her viewpoint as last in line. Embarrassed, she kept her head down and used her hand to shield the side of her face, hoping no one would notice her. When they reached the entrance to the maze, they realized subtlety lay outside their capabilities and they lost all control, giggling and pointing fingers at who they each thought performed the worst impersonation of discretion. Making sure no one was around, they entered the maze, going in far enough behind the hedges to portal unseen.

Phin brought a white crystal out of his pocket, tossed the small stone into the air, and said, "Nikonea City." A portal opened up and spewed out bright light in all directions. He put his hand over his brows for shade. "Whoa. Remind me not to use this kind of crystal at night if we're trying to sneak away. Luckily, it disappears after we go through it."

"There are different crystals? How can you tell what they are?" Mercy asked.

"Man, they're the portal equivalent of gourmet jelly beans. They are all shapes and sizes. Some are bright colors, some are plain, some are even speckled. It's simply a matter of keeping track of them all up here." Phin grinned, tapped his temple, and jumped into the portal. The others followed him and straightaway entered the city through one of Transport Plaza's stationary incoming gateways. Found in Nikonea City's dazzling Central Gardens, Transport Plaza was the sole means of transport to and from the island if traveling by portal. On most occasions, anyone elsewhere on Ara'Ja who specified Nikonea City as their destination, also entered through the plaza portals.

Mercy absorbed the surrounding environment in amazement. Although striking and sophisticated, the size of Nikonea City could not compare against huge impressive metropolitans, such as New York or Paris. But the largest city on Ara'Ja was still mighty impressive. Built along the entire shoreline of a mid-island peninsula, the city boasted a small cove on the west side and a larger gulf on the east. The smaller cove lay between the city and the Tray. From where she stood, Mercy enjoyed an unobstructed view of the larger harbor. The ripples on the sea glistened like gemstones dancing under the intense glare of the sun. The majestic and proud Matacaeton Mountains on the opposite shore stood guard over the capital, always on the lookout for threats. Everything in the city was white and crisp in the brilliant Mediterranean daylight, each building more splendid than the one beside it. Dozens of skyscrapers formed the city's skyline, but were spaced well enough apart that nothing seemed crowded.

Phin examined their surroundings. "Hey. My parents know several people around here. Let's go before anyone recognizes us and snitches."

"The Assembly is this way," Tambora announced and trotted off toward the tallest building.

Mercy followed her. "You've been there before?"

"We live here in Nikonea City." Tambora turned toward Mercy and continued to walk backwards. "Our penthouse is around the corner. The Immaculates take us to the Assembly with them when they aren't away on active duty."

"Who are the Immaculates?" Mercy asked.

Vesuvius chipped in. "That's what we call our parents behind their backs." He paused. "But *lovingly*, behind their backs."

"Because they're neat and tidy?" Mercy giggled at the thought.

"Very much so," said Tambora.

"My parents take me to the Assembly, too," said Phin. "I live in the same high-rise apartment building as Vesu and Tambora, but not in a penthouse. The three of us have been friends for years."

Mercy followed the others to the Assembly offices in silence. Her own modest, unrefined home was in the less impressive town of Athlenan, where fig trees and gas streetlights still lined the brick-paved roads. She deemed herself an outsider. Never did she identify as a bumpkin more than she did in that moment.

Windows lined the curved side of the Assembly building alongside the street and faced east over the gulf where the Matacaeton Mountains stood tall on the far eastern tip of the island. Mercy supposed the windows on the upper floors must have the most incredible views.

A placard placed inside the entrance identified the floor where each department or executive was located. Tambora checked the listing and discovered the offices of High Elder Kadarius occupied the 117th floor. People filled the entrance hall. But thanks to the foresight of the original building committee, dozens of portals lined the perimeter of the lobby, and the Murphy Vestam gang would not have to endure a long, crowded elevator ride. They found the portal to the 117th floor and stood in line. Their turn to pass through the portal came sooner than expected and they stepped through into the front end of a very long passage. A hall veered to their right and another to the left, but the sign above showed the High Elder's office was straight ahead. Tall windows covered one side of the corridor straight ahead. On the opposite side hung life-sized portraits of all the High Elders who served Ara'Ja since the establishment of the first Assembly thousands of years earlier. The portrait closest to them depicted the most recent High Elder, Atticus Kadarius.

"Wow," Phin said, "check this out. It's really interesting to examine these after learning about the High Elders in class. Hey, Mercy. Your eyes are almost the same as your uncle's. Except yours look more like a girl."

"I guess they are. I never noticed before," Mercy said.

"Hey, guys." Vesuvius lowered his voice and pointed to the portrait of Atticus Kadarius's blond-haired and bearded predecessor. "Here is High Elder Caudel, the one everyone says murdered High Elder Broomfield so he could take over his position."

"He has kind eyes," Tambora said. "He doesn't look like a murderer."

"Really?" Phin chuckled. "Because Magister Pappas resembles a complete doofus, and even though he's a jerk, he's literally the most brilliant teacher the Tray has ever had. You can't judge by appearances."

Mercy studied High Elder Broomfield's portrait. He was the first High Elder with a photographed portrait, not painted or drawn. Broomfield's slight grimace and narrowed eyes caught her attention. She suspected something he saw behind the photographer troubled him. "I heard this was taken the day before he died. Something's going on in this picture," she said. "I'm sure he saw something he didn't approve of."

Tambora stepped over and peered closer. "I think you're right. I remember a section in our history textbook showing more photographs from the day they took this portrait. I'll study them tomorrow night after Parents' Day."

"Yes. Tomorrow. We have more important matters to accomplish now. Today," Phin said.

"Impatient much?" asked Vesuvius.

"I don't want to be gone too long from school. The longer we're away, the more of a chance they'll notice we're gone," Phin said.

"He's right," said Mercy. "Let's do this."

Behind a white desk at the far end of the lengthy hall, sat a stern-looking, large woman swathed in a halo of wild red and pink ringlets. Mercy shuddered at the woman's bright orange and yellow plaid suit. The lady peered at them over the lime green reading glasses perched on the tip of her nose. The nameplate read *Ms. Amelia Gochenour.*

Vesuvius bent down close to the nameplate and spelled, "G-O-C-H-E-N-O-U-R. How do you pronounce that?"

The lady ignored the question, but the situation clock floating behind her chimed, "It is 10:45, and it's—" the clock faked-sneezed, "GO-chen-oor."

Ms. Gochenour sniffed. "May I help you?"

"We're here to see the High Elder," Mercy said.

"Do you have an appointment?"

"Um, no, but—"

"You need an appointment to meet with the High Elder."

"But we'll only be a minute, I promise. He's my uncle and I need to speak to him."

"I'm sorry, the High Elder is a very important man and mustn't be disturbed."

"Ugh." Tambora folded her arms across her chest.

"But she's his NIECE!" Phin screeched.

"I don't care if she's the mother of God, she's not getting in without an appointment." Ms. Gochenour's reply sounded harsh and scornful.

Mercy's mouth hung open, wondering what she should do, when a buzzer rang out and the large white door next to them opened. A tall, lean man stepped out and High Elder Atticus Kadarius entered the hall. The children gasped and jumped in surprise at the sudden intrusion from such an important person. His white robe hung open, revealing an impeccably tailored, charcoal gray suit and a deep burgundy tie over a charcoal dress shirt. His clothing was a notable contrast to the gaudy outfit his assistant wore.

"Uncle Atticus!" Mercy ran to him, her arms outstretched.

"Now, what's going on out here?" the High Elder inquired as he hugged Mercy.

"High Elder, sir," Ms. Gochenour said, "these *children* are insisting on seeing you without an appointment. I was just telling them you—"

"Bah. No bother. This is my niece. She's always welcome unless I'm busy saving the world, or something as equally spectacular. And I completed my world-saving escapades an hour ago, so I happen to be free at the moment." He winked at the children. "Come on in, kids. Ms. Gochenour, will you please whip up four lavender lemonades for our young guests?"

"Yes, sir." She huffed and stomped away.

Atticus led the group into his office and closed the door behind them. Mercy looked around in awe at the impressive round white room with flawless marble floors, and, as she suspected, the massive windows offered a fabulous view.

Vesuvius sauntered to the cushy sofa and plopped down, propping his feet on the coffee table as if he were a frequent and favored visitor. "Nice secretary you have there, High Elder, sir."

"Administrative assistant," Tambora grumbled into Mercy's ear.

Atticus sat next to Vesuvius. "Yes, well. She has her good days. And she's decidedly proficient in her duties. So, did someone bring you to town? Do your parents or Miss DeLuca know you're here?"

Mercy and Phin sat in matching chairs on either side of the sofa and Tambora ambled around the office, studying the history throughout the room.

"No. No one knows we're here," Mercy admitted. "We came on our own. We had an incident, and we wanted to ask you about it."

"What happened?" Atticus crossed his legs, clasping his hands around his knee.

"Last week, Tambora and I were in the library at the center, and suddenly, this medallion on the wall started going crazy with rings going every which way. Then a bunch of symbols lit up all over the rings. We thought it was trying to give us a message."

"More like it gave Mercy a message," Tambora said. "She copied all the symbols, hoping you can tell us what they mean."

"Hmm. All right, let me look."

Mercy handed the paper to her uncle. She noticed he glanced down at her cuffs, but she did not wish to talk about them, so she withdrew her hands and held them in her lap covered by her shirt hem. His brows lifted, but he kept silent. She breathed a small sigh of relief. She did not feel up to giving explanations.

The buzzer sounded and the heavy office door opened again. Ms. Gochenour came in, carrying four glasses of purple liquid on a glass tray. An incredible lavender lemon scent wafted up from the tumblers when she passed them around to the children.

"Thank you, Amelia," Atticus said. "You kids haven't experienced lemonade until you've tasted Ms. Gochenour's lavender lemonade."

"Hmph," Ms. Gochenour replied and left the room.

Phin took a drink. "Yum. This is exceptional. Citrusy, yet infused with an organic, herbal, almost flowery essence."

"What on earth does that mean? Why can't you just say, 'Mmm… this tastes good'?" Vesuvius took a big, long drink. "Mmm… this tastes good. See? Not too difficult."

They enjoyed their lemonade and talked about Parents' Day while the High Elder explored Mercy's drawing. Finally, he stood. "I need to check this in my book." He picked up an enormous book from his credenza, took it to his desk, and flipped through the pages. He waved Mercy's paper. "Is this the only copy?"

"No. I have the original in my room at the Tray." Mercy moved to stand next to her uncle.

"I see," he said. "These symbols signify a female, which would most likely be you. The circles are truth and knowledge, or more accurately, truth and wisdom. With the crown, it is fair to presume that all of this means that your time at the Tray is going to be the crown in your education, and the set of wings represents your rise to the top. The other two symbols are life and death and are undoubtedly simply there to signify your lifetime. While this may seem interesting and mysterious, the interpretation is really quite uncomplicated."

"Wow. It's not even close to being ominous. We were sure it meant gloom and doom," Vesuvius said from across the room. "It's a tad disappointing."

The High Elder smiled. "No. No gloom and doom here." He furrowed his brows. "But for now, let's keep this between us." He folded the sheet and stuffed the paper in his trouser pocket. "I don't want a swarm of people thinking there are messages for them in every medallion they come across. Then I would never hear the end of requests to decipher them. Promise me?"

"I promise." Mercy wondered about the concerned look on her uncle's face, despite his words.

"Good," Atticus replied.

"High Elder, sir?" Tambora said. She bent over his credenza and scrutinized a photo displayed there. "Who are these people?"

"They were the apprentices of the Assembly in the 1940s."

"Are you in this picture?"

Mercy and the boys put down their empty cups and moved to get a closer view.

"Of course." Atticus picked up the photo and pointed to a blond young man. "This is me next to High Elder Jonathan Broomfield, God rest his soul."

"It's terrible, what happened," Phin said. "Did High Elder Caudel kill him?"

"No!" the High Elder bellowed. He slammed his fist on his desk, causing Mercy to jump. His tone relaxed as he continued. "I dare not even entertain that thought. All the apprentices loved Jonathan Broomfield. And remember, Broomfield's assistant was Nathaniel Caudel's brother, and he was also killed. A man wouldn't murder his own brother, would he?"

"No. I guess not," said Phin.

An awkward silence filled the room. Mercy went to the window and pretended to be absorbed in the view.

Vesuvius said "Look at how many of the apprentices in this photograph wore dreadlocks."

Atticus roared in laughter. "Yes indeed. Many Ara'Jaeon young men wore them in the 1940s, myself included."

"Do women ever apprentice here? Or get to become a High Elder?" Tambora asked.

Atticus rubbed his chin. "Not historically, but times are changing. Ara'Ja is catching up with the rest of the world on many issues, and I imagine there will be a female High Elder, or rather, High Eldress, in the future. Of course, when one holds this office for decades, or even a century, the prospect of a High Eldress would, presumably, be later rather than sooner."

"That's what I want to do. Just now, this minute, I realized it's what I want to do," Tambora said.

"There is no reason this can't be you. Study hard, get good grades, perfect your skills, and when you've graduated from Academy, you can apply for apprenticeship. You may even be the first female apprentice. Wouldn't that be remarkable? And if I'm lucky enough to still be around, I'll put in a good word for you." Atticus winked. "I know one or two members of the board."

"I hate to be a party pooper, but we need to get back to the Tray before they notice we're not there," Phin said.

"I'll have my driver take you," the High Elder offered.

"Oh no. We're good, thanks," Phin said. "I have a portal crystal."

Atticus lifted a brow. "Did you portal here?"

Phin's cheeks reddened, and he stood at attention. The others averted their eyes and held their breaths at Phin's careless mention of traveling via a portal.

Mercy sensed her uncle slip into his proverbial High Elder persona. "Correct me if I'm wrong, but if memory serves me well, aren't portals forbidden at the Tray? And more specifically, forbidden in order to keep students from leaving the property?"

"Yes, sir," they all answered in unison.

"Well. I'm going to do you a favor and forget you were here for this one time only, but unless you want to hike all those miles and miles—uphill—to the Tray, I suggest you accept my offer of a ride."

Phin nodded. "Offer accepted, thank you, sir."

"And Mercy?" Atticus pulled out a small card from his drawer. "Here's my business card. Next time, have one of your teachers schedule a call or visit." He walked them to the door. "If time permits, I'll be at the Tray tomorrow for Parents' Day."

Mercy gave her great uncle a big hug. "You could hear me sing. I have a solo."

Atticus patted Mercy's back. "Then I must attend. Now go down to the lobby. My car will be outside the door when you get there. When you reach the Tray, the driver will drop you off at the bottom of the drive for you to arrive less conspicuously."

"Okay, thank you." Mercy gave her uncle another quick hug before they left. "Goodbye. I hope to see you tomorrow."

———————◆———————

As the High Elder's limo carried the children to the Tray, a thought troubled Mercy, and she wondered if she should mention her doubt to the others. She cleared her throat. "Do you guys think Uncle Atticus didn't tell us the entire interpretation? Like he hid part of it?"

Phin said, "I thought the same thing, but I presumed he didn't want to bother you with parts of the interpretation that aren't relevant."

"Yes. I suppose you're right." Mercy reclined in her seat and watched the countryside go by as the others babbled on about meeting the High Elder.

CHAPTER 10

THE ANGUISHED PERFORMANCE

Mercy awoke with a jolt. Her immediate thought was *Today is Parents' Day*. "Today is Parents' Day!" she repeated aloud and jumped out of bed. She landed on her feet and hopped over to CJ's bunk. "CJ, wake up. Today is Parents' Day."

"So what," CJ murmured and rolled over to face the wall.

Mercy threw on her brown and gold polka-dotted tights and searched through her closet for her chocolate brown cable knit cardigan and long cream tunic with a lacy flounce at the bottom of the sleeves and at the hem. "Aren't you excited to see your mom and dad?" Mercy asked.

"No," CJ said.

"Why not?"

CJ sat up and rubbed the sleep from her eyes. "Because they can't come."

"Can't come? Where are they? The Chomolhari Summit?" Mercy joked as she pulled the tunic over her head.

The Chomolhari Summit was considered the Ara'Jaeon's ace in the hole. The trump card in the event of a cataclysmic situation. Except for the Island of the Eternal Sun in the Sea of Despair, the summit was the only place on Earth where Ara'Jaeons physically could not portal to or from. Portals could be detected, and although the summit itself was no secret within the Ara'Jaeon community, the exact location and contents were highly classified. For that specific reason, special impenetrable protection cloaks blocked portal functions for hundreds of miles surrounding the area. The facility existed underground, hidden deep inside the Himalayan Mountains on the border of Tibet and Bhutan. A series of intricate unmarked trails and an elevator inside the mountain, ascending and descending to multiple levels, were the only ways to get there. Prior to the invention of modern technology, everyone had to use stairs hewn into the rocks. It was an honor to be stationed at the summit, but a difficult post. Most Ecclesia members both dreaded and yearned for a placement there.

CJ's cheeks whitened. "Yes." She lay down and stuffed her pillow over her face.

Mercy regretted her attempt at humor after she noticed CJ's obvious distress. "I'm sorry," she said. "I didn't know. I shouldn't have made a joke. We'll hang together and you can be part of my family for the day. It'll be fun. Evan my Uncle Atticus might come. You know he's the High Elder." Mercy rarely discussed her connection to the High Elder, but she was not above name-dropping if she considered the situation warranted for her to do so. She fished out a gold fabric flower pin from her drawer and attached it to her sweater.

CJ came out from under the pillow at the mention of Mercy's uncle. "He is? I kind of had my heart set on falling back asleep, but I'd love to meet him. My parents talk about him a lot."

CJ climbed down from her bunk. She sifted through the pile of clothes underneath, pulling out a simple navy pleated skirt and a white blouse.

Mercy sat on her trunk while CJ dressed. "It's odd we don't talk often. I suppose we only chat in the morning and at night. Not a lot of time for conversation. I know almost nothing about you. Tell me about your family. Do you have brothers or sisters?"

"I have one brother. He's twenty. He's at university in Athens, studying archeology."

"He's out in human society?"

"He's still growing and not too tall to need discretion. He would've come today, but he and his classmates are on a dig. He's with them day and night and he can't risk being discovered portaling."

"Of course. Ara'Jaeons should be cautious in human society."

"Right. I'm not blaming him. I know what he and my parents are doing are important." CJ slipped on her shoes. "I'm ready."

Mercy grabbed her tan and cream cloche hat and slipped her arm through CJ's. "Come on, honorary Miss Markos. Let's get some grub."

Tambora was already seated at a table and called them over. They walked past the table where CJ usually ate with her friends. The girls looked at CJ expectedly. CJ nodded toward Mercy and the group broke out in twitters. Mercy fought the urge to be intimidated and continued on to where a breakfast of cheese, Greek yogurt with fruit, sausage pie, and pita toast, awaited them. Mercy sat down and reached for a small chunk of goat cheese.

"Good morning," Tambora said. "Don't you look adorbs."

"Thanks. You, too," Mercy said.

Tambora grinned and glanced down at her simple ivory linen trousers and ivory sleeveless turtleneck. "What? These old things? I have dozens more in my closet."

Mercy chuckled at her friend's mock humbleness. The all-ivory ensemble complemented Tambora's pale blonde hair. She appeared every bit the wealthy young sophisticate her parents groomed her to be, nothing like Mercy's first impression of her, tripping over her shoelaces.

"Well. You look perfectly perfect," Mercy said. "By the way, CJ is going to be my adopted sister today."

"Hey," CJ said, still standing.

"Harmony and balance, CJ." Tambora held out a chair. "Here. You can sit by me. Vesuvius can grab a chair from another table when he gets here."

"Where are the guys?" Mercy asked.

"They're around. I'm sure they'll arrive soon. They probably got distracted by trying to outdo one another in a meaningless activity."

Right on cue, a big clatter sounded followed by a burst of gut-wrenching laughter. Phin stood against the wall, doubled over in a fit of hysterics. On the ground next to him was the pathetic sight of a spread-eagled Petit Serveur. Plopped on the floor nearby, Vesuvius sported an upside-down bowl of fruit salad which oozed from the top of his noggin down to his mismatched socks and shoes. Everyone else in the hall fell silent, and many got to their feet to check out what happened.

"Buggers," Vesuvius said. "I just showered."

From outside the room, a Situation Clock chimed, "It is 8:15, and beware the blundering mess in the mess hall." The proclamation echoed throughout the quieted dining hall, inducing an eruption of whistles and whoops of laughter. Miss Birdie rushed to assist in the matter, followed by a serveur who held two striped kitchen towels. It gave Vesuvius one towel and threw the other down to mop up the mess on the floor. Miss Birdie tugged the towel away from Vesuvius. "Give me that and I'll clean you up," she grunted and wiped him down in half the time it undoubtedly would take Vesuvius to do the job for himself.

"Aw, Birdie. You know you love me," Vesuvius said.

"I love you like I love my hemorrhoid cream. A dose of relief from an otherwise painful existence," she said. "Off you go. No running."

"Thanks, Birdie. You're my heron." Vesuvius leaned into the older woman, pecked her cheek, and took off in the other direction. He turned and ran backwards. "Get it? Birdie. Heron, not heroine?"

She put her hand to her cheek, sporting a slight smile. "I get it, and that's Miss Birdie to you, lad," she called out after him.

Vesuvius skidded to a halt next to Mercy. "Outstanding. Sausage pie," he said. To her chagrin, he took an empty chair from the neighboring table and put it between her and Phin, who just sat down next to her. Vesuvius filled his plate and chowed down.

"Vesu, eat quickly. You need to take another shower and change your clothes before the St. Clair Immaculates get here," Tambora said. "You know they can't tolerate messy."

"On it already." Vesuvius stuffed the last bit of pie in his mouth and ran from the room.

Just as Mercy took a big gulp of chocolate milk, CJ said to Tambora, "I take it you're the only twin to inherit the immaculate gene?"

Milk spewed from Mercy's puckered lips toward Tambora, leaving brown splotches all over the crisp, spring-fresh fabric.

"Bull's eye," Phin laughed.

Mercy almost choked as she attempted to contain her amusement, but squeaked out an apology. "Oh. I'm so sorry." She covered her mouth, hiding her grin. Mercy truly felt badly about the mishap, but the humor in the situation could not be denied.

"Oh great. Now I have to change, too." Tambora got to her feet. "I'll see you later."

"I really am sorry," Mercy said as her friend hurried away.

"Yup, I know you are," Tambora called out and kept walking.

CJ said, "Should I have kept quiet?"

"Don't worry," Mercy said. "She's a little sensitive about the possibility of becoming her parents. But she's a trooper. She'll be okay."

"Children." Miss Carmen stood at the entrance of the hall and clapped her hands together in one thunderous smack. "We have half an hour before your families arrive. Please finish breakfast quickly and assist the serveurs by clearing your tables. Then we'll all meet together in the south lawn. Chop, chop."

Mercy, Phin, and CJ cleared off their table and walked together to the event venue outside. The weather opted to throw a favor toward the festivities and provided delightful conditions. Neither hot nor cold. Sweater weather, Mercy's dad would say. The blue and cloudless sky allowed the sun to radiate splendor onto the festivities below. Mercy and the other students waited in their assigned areas for their families to arrive.

Miss Carmen walked the grounds to make sure all was perfect and in order. The lawn and gardens, manicured to prepare for the day, were pristine except for the ornamental fishpond fountain. Instead of the traditional picturesque spray, chaotic shoots of water sputtered about. Miss Carmen extended her arms, her palms toward the pond. A quick shaft of golden light burst from her hands to the fountain. It happened so fast, Mercy almost missed the surge. The spray adjusted and soon a triumphant geyser shot out. The platinum butterfly koi danced, undulating to the rhythmic beat of the spray as it struck the pond surface. Their silvery white feathered fins glowed against the sapphire lapis lazuli stones which lined the pond, catching glints of sunlight. The surrounding garden rustled in praise, and the grape hyacinths clapped their long leaves together in a gentle round of applause when the soft breeze tickled them.

Spectacular Roman orchids, Mercy's favorite flower, drew her attention. She loved to watch them lift their faces to soak in the morning light. The potted orchids were clothed in the same hues as the colors bequeathed to a setting sun when it paints the sky at nightfall—rose, salmon, gold, and orange. The vibrant colors lifted her spirits, and joy grabbed ahold of her heart before her parents even arrived. She saw them first, walking hand in hand toward the dozens of fussily lined-up rows of white wooden chairs. The couple appeared blissful, content in the company of each other. Mercy experienced a brief stab of envy. She remembered the days when she walked between them. She held their hands as she leapt and seemed to float in the air until they set her back down when they stepped forward. As an older child, she sometimes thought she was invisible to them. She tried to take part in their conversations on several instances over the past few years. She felt ignored, as though she did not speak, or worse, like she was not present. She shook her head and refused to allow foul moods into her so-far perfect day. Mercy's mother looked up and their gazes locked. Mercy waved to her and received a radiant smile in return.

Mercy pointed out her family to CJ.

"Harmony and balance, sweetheart." Emzlie leaned in to kiss Mercy's forehead. "Your pin looks lovely on that tunic."

"Thanks, Mom," Mercy said.

"You look much more alert than when we spoke to you last. You were pretty shaken." Orion bent down to hug her and then tugged her ear. "Let's check out your prisoner's manacles."

Mercy held out her hands to her father. He inspected each of the charms. He fingered the extra charm and glanced up at his wife, who grimaced and gave him a slight nod. The exchange mystified Mercy. What significance was there in a crown? Royalty? Did her family believe they were royal? But before she gave more thought to the subject, her father spoke.

"Well. It appears Magister Pappas has done an excellent job here. How has your training been going?" he asked.

"Mr. Kishan, my instructor, says I'm doing really well."

"I've heard of him. All positive things, of course. You're in fine hands, Mercy." Orion moved closer to her, still in his bent position. He gripped the sides of her arms and looked her straight in the eyes. "I wouldn't leave you here if I didn't believe it with all my heart."

"I know," she whispered.

CJ stayed back and kicked the grass around, her hands behind her.

"Mercy," her mother said, "who is your friend?"

"Mom, this is my roommate, CJ Oliver. Her parents are stationed at Chomolhari and couldn't come. I told her I would share you with her for the day. CJ, these are my parents, Emzlie and Orion."

"Harmony and balance, CJ." Orion took CJ's hand and held it between his own.

CJ's mouth gaped open. Mercy tried not to giggle, remembering Miss Carmen's awkward behavior toward her father when they first met.

"It's lovely to meet you, CJ," Emzlie said in her usual warm and kind tone. "Chomolhari, hmm? How interesting. How long have they been there?"

CJ said, "They've been deployed about a year, but they've returned to visit several times."

Mercy glimpsed a blur of white across the lawn. "Will you please excuse me for a minute? I need to talk to Tambora."

"Of course, honey," Emzlie said and resumed her conversation with CJ.

Mercy approached Tambora and said, "Didn't you say you were going to change?"

"I did. I told you there were more in my closet."

Mercy's brows knitted together. "I thought you were joking. I mean, who does that?"

"I asked my mom that same question." Tambora grimaced. "Hey. I made a few changes to my speech. I hope you'll approve."

"I'm sure I will. You're an amazing public speaker. You really would make a marvelous High Elderess."

"I want to try," Tambora said.

The microphone squealed and Miss Carmen's voice rang out. "Parents, please take your seats. Children, let's get in your places." As the students congregated to their designated areas, Miss Carmen addressed the crowd. "Harmony and balance, everyone. I'm Miss DeLuca, the headmistress. Most of you know me as Miss Carmen. Getting the families of over four hundred students together is no small feat. We thank you for your commitment to our establishment and hope you enjoy your day with us. We'd like to begin by performing a small production the students have prepared. Little Tambora St. Clair won the honor of starting us out by composing an impressive speech, which she will now present to you."

Mercy stood between Tambora and Phin. Phin sputtered. She glanced over at Tambora, who flared her nostrils and tightened her mouth. Mercy bit her lip to keep from laughing and lightly kicked Tambora's shoe. They knew Tambora hated to be called little.

"Don't even," Tambora whispered.

"Tambora, you may proceed." Miss Carmen stepped aside.

Tambora moved ahead of the other students. Mercy spotted Vesuvius in the front row with the St. Clair Immaculates, as the twins called them. The ultra-blond hair and the crisp, clean, and yes, immaculate, white clothing. No wrinkles or hair out of place.

"Family, friends. We are delighted to honor you this day as we…" Tambora said.

A slight commotion arose from the audience. Mercy tuned Tambora out to look over to her own small family in time to catch sight of her Uncle Atticus sneaking a seat next to them. He put his arm around her mother's shoulder, giving her a small squeeze. Atticus was her mother's only living blood relative on Ara'Ja, outside of Mercy. Atticus looked up at Mercy and grinned at her. She beamed in return, glad he could attend.

She hoped he would be true to his promise to not tell anyone she and her friends visited the city unsupervised.

A bee buzzed about Mercy's flower pin and snapped her thoughts to the present. She watched through crossed eyes as the bothersome bug frolicked near her face. She whispered, "Shoo." Her breath hit the bee hard and, thankfully, blew the little stinger away.

"… and so, we will continue to work intensely to make you proud of us, first as your children, and second, as citizens of Ara'Ja." Tambora finished and Mercy realized she missed the entire speech. Even worse, Mercy knew Tambora would ask her for feedback. The audience rose to their feet and Mercy clapped along. Mrs. Immaculate dabbed a handkerchief at her eyes and blew a kiss to her daughter.

"Thank you, Tambora," Miss Carmen said. "Families, you may be seated. Our own Mr. Romani has set the Ara'Jaeon Purpose to music, which our middle grade chorus will now sing. A group of our upper classmen has put together an accompanying drama. Please enjoy." Miss Carmen swept her arm out toward the choir and backed away.

Mercy gulped and tried to calm the sudden appearance of butterflies inside her stomach. It was almost time to sing her solo.

A quartet of older students got in place to pantomime a dramatization of the lyrics. Mr. Romani sat down at the old upright piano the workers dragged out to the garden earlier in the morning and played the first few chords of his composition.

Mercy stepped forward for her solo and closed her eyes. She preferred not to see her dad. She knew he would wave at her, cross his eyes, or behave in some other outlandish manner to get her to laugh. He succeeded several times at past school programs and she needed the fresh start. Another chance to not look the fool in front of her classmates. She sang the first few lines in a sweet high soprano. A hush fell over the crowd. All seemed perfect and idyllic. She was almost to the finish line. Alas, she opened up her eyes too soon. Only three words shy of the end of her solo, she caught sight of the hoard of faces watching her. Her heart throbbed against her chest and a voice inside her, sounding like the robot on an old TV space show, signaled an alarm—*Danger, Mercy Markos, Danger, Mercy*

Markos. Her throat tightened in her effort to smother a fit of hysterical giggles. Instead, the constriction caused a loud, abrupt, and quite noticeable, crack in her voice. A mere three words shy of her solo's ending. Appalled at herself, she stopped singing and returned to stand amongst the other students. Even then, inside the sanctuary of her fellow choral members' presence, she knew she would burst if she tried to vocalize. It was all she could do to just lip sync for the remainder of the choir's performance. Her eyes sought her family in the crowd. Her mother sported a gentle smile. But her father—her easily amused paternal unit— was bent over with his elbows on his knees, looking down. His shoulders shuddered in silent laughter. That image was all it took to set her off. She clenched her teeth to stop herself from the reflex of nervous giggling as she mouthed the lyrics, but horror upon horror piled on her as the pressure of suppressed laughter brought about a mammoth snort which escaped from her nose and out of her mouth.

The choir members around her faltered in their singing and chuckled. Phin cleared his throat, and Tambora, her best friend Tambora, whispered, "Way to go, Mercy."

Mercy's chest heaved in and out and up and down as she struggled to resist a continuous feed of uncontrollable bouts of snickers and snorts. She would never forgive her father for laughing and bringing about the horrendous chain of events. Of course, her own blunder was the primary culprit, but she was not willing to accept personal blame.

After what seemed like a lifetime of misery, Miss Carmen clapped and walked to the mic. "Weren't they terrific? Ladies and gentlemen, your soloist, Mercy Markos. Mercy, please come forward and take a bow."

Mercy choked back a groan, but she took a few tiny steps to stand a few inches in front of the group. A hand from behind pushed her forward. She stumbled, did a quick curtsy, and returned to her place. The audience applauded and Orion whistled. She glared at him.

"Okay, moms and dads." The mic crackled when Miss Carmen spoke too closely. "Our educators are in their classrooms, ready to answer all of your questions. Also, should you need them, there are maps of the buildings and grounds at the table behind you. Our non-teaching staff will roam around, should you require help. You can identify them by their blue blazers with the red pocket squares. A buffet of cheese, meat, fruit platters, baklava, and other sweets will be available in this area shortly. Children, off you go now, attend to your parents."

Mercy grabbed CJ's hand and ran to her mom and dad.

"Mercy." Her mother's arm wrapped around Mercy's shoulders. "Why didn't you tell us you were singing a solo? You did a lovely job."

"I wanted to surprise you. I'm glad you liked it."

"Yes, kiddo. You gave an amazing performance out there, especially those last few notes." Orion planted a kiss on Mercy's forehead. Mercy pulled away. She knew he could not help laughing—it rarely took much. But she was not ready to absolve him.

Atticus stepped in and patted Mercy on the back. "You sang a great solo, Mercy. I think I'll stroll around and greet everyone. The staff has gone through quite a turnover since I last visited the Tray." He addressed Emzlie. "I'll meet you here later and we can catch up."

Mercy's mom hugged her uncle before he ambled off. "I'm looking forward to our visit."

"Hey, Mercy," a voice called out. "We want to meet your parents before we go inside and I want you to meet ours." Mercy looked around. Tambora walked toward them, holding her mother's hand. Vesuvius and their father strolled behind them. "Hi, CJ," Tambora said.

"Hi. You did a good job on your speech," CJ said.

"Thanks," Tambora said. "What did you think, Mercy?"

"It was, uh, it was good. I thought it was good," Mercy said.

Fortunately, Vesuvius saved her from further conversation about it. "Harmony and balance," he said and stuck his hand out to Mercy's dad, then to her mom. "I'm Vesuvius, like the volcano."

"Mom, Dad, that's Vesu and his twin sister, Tambora," said Mercy.

"Like the volcano," said Vesuvius again.

"I remember you from when we dropped Mercy off." Orion grinned. "It's indeed a delight to meet both of you. I've heard a lot about you from your parents. We've been working together." He looked to the St. Clair parents. "It's good to see you again."

Mercy could not be sure, but she glimpsed a sparkle flash from her father's teeth. Yet another outward sign of his dazzling character.

Tambora said, "Mom, Dad, this is my best friend, Mercy. And, this is CJ, Mercy's roommate. These are our parents, Jasper and Enjoli St. Clair."

"Harmony and balance, Mercy, CJ," said the Immaculate mother named Enjoli.

"Harmony and balance, ma'am," said Mercy.

The girls split off from the group to talk, leaving the adults to converse together in low tones. Vesuvius stood alone. "If all you guys are going to do is chit-chat, I'm leaving to go get some food."

"No. No, Vesuvius. We're coming," his mother said. "Emzlie, Orion, we'll see you back at SARA. Harmony and balance."

"And to you," Mercy's mother said.

The St. Clairs headed toward the Tray and Mercy pulled CJ in closer to her family circle. "Mom, Dad, CJ is fourteen and has different classes than mine. Can one of you go with her for a bit and then we can switch?"

"I suppose we could," Emzlie said. "Orion, why don't you accompany CJ first? You mentioned earlier you wanted to speak with Mr. Kishan, and given your gift of gab, that should probably be kept for last."

"Sounds good," Orion said. "CJ, take me away, hey-hey, hey-hey."

"Dad!" Mercy groaned. "Don't show CJ your geeky side."

CJ giggled, grabbed Orion's hand, and dragged him toward the main building. "Come with me, Mr. Markos, I adore geeks."

"Awesome. And you can call me Daddy-O." He looked around at Mercy and wiggled his brows.

Mercy disagreed that CJ liked geeks, but it made her happy to see her father help CJ. She marveled at how lucky she was to have such great parents. She knew she could forgive him anything.

CHAPTER 11

THE FAMILY FRIEND

"Mom, are you ready?" Mercy asked, holding out her hand.

Her mother grasped hold. "Absolutely, let's go."

CJ and Mercy's father were involved in a conversation with a gray-haired couple when Mercy and her mother walked into the lobby. The lit-up expression on CJ's face showed right away they were her parents.

"Mercy, Mrs. Markos," CJ said. "Meet my parents, Hemison and Tempest Oliver."

"Harmony and balance." Mercy's mother shook their hands. "It's a pleasure to meet you."

Although Mr. and Mrs. Oliver greeted her mother, they ignored Mercy. In Mercy's opinion, they wore frozen smiles. Mrs. Oliver, in particular, smiled with her mouth turned down and her nose somewhat wrinkled, as if something did not smell to her liking.

"Emzlie, the Olivers made it here after all, so CJ is well taken care of for her instructor consults," Mercy's father said.

Mercy pulled CJ to the side as their parents conversed. "That's great, CJ," said Mercy. "I'm happy they came. How did they manage it without portals?"

"I don't know, they wouldn't say. It's probably top secret. You know how the Ecclesia works."

"Oh, right." Mercy was quick to agree, although in reality, she knew little about how the Ecclesia operated. She was a toddler the last time her parents were in active service. She spent those days with her mother's parents, which stood to reason why her grandparents became so beloved.

"CJ, let's proceed, we can't stay all day," Mr. Oliver said.

"Okay," CJ said. "See you later, Mercy."

"See ya."

"Hey, guys, Listen," Mercy's dad said. "I'm going to go get a quick bite to eat. I'm famished. I'll catch up to you. I won't be long."

"Mom, I hate for us to start out with this, but Magister Pappas teaches my first class of the day. He's a lot to digest."

"Surely, he can't be that bad," her mom said.

"Oh, he can. Just you wait. He was probably all nice and polite to you when he called you about the restraining, but in class, he's critical and rude."

Emzlie laughed in her charming, ladylike manner, putting her arm through Mercy's. "Come on. Let's go hear what the old meanie has to say."

Mercy studied her mother. Who was this relaxed, girlish woman? Where was her graceful, composed mother?

Magister Pappas was alone in his classroom when Mercy and her mother arrived. He glanced up from his paper when they walked in and smiled bigger than Mercy imagined was possible.

"Emzlie, harmony and balance. How wonderful to see you," he said and kissed the air by each of her cheeks. "How long has it been?"

"Harmony and balance. Far too long, Pelagius, if you don't count the visual call you made to Orion and myself a few weeks ago. How are you doing?"

"Wonderful, my dear. I see Atticus made it."

"Yes. I was surprised to see him. I'm not sure how he heard about today."

Mercy stood by in awkward silence, hoping they would not figure out she visited Nikonea City and invited her uncle to the event, but also puzzled by the odd exchange of greetings and pleasantries between her mother and Pappas. "Do you two know each other?" she asked.

"We trained together for the Ecclesia," her mother explained.

"You were in the Ecclesia?" Mercy asked the magister.

"I was, but I resigned so I could teach," he replied. "I am also acquainted with your father. We were great friends, he and I, long before we met your mother. But enough of me." He turned to Mercy's mother and left a baffled Mercy to stew in her confusion. "Let's discuss Mercy, shall we? She is doing rather well in class. General Abilities is an introductory course and most students will advance to the next level rather quickly. When this term is over, after the winter holidays, Mercy will most likely be assigned to Managing Multiple Abilities. MMA will be the educational complement to her training courses, which will shift over to be a part of her daytime schedule beginning with the next term. As you know, she's been observed to have the aptitude for all four elements. Mr. Kishan, her training instructor, is concentrating on getting Mercy used to one at a time. She's already begun working on Water skills and is progressing nicely."

"Will you be involved in her training at all?" Emzlie said, smiling at her daughter.

Mercy flashed a fake grin in return. She was puzzled. Something was off with the magister which she could not identify. She decided she should pay close attention and listen for more clues about the relationship between Pappas and her parents.

"I've been working in tandem with Mr. Kishan. And if she's ready for remedial training next year, Mr. Romani and I will collaborate to design the best course of action for her," Pappas said. "I won't pad the truth. She's a potential prodigy, and we need to do this right. But she's going to have a long, hard road ahead of her if she wants to excel."

"Mercy's always been able to do whatever she puts her mind to do. I'm sure she'll meet the challenge." Emzlie grabbed one of Mercy's hands. "Sweetheart, would you mind waiting out in the hall for a minute? I'd like to speak with Magister Pappas alone."

Perplexed, Mercy muttered, "Oooh... kay." She raised her brows and left the room. Once outside, she hesitated by the door. Eavesdropping crossed her mind, but as exasperated as she felt about getting tossed out of her own consult, she respected her mother too much, so she looked down over the lobby to observe what went on below. The first floor was a hubbub of excitement as students and their families bustled back and forth. Atticus stood in the center surrounded by admirers. She studied the scene, but grew restless and soon became bored with people-watching. With nothing else to do, she returned to wait outside the classroom door. In the hall, her niggling questions and ideas about Magister Pappas all fell into place. He never used contractions. Ever. But he abandoned his formal speech patterns in favor of a more casual way of speaking when he spoke with her mother. Mercy noticed voices coming from the classroom and realized the door stood ajar. She inched closer as all thoughts of parental respect disappeared. She tried to tune out all other noise to focus only on their voices.

"How should we handle this situation? Has anyone talked to her yet?" Mercy's mom asked.

"Not yet," Pappas said. "We're going to go ahead with the other four first and get her comfortable with them, then we'll address the issue. We don't want you to feel as though we're ignoring the situation. Frankly, we don't think the time is right. And you understand, if word got out to students, pandemonium would ensue when there is no actual need for panic. Ignorance causes that mindset, as you have experienced yourself."

Mercy could not believe her ears. What did her mother experience? It did not sound good. Was she about to experience the same? Her heart raced and her breath became shallow.

Pappas continued on. "Regardless, the Assembly has bound our hands on the general subject and the students are kept oblivious of the reality of it. You know the prophecy, as well as I, and it's not going away. We've already witnessed it manifest so we need to stay mindful of every aspect."

Mercy felt all color drain from her face. "What on earth is happening?" she muttered. She wished she could be home in her bed, never having heard of the Tray.

"Okay, Pelagius. We really hoped this wouldn't happen for another few years, but since it's begun, we'll have to deal with it. Please. Continue to watch over her and contact us if any problems arise. Although we're stationed so far away, and as you know, portaling is limited at outposts, we want to be involved as much as we can."

"It's not a problem, Emzlie. You and Orion are dear friends, and I'll keep a good grip on the situation. It was amazing to visit with you. Hopefully, I'll run into Orion today before you leave. I'd like to wish him well."

Their footsteps approached the door. Mercy scurried to the rail and looked below, pretending she did not overhear their conversation. A hand on her shoulder pulled her into the hall. "Oh, hi, Mom," she said as she turned to find her mother there. "Are you and Papp—I mean, the magister—finished?"

"Yes, dear. We had a pleasant chat."

"Why didn't you tell me before that you knew him?"

"I'm sorry, dear. I was amused by your comments about him, so I kept quiet. Who's next on our list? Mrs. Kishan?"

Mercy was aghast to find her mother was entertained about her earlier remarks regarding Pappas. She yearned to ask about their conversation, but Mercy knew from what she overheard and from the dismissive tone of her mother's voice, it was a subject best left alone. "This way, Mom. It's Ara'Jaeon History. You'll like Mrs. Kishan. She wears the most beautiful saris."

Phin stood outside Mrs. Kishan's room next to a man and woman Mercy presumed were his parents. At first glance, they made an odd couple. The man resembled a lumberjack. His once obviously fair-skinned face was weathered and reddened by a lifetime in the sun, and his wild curly hair sprang out all over his head. His eyes were the same bright color as Phin's. The woman's exotic, dark ebony skin was as flawless as silky velvet. Her burnished golden hair was plaited tightly around her entire hairline and brought up high where the braids entwined together and wrapped high into a bun. She wore an ankle-length caftan made from colorful tribal patterned fabric. Mercy was enchanted by the woman's nose ring. It was attached to a chain of turquoise beads and silver dangles, stretching across her cheek to her ear. She resembled a warrior goddess.

Enthralled, Mercy half-expected a long spear to appear in the woman's hand.

"Um, Mercy?" Phin said.

Mercy realized her rude stare and tore her eyes from the fascinating woman. "Oh. Sorry," she said. "Are you waiting for Mrs. Kishan?"

"Yes. But we're going to skip her for now and go on to another class. This is my dad, Brody, and my mom, Mandisa."

"Harmony and balance," Mercy said. "This is my mom, Emzlie."

Emzlie extended her hand to Phin's parents. "So very nice to meet you."

Brody Jaymes was a hulk of a man, with a grin as jovial as his body was wide. "Happy to meet you. Please take our place here. We're going to see Mrs. Kishan later."

Mercy beamed at Phin. "Thank you."

"See ya later, Mercy," Phin said.

"Okay." Mercy stared after Phin and his parents as they walked away, wondering if they might someday be her in-laws.

Mrs. Kishan called out she was free and Mercy followed her mother into the room. Mrs. Kishan gave a brief report about the subjects of her lessons and said Mercy's grades were good, but she needed to stop flirting with Phin and start paying better attention.

The door cracked open and Mercy's dad peeked into the room. "What's this? Mercy flirts with someone named Phin?" He walked in and stood next to his wife.

Mercy protested. "I do not flirt with Phin."

"Of course not, Mercy." Mrs. Kishan winked at Mercy's parents. "You've got a good girl there, Mr. and Mrs. Markos. She's doing well in her studies, even with the extra time she puts into her nightly training."

"Thank you, Mrs. Kishan." Mercy's father reached out his hand give her teacher a handshake. "We think she's pretty special, too."

Mercy's mother stood. "Come along, Mercy. Time for the next class."

Mercy took her parents around to meet the rest of her teachers. Occasionally, someone mentioned she needed to pay better attention, but she mostly received wonderful compliments.

Finally, they met with Mademoiselle Ginette Manigot, who taught proper behavior and use of abilities in the Abilities Etiquette class. The mademoiselle came from an outpost station on a island in the Caribbean. Only a few thousand occupants lived there, but they shouldered the formidable duty of monitoring North America. Mercy found the mademoiselle to be the most fascinating of all her teachers. Her smooth, deep mahogany complexion, a dark copper afro, and light plum eyes resulted in an astonishing combination. Mlle. Manigot possessed bright and easy, almost carefree mannerisms, as did many who were native to the Caribbean. She appeared almost too laid back to be a teacher, but behind the stereotype, existed a woman who knew how to keep her class in line. Her students, Mercy included, feared her. And loved her. And it thrilled Mercy when her teacher heaped praises on Mercy's character and told her parents their daughter was her most courteous student. By the time they finished the session with Mlle. Manigot, Mercy sported a grin from ear to ear.

"Mercy, your mother and I are going to meet with Mr. Kishan. Why don't you walk around and enjoy some free time?" her father said. Once again, she felt kicked out of the process.

Mercy ambled aimlessly around the property until she thought her parents and Mr. Kishan might be finished. On her way to the food tables to meet them, Mercy remembered she left an art project for them in her room. She ran to retrieve it, passing Atticus on the way.

"Whoa." Atticus grabbed her shoulders. "Where are you going in such a rush?"

"I left something for my mom and dad up in my room."

"Really? And what would that be?"

"I made a sculpture in art class a couple of weeks ago and I wanted to give it to them."

"What a wonderful gesture. Don't let me keep you."

Mercy ran to her room, passing through the cold fifth floor with little notice. She was already used to the phenomenon, and the Regulators almost always prowled around the hallways to watch for anything strange. They usually ignored the students and basically became part of the landscape of floor number five. But they were big and incredibly scary and the children were intimidated by the thought of any kind of close encounter with them. Therefore, the most desirable thing was to not draw their attention, staying hushed when in the area.

Mercy ran to her apothecary, pulling out the drawer designated for her most precious possessions to search for her sculpture of a sleeping foal. The figurine was not the most accurate depiction, but she felt proud of her effort, supposing her parents might use it as a paperweight. She fished it out, noticing something amiss in the drawer. She gasped. The gold nugget she brought back from her abilities test remained where she put it. But the paper she wrapped it in was missing. "Where is it?" She sifted through the contents of the drawer before moving on to all the other drawers. Her heart hammered until she feared it would make its way out of her mouth.

The paper was indeed gone. Her copy of the medallion symbols drawing was not there.

Disturbed, Mercy clutched her sculpture as if someone might take her art project from her at any moment. She reunited with her parents in the food court.

"Are you okay, Mercy?" her father asked. "You look a little peaked."

"I'm fine, Dad. I just misplaced something in my room. I'll find it later." Mercy held out the clay foal to her parents. "I made this for you in art class. I wanted you to have a keepsake to remind you of me."

"Why, it's lovely," said her mother, who took the sculpture and held it close to her heart.

"It's very good, thank you," her father said. "We already think of you day and night. You're our little girl and we love you. We don't need material items to remind us of you. But we'll keep it next to your picture on our nightstand."

Mercy scanned the crowd to make sure no one overheard the little girl moniker. "I love you, too." With so much mystery and intrigue in the air, she suddenly realized her parents, as members of the Ecclesia, could be in danger. "Please be careful at SARA."

"Why is that?" her father asked.

"I don't know exactly. A lot of kids are talking about how there's stuff going on out there and I want you to be careful."

"We always take cautious measures. Don't you worry about us," her dad said.

"Okay. Don't you worry about me either," said Mercy.

"Unlikely scenario." Emzlie kissed Mercy's forehead. "Look, Mercy, I realize you're concerned for us, but we're in a secure place among very accomplished people. Nowhere on Earth is completely and utterly safe. All any of us can do is the best we can with what we have. And that's what you're doing here, correct?"

Mercy nodded.

Mercy's mother looked at her watch. "It's time for us to go. But we'll try to come back next month at Christmas."

It came as a shock to Mercy to realize the holidays were coming up. "Oh. Is it almost Christmas? I forgot about it."

"Na-uh. You did *not* just say that," her dad put his hand on his hip and wagged a finger, as he mimicked teen talk. "Emzlie, I guess we can return all those gifts we purchased."

"Dad, no. I didn't mean it that way." Once again, her father lightened her mood.

"We'll visit again soon, kiddo." Orion rubbed Mercy's shoulder.

Mercy hugged her parents. "Bye. Harmony and balance." She bit her lip and watched them walk away. She did not want them to leave, but she was eager to hunt through her drawers to find her sketch of the symbols. She scrambled to her room once they were out of sight. She emptied every drawer, rummaging through each item. She sat on the floor with everything spread out around her when CJ came in, humming.

"What happened here?" CJ asked.

"I'm looking for something," Mercy said.

"Well. I'd offer to help, but I promised my friends I would go hang out with them. I just came here to change."

"That's okay." Mercy picked up a sweater and folded it. "It's not that important."

CJ finished dressing and opened the door. "Have fun putting all of that away."

"I was pleased your parents attended. It was a lovely surprise, wasn't it?"

"Yup." CJ closed the door behind her.

And just like that, Mercy realized things between CJ and herself were back to normal.

CHAPTER 12

TELYS, HIS NAME IS TELYS

"I'm telling you, the paper was there yesterday morning, and when I hunted around in the drawer in the afternoon, it was gone. I even checked again after my parents left." Mercy lowered her voice. She sat with Phin and the twins at Sunday brunch the day after Parents' Day. "I had it wrapped around the gold nugget I found in my pocket after my abilities test. Whoever took it just tossed the gold aside and grabbed the paper, but nothing else."

"Do you think CJ did it?" Phin bit into his avocado feta sandwich.

Mercy wrinkled her nose. "No. I saw her around the grounds and classrooms all day, hanging on to her mom and dad. She was super excited they showed up. She wouldn't have ditched them for that."

"Besides, CJ wouldn't just leave an enormous chunk of gold there and not say something," Vesuvius said.

"Why not ask your uncle to give back the one he has?" Tambora said.

"I can't. He told me not to tell anyone. And if he finds out my copy is gone, he'll think I wasn't careful. I can't let him discover someone else has it." Mercy buried her face with her hands. "Oh. What am I going to do?"

Vesuvius cocked his head. "Why do you need a copy? I mean, the High Elder already told you the meaning of the symbols."

"I know, and it's true I don't absolutely need to have it. I just wanted one. Just in case."

Tambora leaned in toward Mercy. "In case of what?"

"I can't explain why. I don't even know why myself. The translation doesn't feel complete. It doesn't matter now, anyway. The paper's gone. But that still doesn't solve the mystery about who took it and why."

Phin put the last bite of his sandwich in his mouth. "Mehbee we shud go bek to de liberry—"

Tambora smacked his hand.

"Wad?" Phin rubbed his hand

"Swallow your food before you talk. Don't forget to chew first." Tambora rolled her eyes. "Honestly, there are times I feel like I have to be the mother of you and Vesu."

"More like the anti-fun police," said Vesuvius.

"What did you say?" Tambora asked.

"You're always scolding us when we're having fun," Vesuvius said in a small, intimidated voice.

"No. Do I really?" Tambora appeared stricken.

"You kinda do." Mercy wrinkled her nose. "But we know you don't mean it the way it sounds. We still love you."

"I… I didn't realize it was so bad." Tambora's eyes misted over.

"Tambora, don't get bent out over it," Phin said. "We understand your heart."

"I'm so sorry. I'll make more of an effort to not be as unkind about it." Tambora plucked a tissue from her pocket and blew her nose. "Are we good?"

Vesuvius patted her shoulder. "Always."

"What I tried to say earlier is we should go to the library," Phin said. "We should focus on resolving one question at a time. We can't find the thief. Almost two thousand people attended yesterday. But we *can* try to get the message again."

"It's worth a shot. The medallion was still on the wall the last time I was there, but I was in too much of a hurry to try it out again," Mercy said. "We have the time. Oh, why not? Let's clean up here and get Murphy Vestam to the library."

Mercy led the others to where the medallion hung on the wall at the rear of the library. They were surprised to find Xander on the floor under the medallion, reading a book.

Vesuvius kicked at Xander's shoe. "Hey, mate. Pappas has been looking for you. You better scoot."

Xander jumped to his feet and ran awkwardly toward the portal. "Oh, man. I knew he would find out about how I ditched class the other day."

"Was Pappas really looking for him?" Tambora asked after Xander left the room.

"Nah, I just wanted to see him run. He runs like a chicken." Vesuvius mimicked Xander. "Really, I thought we should be alone in here."

"Good thinking." Mercy turned to the medallion.

The others stood back and scrutinized it. No one spoke until Phin got a closer look. "What did you do to get this thing to spin the last time?"

"I just touched the symbols. Like this." Mercy put her hand out and caressed the medallion.

As before, the medallion came to life and spun around. And as before, when the spins ended, the symbols lit up, but this time, the center section pulsated.

"I forgot paper," Mercy said.

"I'm the fastest, I'll get a few sheets from the front table," said Tambora and she sped off.

Vesuvius reached his hand toward the medallion.

"Vesu—don't touch it!" Mercy cried out, but not in time to stop curious Vesuvius from pushing the beating medallion heart.

At his touch, the medallion sparked and twirled, small at first, then larger and larger until a full-size portal appeared.

"Would you look at that," Phin said.

Vesuvius moved closer to the portal. "Let's find out where this goes."

"No! We don't know what's in there." Mercy pulled Vesuvius away from the portal.

"Nothing's in there. Just step in, step out somewhere else. Like all portals," said Vesuvius.

"I meant on the other side. We could step into outer space, for all we know."

Mercy knew her cautions would fall on deaf ears and she could say nothing to prevent the disaster ahead from happening.

"Cool. I'm going in." Vesuvius put a foot through the sparking mass.

"Vesu—stop!" Mercy said, but Vesuvius vanished through the portal into the unknown.

"Guess we'll have to go after him," said Phin.

"No, Phin. Not you, too," Mercy said, frightened for both of her friends.

Phin shrugged and jumped in after Vesuvius.

"Tambora, come back," Mercy screamed.

Tambora ran up, paper in hand, just as deactivation of the portal initialized. Mercy pushed her toward the opening. "Don't ask—just go." Tambora dropped the paper and jumped through. Mercy followed with mere seconds to spare before the gateway collapsed.

"Vesu, why did you do that?" Mercy demanded when her feet hit the floor on the other side of the portal.

"Because it called to me?" Vesuvius grinned.

"You are making it too difficult to keep the anti-fun police at bay." Tambora glared at her brother.

Mercy studied their surroundings. "Where are we?"

"We're obviously in an office." Phin checked the view out the window. "And apparently, still at the Tray."

"Wowsers. Check out the size of this desk." Vesuvius hoisted himself up to sit on the desktop. "This is massive. This must be Miss Carmen's office. She's the only eight-footer around here."

Mercy picked up an engraved placard on the desk which read *Carmen DeLuca* and flashed the nameplate at Vesuvius. "Ya think?"

"I wonder why the portal brought us here." Phin's eyes darted around the room.

"Maybe there's no reason," Vesuvius said. He swung his legs which dangled several feet above the floor. "Maybe it's all random."

"Perhaps we're supposed to be here," Tambora said.

"Could be. We seem to be involved in a cosmic mystery and everything is happening for a reason." Mercy picked up a small statue from a pedestal table, examined it, and set it down when she realized it might be an antique.

Phin said, "I'd like to figure out why we arrived here, of all places. It's not as though we went through a general portal where you name your destination. The medallion specifically brought us here. Are we supposed to find something?"

"I suppose it's as good a reason as any. Okay. Check around for anything that appears out of place in an office." Mercy walked around the perimeter of the room. "Don't touch anything, Vesu. Don't. Touch."

They each scouted around, but except for the oversized furnishings, nothing appeared out of the ordinary.

"Well. I've come up with zilch," Mercy said.

"I'm a bust too," said Phin.

"Hey, you guys. Miss Carmen is a Miss and not a Mrs., right?" Vesuvius asked.

"You know she is. She's worked at the Tray since before we came here. She lives here. Alone." Tambora clenched her fists and inhaled. "Be nice," she muttered.

"Then why do you suppose she's in a wedding dress with some guy wearing a tux in this picture?" Vesuvius picked up a frame from a side table.

"What?" Mercy cried out. They flocked toward Vesuvius to view the sepia-toned photo he stumbled upon. Sure enough, the picture presented a smiling, almost beaming, younger Miss Carmen. She wore a veil with a circlet of flowers and a man in a tuxedo kissed her cheek.

"Where do you suppose he is?" Vesuvius studied the picture.

"I dunno, maybe he's dead. Or maybe they're divorced." Tambora raised her brows. Divorce happened occasionally within the Ara'Jaeon community, but marital breakups were rare. The assumption was, when you have decades available to find your true love, you have the time to be sure.

The door lock turned and interrupted their speculations.

"Quick, hide," Mercy whispered. She disappeared behind a drape panel on the large picture window and Vesuvius slipped in behind the opposite panel. Phin dove headfirst under the enormous desk and lay down beneath the length of it. Tambora located a small niche just big enough for her to squeeze into between a corner wall and the cabinet behind the desk. From Mercy's vantage point, all the others were within her view. She peeked out and saw the office door hurl open.

Miss Carmen entered and, without switching on the lights, threw her keys on her desk. "Unbelievable," she muttered. She opened a cabinet door to reveal a mini refrigerator and a small bar cart. The contents of Mercy's stomach churned, afraid Tambora would be discovered. But Tambora crouched down next to the cabinet and curled up into herself. The semi-darkness and open cabinet door also did their part to obscure her.

Miss Carmen took out a jar of orange juice and filled a large glass. She topped the juice off with a shot from another bottle she grabbed off the cart. She guzzled down her cocktail in one long gulp, before she let out a monstrous sigh and an even larger belch before she moved to the other side of the room.

A sputter erupted from behind the opposite drape panel. Mercy scowled at Vesuvius, who held his hand over his mouth. Luckily for them, an appearance of a molten silver portal opened next to Miss Carmen, and her surprised yelp covered Vesu's outburst. Mercy almost snorted, but halted at the sight of a white-haired man, dressed in all black, stepping through. Right away, she recognized Telys, the Metalicon. In shock, she stared at him.

Miss Carmen groaned and slammed her glass down. "Telys, how many times do I have to tell you not to barge in on me?"

"Forgive me, love, but we have a bit of a situation."

Miss Carmen attempted to mimic the Metalicon's British accent. "Well. I'm having a situation of my own at the moment."

Telys flinched. "Please never do that again."

Mercy swallowed hard, her brows furrowed. Never in her dreams did she think Miss Carmen and Telys might know each other. A movement from Vesuvius caught her attention. He seemed to be focused on picking at the loose thread of a bright green button on his shirt. Mercy ducked back into the folds of the drapery. "No. Vesu, no. No," she whispered under her breath. He glanced up at her and grinned. She gave him a stern glare of warning. He lowered his eyes to his hands and let go of the button, which by that time was attached to the fabric by only a small thread. Mercy returned her attention to Miss Carmen and Telys. She hoped the Metalicon posed no danger to the headmistress. She stood ready to pounce should the need arise.

Miss Carmen huffed. "Atticus has refused to release the rest of the funds of the already low budget allotted to the Tray. I simply can't continue to run this institution *and* support the cause on what little we've got. You know, he attended Parents' Day yesterday. Poking around into anything and everything."

"Ahem." Telys cleared his throat. "Well. Your office doesn't appear to have suffered much from the budget cut." He went to the cabinet and poured himself a drink. "As for Atticus, he won't be able to find what he's searching for here." He put down his glass and stepped closer to Miss Carmen. "Listen to me. I need for you to make absolutely certain Mercy's abilities have been restrained."

Mercy, surprised to overhear her name mentioned, angled herself to better catch what they said.

"Mercy's been restrained. Trust me, Pelagius knows what he's doing. What's going on?" Miss Carmen asked.

"There are rumblings of escape attempts at the Gates of Vatek. Attempts by those who would try to woo her away. It would be much better for her to remain restrained." Telys paused. "Mercy's smart. Powerful, too. She could easily ruin everything we've worked for. Not to mention we'll still need her, eventually."

Startled, Mercy covered her mouth to keep from making any sound. She was not aware physically leaving Vatek, the land of the dead, was possible. But why would anyone need to? And why would they want her? Who would want her? She glanced at Tambora, eager for her reaction, but the open cabinet door obscured the view of her friend, showing only her fidgeting feet.

"Argh!" Miss Carmen roared. With one hand on her hip and the other rubbing her forehead, she stomped to stand by her desk. Then, she held her hands and grasped at the air with her fingers in a universal Zen-move of calming oneself. She inhaled, then exhaled, and turned until she faced Telys in a calmer manner. "No one will get their hands on the child. This, I promise you."

At that moment, there came the clinking sound of a small item hitting the floor. Alarmed, Mercy watched a little round green object roll across the room. She panicked and struggled to not hyperventilate. Her gaze darted to Vesuvius, whose eyes were squeezed shut. One hand held Miss Carmen's photo and his other held his shirt where the loose button should have been.

"I—" Telys said.

"Shh. I thought I heard something," Miss Carmen whispered.

Vesuvius scrunched his nose and grimaced, retreating further into the drapes. Phin peeked out from under the desk, openmouthed.

"I don't hear anything," Telys said after the long pause. "Look, I just wanted to make you aware of what is going on because we need to map out a plan. But I can see you're in a bit of a mood right now. We can revisit this subject at a later date when you're feeling more—congenial. In the meantime, keep tabs on Mercy Markos."

"I'll do my part and you do yours. And finish up with that orb. My budget simply can't continue to cover the loss any longer. It's bad enough that I've had to pay to hire Regulators for the past four years to give credibility to the rumors I started."

"You mean the rumors of the fifth-floor hauntings?"

Mercy's jaw dropped. Her eyes darted to the boys. They appeared as shocked as herself. She wished she could see Tambora's reaction.

"Exactly. And also as an excuse to keep the walls and doors boarded up to keep you from getting discovered. To make matters worse, I have to find extra jobs to keep the creatures preoccupied whenever you and your Metalicon cronies harvest, so they won't be around to notice you. I can only send them to search the unused portions of the school or hunt for an errant Situation Clock so many times before it becomes suspect."

"We're almost there, love. I think we'll finish in one more visit and the orb will surface."

"See that it does. How did Mercy find you? Weren't you using the invisibility shield?"

"We were. She must have the ability to see through it. It's happened before. It's uncommon, but not impossible."

"Is that so? More reason to finish quickly and carefully. The longer we linger, the more she might grow suspicious."

Mercy closed her eyes, hoping against all hope she would wake up at home in her own bed, with the past few months only a dream. But when she reopened them, she remained trapped behind the drapes of Miss Carmen's office, listening to conspiracies which somehow involved her.

"We'll try to get this last electrical harvest done during the night to reduce the chance of discovery by any of the students."

"Great idea, please make sure of it. Now, I've got a tremendous headache and a meeting coming up, so if you don't mind, I need to prepare."

"All right, I'll get back to you." Telys opened a portal and stepped through. Miss Carmen went to her desk, withdrew her chair to sit down.

Phin, in great danger of being exposed, recoiled when her feet almost crushed his fingers. But fortune smiled yet again, and a rap on the door spared him, for Miss Carmen answered it instead of taking her seat, when she would have kicked him.

"Yes? What is it?"

"Miss Carmen, there is someone in the lobby asking for you," a student responded.

"Do you know who it is?"

"No, ma'am."

"All right, I'm coming." She sighed, exiting the office.

Mercy breathed a little easier, but the kids waited to make sure the coast was clear before they abandoned their hiding spots.

"Man, that was close," Vesuvius said. "I thought for sure they would notice that button roll across the floor."

"What button?" Tambora asked.

"Vesu picked a button off his shirt and it fell to the floor. But that doesn't matter now. We need to get out of here. Do you think we could walk out?" Mercy put her ear up against the door to listen for sounds coming from the hall.

Tambora frowned. "I doubt we could. There's usually a lot of traffic out there." She dropped down and crawled.

"But why would the medallion bring us here and abandon us? And what are you doing?" Phin asked. He hunched down next to Tambora.

"I'm trying to find Vesu's button," Tambora answered. "It's evidence we were in here."

"Oh, man. This situation keeps going from bad to worse." Mercy groaned and joined Tambora and Phin on the floor to search. "It could have rolled under the cabinet. She won't find it for years if it's under there. That cabinet is too heavy to move," Mercy said.

"Hey. There's something over here." Vesuvius crouched down.

The kids crawled across the floor to Vesuvius. Phin picked up the small pebble-sized object and performed a quick inspection. "This is a tiny portal crystal, and it's on the spot where we came into the office. Seems like the medallion gave us a way to escape after all."

"How considerate, considering we never requested to come here," Tambora said.

"Actually, we did kind of agree to come here when we went through the open portal," said Mercy.

"My recollection is of getting pushed, but whatever makes you feel better." Tambora nudged Mercy with her shoulder.

"All right. You win," said Mercy. "But let's get out of here before Miss Carmen returns."

"Where should we portal to?" Vesuvius asked.

"Let's go to Vesu and Phin's room. That's the only place we know will be empty and no one can see us portal in," Tambora said.

Phin tossed the crystal and specified his room. A portal of swirling muck appeared.

Tambora scowled. "Ew. An Earth portal of mud. Really, Phin?"

"Sorry. I didn't know."

"I thought you kept it all up here." Tambora laughed, tapping her forehead.

"Hey. I have a huge assortment. I haven't used all of them yet to know each one," Phin said. "And besides, this isn't my crystal, so it's not technically my fault."

"Do you suppose we'll get filthy going through it?" Tambora scowled.

"There's no reason to think that," Mercy said. "I can't think of any other portal types that have affected anyone."

"I'll go first." Vesuvius leaped into the gunk, and Phin hopped in after him.

"We might as well go," Mercy said. "Let's jump together on the count of three."

Mercy and Tambora grabbed each other's hand, counted to three, and ran through. They gave themselves a quick once-over after they went through the portal, delighted to find themselves still clean.

Perplexed, Mercy realized they were back in the library next to the medallion. "I thought we were going to your dorm?"

"Yeah. What's going on?" Vesuvius asked.

"It must not have been a regular crystal. It was probably a homing crystal," Phin said. "I didn't know they were real. I always thought they were a myth."

"What's a homing crystal?" Mercy said.

"A crystal left behind by a closing portal. You'll return to the original location where you jumped from," Phin answered. "I've never seen one before."

"Hey, guys. I still have Miss Carmen's wedding picture." Vesuvius held out the photo.

Mercy's heart dropped. They could not catch a break.

"Oh no," Tambora said. "How can we put that back? Surely, she'll notice it's gone, and we'll be skunked if we're caught with it."

"Let's just leave it where we can be sure someone will find it, and no one will know we were involved," Phin suggested.

Mercy took the picture from Vesuvius and examined it. "This guy looks familiar. And he has blond dreadlocks." Dreadlocks amused Mercy. In her opinion, few could pull off the quirky style. *But Phin could, and so could Pip*, she thought. She shivered when she recalled the ominous dark-haired Metalicon. She hoped their first meeting would be their last.

Tambora said, "Remember several apprentices wore them in the photo in your uncle's office? He said they were popular in the 1940s. This picture of Miss Carmen must've been taken around the same time. This means she could be a hundred years old."

"Eh, she still has at least a good 250 birthdays left in her. Those stern types have a tendency to hang on longer," Phin said.

Laughter broke out from entrance of the library. "Psst. We've got company," Tambora said. "We need to talk about this elsewhere."

Phin and Vesuvius rushed to the aisle between the book shelves and the wall to get to the front without running into the intruders. Mercy and Tambora couldn't follow, because Mercy dropped Miss Carmen's photo, and they stopped to get it. A rowdy group of upper-level students came into view, shoving each other and joking around. Beau and Conrad tagged along behind them, acting eager to belong.

Mercy clutched the frame close to her chest, making sure the front of the photo was pressed next to her body.

"Look who's here," a boy said. "The mystery power girl and a third of her fan club. What are you guys whispering about? Are you planning how to save the world?"

The other boys chuckled, but no one would make eye contact with her.

Mercy flushed. Fatigue overcame her, and she possessed no desire to stand and fight. Why did kids make fun of her? She thought she was supposed to be some kind of prodigy. Although Mercy understood they were probably envious of her abilities, she did not know how to deal with it.

Tambora looped her arm through Mercy's and walked her past the boys where Phin and Vesuvius waited. They all passed through the portal to the library entrance. "Mercy, don't pay attention to them. The green in their purple eyes is showing," she said.

"What? I don't get it," Vesuvius said.

"They're jealous, nimrod. Honestly, how are you my twin?" Tambora let go of Mercy and slapped herself on the wrist. "Be nice to Vesu," she whispered.

"What about this photograph? Why don't we leave it here in the library?" Phin asked.

"We can't do that. Those guys back there have seen us, and besides, there's a video camera right there at the checkout desk that shows we've been in here. Someone will figure out we did it," Mercy said in a soft tone. Fresh from her sting of embarrassment, her cheeks still burned, rosy and hot.

"We'll think of a way, Mercy. When we get out of the camera's view, give the picture back to Vesu. He can hide it under his shirt." Tambora grabbed a couple of sheets of paper and a pen from the stationary table. "Let's go find a spot to sit outdoors where we can talk minus the company of any big ears."

When outside, they located a lush grassy spot under a magnificent Persian silk tree blanketed with feathery pink blossoms. In nature, Persian silk trees bloomed only in the spring and summer, but the Tray gardener possessed incredible Earth skills. He was a whiz at skirting around nature's directives when he had a mind to do so. Tiny lily-of-the-valley grew around the base of the tree, producing a sweet fragrance which stirred up memories. Memories of being wrapped in your mother's arms as she rocks you to sleep on the back porch during a warm summer evening.

Mercy lifted her head high to clear her thoughts and let the fresh air envelop her. When she finished, she realized the others plopped down on the lawn, sitting in a circle. "Here, Vesu. Take this." Mercy handed Miss Carmen's photo to Vesuvius, who hid it beneath his sweater. "I have a lot of questions from when we were in Miss Carmen's office." Mercy sat down on the grass and stretched her legs out. "I don't even know where to begin."

A good long minute lapsed before anyone spoke.

"Let's go with the easiest first." Tambora reached over to Vesuvius and used her stack of paper to whack him on the head.

"Ow. Why did you do that?" Vesuvius cowered under his arms.

"That is for almost getting us caught with that loose button stunt you pulled. The one that's still missing in her office, so we're not completely safe yet. And for nipping the photo to boot."

Mercy chuckled, despite her attempt to hold back. Tambora's pledge to rein in the fun police did not last long. But in that instance, she was on target.

Tambora settled back and laid out her paper and pencils in her usual ordered manner. "Sometimes the fun police have no choice but to give out tickets. Okay. Now that's been taken care of, let's get down to real business. Who was that Metalicon and why did he talk to Miss Carmen about Mercy?"

"Telys. His name is Telys," Mercy whispered.

CHAPTER 13

FLIGHT OF A GUTLESS TAIL

Mercy sighed. "Telys is a Metalicon I met on the day I arrived. The others were Pip and Patina. From what we heard, it sounds as if some kind of orb is hidden at the Tray and the Metalicons are trying to get to it by taking electricity. It makes sense when I think about what I witnessed in that room my first day here."

"And we can also assume Miss Carmen is in cahoots with them," Phin said as he sifted through the stones and rocks strewn around the trunk of the tree.

"She said she sends the Regulators on errands when the Metalicons are working. That's why they weren't around that day," said Mercy.

"This means the fifth floor isn't actually haunted and all those shakings and lights came from the Metalicons taking the electricity." Vesuvius plucked a long blade of grass and chewed on the end. "Bummer. I kind of enjoyed getting scared going through there."

"Think, Vesu." Phin picked up a small flat stone, inspected it, and put it in his pocket. "The Metalicons are taking our electricity. Trust me, you can still be scared."

"At least now we know you weren't kidding on your first day here when you said you saw Metalicons," Tambora said.

"You didn't believe me?" Disappointment dripped from Mercy's question.

Tambora placed Mercy's hand between her own. "It's not so much that we didn't believe you, as much as it was that we couldn't understand what you saw, or how important it was."

Phin chimed in. "Is anyone else not surprised that Mercy can see through invisibility shields? I mean, her abilities just keep adding up."

Mercy stifled a giggle. She felt like a boy-crazy school girl and she did not enjoy the sensation.

Tambora gasped and raised her hands to her cheeks. "Oh, my goodness. I just realized what the orb is. I heard my mom and dad talking once about how the spirit of each element inhabits an orb."

"Yeah, I've overheard my parents, too." Phin sat up straighter. "And no one should ever have possession of all the orbs because the four together gives them too much power. My mom said they were all separated and hidden thousands of years ago. No one alive knows where they are. Not even the Assembly knows."

"Eureka!" Mercy shouted, then glanced around to see if anyone outside of her friends heard her. They were safe, but she lowered her voice, anyway. "Don't you see?"

"What is it, Mercy?" said Vesuvius.

Mercy jumped to her feet and paced under the tree. "The Metalicons are attempting to retrieve all the orbs to gain absolute power. And Miss Carmen is helping Telys. She's helping the Metalicons."

Vesuvius gulped and the blade of grass fell from his mouth. "No way."

"Telys said the orb will surface soon. That means the orb is somewhere at the Tray. Probably on the fifth floor. And if they're taking electricity, it must be the Fire orb," Mercy said. "The Tray isn't thousands of years old, though. Someone must've moved it at some point."

"Not unless it's coming from underground, and they're mining it from the fifth floor," Phin said.

Tambora pulled her knees to her chest, wrapped her arms around them and rocked. "Oh. This is bad."

"We've got to tell someone," Phin said.

"Who could we tell?" Mercy frowned. "We can't call our parents from the Visual Communications Room without permission and we don't know who we can trust. Miss Carmen is most likely helping the Metalicons, and maybe Pappas is too. Restraining me was his idea. The Emissary told me sometimes honorable places don't hold honor. This has to be what it meant. And did you hear Telys say some inhabitants of Vatek are trying to get to me? He and Miss Carmen want my powers restrained so I can't fight."

"So, what do we do now?" Phin asked.

They all looked to Mercy for an answer she could not provide. She shook her head. "I just don't know."

"Don't stew over it. The next step will surface when it's time," Tambora said.

Vesuvius pulled Miss Carmen's photo out from under his jacket. "What do we do with this picture?"

Tambora gathered up her unused paper and reached out for the photo. "I'll take this. I have an idea on where to leave it."

The dinner bell sounded, echoing throughout the gardens and grounds. Children emerged from all over the property, hurrying toward the building. Vesuvius and Phin jumped up, stumbling over the girls, frenzied to get to their next meal. Mercy and Tambora strolled in calm silence. Mercy's mind spun, filled by deliberations of Miss Carmen, Telys, and all the implications of what their acquaintance might mean. She was certain Tambora suffered the same thoughts. They stepped through the red revolving door and into the crowded lobby of students, heading to dining hall.

Tambora said, "I'm going to take care of that *thing* Vesu gave to me. I'll be down for dinner in a few minutes."

"What will you do with it?"

"I'll tell you later. Save my seat."

Mercy nodded and made her way to the dining hall where the boys already sat.

Vesuvius sent a spitball to the next table, hit a girl whose back was toward him, then quickly spun around, acting innocent. She glared at Mercy, who cocked an eyebrow back at her.

"What are we having?" Mercy opened her napkin and set it on her lap.

"Potpourri stew," said Phin.

"What kind of stew?" Mercy said.

"Potpourri stew. You know, made using leftovers from other meals? There was a lot of food left from Parents' Day. Meats, vegetables, cheese." Phin sent his own spitball flying aimlessly through the air. "As Miss Carmen says, 'Waste not, want not.' She must really be tweaking the budget to fund those extra activities."

"Shush," Mercy said. "You guys are going to have to be more careful about what you say in public or Tambora and I will have to solve these mysteries minus you both."

"You're absolutely right," said Vesuvius in a rare logical moment. "Isn't she, Loy-Roy?"

A few weeks earlier, the kids realized the chipped Petit Serveur faithfully showed up at their table for every meal. They named him Loyal Royal. The word royal referred to the rich blue of his platter-shaped body. They called him Loy-Roy for short. Loy-Roy appeared to respond to the moniker, and the nickname stuck. Loy-Roy finished setting the table then rotated toward Vesuvius, his wings upturned as though he held his palms up at his side in an I-don't-know pose.

"Just say yes," Phin said.

Loy-Roy bobbed and pointed one wing to the empty chair.

"Tambora's coming. You can set up for her," Mercy said to the serveur.

Loy-Roy dipped, set the fourth-place setting, and returned to the kitchen.

"Where is Tam?" Vesuvius asked.

"She's taking care of *your* mistake," Mercy answered just as a serious-faced Tambora arrived.

"Did everything go okay?" Vesuvius asked his sister.

"It's fine." Tambora's answer was short and clipped. She hissed, her voice low. "But you need to think about what you do or you're going to get us all in trouble."

"That's exactly what I said to them." Mercy also spoke in a quiet tone.

"I'm aware we've been messing up and treating this like an adventure instead of a serious situation," Phin said. "Please don't leave us out. We'll do better, right, Vesu?"

"To the best of our ability," said Vesuvius.

Mercy frowned. "That's exactly what scares me."

Phin reddened. "Well stated."

Tambora laughed, and the mood shifted into a lively chatter by the time Loy-Roy brought out their meal, followed by jamun pie, which was made using Miss Carmen's recipe.

After dinner, Phin and Vesuvius went to hang outside before nightfall. Tambora grabbed Mercy. "Come with me."

She led Mercy up to the student lounge. The room was almost empty as most students went outdoors before the sun set. They sat in a corner far from the few students who studied there.

"What's going on?" Mercy scooted back in the comfortable chair.

"I wanted to tell you what I did with the photo. I thought it would be better for just the two of us to know," Tambora said. "I wrapped it in a pillowcase and propped it up against Miss Carmen's office door.

"You made sure no one saw you?"

"No one was around."

"Good." Mercy stared out of the wall of windows and spotted Phin and Vesuvius in a game of American baseball with a group of kids. The sun settled low in the horizon, and rosy hues spread across the distant sky to signal nightfall's approach. She sat upright. "I know we've got a lot on our minds right now, but what do you think about running outside and playing ball with the guys for a bit. It might help to clear our heads."

"Let's do it," Tambora said.

"I'll race you down the first flight of stairs." Mercy jumped out of her chair and sprinted toward the door and down the stairs to the sixth-floor. "I won," she shouted.

"For now," Tambora said.

"Let's race again," Mercy yelled and ran for the next set of stairs.

"Get set, go," Tambora shouted.

Still ahead of Tambora, Mercy was almost at the stairwell between the sixth and fifth floor when she met Beaumont and Conrad, coming up the stairs toward her.

"Those bracelets are amazing, Mercy," Beau scoffed and smirked at Conrad, who snickered. "Gosh. Don't things just keep getting better and better," Beau said as Tambora caught up to Mercy.

Mercy brushed past the boys and took a few steps down the stairs. She stopped and turned around. "Tambora, let's go. They're not important enough to bring us down."

Tambora followed Mercy, but when she took her first step, Conrad said, "I think I'm important enough. Down you go." He stuck out his foot and tripped Tambora.

Tambora shrieked and plummeted into Mercy, whose good grasp on the railing kept them both from tumbling down the entire flight of stairs. Mercy helped her friend get up from her fall, and Tambora sat down, trembling on the steps.

"What do you think you're doing!" Mercy yelled at the top of her lungs. "You could've killed someone!"

"But we didn't, did we?" Conrad said with a big toothy Cheshire Cat grin.

"Hey. There's no *we* here. You did this on your own," Beau said, inching away from his rogue disciple.

BOOM—BOOM—BOOM.

They quieted as the sound of powerful footsteps came up the stairs. The thunderous, resonating steps of a Regulator. Beau's face drained of all color and he ran the other direction, leaving the others to cope with the formidable creature.

Mercy's knees knocked together. "They must've heard the ruckus and are coming to check it out. Whatarewegonnado whatarewegonnado?" Mercy's words ran together. But Tambora gave no response. She simply sat with her head down on her lap, covered by her arms.

The weighty steps got closer. Conrad fidgeted. "Umm, look, ladies. It was an accident. Just a joke. I didn't mean anything by it, you know? You can just tell them it's all been taken care of, okay? Okay. See ya. Bye." As that statement still rang in Mercy's ears, Conrad Montague twirled his gutless tail around and ran.

Mercy trembled in fear, too paralyzed to run. Even if flight was possible, Tambora was in no state to get up yet and Mercy would never leave her there alone. Mercy closed her eyes. To calm herself, she shakily, but bravely, sang out the Ara'Jaeon anthem the chorus performed the previous day for the parents. The footsteps stopped just before they reached the girls. Mercy's singing faltered when she detected a presence nearby. Trembling, she halfway opened one eye. She peered through her squint and found nothing out of the ordinary, so she held her breath and took a bigger peek. On the stairs, a few steps down, were none other than Phin and Vesuvius, and they each carried a long, heavy metal baseball bat. "Oh!" Mercy let out a sigh of relief. "You frightened us half to death. We thought you were Regulators coming up to investigate the noise. I'm still shaking. Those creeps, Beau and Conrad, tried to make Tambora fall down the stairs. Well, Conrad did. Beau is just a creep."

"Are you okay?" Vesuvius helped Tambora up from her seated position.

Tambora nodded.

"We just came in from outside. We were right below you and heard what was going on," Phin said. "We had our bats and wanted to put a scare in those guys."

BOOM—BOOM—BOOM.

"Guys, stop. That only works once." Mercy gulped a large bit of air when she realized the boys held their bats motionless in their hands. The sound did not come from them.

Phin and Vesuvius turned to each other, their faces awash in horror. "Argh!" they yelled in unison.

Tambora dried her tears, recovering enough to dust off her skirt and say, "Friends, family, we gotta run."

The foursome shrieked and scurried as fast as they could. No one wanted to come face to face with a Regulator on a mission. Mercy's room was the closest. They slammed the door shut, kept the lights off, and waited. Mercy was thankful CJ was out so she would not feel the need to do any explaining.

"Oh man, oh man, o-man-o-man-o-man." Vesuvius bounced in place.

"Shh." Mercy whispered. "They're right down the hall." The low groaning of the Regulators grew closer. She cringed. It was the first time she experienced it for herself and it caused her a great discomfort. It sounded similar to the old, squeaky, wooden ships in the movies when they creaked and clunked as they rode the high ocean waves.

They listened to the stomps and moans for what felt like an eternity and focused their attention on the door. The heavy footsteps advanced closer and closer, until they paused outside the door. The kids froze. No one moved a muscle except for the quivering of Mercy's legs. She was terrified the Regulators would hear her bones rattle. The footsteps marched back and forth a few times outside her door, but eventually ebbed away until they were out of earshot.

"That was clo—" Vesuvius said.

Mercy interrupted him with a whisper. "Be quiet. We need to wait and be sure they've left." She held off for a few minutes before she cracked the door open and peered out. All was quiet. "I think they're gone."

Vesuvius and Phin also popped their heads out the door before they raced off to wherever boys go to recuperate from the fright of their lives.

"This would be a good time to get outside for some fresh air," Mercy said. "But I don't think you should try the stairs right now. You're still trembling."

"I am. But someone has to report what Conrad did," Tambora said.

"I'll go find Miss Carmen and let her know."

"Aren't you afraid of her?"

"A little, but I heard somewhere there's a best friend code that says you have to confront your fright directly in the face to help a friend." Mercy hoped her attempt at humor would bring a smile out of Tambora and it did. "Besides, Miss Carmen is still the headmistress around here and she *is* doing her job. We have to act like we don't suspect her of anything." Mercy wrapped her arm around Tambora and walked her to her room. "You get some rest now and we'll talk tomorrow."

"Okay, Mercy. Be careful. See you tomorrow." Tambora withdrew into her room.

Mercy stood alone in the hall, attempting to compose herself. Her chest heaved with several deep breaths. When her courage reached beyond her fear, she proceeded toward the lower floors to find her supposed nemesis.

Mercy found Miss Carmen in the main lobby, sitting on the stone ledge of the water garden and crooning over the flora which stretched toward her while she sang to them. However, the moment Mercy stepped down from the stairs, the faces of all the flowers veered away from Miss Carmen and toward Mercy. A few leaves even extended in her direction. Rock Star Mercy reached out to pat the outstretched hands of her adoring fans, but when she thought she spotted a flicker of a tightening on Miss Carmen's lips, she drew back from her admirers to keep from offending the headmistress.

"Miss Carmen?" Mercy clasped her hands.

"Yes, Mercy?"

"There's been an incident."

Miss Carmen patted the ledge next to her. "Have a seat, then. Tell me about it."

"It's all okay now. But it could've been really serious." Mercy averted her gaze, unsure if she could look at Miss Carmen straight on. It was bad enough she was uncomfortable over what she overheard earlier in the day, but the flowers shifting their attention from Miss Carmen to Mercy, created a doubly awkward situation. She sat down and met the eyes of the older woman.

"Tambora and I were on the stairs when Beau Chamberlain and Conrad Montague harassed us. I can take it and Tambora can take it. But Conrad went too far and deliberately tripped Tambora when she tried to go down the stairs. Luckily, I stood right below her on the steps, so she didn't fall far."

Miss Carmen stood and wrung her hands. "Where is she? Is she injured?"

"No. She's okay, just shaken up. She's resting in her room. But we thought you should know about it because she could have been hurt badly."

"You did the right thing to come to me," Miss Carmen said. "I'll take care of the situation, but first, I'll check on Tambora. Thank you for bringing this to my attention."

The students were abuzz the next morning. Mercy caught sight of Beau in the hallway after breakfast. He kept his gaze down. No one saw Conrad since the night before. The whispers going around alleged he was expelled for a physical attack on another student. Miss Carmen visited each first period classroom to address bullying in all its forms and how it would always be dealt with in the strictest of penalties, namely expulsion from the Tray. She did not mention Conrad by name, but made it clear an unacceptable event occurred, and the Tray had to take active measures. The manner in which Miss Carmen handled the situation impressed Mercy, and she struggled to remind herself the headmistress was not completely trustworthy.

On her way to her second class, a Situation Clock chimed in her ear, interrupting her thoughts of Miss Carmen. The quiet whisper was barely loud enough for her alone to hear, "It is 9:05, and time will forever tell all things."

She peered over her shoulder and said, "I fear you are correct."

CHAPTER 14

Late October on Ara'Ja still produced many sunny days and the sunshine boosted Mercy's dispostion. It was a Saturday, and the previous two weeks flew by with no unusual events. She felt free. And strong. Tambora went off by herself to study, leaving Mercy on her own. She caught up on her journaling. In her written musings, she told how her paper of symbols was gone and her uncle had the other copy. She stopped writing, wondering why she never searched for any books in the library on ancient symbols. She resumed her journaling, but the idea of a book of symbols nagged at her until she could no longer focus. She decided she would make use of the extra time and energy to visit the medallion to get the symbols again. Then she would look for a library book. She entered the portal to the empty reference room. She found a dark room with no other students present. Flipping the switch on the wall, she was relieved when the lights flickered to life. She had no reason to think they would not come on, but the only thing spookier than a shadowy, uninhabited library was a shadowy, uninhabited church, or so she heard. Odd, how the places meant to bring the most joy could be the most eerie in the absence of light.

Mercy grabbed paper and pencils from the front table. She omitted her typical library routine of walking through the aisles, running her fingertips over the book spines. She came with another purpose. She made her way to the medallion and put her hand out to touch the relic. Again, there were lights and spinning. She hoped it would not bring up a portal. She was unsure if she possessed enough willpower to not go through. Her luck held out, and when the spinning stopped, she recognized the lit symbols as the same characters she was previously given. In her mind, it verified they meant something crucial to her, regardless of the generic interpretation her Uncle Atticus gave her. She did not doubt his explanation of each symbol's meaning as much as she believed he did not give her a full interpretation of them as a whole. She copied down the symbols as before and searched in the Ancient Ara'Ja section for a book on ancient symbols. She located one a few minutes into her search and pulled the volume from the shelf to take with her to a table in the corner. Mercy admired the craftsmanship of the book. A worn black and gray snakeskin cover, embossed with the element symbols, protected the delicate parchment. She positioned the paper and pencil front of her on the table, the book to the left, and her sheet of symbols to the right. At that moment, she thought she could attain the proficiency of the ultra-organized Tambora. She savored the notion.

There were eight symbols. She did not bother to look up the first one. It no doubt represented a female. The next one was a spiraled circle and the one after was a circle with two consecutively smaller circles inside. She flipped through the book and found a section filled with circles. She ran her finger across every symbol on the first page, searching for the two. She did not realize there could be so many ways a circle could be made into a symbol. She found the spiral on the second page. The connotation said it stood for either wisdom or knowledge. That concept made sense, she thought. Her Uncle Atticus mentioned knowledge. She wrote the meaning and went back to the book to find the second circle. She found it halfway down the third page. Truth or integrity was written under it. Again, Mercy thought everything so far lined up with what her uncle told her. A girl, knowledge or wisdom, and truth or integrity. "Maybe this won't be so complicated after all," she muttered aloud as she wrote in her notes then began her search for the fourth symbol. The last icon was identical to the fourth, but upside down. She hoped she would locate both on the same page. She explored the old manuscript, hoping to find anything which resembled the two symbols. But before she did, she discovered a section on wings. Several variations were listed, but most of them meant the same thing. Life or resurrection. She came across the shape of her pair of wing symbols right away and the significance matched that of the others. She made her notations and turned her attention to symbols number four and eight. A peace sign and its upside-down counterpart. The thought crossed her mind they might mean war and peace. But she knew the peace sign was developed in the mid-twentieth century. It was too new to be part of an ancient collection of symbols.

After she rifled through a few more sections, she found a page of images of various types of lines with what Mercy might loosely call legs and arms. She found hers next to each other. The first one—the upside-down peace sign, or the one with its arms stretched upward—meant life or to renew. The other meant death. At first, she was afraid. Her heart pounded harder, making it difficult to breathe, until she remembered her uncle said some symbols represented her lifetime. She reasoned they could be symbols which represented her life span from birth to death. Once again, it all fit. Perhaps her uncle truly told her everything.

She almost quit the search, as she only had one more to go, and it was simply a crown. Her Uncle Atticus mentioned a crown. But so did the voice in her head on that first day. That crown did not have such a pleasant meaning, so she kept on with her search. She easily discovered the section of crowns. Again, there were multiple versions. She quickly identified the crown with a line under it. A chill ran through her when she read the significance. Crown of Reward. She sat straighter. It felt ominous. But Atticus said her time at the Tray would be the crown of her education. Still, she mused it worked within his interpretation, and she talked herself into remaining calm.

She wrote the meaning of the symbols in order. Female. Knowledge or wisdom. Truth or integrity. Life or to renew. Crown of Reward. Life or arise. Death. These symbols put together reminded her of words spoken to her on her first night at the Tray. She would never forget them.

"The prophecy of the Council declares the lines of Kadius and Marokos shall unite and produce a daughter. But beware, she shall restore the Iron Crown and bring forth death."

She thought she should look up her family names in a lineage and genealogy book to find out if there was a connection to Kadius and Marokos. She knew right where those books were. She skimmed past them earlier while searching for the book of symbols. She ran to retrieve one and eagerly returned to her study area, only to realize her carefully organized table no longer resembled the neat workplace Tambora might maintain. She did not remember creating such a mess. She sighed at her failed attempt for an ordered task. She scanned through the pages for Kadarius or Markos and found Markos first. She read aloud.

The Markos family name was first established as Marokos. They were known for being bearers of truth and integrity.

That find confirmed her suspicions of the similarity between her family names and the ones she heard on her first day. Her breath caught in her throat as she searched for Kadarius. She did not think her heart could pound any harder, but when she read the history, she was near distraught. The Kadarius family name originated as Kadius and they were legendary for their wisdom and pursuit of knowledge. And there, under the Kadius surname, was a prophecy made in the ancient times of the original Council of Apotheosis along with a depiction of the symbols the medallion gave to her, but arranged together to form a complete meaning. A meaning which matched the prophecy.

The Daughter shall place her feet on Truth and carry Wisdom in her hands. And she will make new the Iron Crown of Reward and give rise to Death.

Markos signified Truth and Kadarius represented Wisdom. She, Mercy Markos, was the living embodiment of the unification of Wisdom and Integrity. What was the iron crown and how would its restoration bring death? Death to her? Death to her family or friends? How was it even possible for her to be involved? Confident she made the correct interpretation, she needed to find Tambora and say the words out loud to determine if her analysis sounded as preposterous as it did in her thoughts. Mercy put her head down on the table. She did not wish to fix any stupid crown. She desired to have nothing to do with any of it. Her hands shook as she set aside her emotions and put the books away instead of leaving them and running off. When she finished, she grabbed her notes to search for Tambora.

She came across Vesuvius in the lobby. Out of breath, she asked, "Where's Tambora?"

"She's outside under the mimosa tree."

Without so much as a thank you, Mercy took off at top speed to find her friend. She was aware of a distant "Are you okay?" called out from behind her, but she ignored the question and raced to Tambora to spill what she found.

Mercy stopped short of careening into her friend. She bent over with her hands on her knees as she tried to catch her breath. She stood before she was fully ready, fanned her notes at Tambora, and sputtered the best she could, "It's me. Wisdom and Truth are Kadarius and Markos. Together, it's me. And somehow, I'm going to restore some type of death crown."

"What?" Tambora said. "Slow down, I didn't catch all of that."

"Tambora, I went to the medallion again and touched it. It gave me the same symbols as before and then I found them in a book."

"Why didn't you take me with you? I could've helped," said Tambora.

"It was a spur-of-the-moment thing. Listen, there's something I didn't tell you. Something about my first day here."

Tambora gave Mercy a quizzical look.

"At dinner, on my first day, a voice in my mind called to me from a great distance. No. It was more of an echo from the past, ancient and old."

"What did the voice say?"

"It basically said there was a prophecy that Kadius and Marokos will join to have a daughter, but she'll restore a crown and it will bring death. I uncovered proof that the surnames of Kadius and Marokos are the old versions of Kadarius and Markos. My parents are both only children, the last of their lines. I'm the daughter." Mercy burst into tears. "And I'm probably going to help destroy the world."

Tambora set her book down and rose to her feet. "What prophecy?"

"The one that says *The Daughter shall stand on Truth and hold Wisdom in her hands. She will renew the Iron Crown and give rise to Death.* It's all right here. I've written everything down."

"Give rise to death? That's terrifying. It's nothing close to what the High Elder said. Can you show me your notes? Maybe you're missing something."

Mercy gave her papers to Tambora who examined them. Her eyes grew larger and larger as she read. "Well. Your conclusions seem logical when compared to these notes."

"See? I'm going to do awful things. *Give rise to death,*" Mercy screeched. She gasped as she recalled Azrael, her childhood Metalicon boogeyman. He hid under her bed nightly for years until she decided she was too old to believe in such silliness. She had not seen him since. But she looked up the meaning of the name of his name once, when she got curious. "Tambora. Azrael. It means Angel of Death! The Metalicon who terrified me every night when I was small was probably the Death Angel. And I'm going to bring him back. Could it get any worse than that? I'm going to turn into a monster!"

"Mercy, you won't. Besides, we don't know for sure the prophecy will happen. Prophecies can be… they can be subjective. You're aware of it now, so just don't do whatever it is to the crown that destroys everything."

"We can't talk to any of our parents." Mercy sat next to Tambora and wiped her tears. "There's no way to get into the communications room without Miss Carmen finding out. She keeps a tight rein on that room. Besides, since she's working with the Metalicons, she's probably put a bug in there so she knows what all outside conversations are about. And we can't portal to them because we can only portal off the island from

Transport Plaza in Nikonea City. And we'd get caught because we're not thirteen yet."

"Not to mention there are special codes you have to use to get to the outposts. We don't know what those are," said Tambora. "Mercy, you need to calm down. The world is not ending tomorrow."

Mercy crossed her arms and stared at Tambora, her lips clenched in frustration. She stood and leaned up against the tree to steady herself as she struggled to decide what to do. The girls stared at each other. The wind picked up, disturbing an unseasonal kaleidoscope of Holly Blue butterflies perched in a nearby lavender patch, another unseasonal phenomenon among many on Ara'Ja. Thousands of pale silvery blue beating wings saturated the air as they pirouetted in tandem with the hum of nature. They flocked around Mercy and Tambora, like flower petals, raining down from the heavens.

With a respite from their standoff, Mercy and Tambora held out their hands as an invitation to the splendid creatures. Butterflies soon covered their arms and torsos. Their eyes met in a playful glance and they both burst out into a fit of giggles. Mercy pretended to be a model in a photo shoot and randomly changed poses. She could visualize the magazine spread, featuring two pretty girls, a radiant redhead and a platinum blonde, covered in butterflies and vogueing under a spectacular flowering tree.

"All right." Mercy finished playacting. "I'm not going to argue." Mercy frowned as she continued to think. "We'll just have to go visit Uncle Atticus again."

Tambora wrinkled her nose. "But he already gave you a wrong interpretation of the symbols. Why would he change what he said?"

"I'll be honest with him and tell him I looked up the meanings of the symbols and I found out about the prophecy. He's my uncle. I've known him my entire life. He'll tell me the truth. He wouldn't deliberately lie to me," said Mercy.

"Do you think any of this has to do with the Metalicons trying to get the orbs?" Tambora shook off the butterflies which flew off together in a massive cloud of blue to the nearby gardens.

"It has to. It's like all of this is purposefully happening at once," Mercy replied.

"This situation is bigger than us. I think we need to be extra careful and take our time to think this out."

"I know. We should visit my uncle soon and find out what he has to say before we decide what to do. But we'll have to go in secret again."

"Great idea. Let's talk to Phin at dinner about getting one of his portal crystals."

Mercy noticed the students were more animated than usual. Many yelled across the dining room, still others tossed crumpled napkins into the air. Adele ran up to them, her perfect golden curls bounced with every step.

"Did you hear? Miss Carmen is going to make a big announcement," she said and ran away without waiting for a reply.

"We haven't heard anything. But thanks for the info," Mercy said loudly to Adele's back.

Tambora chuckled. "She deserved that. Come on. The guys are already at the table."

Mercy and Tambora sat down as Loy-Roy arrived, carrying glasses and a pitcher of water. He bounced to greet them.

Loy-Roy acted as an unofficial member of their little group. They spoke freely in front of the serveur, confident he would keep their secrets. He already knew they were in Miss Carmen's office and he knew about their trip to the Assembly. He knew it all.

"Hey, Loy-Roy. How's it going?" Mercy poured herself a glass of water and took a long drink.

Loy-Roy set down his cargo, spun around, and landed with his gilded edge on the table with one wing up and one out to the side.

"Ta-da!" Vesuvius sang out.

"That good, huh?" Mercy laughed. "What's for dinner tonight?"

Loy-Roy sped away and returned with a load of food. He set a large platter of souvlaki, skewered chicken and pork, on the table for the kids to share. He placed a bowl of tzatziki sauce alongside it. Then he set out individual bowls of salad made with vegetables harvested from the Tray's own garden.

Mercy closed her eyes, picturing the day her grandmother and mother taught her to make souvlaki. The adult women sliced the meat and let it marinate for a few hours, then they showed her how to thread the meat onto the skewers before her father set them on the grill to cook. While the meat cooked, she and her grandmother made the delicious yogurt and cucumber sauce traditionally served with the dish. Once again, Mercy's heart ached for her grandmother and she felt the heavy weight of the prophecy.

Loy-Roy placed himself in front of Mercy, raised her chin with one of his wings, and tapped the end of her nose before he flew off. She made a sad attempt at a smile.

"What's wrong, Mercy?" Phin asked.

"She's come across interesting information about the symbols from the library medallion." Tambora reached for the sauce and heaped a generous amount onto her plate. "High Elder Atticus didn't tell her the entire interpretation and we need to talk to him again."

"Some of what I discovered seems pretty serious and we need to have him confirm what I found. Basically, there's some kind of prophecy about me." Mercy leaned in, lowered her voice, and repeated the prophecy she told Tambora.

"Wowsers. That is so cool. I wish there was a prophecy about me." Vesuvius forked a sizeable chunk of chicken. "Why can't we just go tell Miss Carmen?"

Tambora quieted her voice. "Vesu, do you not remember what happened only a few weeks ago? We caught her plotting with a Metalicon."

"Right," said Vesuvius. "There is that."

"Maybe I could come up with an excuse for me to call him, a reason so important, they would have to let me into the communication room. Then I can tell him we need to see him urgently," Mercy said.

She was interrupted by the clap of Miss Carmen's hands. The single, loud crack rattled the chandeliers which hung from the ceiling. "Attention, please. I have an announcement."

The room hushed.

"As most of you know, High Elder Kadarius was here during our Parents' Day event. He was very impressed and wants to take a more active part in our institution. He left Ara'Ja this morning for a month-long tour of all the Ecclesia outposts. But upon his return, he has agreed to host a Fall's End banquet for the Tray students, followed by a symposium."

Tambora leaned over to Mercy. "Did you know about this?"

"No. I haven't seen him since Parents' Day," Mercy replied. She scowled, unsure of what she should do next.

Miss Carmen continued, "Most of you have parents in the Ecclesia and this will be an excellent opportunity to learn more about their duties and the facilities where they live and work. Many of you will follow in your parents' footsteps to become members of the Ecclesia yourself, thus, you will want to pay close attention at the symposium. The High Elder has promised a question-and-answer session after his talk. Take these next few weeks and *thoughtfully* prepare questions you want to ask. Trick questions and ignorant remarks will not be tolerated. Am I understood?"

"Yes, Miss Carmen," came the unified answer from the students.

"Am I understood, Beaumont?"

Beau slunk down in his chair and nodded.

"Excellent. You may continue with your meals." Miss Carmen returned to her seat and chatted with her constituents. Mercy detected a hint of panic in the way the headmistress did not blink and in the frozen smile she wore.

The usual dull roar of the dining hall resumed, this time with more excitement. But the mood around the Murphy Vestam table deflated like a beach ball when it saw the end of summer.

"There goes that idea," said Phin. "What now?"

"I say we go there, anyway, and have Ms. Grouchypants contact him," said Vesuvius.

"No," Mercy said.

"What's that?" asked Vesuvius.

"I said, no. We're not doing anything right now. Check out Miss Carmen's expression. She's terrified of Uncle Atticus. She knows she's going to get caught working for the Metalicons. We have to be smart. Let's just keep alert until he returns, then we can go to him with evidence."

"Mercy's right," Tambora said. "That's all we can do for now. We'll need to be extra cautious and stick together."

"I'll watch over you, Mercy." Vesuvius patted her back.

"I will, too," said Phin, throwing out his hand for a team hand stack. "Murphy Vestam."

"We all will." Tambora put her hand in. "Murphy Vestam."

"Murphy Vestam." Vesuvius joined his hand with the others.

Mercy teared up, wiped her face with her sleeve, and topped off the hand stack with her own. "You guys are the greatest friends ever." Not to be excluded, Loy-Roy flew to the center of their circle and set his wing on Mercy's hand. "Loy-Roy, how could we ever forget you?" Mercy laughed.

CHAPTER 15

FOUR FEET OF CONSPIRACY

Mercy slumped forward, her elbow on her desk, and her chin placed in her palm. Her other hand held a pencil which she idly tapped over and over on her Language Arts textbook. Tambora sat in a similar pose across the aisle from Mercy. As lovers of words and books, both girls favored the once-a-week class, focusing on reading, writing composition, public speaking, and listening. But on that specific Monday, Mercy's attention span plummeted. She could tell by Tambora's fidgeting, her friend was in the same predicament. Mercy shook herself to bring her attention back to Mrs. Savalas, a teacher in the general studies rotation. A scrunched-up piece of paper landed on her desk and bounced twice before it stopped. Mercy straightened, twisting her head to see if Tambora was the culprit. Tambora raised a brow and darted her eyes back and forth between the crinkled missile and Mercy. Mercy picked up the paper wad and smoothed it open.

Dear Mercy… my very best friend,

I'm crawling out of my skin. There's a best friend rule that says if your best friend is stir crazy, you need to think of a solution. Let's get out of here! Are you in?

Circle one.

Yes No

Mercy grinned and circled yes. She re-wadded the paper and waited for Mrs. Savalas to turn to the blackboard, then tossed it to Tambora. She took a side glance at her friend, who looked back with hard, wide-opened eyes. Tambora's head bobbed toward the teacher. Mercy pointed to herself and mouthed, "Me?"

Tambora nodded, pointed at Mercy and then to Mrs. Savalas.

Mercy wondered why she should be the one to think of a valid reason to get out of class when Tambora's imagination could create a more plausible cause. But she was Tambora's best friend; and therefore, required to fix the situation. She bit her lip and tried to think about what excuse she could use to get them out of class. She ran her fingers through her hair while she thought, which gave her a most magnificent idea. She knew her plan would mortify Tambora, but it was brilliant. Mercy was excited to see her friend's face when she heard Mercy's request. When Mrs. Savalas finished at the blackboard, Mercy raised her hand and waved.

"What is it, Mercy?" Mrs. Savalas asked.

Mercy put on her best worried expression. "Mrs. Savalas, my scalp itches." She pointed at Tambora and watched for her reaction. "I noticed Tambora is scratching her scalp, too. I think we have lice. We should go to the nurse and get checked out," Mercy said with all the sincerity she could muster.

The class burst out in laughter. Tambora's mouth dropped open, and she sat motionless, an expression of horror and shame frozen on her pale face.

"Oh, my. Yes. You better go immediately. You're excused." Mrs. Savalas scratched her own scalp, then inspected her fingernails.

"Thank you." Mercy choked back a giggle, and she gathered her books and supplies. "We'll go straight away." Mercy straightened her stature and walked past the other students who covered their heads and recoiled away from them. Phin retreated into a corner, appearing shocked and appalled. She winked in his direction. An expression of realization came over him. He grinned and nodded. Tambora kept her head down and, without a word, followed Mercy.

When they entered the hall, Mercy put her finger to her puckered lips and whispered, "Shh. Let's go outside."

They tiptoed through the corridor and down the three flights to the lobby. The same pesky Situation Clock with the fancy scrollwork which bugged her when she arrived at the Tray made a bee-line toward her, chiming all the way. "It is 1:13, and two of four are out the door."

Mercy batted at it. "Shush, now. You're going to get us in trouble." Out of the hundreds of students at the Tray, she could never figure out why Situation Clocks seemed to single her out. She wondered if she might give off a vibe which advertised open season on girls named Mercy. Mercy and Tambora hurried to the door, the clock hot on their heels. Before she stepped into the revolving door, Mercy pointed her finger at the clock and said, "Not a word." The clock remained inside, but pressed its face against the massive picture window. It looked forlorn, and Mercy thought perhaps it wanted to experience nature. It was not her place to give the clock free rein, so she left it inside. She hoped it would not go around in jealous retaliation, using their business in a state of affairs proclamation.

Once outside, she and Tambora burst into a hard run and did not stop until they were inside the maze. They did not need to venture too far in to keep hidden, as they were much shorter than the tall lilac hedges. Out of breath, they plopped down on the soft green grass of the pathway. Mercy laid out flat and spread her arms to her sides. She gazed upward. Even though they were nearing December, the sun-filled sky was colored a brilliant baby blue, speckled with perfect, white, fluffy clouds. The type of sky you witness on the most flawless of days. "I love these lilacs bloom all year instead of only for a few weeks," she said. "I love this time of year, it's not hot, not cold. I love Christmas is right around the corner. What do you love?"

Tambora pulled a small bag of M&M's from her pocket. "I sure don't love the entire school thinking I have lice. Why did you humiliate me like that?" She wrinkled her nose.

"If you wanted something less disgraceful, you should have been the best friend to think up an excuse. But at least I shared your shame, and you know how I hate attention. It was simply too perfect to pass up. Maybe my dad's pranking is rubbing off on me."

"Yes. I can detect your dad's spirit in that prank. Here, have some chocolate," Tambora said. "What I truly love is that we can get products here from the outside realm. What would life be without chocolate?"

Although there were candy-makers on the island, the only way to get name brand sweets was to have them imported. Children all over Ara'Ja scrambled to get to the stores whenever a shipment arrived by Ara'Jaeon import and export freighters, which operated with the capability to create a temporary rift in the cloaking of Ara'Ja and its outposts.

"Thank you." Mercy sat up and held out her hand. "So now what? I got us out here, you choose what to do. I figure we have a couple of hours before they realize we're gone and send out the Regulators."

"Don't even joke about them. Hearing them come toward us the other day was closer than I ever wanted to get to meeting one."

"Me too. But we pass by them every day, aren't you scared then?" Mercy threw a candy up into the air and caught it in her mouth.

"Yes and no. They're standing still. At attention. They're like statues. You get used to it. And honestly, we were too caught up with being scared by the other strange things. The cold, the dark, the stories. We've always hurried through there without giving much thought to the Regulators. They're here for our protection, or we thought they were, but to have an actual encounter with one? The very thought frightens any desire for adventure out of me."

"Right. The ruse is that they are protecting us. Miss Carmen put them there to give credibility to her haunting stories, so the Metalicons could work on getting the orb. I wonder when they'll be finished. I hope it's not before Uncle Atticus returns. We just can't let them take it. Once they have it, we may never get it back, and they'll be one step closer to ruling the world."

Voices drifted in from outside the maze and they grew closer to where the girls sat. Mercy recognized them as Miss Carmen and Magister Pappas. "We can't let them find us here," Mercy said. She and Tambora scurried around on their hands and knees to find a hiding place. They found a small opening nestled at the bottom of a couple of bushes. The gap was perfect for the two of them to crawl into and they hurried inside.

Several stray twigs stuck out into every cranny of their small hollowed nook, poking into Mercy. She twisted this way and that, while she attempted to avoid getting further stabbed. She kicked Tambora's shin, who groaned in semi-silent protest. "Sorry," Mercy whispered.

The voices became clearer as they neared. "It's nice to get away for a minute," Miss Carmen said. "We haven't talked privately in a while. I've been meaning to tell you. Telys came to visit me the other day."

Just then, Mercy spotted her books and journal out in the open, but within reach. She stuck out her arm and snatched them, hoping she was quick enough to grab them before they were noticed.

"And what was his report?" asked Magister Pappas.

Flabbergasted, Mercy leaned over as best she could to whisper in Tambora's ear. "I knew it. Pappas *is* involved. He knows Telys too."

Tambora wrinkled her nose and nodded. The voices came precariously close to their hiding spot and Mercy saw two sets of shoes stop close to where she and Tambora hid. She took deep slow breaths, for she feared the adults would hear the deafening thumps of her pounding heart.

"He and his cronies are nearly finished fishing out the Fire orb from where it's been concealed on the fifth floor for the past few centuries. It hasn't been easy. It was buried pretty deeply under several layers of static electricity. He expects one more session should finish the job," said Miss Carmen.

"Excellent. They need to accomplish this before we can proceed with the next step. I am working on a theory of where the Water orb may be hiding."

"After all these decades of planning and searching, it's almost surreal to think this whole situation could be over within the next year or two."

"Carmen, I must caution you not to get too comfortable. Many tasks have been forfeited at the finish line due to complacency and loss of vigilance. We must stay guarded, lest Atticus uncover our actions."

Mercy threw both hands over her mouth and glanced over at her friend. Tambora's forehead wrinkled and her mouth hung open. Tambora appeared as shocked and disappointed as Mercy. Since their accidental portal into Miss Carmen's office, Mercy suspected there might be other staff members at the Tray involved in the dubious activity. But the discovery that her suspicions were certain still hit hard.

Tambora grabbed onto Mercy's hand.

"Pelagius, there's more," Miss Carmen continued. "Telys informed me there have been attempts of escape from Vatek using astral projections. We can only assume they are trying to get Mercy."

"Yes. I see how this could be disastrous if we did not have restraints in place," Pappas said. "But as long as Mercy's abilities remain bound, there should not be any trouble. Still, she *is* unbound during her training sessions. I shall start attending them to keep watch over things. But I will need to show up with a reason to observe as to not arouse Nedim's suspicions."

The four feet walked away and out of Mercy's line of sight.

Miss Carmen said, "I think someone's been snooping around in my office."

"What makes you say that?"

The voices ebbed and Mercy no longer heard their voices. "Do you think she knows it was us in her office?" she mumbled to Tambora.

"I don't think so, how could she?"

"Fingerprints?"

"Don't be silly. People don't just keep fingerprinting kits around."

"I guess not." Mercy dared poke her head out to make certain they were gone. "Oof," she grunted and made a hasty escape from their diminutive, short-term prison. "I didn't expect to be that uncomfortable." She brushed dirt from her clothing. "Our uniforms are the wrong color to be crawling around in the dirt."

"Right. Now, it's filthy, and no longer matches my hair." Tambora crawled out. "I don't think I could tolerate having your foot in my side for one more minute."

Mercy sat cross-legged on the grass. "I can't tell anymore who the good guys are." She took a sharp breath when a new thought entered her mind. "Pappas is friends with my parents. I wonder if they know about him. I should try to contact them. And we need to tell Uncle Atticus of this, too. I hope he comes back soon."

"I suspect he's already suspicious from what was said in the conversation between Miss Carmen and Telys, and now the one between her and Pappas. And maybe your uncle is even already working on a plan. He and the Assembly could take care of this without getting us mixed up in it any further. Let *him* talk to your parents. Wouldn't that be a better option? We're only kids. We don't need this. And if we end up having no other choice, we can always secretly portal to the city and try to get ahold of your parents."

"You're right. Of course, you're right." Mercy swept a clump of dirt from Tambora's shoulder. "I hope Miss Carmen doesn't figure out we're the ones who were in her office." She glanced up to notice Tambora watching her. She appeared tired. Mercy realized, although she had been making the whole situation about herself, she was not the only one affected by whatever was going on.

"Me too."

Mercy gave Tambora a wry smile and looked away. "Our time out of class didn't end up very enjoyable, did it?"

"No."

"But we got more information, didn't we?"

"Yes."

Mercy rose to her feet. "I suppose we should get to our next class." She held out her hand to help Tambora get up.

"Probably so."

"They're going to notice how filthy we are."

"I suspect they will."

"What should we say about the lice?" Mercy ventured a glance at her friend and they burst into laughter. They each put an arm around the other and made their way toward Abilities Etiquette class, knowing there would be a price to pay for skipping out on Language Arts, but still confident in their friendship and alliance.

CHAPTER 16

A PLACE IN VATEK

Mercy and Tambora slid onto their seats in Abilities Etiquette just as the bell rang. They enjoyed the class, as Mlle. Manigot, their favorite teacher, taught the subject. Mlle. Manigot—fun, charming, and full of *jwa lavi*, as the Haitians say—sat on the edge of her desk. Her full, brightly colored skirt almost hid the canvas espadrilles on her feet which swung freely above the floor. Mercy could not pull her eyes away from the flowered scarf wrapped and tied around her teacher's hair and the big hoop earrings, dangling out from under it. Mlle. Manigot smiled, her white teeth glistened against the darkness of her skin. When she spoke, it was in an enchanting, laid back, Caribbean accent. "Students, today, we will discuss how it's important to understand when to stand back and out of the way of others who are working in tandem with you, in order to stay out of the line of fire and end up in Vatek prematurely."

Angela raised her hand.

"Yes, Miss Juneau?"

"What exactly *is* Vatek?"

Titters and snickers made their way around the classroom. One student chirped, "Oh, come on. Surely, you're not that ignorant."

Mercy's cheeks flushed on behalf of Tambora's roommate, but also because she, herself, did not understand all the details of Vatek. She knew Ara'Jaeons went to Vatek when they died, but little else.

"Ara'Jaeons, although we live long lives and carry certain self-healing attributes, are mortal. Our physical bodies are composed of flesh and blood. But when we die, we go through the Gates of Vatek into a more spiritual, immortal life. There are those in Vatek, whose mortal lives were too corrupt, who are imprisoned there. The others, as far as we can tell, are free to roam about Vatek, enjoying the activities they love best."

Vesuvius raised his hand. Mlle. Manigot gave him permission to speak.

"Does anyone ever leave Vatek?" Vesuvius asked.

"Not that we are aware of. Many believe those in Vatek, who are very strong, could perform astral projections. And there are legends of a crown that can reward someone in Vatek to come back to Earth. But this is just a legend. No one knows where this supposed crown may be."

Mercy perked up. A symbol from the medallion was a crown of reward. She looked to Tambora and widened her eyes. Tambora looked confused and mouthed 'what'. Mercy put her hands on her head to mimic a crown, but Tambora's bewildered look remained and she wrinkled her nose and shrugged.

Mercy ripped a sheet of paper from her notebook and drew a replica of the symbol. She held it up discreetly, facing Tambora. Tambora's mouth dropped open, as her eyes widened and she straightened her back. Obviously disturbed, Tambora turned toward the front of the class, not blinking.

Equally troubled, Mercy spent the rest of the class outlining a story of a villain, freed from the realm of Vatek who wreaked havoc on the world and of the young Ara'Jaeon girl who defeated him.

———————◆———————

Mercy hesitated outside the open doorway of her training room. Mr. Kishan stood across the room with his back to her. Mercy rapped on the doorframe. "Hi, Mr. Kishan."

"Good afternoon, Mercy. Come on in." He carried a fire extinguisher to the training mat. "As you can probably tell, we're going to introduce a few exercises using Fire skills today."

The news thrilled Mercy. When she first came to the Tray, Tambora and Vesuvius conjured up lights during their trek through the darkened fifth floor. She yearned to do the same.

She hurried toward Mr. Kishan, holding out her hands for him to unlock the Fire talismans on her wrist cuffs. She noticed a movement out of the corner of her eye. She twisted around to see Magister Pappas enter the room. He did not speak, but stayed near the exit, leaning against the wall, his arms crossed. He looked bored, as though being there was beneath him. That notion agitated Mercy. How her parents could befriend such an arrogant, moody, and probably traitorous person was beyond her reasoning.

Mr. Kishan greeted him. "Good afternoon, Pelagius. We are just beginning."

Pappas nodded, but remained wordless.

"The magister is going to observe our sessions for a while. He promised your parents he would monitor your progress."

Mercy spun to face Pappas. He stared at her with one brow raised and his demeanor hard, but he remained quiet. She frowned, not caring if he felt her loathing. Her opinion of him plummeted to an all-time low in the hours since she and Tambora overheard his conversation with Miss Carmen. She returned her attention to Mr. Kishan, her excitement for the Fire sessions no longer existed. In its place dwelled suspicion and disgust.

"We're going to begin today with the simple lighting of a match." Mr. Kishan pulled out a box of long matchsticks. He held one up. "As before, on your first Water lesson, close your eyes and envision your action within your mind. Now, visualize the match and imagine it igniting. When you have confidence in your vision, open your eyes and lock them onto this match. Then reach out and wave your hand."

Mercy hung her head and scrunched her eyes, closing them as tight as she could. She knew from experience that frustration hindered her performance, so she put her opinions of Magister Pappas aside and focused her thoughts on the match. She imagined an unseen force strike against the small wooden stick, causing it to spark to life. She waited for a moment to watch inside her mind for a tiny flame to flare. Ready for reality, she inhaled, lifted her gaze, and stared at the match Mr. Kishan held. She willed herself to be confident, extended her arm, and waved her hand at the match. A big zero happened. Not even a little sizzle. She groaned and rubbed her forehead.

"This is okay," Mr. Kishan said. "It's possible a wave of the hand isn't the right technique for you in this exercise. You must remember all you do is ultimately and inherently personal to you. Let's try this again, and this time, don't think too hard about how you will get the match to light. When you're ready, simply let it happen."

Mercy followed the instructions, opening her eyes when she envisioned the match flare up. She did nothing, hoping her inaction would suffice for a simple solution. But it did not. She dropped her head again to meditate on the lit match. In her vision, Pappas emerged in the surroundings. His unwelcome appearance in her mind infuriated her. Angered, she kept her head down, lifting only her eyes to glare at her target. She took deep breaths, in and out, through her flared nostrils for several seconds—not unlike an angry bull. She could think of no other appropriate analogy, for she contemplated how she might feel if she charged at him. When she decided the time was right, she stretched her arm toward the match and snapped her fingers, using the fiercest crack she could manage. The sound vibrated throughout the silent room, hitting the match with such an intense force, the energy of the strike knocked it out of Mr. Kishan's grasp. The entire match burst into hot blue flames. Mercy let out a startled yelp, remorseful that she nearly injured Mr. Kishan.

"Yikes." Mr. Kishan stomped out the small fire with his sandaled foot and rubbed his almost singed hand on his loose cotton trousers. He chuckled. "Close. Anything more and I would have had to grab the fire extinguisher."

Mercy risked a peek at Pappas. He no longer rested against the wall, but assumed a military stance, his hands behind him and his legs slightly spread apart. He looked ready to pounce into action if needed. She experienced an odd satisfaction at having gotten the attention of the pompous magister.

"Mercy, that was a bit overdone. Do you remember what I told you at our first lesson about keeping a balance when using our powers? This includes our emotions." Mr. Kishan took Mercy's shoulders in his hands and looked at her straight on. "It's obvious to me you are out of sync today. Do you need to talk?"

Mercy shook her head, her hand clenched at her sides. Even if she wanted to, she could not talk while Pappas remained in the room.

"All right. The invitation is open for whenever you are ready." Mr. Kishan let loose of Mercy. "When using your abilities, it's important to separate yourself from whatever is bothering you, especially in these early learning stages. Do you believe you can put aside whatever is troubling you long enough to continue our lesson or should we cancel for today?"

Mercy unclenched her fists and steadied herself. "I would really prefer to keep going. What do I need to do to get myself settled?"

"Breathing exercises work wonders for stress. An easy way is to relax your shoulders and inhale through your nose for a count of two. Then pucker your lips and exhale through your mouth for a count of four. Do this for a few minutes. Exhaling this way releases the trapped air in your lungs which causes gasping for breath, which triggers a fight-or-flight response from our brains. Thus, the goal is actually to calm our air intake and release. The rest will follow."

Mercy did as directed. "I'm a lot better now. My Grandma Yvonne used to have me breathe when I was stressed, but not the same as this. Breathing must be really important."

Mr. Kishan tapped Mercy on the nose. "Breathing is always important. Many people from the East Indies, including myself, routinely perform yoga and/or meditation to stay focused and strong-minded. Many respiration exercises can be used during these practices. If you are ever interested, I will be happy to show some of them to you."

Mercy's interest piqued. "I think I would like to learn more."

"All right, I'll put together a little guide for you and we can go over it when it's ready. For now, do a few more minutes of the breathing exercise I just showed you, and then we'll continue the match-lighting training. Fire can be tricky. You'll need to conquer this one consistently before we can proceed."

After a few more rounds of inhaling and exhaling, Mercy calmed herself enough to continue her Fire lesson. She ignored Magister Pappas, putting her sole concentration into her goal of lighting the match. She tried a few more hand motions, but none worked. She wanted to try the finger snap again. She performed another cycle of breathing and repeated the closed sight visualization ritual. She opened her eyes and stretched out her arm. She snapped her fingers lightly and gently, feeling newly confident. A slight jolt of electricity rushed through her body, down her arm, tickling her palm when it raced out through her fingertips. The match in Mr. Kishan's hold crackled, and a flame came to life from the red tip. Relief spread through her as she realized she was not broken.

"Perfect." Mr. Kishan beamed at Mercy. "Now, do this twenty more times. In a row. Prove to me it wasn't a fluke."

"What about five?" She grinned and rubbed the itching on her palm.

"Twenty-five. Keep bartering and it will keep going up." Mr. Kishan grinned, his smile bright against his dark complexion.

Mercy groaned in false protest. Her minor achievement provided a respite from her anxiety. She successfully performed her task ten more times, when Magister Pappas interrupted with a short applause.

"I am going to throw in a bit of a challenge," he said. He pulled out a huge chunk of clay from the supply cabinet, grabbed a nearby folding tray, and took the items to where Mercy and Mr. Kishan stood. "Nedim, help me press out this clay, then we are going to stick matches in throughout. Keep them about two inches apart."

When they finished, Mercy stood before a clay covered tray spiked with dozens of matchsticks.

"Okay, Mercy. Now light them." Pappas crossed his arms over his chest.

"How am I supposed to do that?"

"That is *your* problem," he answered.

Mr. Kishan said, "Pelagius, I don't think she's ready—"

"Poppycock," Pappas said. "There will be times she is going to need to fend for herself. She needs to figure out now if, and how, she will do it."

Mercy, full of uncertainty, stared at the tray before her.

"What about it, Mercy?" said the magister. "Will you stand on your own? Or will you always be dependent on others to tell you what to do?"

How dare he be so condescending, Mercy thought. She traded barbed glares with the magister and boldly said, "Challenge. Accepted."

Pappas's thin lips curled into a shape resembling a smile. He nodded once and backed away without breaking visual contact with her.

Mr. Kishan put his hand on Mercy's shoulder. "Okay, Mercy. Don't be overwhelmed, just breathe and concentrate. You can do this."

Despite Mr. Kishan's encouragement, deep down, Mercy panicked. But she made use of her new breathing technique, then closed her eyes and took her time until she cleared her mind from all distraction. When ready, she steadied herself and visualized the field of matchsticks bursting into flame. Then she focused her gaze onto the matches and snapped her fingers. One match, in the corner, lit up and sputtered out right away. She bit her lower lip and looked to Mr. Kishan in a silent plea for help. He urged her to try again. She tried once more. One match in the opposite corner flamed up high, but fizzled. Again, she steadied her thoughts onto the matches. In her mind's view, the matches lit up one by one until they were all on fire. She opened her eyes, looking neither right nor left. She focused only on the matches. She held out her arm and snapped her fingers hard. Instinctively, she then raised her other arm and with both of her palms facing forward, she pushed them toward the tray. One by one, the matches came to life as she envisioned. She stood motionless, observing them as they continued to flame without being consumed. A sense of accomplishment swept over her. But she suspected her teachers' attention was not on her victory, as they whispered to each other instead of paying any notice to her. Disappointment threatened her elation. On a whim, she sucked in a generous amount of air and blew toward the fire. Her exhale sent out a sizeable wind, putting out every flame in unison.

She flinched in surprise. Magister Pappas and Mr. Kishan ran toward her. Each of them picked up one of her wrists to examine the Wind charms. Despite of her use of Wind, the talismans remained restrained. Mercy stood still, afraid to move.

"Did I—did I just use Wind?" Mercy asked.

"I don't understand," Mr. Kishan said to Pappas.

"Get her Fire restraints reactivated quickly, and do not mention this to anyone. I need to confer with the Council of the Apotheosis." Pappas ran toward the door, but stopped to address Mercy before he went through. "Mercy, I repeat. Do *not* talk to anyone about this. No one. I mean it. No. One."

Mercy's breathing became labored. She could feel herself enter a panic attack. The Council of the Apotheosis was a mystical fellowship of wise, noble, academic, and spiritual Ara'Jaeons. Almost as revered as the Firsts, and more elite than the Assembly or the Ecclesia, they were the most aloof and superior sect of Ara'Jaeon society. It was rumored that they lived in seclusion somewhere in the Matacaeton Mountains. In her wildest dreams and fantasies, she never imagined she might become a subject of conversation among them.

"Breathe, Mercy. Breathe." Mr. Kishan locked the Fire restraints. "There is naught here to be anxious about. Magister Pappas is a brilliant man, more gifted and knowledgeable than even the most brilliant of us all, and he will work this out with the Council. But remember, do not tell anybody. There is nothing to be ashamed or afraid of, and although we may not have a dilemma right now, we may have one on our hands if the wrong people find out about this. Not everyone would have your best interests in mind. Which is why, for now, we must choose caution. It is critical to not speak of this. Not even to your friends. They would mean you no harm, but they could unintentionally say something to cause others to take notice. Can we agree?"

Mercy already thought she held too many secrets, and once again, she was forced to make a promise to keep quiet about an exciting event. But an awareness of duty hung heavy around her neck like a large piece of gold jewelry. "Yes. I won't mention it."

"Perfect. Come here tomorrow at the same time unless you are told differently by either the magister or myself."

Mercy nodded and ran from the room. She continued to run until she reached the overpass to the main building. Once there, she pressed her spine against the wall and flattened herself. Confused thoughts about prophecies, schemes, and unexplainable events spun around in her mind, attempting to find a stronghold. Was Pappas there to help her or was he complicit in the conspiracy against her? And what about Mr. Kishan? Was he also involved? And if so, on which side? Mercy performed her new breathing exercise and minutes later, became calmer. Her panic subsided. She recognized there was no time to wait for her Uncle Atticus to return to Ara'Ja. She needed to confide in someone and resolved to contact her parents. Surely the ban on her talking about what happened did not include her family. The decision comforted Mercy. She inspected her hands, wondering what else she could do while restrained. She spotted a marble on the floor and blew toward it, hoping it would roll on its own. Unsuccessful, she flung her hands out and blew again. Nothing happened. She would have to watch for other opportunities to test it out. She picked up the marble and readied herself to meet her friends and pretend nothing exceptional happened during training. She encountered Phin in the lobby and they walked the rest of the way together.

"How was training, Mercy?" asked Phin.

"It was… interesting. I had my first Fire lesson, and I learned to light matches. Exciting, huh?" Mercy said, eager to avoid further questions.

"Actually, it is," Phin said. "Fire would be a cool ability. Mine are Wind and Water. The girly ones. Earth and Fire are manly abilities."

Mercy thought she detected a literal twinkle in Phin's eye. "I've never heard of this before."

Phin leaned in to whisper in her ear. "It's true. Wind and Water are the same abilities Pappas has."

Mercy flushed. "I believe he also has Fire, so your feminine and masculine element theory is shot. Besides, what's so womanly about hurricanes and tsunamis?"

"It's not necessarily about what the elements can do, but more of what their individual personalities are."

"Personalities?"

"Haven't you ever heard the phrase *Graceful Wind, Soothing Water, Valiant Earth, Conquering Fire*?" Phin teased.

Mercy chuckled. "You're incorrigible and incredibly prone to stereotyping genders."

"Face it, you love my feminine side." Phin winked.

"Oh, look. The others are already here," Mercy said, hoping to steer the conversation in a new direction. Her cheeks warmed, and she rushed to get to their table before she said anything stupid.

"I've been talking to Tambora about your little lice attack," Vesuvius said to Mercy.

"How do you know about this?" Mercy asked.

"EV-erybody knows," Vesuvius said.

Tambora's face grew red.

Vesuvius snickered. "Aw. Don't worry none. All the kids know it was a ruse to get out of class. And they also know you two were told you have to wash all the classroom windows on the third floor."

Tambora growled and covered her face. "Don't remind me."

Mercy groaned. "I'm really not looking forward to it."

"Who would?" Phin said.

Mercy and Phin sat down. Loy-Roy arrived soon after, carrying the dinner plates. The serveur made a little curtsy to Mercy and placed one in front of her.

"Hey, Loy-Roy. Have any new tricks today?" she asked.

Loy-Roy set the plates down, tilted on his side, folded his wings to the front, and bounced a few times to his right. He extended his wings out to his side, then crossed them in front, and back out again. He tilted the other way and bounced left to his original position. The children laughed, patted Loy-Roy's platter body, and offered their congratulations on his dance moves.

"Did Tambora tell you guys we overheard Miss Carmen say she thought somebody had been snooping in her office?" Mercy asked. They talked in hushed tones while Loy-Roy continued to set their table. They were never afraid to talk in front of him anymore. Mercy supposed he knew all about their covert affairs, but she did not mind. After all, how would he be able to spill their secrets?

"Really?" Vesuvius responded. "I wonder how she could tell. We were really careful to not disturb anything."

"No. We didn't disturb anything except for your lost button and the photograph you stole." Tambora scoffed at her brother. "I left it by her office door, wrapped in a pillowcase because I thought she may want to keep it private. When she found it, she would have realized someone had been there."

As if aware of their conversation, Miss Carmen entered the room. She stood at her full height, her demeanor emotionless, her posture straight and lips compressed. She strolled to the nearest table and set down an object. The room hushed. Many students strained to get a glimpse. Several rose to their feet to get a better view. Others stood on chairs, looking over everyone. From her vantage point, Mercy could not see what the item was, except it was small enough to fit in Miss Carmen's fist. The students at the table where the Tray's leader stood, gawking at one another in apparent confusion. Miss Carmen picked up the article, progressed to the next table, and set it down. Similar to the previous table, the students seemed baffled. She picked up the object again, and went table by table, repeating the procedure. The students looked mystified.

Loy-Roy wandered through the room, keeping low to the ground, until he came near to the action. He hovered for a moment before he flew to Mercy, staying close to the floor. He lingered by her feet, yanking on her pant leg with his wing.

She leaned over. "What is it, Loy-Roy?"

Loy-Roy slowly rose to the tabletop. He seemed to study the shirt Vesuvius wore. His wing wiped back and forth across the front of the shirt, using his tray body to keep his motions hidden from anyone positioned behind him.

"Hey. What's going on?" Vesuvius said.

"What are you trying to say? Is it about Vesu's shirt?" Mercy softly asked. She did not want to draw attention to their table.

Loy-Roy bobbed up and down.

"What is it?" Phin asked.

Loy-Roy again wiped at the shirt, pausing his wing over a button.

Mercy further lowered her voice. "Vesu's button?"

Loy-Roy bobbed again.

Tambora paled and whispered. "Vesu's button."

Loy-Roy shuddered. He lay down spread-eagled on the table, looking thoroughly exhausted from his game of charades.

"Oh no," Vesuvius muttered when Miss Carmen set the object on the table next to theirs. They glued their somber eyes onto the bright green button she put there. The bright green button. The button Vesu lost in Miss Carmen's office.

"What are we going to do?" Phin whispered.

Without moving her lips, Mercy spoke between clenched teeth. "Look confused, just like all the other students."

Loy-Roy picked himself up from the table and hovered, trembling, between Mercy and Vesuvius.

Miss Carmen took the few steps necessary to get to the table of the mortified party of four. She placed the button dead in the center, speaking for the first time since her arrival arrived in the dining room. "What say you?"

Tambora looked at the button, up at Miss Carmen, and back at the button. "That's not my button," she said. "Mercy, is it your button?"

Mercy shook her head. "No. No, that's not my button. Phin, is it your button?"

"It is absolutely not my button," Phin stated. "Vesu, is it your—"

Loy-Roy, who still quivered next to Mercy, suddenly plummeted to the hard floor and shattered into smithereens. The sound echoed throughout the quieted room. A collective gasp erupted from every table, then silence again.

"Noooo!" Mercy cried out. Sobbing uncontrollably, she dropped to the floor to pick up the fragments. But the situation held no hope. Loy-

Roy, her kind and quirky friend, was destroyed. She gathered up a few of the larger shards and stuck them into her pocket.

Two Petit Serveurs with a broom and a dust pan made their way to the site of poor Loy-Roy's misfortune. They each placed one wing over the center of their platter bodies. Over the place where a heart might reside. They cleared up the pieces of their fallen comrade and returned to the kitchen through a gauntlet of serveurs offering winged salutes as the procession passed by.

A situation clock wailed in the distance, "It is 6:15, and the time to dance is passed."

Tambora kneeled down beside Mercy, holding her friend as Mercy continued to weep. "Come on, let's go for a walk."

Mercy nodded. Phin and Vesuvius got up to go along, but Tambora told them to stay put.

"Ah, girls, we need to finish this little chit chat," Miss Carmen said.

Mr. Kishan rushed to Mercy's side, giving her a hand to lean on as she stood. "Miss Carmen, perhaps it would be wise to give them a little space right now. The conversation isn't going anywhere. You could continue it tomorrow."

"Give that back to me," someone shrieked from across the room.

A group of boys volleyed an object over a group of girls, catching the attention of Miss Carmen. She moved to deal with the situation. Phin and Vesuvius looked at each other, nodded, then scooted out of the room behind her back.

"Go. I'll cover for you," Mr. Kishan whispered to Tambora and Mercy.

Tambora led Mercy outside to a white marble bench in the garden.

"I'm sorry," Mercy blubbered. "I don't know why I'm this upset over an accident involving an object that's not even alive."

"Mercy, you're allowed. You were attached to Loy-Roy. Friends, in fact. I'd like to think he might even have had a soul." Tambora's cheeks were wet with tears. "But this was no accident."

"Why do you say that?" Mercy reached into her pocket for a tissue.

"Loy-Roy is a hero. He purposely threw himself on the floor to create a distraction. I watched him. He saved Vesu from having to answer with a lie and us from being found out."

Mercy pulled out the pieces of the platter from her pocket. "It's ironic we discussed Vatek in class today. Do you suppose there's a place in Vatek for Petit Serveurs?" Not waiting for an answer, she used her hands to burrow a hole behind the bench. "Could you help me bury him?

"Of course." Tambora kneeled beside Mercy and helped dig a deep hole.

Mercy set the china pieces into the hole with utmost care and covered them with dirt.

"Loy-Roy, my friend. You always brightened my day. I hope life is better for you, wherever you are." Mercy held her stomach and doubled over in grief. She and Tambora held each other and wept for what seemed like hours while forget-me-nots grew where their tears soaked into the ground.

CHAPTER 17

THE FIRE ORB

Sleep eluded Mercy. The culmination of the events of the day troubled her—the shock of a betrayal, the override of the restraints, the anxiety of almost getting discovered by Miss Carmen, and the horrific death of her beloved Petit Serveur. She sobbed for hours after the loss of Loy-Roy until her tears were spent and she could no longer even seek comfort by burying her face in her pillow to cry. She desired no company, pretending to be asleep when CJ came in. During the night, a void invaded her mind, heart, and spirit. Restless and hollow, she thrashed around in bed, unable to find rest. She looked to the bunk where CJ slept. Her roommate's breathing seemed extra loud. Or perhaps Mercy's sensitivities were more delicate than usual. The sounds of CJ's deep sleep mocked her own failed attempt at slumber. Her stomach growled, making her aware she did not eat dinner. She supposed her hunger contributed to her sense of emptiness. A secret raid of the refrigerator became her primary focus when she could no longer deny the gnawing in her stomach.

She wondered if Tambora was asleep yet. Most likely. She opted to go alone and not risk waking her friend. She slipped down from her bunk, pulled on her robe, and grabbed a flashlight from her drawer before she tiptoed out. She left her slippers behind. They made a small scuffing noise when she walked, and she knew she would have to be extra quiet in the kitchen. All the Petit Serveurs—all except one special friend—were stored upright in a cabinet covered by glass doors. She spotted them one evening when Miss Birdie asked her to retrieve an item from the kitchen supply closet. They seemed at peace, asleep, or whatever version of sleep they experienced, with their wings folded in front of them. She had made a slight noise, and they awoke. Petit Serveurs were soundless within themselves, but the attempted flutters in their confined space made a racket. So, she needed to be cautious to not disturb the serveurs which could wake the cooks in their rooms behind the kitchen.

On her way down, Mercy found the Regulators were, once again, absent from the fifth floor. It was only the second time she noticed them away from their posts. The first being the day her confrontation with a few Metalicons turned her whole life topsy-turvy. She thought Miss Carmen might have sent the Regulators on another task while the Metalicons finished their work. She switched on her flashlight and tiptoed forward. Done, perhaps out of habit, because she experienced neither fear nor excitement. She felt nothing. About halfway through to the next stairwell, she noticed a faint bluish light pulsate from an open door. The same door, which was not supposed to be there on her first day. Mercy suffered little concern about what the Metalicons did, or so she told herself. A pack of emotions vied for her attention. The void in her urged her to ignore the whole incident and walk on by. Responsibility advised her to run and wake the others. But curiosity was unwilling to lose the potential opportunity to learn more about the threats to disrupt her life and pressed her to go in on her own. In the end, desolation and curiosity agreed to override caution, suggesting she disregard the danger. After all, desolation reasoned, she did not care anymore. Mercy listened and opted to go on by herself to check out the situation. "Emptiness can be a catalyst for bravery. Or stupidity," Mercy said to herself. She raised her brows at the thought. She liked to come up with new sayings. She would write the adage down in her journal as soon as possible. She could use the phrase when she wrote her novel. Maybe her first one would be a novel about a prophecy which messes up the life of a young Ara'Jaeon girl. So many ideas. It was hard to decide.

Mercy went through the door, recognizing the light and sounds in the same long, dark hall she went down on that first day, a lifetime ago.

Emboldened by familiarity and also the fact she carried a flashlight, she hurried on in confidence. She knew what to expect. Nearing the room, she could make out the voices of Pip and Patina, heckling each other as Telys intermittently called out instructions. She came to a stop outside the open door, questioning her sanity. On the verge of retreating, she hesitated when Telys addressed his cohorts.

"Let's finish up here. Once we've accomplished today's task, we'll have the Fire orb, and this part of Azrael's plan will be complete. We won't need to come here again."

Shock and righteous indignity overcame the empty sensation in Mercy. Who was the real-life Azrael? What type of evil plan was afoot? She would not allow the Metalicons to take the orb and get away with their treachery. She realized there was no time to run and find help. Even if she could, who would she get? Miss Carmen and Pappas were the two obvious choices, but Miss Carmen was in cahoots with Telys, and Magister Pappas was in an alliance with Miss Carmen. No. Prevention was up to her. She knew she needed to stop the situation straightaway.

Mercy, with brazen abandon, stepped into the room. "Halt!"

Pip and Patina swung around to look at Mercy and burst into laughter. Pip's was a loud, insulting snicker. Patina's a charming, tinkling giggle. The two were a perfect contrasting complement to each other.

"Halt?" Pip opened his arms to his sides. "What are you? A knight?"

Mercy's cheeks burned. She did not intend to be geeky. "I mean stop. What you're doing here is wrong. You need to leave and don't come back." The gaiety of the two Metalicons grew stronger. Mercy groaned within herself, biting her lip. Good gracious, she thought. She sounded like Gollum in the Lord of the Rings movie. She could hear the high-pitched, scratchy voice in her head and hoped her tone, at least, was more pleasant.

Patina pranced toward Mercy. Arrayed in a mid-length, ruffled royal blue dress, she easily could have been the model of a tall, exotic can-can dancer on Mercy's father's old Toulouse Lautrec posters from the late nineteenth century. With an Ara'Jaeon's ability to live for several hundred years, she supposed it was a real possibility.

"Oh, Pipeous. Our little prodigal dove has become daring and has made her way into our nest, once again," Patina said.

Nervous at Patina's approach, Mercy edged nearer to Telys. He at least was cordial to her on their previous encounter, and he appeared jovial when she overheard him in Miss Carmen's office. He did not act one hundred percent evil. Mercy hoped perhaps a certain amount of morality remained in him. She felt a strange affection for him. Telys glanced up at her for the briefest of seconds, but otherwise ignored her as he gathered electricity, directing the energy into his console.

"You know, little one," Pip said as Patina circled around Mercy. "You should never have returned here. We may not let you fly away this time."

Mercy's eyes widened and her bravado faltered. She never thought they may not let her go. With an unexpected suddenness, the electrical crackles and beams disappeared and the only light came from Mercy's flashlight.

Telys packed up the equipment. "Let her alone, Pip. It doesn't matter now. There's nothing she can do. I'm finished here and we won't be returning. I have the orb."

Mercy looked toward Telys, expecting a big display. Telys smiled and held up a small, round red object, the size of a baseball, and put it inside his case. The orb resembled a big marble filled with molten lava. The small size surprised her. When Tambora talked about the orbs, Mercy envisioned them to be large, too large to carry. She wondered how the Metalicons could transport them.

"Aw." Pip gave Mercy a wicked grin and tweaked her nose. "No harm in having a bit of fun."

Mercy recoiled from his touch. As she flinched, the thunderous footsteps of a Regulator sounded. BOOM—BOOM—BOOM. A shadowed figure came around the corner into the room. She gasped, afraid she would be judged as a Metalicon by the dark guard. She edged away from the door, her knees shaky. Telys grabbed Mercy by the waist, heaving her up on his shoulder. He opened a portal and leaped through, taking Mercy with him. The jump was over in an instant and the portal closed moments after Pip and Patina came through behind them. Mercy screamed and kicked until Telys put her down with an unceremonious dump.

"You're welcome," he said.

"For what?"

"For saving your bum from the Regulator."

"The Regulator never would have shown up if you weren't there to begin with," Mercy retorted.

Telys took a hard look at Mercy. "Fair enough," he said after a lengthy pause.

Mercy surveyed her surroundings. They were in a dank cave lit by electric lights on the cave walls. They were fashioned to resemble old torches, even down to the flickering. Niches, carved into one wall, formed a row of workstations. The recesses contained tables, chairs, computers, and shelves. Everything a normal workstation would have, except workers. The cave was uninhabited, save Mercy and her three Metalicon companions. It was the middle of the night and she reasoned the others must be asleep. Funny, that. It never crossed her mind before that Metalicons were basically the same as the rest of the Ara'Jaeons. She always thought of them as mystical. Four large vats, taller than Mercy, filled one side of the chamber. A thin stairway led up the side of each where a small empty crystal cup extended up through the center. Clear pipes, attached to every tank, merged into a single, upright, glass box with a door on the front. It was large enough for a tall Ara'Jaeon to stand in. Emptiness abandoned Mercy, leaving her alone with fear. Her heart pounded hard, and she wondered if the box was her destination.

"Don't let her move from this spot," Telys commanded the others.

A Situation Clock, covered in gears and other metal fixtures, soared across the room and stationed itself nose-to-nose with Mercy. "It is 12:08, and not yet time to restore the crown," the clock screeched.

Mercy blinked. "What did you say to me?"

"It is 12:08, and you're very early."

"Pip, get that thing out of here," Telys demanded as he climbed the steps to a vat.

Pip swung at the clock. "Scat, you little time-telling nuisance." The clock flew off, but not before it spun around to Mercy and pointed a wing fashioned from at least a half a dozen skeleton-keys.

"It is 12:09, and when you return to this place, Azrael will be waiting."

"I said to get that blasted clock out of here!" Telys roared and Pip scooted the clock away from the room.

Mercy held her stomach. She was hungry, worried, and after the run-in with the clock, she felt ill with no appetite, but oddly, still hungry. According to the prophecy, a girl would restore a crown and then there would be destruction. She knew she was that girl. It took little intelligence to realize the clock also believed, but said it was too soon and that she would someday return. She hoped the time was a long way off, because if this Azrael behaved similar to *her* Azrael, she would be in deep trouble. She needed to have a lot more training under her belt if she was supposed to save the world.

Telys took the Fire orb from his case, placing it onto the crystal cup holder. Fire and electricity emitted from the orb, filling the pipes connected to the glass case. Mercy concluded the other holders waited for the orbs of the other three elements. Curious, Mercy tried to get closer for a better view, but Pip and Patina blocked her way.

"What were you doing, bringing *her* here?" Pip questioned.

"She's here for me." Patina hopped up and down and clapped her hands. "She's my tiny dancing partner."

"I'm not really here for anyone," Mercy said, feeling disregarded, even though they talked about her. She realized her feet were bare and cold.

Pip scolded Patina. "Honestly, Patina. Grow up. Life isn't always about fun and games." He scrutinized his black, polished fingernails.

Patina pouted, her eyes glazing over to a vacant stare.

"Pip, you were there, I brought her here to keep her away from the Regulator," said Telys.

Pip's eyes widened. "Of course, we can't have her getting hurt, can we? We need her for the crown." Pip's voice was sarcastic.

"No. We can't," Telys quipped curtly. He glanced at Mercy, then looked away. "And yes. We do," he added quietly.

Mercy's thoughts raced. Everyone seemed to need her to fix the crown. Well. She would simply refuse to do it. They could beg all they wanted to, but she was strong. She could be resolute.

"What will we do with her now?" Pip glared at Mercy. She squinted and responded with a fierce grimace in Pip's direction, trying to overcome the fear in the pit of her stomach.

"Give me a few minutes to shut this down, then I'm taking her back," Telys replied.

The weight of the unknown lifted off Mercy's shoulders. She would go back to the Tray, but she knew she would revisit the cave in the future. The next time would not be for a social call. The significance of her mother's adage, *live to fight another day,* did not get lost on Mercy.

"Taking her back?" Patina positioned herself between Mercy and Pip. "Why can't we keep her? We do love company, especially that of our little dove."

"She's not a pet, Patina." Pip shifted closer to Telys. "Listen, Telys. She can't go back. She'll talk."

"I'm taking her to the Tray. That's final," said Telys. Decisiveness filled his tone, and he continued to work. "It would bring too much attention if she disappeared. And she can talk all she wants. She's just a stupid kid. Who'll listen to her? She hasn't seen anything that everyone won't already know by morning."

Mercy flushed when Telys called her a stupid kid, and for whatever reason, the reference crushed her. She stared down at her shoes, hoping no one would notice the blow she felt.

Telys grabbed Mercy by the hand, pulling her out from her thoughts. "Let's get you home, Miss Markos."

Before she could react, he opened a portal and led her through. The last sound she heard was Patina's voice, calling out to her, "We'll dance again soon, little dove. Don't forget me."

As if I could, Mercy thought. If she knew anything at all, she knew those Metalicons were unforgettable and she would meet them again. Telys and Mercy stepped out of the portal into an eerie, silent, and darkened room. A familiar smell charged at her, kind of old, but more nostalgic than stale—like a cozy gathering of old friends. "Where are we?" she asked.

"We're in the Tray library."

Upon the discovery that she stood in her beloved library at the Tray, her sense of the familiar took over and her bearings returned to her.

Lights flickered in the dark behind her. She realized they just entered through the wall medallion. "How did you know to use that?" she demanded.

"I know a lot of things." Telys cupped his hands and produced the same ball of light Vesuvius and Tambora created each time they went through the fifth floor. Just in time, too, for the bit of light they received from the medallion went out.

Astonished, Mercy asked, "How do you have Fire? Aren't you a Metalicon?"

"Ah. I have more skills than just metal, the same way you have multiple skills. I inherited them. Many Metalicons are not strictly Metalicon, you know. They descend from ancestors with other skills, as do almost all other Ara'Jaeons. There aren't many pure bloodlines anymore, although there seems to be more pure Metals than any of the other elements. Possibly because there isn't much social interaction between the Metals and the others, what with the Metalicons being evil and such." Telys chuckled.

Mercy cocked her head and studied the man. "I guess I never thought of that before. So, you *chose* to be evil?"

Telys cleared his throat. "I guess you could put it that way. But whatever the Metalicons do is entirely logical to them. If you want to call it evil, I would counter to say they think it is a necessary evil."

Mercy thought he possessed a pleasant laugh, but she needed to remember—evil was evil, necessary or not. Still, many questions filled her mind. "What do you plan to do with the Fire orb?"

"Metalicon stuff."

"Truly evil stuff?"

"To some, perhaps. Orb talk is off the table. Next question."

Mercy wanted to keep him talking, as she hoped he would make a mistake and disclose needed information. "Ara'Jaeons are born with red or blond hair. If the Metalicons are the same as us, why is theirs dark?"

"It works similarly as DNA. The full blood Metalicons have dark hair. There are many mixed bloods. Most of them identify as Metalicons, but they could have dark, red, or even blond hair. Some dye their hair dark. In my case, it's pretty much white." He patted his hair and pretended to boast. "It's all natural."

Mercy rolled her eyes. "How nice for you. So, if someone with just one Metalicon ancestor is born with dark hair, they automatically become a Metalicon?"

"Have you seen very young children around with bald heads or wearing wigs? Their families shave or cover it until they're old enough to dye it blond or red. Or, the child may decide to leave the conventional Ara'Jaeon community and become a full-fledged Metalicon when it grows up."

"I've wondered about it. I asked my mom about the wigs and bald heads and she told me those kids were born with a hair problem, but it wasn't serious and it usually took care of itself in time. She also once told me a Metalicon was in our family a long, long time ago. Does this mean I could be a Metalicon, too, if I wanted?"

"If this is true, and you have Metal abilities, then yes. But do you think you would ever want to be seen as truly evil?" Telys looked away.

Mercy could see no reason for the discomfort he showed during the entire conversation. "No," she answered. "I would never choose to be a Metalicon. I'm only curious." She did not know why she asked the question. Would she ever consider it? The fact she could choose to be a Metalicon elated Mercy, but she felt creepy even harboring such thoughts.

Telys handed the ball of light to Mercy. "It's well after midnight. You need to go to your room. You dropped your flashlight earlier. Take this with you to find your way in the dark. Toss it in the air when you're finished, and it will go out."

"I've seen my friends do it before," Mercy bragged. She wanted to appear sophisticated.

He kneeled down on one knee in front of Mercy and clasped his hands around hers as she held the light. "Listen, let's keep what happened tonight between us. It is needless to cause panic to the other students. And the adults will know we possess the Fire orb soon enough."

The directive angered Mercy. She wished she could wag her finger at him, but he held her hands down around the globe. "You told Pip it didn't matter if I talked."

"I told Pip what I needed to tell him because I didn't want him to question my decisions."

"Why are you insisting I keep my mouth shut? I'm fed up with everybody telling me what to do. So. What if I don't?"

Spittle spewed from Mercy's mouth during her rant and hit his cheek. He grimaced and let go of her hands to pull out a tissue from his pocket. Without a word, he wiped his face, wadded up the tissue, stuffed it back into his pocket, and stood straight and tall to his full height. He towered over Mercy. He must have been about seven feet tall, the same height as her parents.

He glowered down at her. "It would do well for you to remember your place. You're merely a child and there are many things outside of your miniscule realm of wisdom."

Mercy's breath seized in her throat and she sensed the color ebb from her face, starting at her forehead and down her cheeks and neck where it transformed to fire in her throat. Right then, he reminded her of Magister Pappas. Hot tears of anger and humiliation flooded her eyes and threatened to spill over.

Telys put a fist on his hip and rubbed his brow with his other hand. He turned away from her. "Oh, come on, now. Don't do that. I don't need to see that."

The dam broke. She thought she was all cried out from Loy-Roy's demise, but hot tears fell down her cheeks. "I *hate* you! You're a cruel, mean, awful man. A thief. And as cold as—as—metal, and I *hate* you!"

Mercy heard Telys take a big breath. He circled around to address Mercy, and a hardened expression came over him. "Hate is an awfully strong word, Miss Markos. You'd best return to your room now and forget about tonight. I *will* know if you've been talking." He selected a sequence of symbols on the medallion, causing the portal to open. Just before he jumped through, he hesitated. "You're probably hungry." He pulled a chocolate bar from his pocket. "Take this." He tossed the candy at her and departed without speaking another word.

Mercy tucked the ball of light under her arm and picked the candy bar up from where the treat landed on the floor. It was a Sweetest Kaju, a chocolate bar full of cashew butter fudge and dried tropical fruit. Her favorite. Too upset to eat, she took the chocolate with her for another time. It was, after all, her favorite. She sniffled all the way to her room, climbed into bed, and curled up in a ball, feeling small, childish, and more helpless than ever in the world of adult intrigue. She yearned to be a little kid again. Before she knew about the stupid prophecy and experienced the tug of war around her. Back when she only cared about playing.

CHAPTER 18

A LIGHT SHINES IN THE DARK

Mercy sat, staring vacantly as a Petit Serveur set the table and served breakfast. The serveur hovered in front of Mercy as though expecting a greeting. She opened her mouth to talk, but closed it again. A few days prior, Loy-Roy sacrificed himself to save her and her friends from certain doom. The wound was still too fresh and she could think of nothing to say. Instead, she offered a small smile and nodded at the little guy, who then dipped in acknowledgement and exited the room.

"I'm just not ready to welcome a replacement for Loy-Roy with open arms," she explained to the others. "But it's not the serveur's fault. I should probably be kinder to it."

"I think you were plenty kind," Phin said. "I mean, you didn't kick it out or anything. You smiled at it."

"Mercy, are you okay?" Tambora said. "You're awfully quiet this morning."

"Yes. I've experienced a rough couple of days, but I'll be fine," said Mercy. The decision to keep quiet and not share her visit to the Metalicon cave a few nights earlier came easier for Mercy than she originally thought. She was used to making promises to stay silent. She chose not to divulge the secret, and her friends did not press her. Phin and Vesuvius talked about how they escaped the dining hall before Miss Carmen could continue her confrontation about the button, and they wondered when or if the axe would fall. Mercy did not partake in the conversation. She watched Miss Carmen and Pappas at the head table, wondering if either of them knew the Metalicons finally retrieved the Fire orb. Nothing unusual manifested in their behavior toward each other, as if secret collusions did not even exist.

In class, she pulled a piece of gum from her pocket, opening the foil wrapper with as much soundless discretion as she could manage. She hoped the sugary chew might help to keep her awake and peppy, at least until the conclusion of General Abilities. But even the most hyper person could be put to sleep while listening to Magister Pappas drone on and on about synergy and how different abilities used together could be an effective tool to accomplish a goal. Mercy nodded off more than once.

The classroom door opened and Miss Carmen peered in. "Excuse me, magister. May I please borrow Mercy Markos?"

Pappas nodded his approval.

"Mercy, grab your books," Miss Carmen said.

Mercy swallowed her gum, her stomach in knots. She managed a quick glance at Tambora, Phin, and Vesuvius. They seemed to be as uneasy as herself. They were all edgy since the button incident. It appeared the wait was over. She supposed Miss Carmen intended to summon each of them separately to confront them. She pulled her books into her arms.

"Come with me, please." Miss Carmen gestured to Mercy and held the door open.

Once out in the hall, Miss Carmen took the lead. Mercy trailed behind, dreading what was to come. Her stomach rolled in circles and her body throbbed with each heavy beat of her heart. They walked in silence, passing by Miss Carmen's office. She always used her office to talk to students who were in trouble, which Mercy believed to be her present situation.

"Miss Carmen, aren't you taking me to your office?"

The headmistress slowed her pace. "No. We're going to Visual Communications. You have a call."

Mercy's heart soared. "A call? For me?" A hint of a smile forged through her fatigue. "Who is it?"

"I thought you might enjoy a surprise. Come along."

They continued on, again, without speaking. Mercy did not know whether to be excited or anxious. She was not too keen on surprises since she got to the Tray.

Once there, Miss Carmen unlocked the room and let Mercy in. "I'll wait in the hall until you're finished."

Mercy stepped into the room and the door closed behind her. She located the activated comm unit and stood on the sensor mark to open the call.

"Good afternoon, Mercy." The communications synth appeared on the monitor screen. "Are you set for your call?"

"Yes, please." Mercy fixed her gaze on the monitor, eager to discover who called her.

The synth faded out, replaced by an individual Mercy knew all too well. Her heart almost burst out of her chest, and she squealed, "Grandma!"

Her grandmother held a peeling knife and appeared to be in her kitchen with an array of fruits and vegetables on a kitchen island. Mercy wondered how she got ahold of a portable comm. The comms were Ara'Jaeon technology and the outside world did not have access to them.

"Hello, Mercy, harmony and balance. How are you, dear?" Yvonne Kadarius smiled into the camera at Mercy, who burst into tears. Whenever she was upset, hearing her grandma's voice made her weep.

"Are you all right? I suspect you're going through a difficult time right now and you believe you're all alone."

"Grandma, how did you know?" she squeaked.

"A grandmother knows."

"It's been so hard. I feel as though there are no adults I can talk to." Mercy tried to stop her tears, but could not repress the catch in her voice.

Her grandmother picked up a stunning kumquat and sliced into the citrusy fruit. "I know, dear. That's why I'm coming to Ara'Ja. I'll be there late tomorrow afternoon, in time to spend the weekend with you."

Mercy straightened her spine. The surrounding air smelled of joy, and the joy seeped into her skin and touched every cell of her body. But logic pointed an unforgiving finger at her and her delight suffered a quick and painful death. "How can you do that? Mom and Dad aren't around to portal you in."

"Sweetheart, your parents aren't the only individuals I know in Ara'Ja. Remember, I lived there for over forty years." She chopped her vegetables, peering straight into the camera between cuts. "Now, I need for you to calm down and act like nothing is wrong. You don't want whomever is causing your distress to see you vulnerable. That's when enemies are most apt to strike out. Keep being strong and confident. And it's important you don't tell anyone I'm coming. I don't want anyone to know before I get there."

A sudden fear jabbed at Mercy. The word enemy struck her like a slap in the face. "Why not? What enemy?"

"Mercy, enemy was perhaps not the correct word to use, but this whole situation is being taken care of and I don't want you to think about this any longer. The whys don't matter."

"But I keep hearing that from people and things keep getting worse instead of better." Mercy grunted and dragged her open hands over her face in frustration. Her palms distorted her features as they traveled down, smearing her tears on her cheeks.

"I know, dear. But I also know there are people working behind the scenes to keep you safe. Just promise me you won't talk to anyone about my visit, and we'll have a nice heart-to-heart chat tomorrow night. I would rather not have this discussion over the open comm."

"I promise, if *you* promise we'll have that talk." Mercy negotiated her terms.

"I promise. I need to cut this short, sweetie. I have a guest. And I need to pack a bag. I love you and I'll see you tomorrow night."

"I love you, too, Grandma. I'm glad you're coming. Who is bringing you in?"

"Mercy—"

"Yes?"

"Don't ask too many questions. Some information is better left unknown."

Mercy knew better than to ask again. Although she and her grandmother shared a close bond, and she itched to know more, Mercy respected the boundaries between grandparent and grandchild.

"Mercy, your parents and grandfather would be very proud right now if they could see how grown up you've become. And I'm proud too. Harmony and balance, my dear. Until tomorrow."

Her grandmother glanced past the camera, gave a slight nod, and whispered, "I'm finished."

"Bye, Gram." Mercy's chest swelled at the possibility she could make anyone proud. Her grandmother was not alone. It had to be an Ara'Jaeon with her. Someone with a portable comm. Maybe her great-uncle Atticus was there. After all, he and her grandmother were in-laws. Certainly, they would have kept in touch after she left the island. But Atticus was on his outpost tour. He could not have been the visitor. Contemplating the puzzle, she concluded someone on Ara'Ja had her back, and the thought warmed her.

Once again, Mercy and Miss Carmen walked without speaking. Mercy took three steps to every one of Miss Carmen's long strides, and their combined footsteps created the beat of a rhythmic waltz. Although relieved in the fact she dodged a lightning strike regarding the button, she thought Miss Carmen acted a bit off. But it was no surprise, considering the headmistress knew someone broke into her office.

Miss Birdie passed by them as Miss Carmen unlocked her office door.

"Birgitta?" Miss Carmen always used Miss Birdie's given name.

"Yes, miss?"

"Please pull the St. Clair twins and Phineas Jaymes out of class and escort them to my office."

"Of course, miss."

Mercy almost groaned aloud. The reprieve was over.

Once inside, Miss Carmen asked Mercy to grab a few chairs from across the room and put them before her desk.

Mercy picked up a lightweight armchair. "You're not taking me back to class?" She struggled to keep her voice light.

"I am not. We have a breach of trust to discuss." Miss Carmen rummaged through one of her desk drawers.

Mercy's cheeks grew hot. She opted to sit in the chair farthest away from the headmistress. She hoped her positioning would shield her from the initial blast of Miss Carmen's wrath. She experienced no qualms in putting one of her friends in the hotter seat. We are *so* in trouble, Mercy thought. She tried to figure out how they should handle the situation. She was not comfortable with straight out lying. She regretted they could not come up with a reasonable and believable explanation of why they trespassed in Miss Carmen's office, not that they did not try. Every scenario they speculated over was passed on as neither reasonable nor believable. She held her hands tight against her stomach to calm the protests as they gathered there and built a bonfire. She hoped she would not throw up—or toss her cookies, as her father would say—on any of the beautiful old throw rugs layered over the hardwood floor under her chair.

Miss Carmen moved to the edge of her desktop, sitting with her arms crossed and one foot on the floor, which tapped out a steady, deafening tempo of doom. She stared at Mercy with a coldness Mercy feared more than anger. She hoped the others would get there soon. The full concentrated discharge of Miss Carmen's iciness was directed at her. She reasoned they would each get a more diluted portion when they were all in attendance. A small rap on the door broke the uncomfortable stare.

"Enter," Miss Carmen called out. She instructed the hushed group of Mercy's best friends to sit as they entered the room with the tentative walk of those who expected to meet their demise.

Miss Carmen stood. By far the tallest Ara'Jaeon Mercy knew of, the children needed to crane their necks to look up at her from their seated positions. Miss Carmen pulled out her desk chair and sat down. Without taking her eyes away from her students, she put a green button on her desk top. Then, she opened a drawer and withdrew a white cloth.

Horrified, Mercy realized Miss Carmen held a pillowcase. She threw her hands to her face, peering over her fingertips to risk a peek at

Tambora, who looked about as white as the bed linen in the somber woman's hand.

With wet and shiny eyes, Miss Carmen pulled a photo frame from within the pillowcase. In a display of unexpected tenderness, she wiped down the edges of the frame before she set it next to the button. She lifted her head high and seemed to gather her thoughts before she imposed a hardened smile on the children. "It appears there has been a break-in to my office. Do any of you know about this?" She glared from one child to the next, until at last, her eyes fell upon Mercy and lingered there. The children sat in unified muteness.

Miss Carmen picked up the photo and spoke in a quiet voice. "I discovered this in the hall by my door. Can you imagine how it might have gotten there? Quite irresponsible to put an item on the floor where anyone could have kicked it, correct? It could have been damaged, don't you agree?"

Mercy solemnly nodded and Tambora muttered a small, quiet yes. Vesuvius and Phin remained dumbstruck.

"I have no proof, but from my observations, every instinct in me believes the four of you were involved. You can deny it. But the situation would go better for you if you tell the truth. Who will speak on behalf of you all?"

Tambora glanced at Mercy. Vesuvius and Phin also both directed their attention to Mercy. She moaned and stood to address Miss Carmen. She took a big breath and in a show of bravery, she came clean. "We did it." Tambora dropped her head, and the boys groaned. Mercy thought they looked to her to confess for all them, but too late, she realized their actual intent. They thought she would come up with the best cover-up. She kicked herself for missing the hint, believing her sole remaining choice was to continue on. "We didn't mean to. We found an open portal and jumped into it, and before we knew it, we were in here. We picked up the picture to look at it and the portal opened back up, so we jumped through. We didn't mean to take the picture with us, and we thought if we set it by your door, you would find it and not be able to trace it back to us. We wrapped it, though, because we thought maybe it was private and you wouldn't want anyone to see it. We're sorry. We're truly sorry. We didn't mean any harm. It will never, ever happen again." Mercy's composure fell, and she sobbed. "And now Loy-Roy is gone, and it was all for nothing."

Miss Carmen raised her brows. "Loy-Roy?"

Tambora spoke out. "Loyal Royal, our Petit Serveur. He knew what we did, and he sacrificed himself to distract you from finding us out."

"I see. This is the, uh, *platter* that fell when I put the button on your table. I assumed Mercy broke down to get you all out of the room. Well. I can assure you this Loy-Roy, as you call it, had no capability to provide any type of response. But as it is, the serveur most likely isn't gone. Our kitchen staff has repaired dozens of serveurs over the years. I'm sure he— er, it—has been restored by now. *If* all the pieces were accounted for."

Mercy gasped. "Oh no. I took a couple of pieces and buried them out in the garden. Can I go get them?"

"Not right now. Know this. I am deeply disappointed in all of you and you leave me with no options but to provide you with an appropriate punishment along with the windows you and Tambora already need to clean. Until I am convinced you have been satisfactorily disciplined, there will be no extracurricular activities for any of you. And, for the rest of this week only, there will be no after-class training. Girls, you can clean the windows tonight after class, then go to your rooms. Until I say otherwise, you may not leave this building unless it's for class or training, which will resume next week. When classes are not in session, you will be in your rooms—your *own* rooms—or the library. You may take your meals in the kitchen. Questions? No?" Miss Carmen continued without waiting for any remarks from her students. She handed each of the children a piece of paper with her signature on it. "You are now dismissed to go to your classes. Here are your passes to return to class."

Mercy let out the breath she did not realize she held in. She did it. She told half the story and got away with it. She reminded herself everything she said came from an account steeped in truth. The break-in *was* accidental. The thought that Miss Carmen might learn what they overheard while they hid in her office terrified her. But now the cover-up was over. They could accept the punishment and Miss Carmen would forget all about their little indiscretion.

"By the way," Miss Carmen said. "Where was this portal you took to get into my office?"

Mercy's mind raced to think of a way to not give up the medallion. They might need to use the portal again at another time. But Phin piped up. "It was a medallion on the wall in the back of the library reference room. It just opened up. Like magic."

"Then the library will be off limits to you also, at least until I can get that taken care of. You may return to your classes now, but don't forget, when they're over for the day, you're grounded."

The dejected group proceeded toward their respective second period classrooms—first period having ended during the inquisition. Vesuvius complained over and over he would have nothing to do.

"Why?" Tambora said. "Aren't you rooming with your best friend? You two get to be together, playing games, talking, and goofing off. Mercy and I will be all alone in our dorms while our roommates are out having fun. Quit complaining. This is all your doing."

"Okay, guys," said Mercy. "It doesn't matter who's at fault. Let's be mature and get it over with."

Phin stopped and pulled at Mercy's arm. "Mercy, here's our class. Mrs. Kishan has already gotten started."

Mercy said, "Tambora, let's talk at lunch about the window washing. We'll probably have to ask Miss Birdie where the supplies are kept."

"I know where they are," Tambora said.

Mercy was not surprised. "Of course, you do. Okay. We'll meet up later." Although relieved with the general outcome of the meeting, the realization that the medallion would likely not be there much longer saddened her. And of course, the bigger disappointment was she could not retrieve the pieces of Loy-Roy from their resting place. She needed to decide on a strategy. Maybe CJ would get them for her. CJ was the answer, Mercy decided. She would speak to CJ after dinner.

———

Mercy stood on a five-foot tall stool with a long squeegee in hand and stretched as far as she could to reach the top of the window. She wished she were older and at her full height. Window washing would be much easier. She stopped for a moment and watched Tambora, who was a few inches shorter than herself. It was enough of a difference to make the task even more difficult.

Tambora grunted and sat down on her stool. "We're almost finished, right?"

Mercy laughed. "No, dear. Maybe half. I don't think we're going to finish tonight. Maybe Miss Carmen will let us wrap up next week."

"I sure hope so. I'm tuckered out and my stomach is growling."

Mercy dragged her stool next to Tambora and plopped down. "Mine too. There's no way all these windows can be completed in one night. I think we should stop for now and take our showers before dinner. We can discuss it with her then."

The girls tidied up their cleaning supplies before they left the room.

"Tambora?" Mercy said. "I don't think you should wash your face."

Tambora grimaced. "Why ever not? That would be gross."

"Because you look really cute with that smudge of grime running all the way down from your forehead to your chin." Mercy nudged Tambora and took off running with Tambora in hot pursuit.

CHAPTER 19

THE ACCOUNT OF ONESIPHORUS

Mercy tossed in bed for the fourth evening in a row that night. Sleep took forever to override her many thoughts. Earlier at dinner, Miss Carmen agreed to let the girls finish the windows another time, which created one less situation battling for Mercy's attention. But the movie screen in her mind still played so many emotions, guilt, and baffling circumstances. Late into the night, exhaustion won out, and she fell into an uneasy sleep. Mercy woke up to a new day after her fitful night. She staggered through the morning and afternoon in a complete haze from lack of quality sleep. She heard her teachers and friends speak, but could not comprehend what they said. The entire day sounded like gobbledygook. At one point, Tambora's distorted face zoomed in close, asking in a far-away voice if she was okay. Mercy blinked and responded she was fine. Her voice echoed, sounding weak and unwell.

After classes finished and despite her restrictions, Mercy slipped away from school grounds. She was startled to find herself at Transport Plaza in Nikonea City to meet her grandmother, having no recollection of how she got there. All around her, a bustle of people entered and exited the dedicated portals for transport on and off the island and in and out of the city. She moved to a higher position and saw her grandma arrive through an entrance portal. She could not come in alone. That decree was the rule for humans. Humans were required to have an Ara'Jaeon adult escort. Weaving her way through the crowd toward the row of portals, Mercy strained her neck to find out who brought her grandmother in and observed a man in sunglasses and a newsboy cap come in through the same portal right behind her. He dressed casually in a tee shirt and jeans and carried two suitcases. Mercy recognized them as belonging to her grandmother. He assisted the older woman to another portal, gave the luggage a gentle toss through the portal, and hugged her before she stepped through. Mercy followed him as he walked away from the plaza and toward a thick white marble column which bordered Central Gardens. He took off his cap and ran his hand through his icy blond hair. She was dumbfounded. It could not be. But it was. Telys escorted her grandmother into Ara'Ja. He slipped behind the pillar and out of sight. She ran and ran and ran to catch up to him until she was sure her legs would give out beneath her. She shouted for him to wait, but no sound escaped her lips. She arrived in time to witness the last fragment of a metal portal disappear. Her gaze wandered around the gardens. She looked around for help, but no one paid attention. No one cared. He escaped unnoticed. A hand from behind her grasped her shoulder. She shrieked and sat straight up in bed, drenched with sweat. CJ stood next to her bunk, shaking her. Mercy's heart dropped a beat.

"Are you okay? You were yelling."

"Yes. I'm fine. I had a bad dream." Mercy yawned and rubbed her eyes. "What time is it?"

"It's 7:00. You need to get up," CJ said with an air of authority.

"I think I'll just lay here for a bit, thanks." Still shaken, Mercy pulled her covers over her head. "Mercy, pull yourself together. It was only a dream," she muttered to herself.

"Did you say something?" CJ asked.

"I told myself I need to get up. Tomorrow's Saturday. I can sleep in then." Mercy groaned. She turned on her side to watch CJ crouch down, burrowing in a pile of clothes under her loft.

"Found it." CJ raised a red hiking boot and waved it in the air.

"Those don't fit the school dress code, you know," Mercy said. She climbed down from her bunk and landed on the floor with a soft thud when she skipped the last two rungs of the built-in ladder.

"Of course, I know that. I want to wear them later today. A bunch of us have gotten approval to hike down the Simm Bhalid Trails right after school and have a picnic dinner on the beach." CJ put down her boots and furrowed her brows. "You probably wouldn't want to go with us, would you?"

Mercy's heart leapt, followed by a wave of immediate disappointment. She yearned to go. She had not yet been on the trails. They led from the Tray down through the hilly forest to the bay. She heard most of them were nice, easy hikes. Although, a few paths presented more of a challenge. "I would love to, but I can't. I'm not allow—um, my grandma is arriving tonight from Crete and I need to stick around here."

"Your grandmother is coming? Here?"

Mercy bit her lip. In her haste to cover up the humiliating fact she was the equivalent of grounded, she forgot she was not supposed to talk about the visit. Of all the secrets she promised to keep, her grandmother was the last person she wanted to betray.

"Why is she coming here?" CJ said.

Mercy tried to downplay the situation. "Oh. It's only for a quick stopover. Not really worth mentioning at all. Really, she might only be here for a couple of hours, maybe not even that long. Just in and out to say hi, and then she'll go home." She was desperate to deflect further inquiries about her grandmother's stay. She already blew her promise when she mentioned the visit. But CJ was merely a kid, like herself, and Mercy surmised CJ may not have noticed her cover-up attempt. Still, she needed to be more careful.

"Maybe I can meet her while she's here." CJ set her hiking boots next to her desk and laid out a change of clothes on her bed.

"She'll probably be gone by the time you come back from your hike, but if she's still here, I'll introduce you. But please don't tell anyone. My grandma didn't want to make a big deal of her visit."

"Well. I have to go. I need to make a call to my parents before breakfast. Since it's hard for them to leave the Summit, I have special permission to call them once a week. They carry around a little portable comm so we don't have to make any pre-arranged calls." CJ opened the door. "Later." She did not wait for a response from Mercy and left.

Mercy dressed as she fought tears and realized two things. One, she forgot to ask CJ to dig up the fragments of Loy-Roy, and two, her grandmother was visiting while Mercy was grounded. Mercy's stomach gurgled, and she noticed how hungry she was. She grabbed her stack of books and opened the door to rush down to breakfast. She almost plowed into Tambora, who stood by the door with a raised fist, ready to knock.

"Whoa!" Tambora reached out and grabbed Mercy's shoulders to prevent the collision.

"Let's go. I need to eat." Mercy seized Tambora's hand and dragged her down the hall.

"I know. Me too, but listen." Tambora pulled away. "We need to talk."

"What is it?"

Tambora looked around. No one was in the hall except the two of them. She pulled out her Ara'Jaeon history book from her backpack and flipped through the pages. "I want to show this to you. I came across this section about the High Elders. These pages show all their portraits. Here's High Elder Broomfield. Do you remember we thought he looked strange when we saw his portrait at the Assembly? Almost as if he observed something he didn't like?"

"Yes. Of course, I remember. We talked about studying the picture more closely."

Tambora directed Mercy's attention to another photograph on the page. It appeared to be almost the same picture as the portrait, but less formal and taken from a different angle. "Somebody took this photograph of the Elder while he sat for his portrait. Check out the picture on the wall behind him. You can glimpse a reflection in the frame."

Mercy pulled the book closer to better inspect the picture. "This person has blond dreadlocks. How on Broomfield's beard did you notice this?"

Tambora shrugged. "I don't know, but he resembles the man in Miss Carmen's wedding photograph, don't you think?"

"This reflection is a little blurry, but I can see how it could be him. Wow. The High Elder was staring right at him."

Tambora closed her book. She put her hand on her chest and took a deep, unsteady breath. "Didn't you say you heard he was killed the day after this picture was taken?"

Tambora's trembling concerned Mercy. "Yes. Tam, do you think this was all a coincidence, or do you think this guy with the dreads was the murderer?"

"Maybe. Maybe not. But I think it's a big possibility. And I also think he was Miss Carmen's husband."

Mercy's shoulders dropped when she took in this new information. "Which means Miss Carmen was almost certainly involved in the murder."

"Mercy." Tambora's voice quivered. "I don't think we can wait until your uncle Atticus returns from his trip."

"I know," Mercy said. "Look, there is somebody I can talk to, but not until tonight or tomorrow."

"Who? There isn't anyone around here whose allegiance isn't questionable."

"I know. It's—I can't talk about it yet. I'm sworn to secrecy. You'll find out tonight, I'm sure of it."

Tambora stood still for a moment before she rushed to catch up to Mercy. "I haven't pulled the best friend code on you in a long time. Need I remind you of code 48? Best friends are exempt from vows of secrecy."

Mercy sighed and held her armload of textbooks close to her chest. "I don't know why I'm surprised you even brought it up." She leaned in closer to Tambora and lowered her voice. "I'm not supposed to tell. But my Grandma Yvonne is coming to Ara'Ja tonight to visit me."

Tambora squealed, "What? Your human grandma?"

"Shh. Keep your voice down." Mercy held her hand over Tambora's mouth, who yanked it away.

"I'm sorry, but I'm super stoked. I've never met a human before and the way you talk about her makes her out to be wonderfully and fantastically normal. Not in a boring way, but in a cozy, dependable way, like wrapping yourself in a warm blanket on a cold, winter night. My grandparents, on both sides, spawned the Immaculates, so you can guess how comfortable and cozy they aren't. For Fire people, you'd think they would be warmer. Why aren't you more excited about her coming here?"

"I *am* excited. But what if Miss Carmen won't let her stay because of our punishment?" Mercy's voice trembled. "That would be the worst thing she could ever do to me. It would break my heart to know Grandma was on the island and I couldn't see her."

"Come on, even Miss Carmen wouldn't be so cruel to a student. Would she? No. I can't believe she would. Why don't you ask her at breakfast?"

"Because my grandma asked me not to speak about her visit."

"But Miss Carmen let you take her call. Don't you think she already knew your grandma was coming?"

"Maybe, but I've already broken my promise twice."

Tambora blinked. "Who else did you tell?"

"CJ. I didn't mean to. I wasn't thinking, and I blurted it out. I asked her not to tell anyone." Mercy frowned. "But she really didn't answer me, she just left the room. I've made a mess of this whole thing."

Tambora said, "I don't think CJ would say anything. Why would she? Your grandma's visit wouldn't be high on her list of favorite conversation topics. She and her friends have other interests, like hair and fashion and boys. You should have no worries about her."

Mercy chuckled. "This is true."

"I still believe you need to talk to Miss Carmen about your grandma's visit. You don't want her blindsided by it."

"I need to think about this some more. I'm nervous about telling Miss Carmen. She could stop my grandma from coming to the Tray, period. But if I don't talk to her, at least Grandma can show up here and I might have a chance to at least see her before she gets sent away." Mercy hugged Tambora. "In theory, you're right, though. You always provide me with a good balance of information. I don't know what I would do without you."

"Probably wallow in the Sea of Despair, praying for a friend to take pity on you." Tambora giggled and punched Mercy's arm.

Mercy snickered, although in reality, the Sea of Despair was not an amusing subject. Off the uninhabited and undeveloped south shore of the island, the sea claimed the lives of many Ara'Jaeons over the centuries. Throughout time, many citizens of Ara'Ja attempted to cross the treacherous Sea of Despair to reach the small isle, Isola del Sole Eterno, a few miles out. Considered a part of Ara'Ja, Isola del Sole Eterno, which many simplified to Island of the Eternal Sun, was a land Ara'Jaeons knew only from legend and myths. Legend handed down narratives revealing the island as the birthplace of the Ara'Jaeon race. While the stories of myth promised if any Ara'Jaeon could make their way to the island, they could petition the elements and the supplication would be granted. No one knew of anyone who actually accomplished the journey. They either returned defeated by the strong winds and high gales of the sea, or they did not come back at all.

The boys met Mercy and Tambora at the dining-room door and shuffled along behind the girls to the kitchen in the basement below. They marched through the room to the door on the opposite wall as though the kitchen was their routine destination. When the door closed behind them, they raced down the stairwell. Tambora got there first, her cheeks ruddy from the exercise.

A cook escorted the group to a small table in the corner and gave them their meals with the warning to keep quiet and not disturb the goings-on in the kitchen. Meals at the Tray were prepared in the traditional manner. Most Ara'Jaeons believed meals made the old-fashioned way, by hand, were infused with a high measure of love and pride, which transferred to those who dined on them. Of course, once in a while, a spice flew across the room, or a cook used a Fire skill to light an oven with a faulty igniter. But most Ara'Jaeon kitchens buzzed with physical activity from actual cooking.

The children sat in relative silence while they ate. They dared not speak of Tambora's theory with the kitchen staff all around them. But no one in their group gave the impression they wanted to talk, anyway. Perhaps they reflected on past sins, or in Mercy's case, remembered a lost friend. Many Petit Serveurs bustled about. But none was her beloved Loy-Roy. Her heart lurched when she realized if she could not retrieve the buried pieces soon, he was forever gone.

After breakfast, they made their way to General Abilities, the only class all four attended together. The class made Mercy uncomfortable ever since the theatrics of her abilities reveal. Most days, she tried to keep her head down, staring at her book to keep from locking eyes with any of the students. She imagined they watched her, waiting for more dramatic demonstrations. The fact Magister Pappas did not call on her again after the fateful day of the aptitude tests helped, but she lived in the fear the amnesty would not last. Mercy rested her elbow on her desk with her chin on her hand while Pappas lectured about how to daily use elemental abilities and how regular dependence on one's abilities to perform everyday duties led to laziness. He used the speech as a precursor to Managing Multiple Abilities class, known as MMA, which would replace General Abilities after the Christmas holidays for many of the students, including Mercy and Phin.

All students who possessed a single ability would be relegated to classes specific to their element. Many Ara'Jaeons considered a solitary element gift to be a source of shame, except with pure bloods, when the talent of a singular skill source was never scorned. If a pure blood was serious about training, his or her skills in the particular element were apt to be superior to most. As Fire pure bloods, the twins fell into the single ability category and would not attend MMA with Mercy and Phin. Instead, they would go to the Fire Management class.

As Pappas finished his speech, Mercy relaxed. She made it through another day of General Abilities without getting called upon.

"Mercy." The magister's voice cut through Mercy's thoughts.

"Yes, sir?"

"Please stick around after class, I wish to speak with you. The rest of you may leave."

Mercy exchanged glances with Tambora and grimaced. "Go on ahead, I'll meet you later."

She pushed through the hoard of students who flowed in the opposite direction until she reached Pappas, who sat down behind his desk and folded his hands.

"There was no training for you last evening due to Miss Carmen's restrictions on your free time, so I could not tell you Mr. Kishan took an unexpected leave of absence yesterday. Beginning Monday, I will take over your training."

Mercy's stomach twisted in knots. The thought of working with Pappas made her nervous, especially after what she and Tambora overheard in the maze. But curiosity won over trepidation and she blurted out, "Where did Mr. Kishan go?"

"Now, Mercy, you know Mr. Kishan has the right to keep his personal life private." Pappas took a schedule planner from his desk drawer and reached for a pen.

"Could you at least let me know what happened when you went to see the Council of the Apotheosis about me? About my using Wind?"

Pappas put down his pen. "That is an acceptable question, although, not easily answered. But the short version is, after hours of contemplation and research, we could not devise a conclusive and logical explanation. Many believe, because you are naturally gifted in all four element areas, perhaps your powers overlap to a certain extent. Others thought the anomaly was merely a fluke. Regardless, no one thinks you are in any danger because of it. I am sure, once you have gotten reasonable control over your abilities, we will not have any more of these—episodes. In the meantime, do not breathe."

Mercy's jaw dropped, unsure of how to respond.

"That was... uh... supposed to be a joke," Pappas said, his pasty cheeks flushed.

"Oh. Ha-ha." Mercy pretended to laugh.

"Yes, well. I am spending a sabbatical weekend in my private quarters and won't be available until Monday, so I wanted to make sure I talked to you today." Pappas stood and erased the blackboard behind his desk. "You better get to your next class."

"Yes, sir," Mercy said. Relieved her talk with Pappas was finished, she fled the room, hurrying to her history class. She scooted through the door before Mrs. Kishan reached out to pull it closed.

Mercy sat down at her desk and arranged her books and paper in front of her.

"Good morning, students," Mrs. Kishan said.

"Good morning, Mrs. Kishan," the students responded in unison.

Mercy looked up to discover her teacher's swollen and red-ringed eyes upon her. Mercy wondered why Mrs. Kishan did not accompany Mr. Kishan on his sudden trip and if her distressed condition was related. She hoped their family was okay. She held a genuine fondness and admiration for the couple. They produced an aura of calm and stillness, not only for her but also on the Tray. If they ever left, the balance of temperament at the Tray would change, and the scale would not tip toward the better. Mercy sensed she intruded on a private matter and looked away.

"Please open your books to chapter twelve. Today, we will study the Ara'Jaeon Firsts. Who can name them?" Mrs. Kishan asked.

Many hands flew into the air, Mercy's included.

Mrs. Kishan called on Adele to answer.

Adele stood and spoke in a loud voice. "Nayavu, Zephyrine, Kenwei, and Canicus."

"Correct." Mrs. Kishan picked up a book from her desk. "The Ara'Jaeon philosopher Onesiphorus chronicled the inception of the Ara'Jaeons. He called it *The Birthing*. This excerpt is from his writings."

The whirlwind began as a tiny speck, barely visible over the horizon, raised high above the snow-covered mountains which surrounded most of the grassy field. The twister increased in size and strength as it approached the natural arena, which was created when the pine forest at the less mountainous south side of the field effectively cut the pasture off from the rest of the world. The wind located a perfect spot to settle near the quiet stream flowing through the very heart of the meadow. It danced around and around, enjoying the pulsating concerto of nature's heartbeat. Slowly, it took tangible shape, until the air became still, and in place of the mayhem, an exquisite woman, who stood no lower than the most majestic of sunflowers, remained steadfast and sure. Her lovely amethyst eyes shone bright with exuberance, and soft pink curls, tipped in silver white, cascaded down her back. Her tresses eagerly blew about by a breeze no longer discernable. Similarly, her graceful white gown billowed and swirled around her, until logic deemed it should become ruined and tattered. She lifted her delicate arms and fervently declared, "I am the Wind Rider, Zephyrine, of the west wind!"

Earth heard Zephyrine and trembled with all its might, and its mouth opened inside a nearby patch of lush flowers. Dozens of tree limbs collectively emerged from the orifice, intertwining as they grew, until they became one. The trunk split in two and formed thick, muscular legs. Branches developed into tanned, muscular arms, reaching gracefully to the sky. Finally, there stood a bronzed man, as tall as Zephyrine, with hair the color of dark red clay, tied back in a ponytail, and intense eyes rendered with the deepest purple. Bleached white animal skins, adorned with simple designs, clothed him. His hands already raised, he cried out to the sky, "I am called Nayavu, made of clay. I am the Earth Watcher!"

Lightning, not known for its subtlety, theatrically struck the ground not too far away, and a pillar of fire and smoke appeared. It burned for a time, then took on the form of a massive, towering man, sturdy and robust. He sported a spirited grin and a shock of unruly, bright copper hair. Like the others, he wore white and his eyes were of a purple hue. And, as the others did before him, he lifted his head and raised his fisted hands to the heavens. "I am Canicus, born of Fire. I am the Fire Eater!" he enthusiastically shouted. The pine trees in the south overheard Canicus and whispered warnings among themselves to be cautious and alert.

The gentle, meandering brook previously kept quiet, content to watch the handiwork of the other elements. Suddenly, Water was no longer satisfied with its bystander status. It sprouted a high fountain and spit it out to the grassy earth, where it shattered into millions of droplets, bonding together to fashion another tall woman. Her velvety mahogany skin was smooth and shimmering. Thousands of tight white curls covered her head in a massive crown. Her raiment consisted of a short sinuous white dress that echoed the glistening of still waters, basking in the morning sun. Her kind, gentle smile caused the birds to hush their melodies in awestruck admiration. She lifted her arms and pale violet eyes, and she took in a deep breath. "My name is Kenwei, the water's lily. I am the Water Dancer! We are the Firsts."

"We are the Guardians," Nayavu proclaimed.

"We are the Accountable," said Canicus.

Zephyrine looked at her sister and brothers and cried out, "We are—the Ara'Jaeons!"

The Firsts formed a circle facing outward and beheld as each element created a hundred more Ara'Jaeons for them to lead.

Thus transpired the birthing of the Ara'Jaeons.

The class hushed. The picturesque narrative overwhelmed Mercy and she was moved almost to tears. The descriptive story was new to her, and, she suspected, to most of the others, as well. Until then, she only heard the most generic of accounts, one which barely registered on any scale of interesting.

Mrs. Kishan put down her book. "Does anyone know the meanings of the names of the Firsts? If you listened closely, the story provided all the answers,"

No one raised a hand. Mercy never thought about what the names might mean and she doubted the others had either. She peered down at her textbook and found the descriptions there, printed in black and white. She read along in silence while Mrs. Kishan spoke, her voice quiet and shaky. "Zephyrine means west wind. Kenwei is water lily. Nayavu means clay, and Canicus signifies born of Fire."

Mercy looked around the room to see if anyone else perceived the subtle change in their teacher. She saw no signs that the other kids noticed anything out of the ordinary.

"Azrael, the First Metalicon. He who will wear the crown of reward. The Iron Crown of Sachar."

The same distant and ancient voice Mercy heard a few months earlier called out to her again. Startled, she gasped, none too quietly, and her head shot up. Students all around the room turned to her with inquisitive looks, but she did not care. Her attention focused solely on Mrs. Kishan, who soared at such a high speed to stand motionless before her, Mercy thought the teacher used some type of transport trick. Mercy recoiled when Mrs. Kishan bent down and hissed, "You've heard the voice. The primordial one which calls from the beginning. I've heard it too. Azrael is coming. When you restore the crown, death cannot be stopped."

Mrs. Kishan turned away and collapsed to the floor. Mercy sat in shock, unable to move. Several students jumped up to assist their instructor while others ran from the room and yelled they would get help.

A few minutes later, Magister Pappas rushed in, followed by Miss Carmen.

"What happened here?" he asked.

All the students talked at once. Phin left his seat and knelt next to Mercy, who sat frozen in her chair.

"She talked about the Firsts and she collapsed," said one student.

Another said, "She looked possessed."

"She told Mercy Azrael was coming and said something about fixing some kind of crown," said Adele, who sat next to Mercy.

Mercy groaned inside. Of course, Adele would be the one to overhear and tattle.

Pappas's head jerked up and looked in Mercy's direction. "She said what?"

Mercy stiffened. She hated how everything out of the ordinary always pointed back to her.

"Mrs. Kishan said Azrael is going to come and Mercy is going to restore a crown," Adele repeated. "And there's going to be death. Are we sure she should be here?"

"Who is Azrael?" a student asked.

"I don't know," another responded. "Apparently, some kind of troublemaker."

Pappas and Miss Carmen traded glances Mercy could only interpret as alarm. The magister lifted Mrs. Kishan up into his arms and carried her out. For such a slight man, he seemed quite strong.

Miss Carmen stayed behind and addressed the students. "Mrs. Kishan is going to be fine. She's been under a great deal of stress with a family situation, so don't take her ramblings too seriously. Death is *not* coming to the Tray." She instructed the students to return to their seats and said she personally would resume Mrs. Kishan's classes for the day.

"Are you okay, Mercy?" Phin asked.

Mercy nodded and attempted a smile.

Phin patted her back and moved to his desk.

Mercy fidgeted until class ended and barely registered Miss Carmen's lesson. Her mind raced back and forth between worry for Mrs. Kishan, anticipation for her grandmother's visit, and apprehension at the discovery Azrael was the First Metalicon. Azrael... who was most likely connected to the iron crown referenced in the prophecy. The crown she was supposed to restore. Her concentration existed at an all-time low.

The class bell rang and Mercy grabbed her books and hurried to her next class, eager for the school day to be over.

Mercy waited outside Miss Carmen's office for what seemed like hours. She hoped to talk to the headmistress about her grandmother's visit before she went back to her room to wait for dinner. She knocked on the door and called her name, she looked up and down the hall and over the rail to search for Miss Carmen. Mercy took a seat on the floor, worked on her class assignments, then stood up to stretch. She pounded on the door again. "Well. I guess there's nothing left to do, but go to my room until supper," she muttered, and climbed the five floors to her room.

Several thuds and grunts came from inside Mercy's dorm room. She hesitated to enter, but concern for her belongings got the better of her. She gripped the door handle and opened the door. She walked in to find CJ stomping around and throwing her hiking gear, squawking like a mad magpie the entire time. Mercy detected an errant boot tossed in her direction. She ducked in time to avoid a direct hit to her nose. "Hey! What are you doing?" Troubled by what she saw, Mercy did a quick assessment to check the status of her possessions. To her relief, she found nothing out of place on her side of the room.

CJ paused her tantrum. "It's pouring buckets outside, and we had to cancel our hike down to the beach."

Mercy stifled a grin. She almost felt horrible at her elation in discovering no one could go on a picnic, when she, herself, could not take part. She *almost* felt horrible. Not quite. And so, she feigned sympathy. "Aw. That's too bad. But focus on the bright side, at least you'll stay dry, and the beach isn't going anywhere. There's always another day."

CJ glared at Mercy. "Well. *Some* of us aren't important enough to have a grandmother come for a visit."

"What?" That statement was the first time Mercy detected bitterness from CJ and she stood motionless in disbelief.

"You heard me," CJ said. "When I told my parents your grandmother was coming here, they said you get away with too much because the High Elder is your great uncle. And all the teachers think you're so special. And I realized my parents were right. Everyone knows you're a favorite of Pappas and Miss Carmen."

Mercy's jaw dropped. "You told your parents my grandmother was visiting?"

"I did, and they were none too happy about it either."

"But I asked you not to tell anyone," Mercy said, close to tears.

"I tell them everything. And I think they are going to file a complaint, because the minute I told them, they were quick to end our call."

"Why would they complain? It's not against the rules for family to visit."

"*Ara'Jaeon* family. Your grandmother is a flawed human and not worthy to be here. My mother said so."

Mercy stiffened. "That's not true," she cried. "We're here to keep the world a safe place for everyone, especially humans. And if you saw the way Pappas and Miss Carmen really treated me, you would know I'm not their favorite." She always thought she and CJ got along fairly well, despite their differences. Mercy even tried to include her roommate on Parents' Day and CJ appeared pretty happy then. She tossed her books under her bunk and backed out of the room without another word.

Mercy ran, but she did not know where to go. She could not be anywhere except her room, so she ran toward a remote area on the student housing floor and soon found herself in an unused corridor.

For the second time within an hour, she sat down on a hall floor. She brought her knees up, folded her arms around them, and buried her face. She sat there for what seemed like ages.

"There you are. What are you doing down here?" Mercy heard Tambora ask.

Mercy brought her face out of hiding. "Hanging out for a bit. CJ's having a meltdown right now, and I'm trying to avoid her."

"She's acting strange. I went to your room, and she snapped at me."

"What's going on? Why are you wandering around?" Mercy asked.

Tambora sat next to Mercy, stretching her legs out. "Nothing's going on. I thought I would wait with you until dinner. No one will know. We still have about half an hour. I also wanted to check on you to make sure you're okay. I heard about what happened this morning with Mrs. Kishan."

"I was stunned at the whole thing. But I'm fine now."

"Have you thought at all about what I showed you this morning? About Miss Carmen's husband?"

"No. It's been an odd day, and it wasn't at the top of my mind. Let's not talk about this right now. It feels nice to sit and not worry for a change, right?"

"It does," Tambora replied.

In the stillness, Mercy played with her shoelaces and tried to empty her mind. She hoped for an escape from the many situations which bombarded her every day for the past few weeks.

Tambora broke the silence. "Who's escorting your grandmother into Ara'Ja?"

"I don't know. She wouldn't say. When I asked her, she reminded me she lived here for decades and she knows more people than me and my parents."

"That makes sense," Tambora said, and both girls gave themselves over to the quiet once more.

Again, Tambora spoke first. "Do you think a half an hour has passed yet?"

"No," Mercy said. "But let's go. I'm too restless to continue to sit here."

CHAPTER 20

FAIRY TALES AND NIGHTMARES

Mercy and Tambora sat down on the towering chairs at the kitchen table to await their meal. The table was meant to be used by tall Ara'Jaeon adults, not by children, and their legs swung in mid-air, because their feet came nowhere close to reaching the floor. Miss Carmen was not around when they made their way down to dinner, and Mercy feared time to plead her case would run out. She did not know when her grandmother planned to arrive. Since early evening was already upon them, Mercy thought chances were good she would get there soon or not at all. She hoped her grandmother could at least send a message when she arrived on the island. "Where are the boys?" she asked Tambora.

"I don't know. I expected them to be here," Tambora said.

Miss Carmen entered the room and graciously acknowledged the staff before she moved closer to the girls. Mercy could not discern the older woman's mood, but whatever the case, she prepared herself to ask the all-important question. *Can I visit with my grandma?*

Miss Carmen spoke before Mercy could open her mouth. "Girls, you'll be eating dinner upstairs in the dining hall tonight. Mercy has a visitor, and since it's unfair to excuse only her from your punishment, I've postponed the grounding until Monday for all of you." Miss Carmen stepped to the side to reveal a pleasant older woman with snow white hair and icy, blue eyes, twinkling like holiday lights. She was the Christmas spirit personified.

"Grandma!" Mercy jumped down from her perch and sailed over the few steps between them. She flung herself into her grandmother's open arms and burrowed into her, weeping hot tears mixed with both pain and relief.

Grandma held Mercy close and caressed her granddaughter's wild curls before she cupped Mercy's cheeks in her hands, pulling her face close to her own. "My, look at you, growing like a weed. You're almost as tall as I am."

Mercy smiled and used the sleeve of her sweater to wipe her nose. "Pretty soon, I'll be taller than you."

"And in a few years' time, you'll start shooting up to your adult height. I'll have to crank my neck to look at you, just as I do your mother. She never let me forget it once she reached her hyper growth years."

The thought of her mother as a rebel teenager amused Mercy. She sniffled away the rest of her tears. "Grandma, this is my best friend, Tambora. Tambora, my grandma, Yvonne Kadarius."

"Harmony and balance. How very nice to meet you, Tambora." Grandma's blue eyes brightened and lit up the room when she extended her hand to Tambora.

"Harmony and balance, Mrs. Kadarius," Tambora said. "Mercy talks about you all the time."

"Please, call me Grandma."

Tambora grinned ear to ear. "Thank you, I will."

Mercy took her grandmother's arm and led her to the dining room with Tambora and Miss Carmen following. Mercy overheard Tambora say, "Miss Carmen, this was really nice of you to let Mercy and her grandmother have a visit."

"I realize Mercy has been struggling," Miss Carmen said. "I'm hoping this will help her out a bit. However, this weekend's reprieve expires Monday."

"I know," Tambora said. "Still, it was a kind gesture."

Phin and Vesuvius already sat at their usual table and Miss Carmen left them to join the other staff.

"Hey, guys. Grandma, this is Phin and Vesuvius. Vesu and Tambora are twins. Guys, this is my Grandma Yvonne. She's visiting from Crete." Mercy made a quick scan around the room to find CJ, wondering if she should introduce them. Perhaps it should wait until the next day. CJ was not so kind to Mercy an hour earlier.

"Ecxellent," Vesuvius said. "You're the human?"

Tambora reached over and pinched Vesuvius hard on the arm.

"Ow. What did I do?"

"Try to be a little more polite, she's not an oddity. Several humans live on Ara'Ja. We're not much different," Tambora said.

"Except for our hair, our eyes, our height, our life span, and our elemental abilities. Shall I go on?" Vesuvius asked.

Grandma beamed at the children and the sparkle in her eyes remained bright.

"No, Vesu. I think you covered it all." Mercy laughed. "Grandma, this is what I have to deal with every day."

"You are absolutely correct, young man," Mercy's grandmother said. "There are plenty of differences. But there are plenty of similarities, too. We all can hate and we all can do good. But most of all, we all have the power to forgive and to love. This is what's most important. You have enjoyable friends, Mercy. I'm pleased to meet you all." Grandma Kadarius sat down next to Mercy and squeezed her hand. Mercy felt at peace for the first time in weeks. She knew grandchild heaven existed.

A Petit Serveur approached them and set the table.

"Grandma, this is a Petit Serveur. They help at mealtimes."

"I'm familiar with Petit Serveurs. Your grandfather and I used to have one. We enjoyed the interaction. The serveur was quite entertaining. But I had to give it up when I left the island. Certain objects you have here on Ara'Ja and at the outposts, like Petit Serveurs and Situation Clocks, don't operate the same outside of the Ara'Jaeon realm. They become ordinary and inanimate in the human world."

"We had a favorite here too, but he fell to the floor and smashed," Mercy said in a dejected voice.

"Ah, too bad. Weren't they able to fix it? Ours broke once," Grandma said. "We found all the pieces except one little chip. Although the fact the piece went missing didn't matter much because your grandfather was still able to get it mended."

Mercy perked up. "Maybe we could get ours fixed. Tambora and I buried some pieces out in the garden. If we can get them to the kitchen staff, just maybe—"

"We'll find a way, Mercy. I promise," said Tambora.

Phin plopped his elbows on the table. "Mrs. Kadarius, how did you meet Mr. Kadarius?"

Mercy almost jumped out of her chair. "This is a *great* story."

Grandma Kadarius chuckled. "You kids don't want to be bored by my anecdotes. You must have much more exciting escapades to talk about. And you don't need to call me Mrs. Kadarius. Grandma is fine."

"Woof—Grandma K in the houuuuse," Vesuvius shouted, his voice hardened to mimic a wrestling announcer.

A hush filled the room as the faces of four-hundred plus students turned toward the Murphy Vestam table. Mercy froze, but to her relief, the attention to their table lasted a mere five seconds and then everyone resumed whatever activity they did before the outburst.

"Oh. Please tell us, Grandma K," Tambora said. "It must be fascinating. Human-Ara'Jaeon marriages are rare."

"I'm not sure how much Mercy has told you about me, but I'm from the United States. Northern Indiana, specifically. The area is almost completely flat farmland. No beautiful mountains, no oceans. Although we had access to Lake Michigan, one of the largest freshwater lakes in the world. The lake is so big, waves like what you would find on the ocean crash along the shore. So, there I was, a naïve, small-town girl who had never been outside of the State of Indiana. The year was 1969. I was nineteen. Not much older than the lot of you. The Vietnam War raged in southern Asia, and humankind grew restless. But in my small part of the world, life remained pretty much untouched by the cares of the times, except for the occasional patriotic boy who enlisted into the military or whose number came up in the draft. One early summer night, I was strolling home from a community dance, taking my time. You see, we lived outside of town, and I didn't own a car. I had a long way to go on mostly unlit and unpaved roads. Back roads, we called them. Times were different, and we didn't think much about the dangers of going out alone at night. The evening was dark, but pleasant. A soft breeze chased away the heat from the day, and the crickets and frogs in the swamps along the roadside called out to one another. It was the type of night where you simply took a deep breath to drink in the sheer and modest tranquility of your surroundings."

"It sounds wonderful." Tambora placed her elbow on the table, resting her chin in her palm.

Grandma sighed. "Oh, it was, it was. But remember this. Sometimes you don't appreciate what you have until you no longer have it."

"That's brilliant advice," said Phin. "We shouldn't worry about the future and enjoy today. Right, Mercy?"

Mercy wrinkled her nose and stuck out her tongue. "I enjoy plenty."

"Sure, you do." Phin laughed.

Grandma K took Mercy's hand between her own. "I was blessed with a good life, but, oh… I so longed to leave the small town for bigger things, for adventure. Sewing and baking and gardening, they filled my time, and all continue to be interests I enjoy to this day. But I prayed for more. And I prayed that night on my way home from the dance. Well. God must've listened to me. I traveled on an empty section of the road and was almost home, when I thought I heard a small moan coming out from the bushes. I stopped and listened. It sounded again. Only the second time, it was a definite cry for help."

Tambora gasped, her gaze fixed on Grandma K.

"Without hesitation, I ran to the bushes and brushed aside the branches and overgrowth. Then the moon came out from behind the clouds and shone a spotlight onto the exact area I cleared away. What I saw both amazed and terrified me, and I froze. For on the ground in front of me lay the most beautiful man I ever laid eyes on. Not beautiful in the typical implication of the word. Of course, he was physically quite stunning, but beautiful in the sense there was a pure and unadulterated goodness in his expression. I can still visualize those vibrant purple eyes shining bright in the moonlight. And he was tall. Even though he was crumpled up, I realized straight away he was much taller than anyone I knew. His legs went on and on, they did. At first, I wondered if I was being pranked, but then I noticed the gash in his blood-soaked shirt."

Mercy watched her friends, her lips stuck in a grin, not a grin at her grandfather's misfortune, but a genuine beam of delight in witnessing her friends experience her favorite story for the first time. Tambora had not moved at all. Mercy knew the enchanted moment engrossed her friend. As for the boys, the mention of blood clearly hooked them into the narrative. Grandma knew how to tell the tale.

"He asked if I could help him bind his wound and he would be on his way. Of course, he had a tantalizing British accent. How could a midwestern American girl resist? I took off his shirt and wrapped it tightly around the injury to lessen the bleeding, but I could tell he was in no condition to walk. I told him I was close to home and would return soon with help. I begged him not to move. He thanked me for my aid, but said he didn't want folks to know about him being there, and he declined further help from me. But I insisted. I ran as though my life depended on it, straight into our house and up the stairs to my brother, Ben's room. Luckily, he was there. I grabbed his truck keys from his dresser top, told him there was an emergency, and I dragged him out of the house to his truck before he could say a word. I was gone less than ten minutes, but when we returned, the man wasn't there. Ben used his flashlight to scan the area and noticed a bloody trail leading away from the site, which we followed. We found the man unconscious a few yards away. My brother got into his truck and parked as close as he could, then we pulled the man into the bed of the truck, but not without a struggle. Because, as I suspected, he was *very* tall."

"Because he was a fabulous Ara'Jaeon," Tambora said.

Grandma nodded. "Yes. Precisely for that reason. But we didn't know it yet. I told Ben I thought the man was in trouble and he didn't want to go to the hospital. So, we took him to an abandoned barn on the far corner of our property, and Ben retrieved blankets and first aid supplies from the house. We did our best to clean and dress his wounds and to make him comfortable, but we didn't think he was going to survive. We were discussing what our options would be if he died, when he called out to us. The man insisted he would be okay, but if the worst would happen, if he died, there was a phone number written on a card in his pocket. He instructed us to call the number, tell them Augustus had fallen, and someone would be there to retrieve him within a few hours."

"Like spies!" Vesuvius slapped his hand on the table.

Grandma smiled. "Kind of, but it turned out to be an elite group within the Ecclesia. I took care of Augustus for several weeks while he was on the mend, because Ara'Jaeons don't heal as quickly off of the island. We talked a lot, conversations which opened up my little world to a whole secret society right here on earth. It fascinated me. He wasn't supposed to talk to me about his life or about the mission he was on, but we developed a close bond and quick trust of each other. I discovered Ara'Jaeons aged much more slowly than humans, and even though he appeared and acted only a few years older than myself, he was, in fact, almost sixty. When he was well enough to leave, he promised he would return to call on me and he kissed me goodbye." Grandma paused and touched her lips. She seemed to be elsewhere. "The age difference actually worked out well for us in the long run, as our physical stages eventually evened out, and I had only just passed his physical maturity when he died."

Tambora sighed, her smile wistful and completely engrossed in Grandma K's personal fairytale.

Mercy's hand flew to her mouth to hide the giggle about to burst out. Tambora, the hopeless romantic. Who knew?

"He kept his promise," Grandma K said. "And over the next year, he secretly visited once or twice a month. Before long, we fell in love, and after a lot of soul searching, we married. Although unusual, Ara'Jaeons did not forbid intermarriage with humans. Regardless, his family welcomed me, and mine accepted him, or at least the version of him we presented to them. We made up a story about his upbringing and he wore glasses with tinted lenses to disguise his bright purple eyes. My brother was a fiercely loyal man who kept quiet about what he knew of Augustus and no one was ever the wiser."

"How majestic. I can't wait to fall in love," Tambora said in a dreamy stupor.

"Pfft—love. I liked he was a spy." Vesuvius jumped up and made a James Bond pose, using one hand to resemble a gun. Phin hopped onto his chair and challenged Vesuvius with his own version of an invisible weapon.

"This is going to be my first novel," declared Mercy.

"This will be a great story for you to write about, Mercy," Tambora said. "You should make notes. Why not write your book sooner rather than later? You're always talking about becoming an author, but I never see you writing."

"I know. Things have been crazy since I got here. I need to make more of an effort." Mercy glanced down at the notebook she carried around everywhere she went. When was the last time she wrote in it?

"Where are you staying while you're in Ara'Ja, Grandma K?" asked Phin.

"I'm staying here at the center. Miss Carmen set up an empty room for me a few doors down the hall from Mercy."

Mercy brightened. She already envisioned herself and her grandma having a girls' overnight together. She would invite Tambora, of course, but she would not ask CJ. She did not understand what she did to make her roommate treat her with such hatred. But three made a good number for a sleepover. She figured, after lights out, she and Tambora would sneak out of their respective rooms, unseen by their roommates, who would most likely expect to be included. She only needed to wait for CJ to fall asleep. Her thoughts were broken when their Petit Serveur delivered dinner of braised lamb and colorful, herb-roasted root vegetables. Mercy studied her grandmother while they ate.

"What do you think, Grandma? Good, huh?"

"It's lovely," her grandmother replied. "The lamb is quite tender and the root vegetables are especially fragrant. I'm on my second serving and

I'll have difficulty to not grab a third. I should ask the cooks about their preparation methods."

"Attention, please." Miss Carmen stood up and clapped her hands together. "I have received word, because of unforeseen circumstances, High Elder Kadarius cut short his trip after only a few days and has already returned to the island. Once he settles in, we will set a date for the banquet and symposium he will host for us. I realize we thought we had a month to prepare, but time is now shorter. Therefore, if you haven't already, please work on your questions for him."

Mercy gasped, excited at the news, which meant a visit would be possible between her uncle and her grandma. "Grandma, Uncle Atticus has returned. Now you'll be able to see him while you're here."

Grandma K hesitated before she answered. "Yes, dear. If I have the time."

Mercy wondered what might be important enough to keep her from fitting in rare time with her brother-in-law. She bit her lip to keep herself from asking. She remembered getting chastised the day before and did not want to be told again, in public, she did not need to know everything.

Mercy tried to listen in on the rousing discussion between Tambora and the boys about what questions they should ask the High Elder, but her grandmother's obvious change in mood caught her attention. Mercy grew concerned by her grandma's silence, her flushed cheeks, and her gaze focused down on her plate.

Mercy touched her grandmother's shoulder. "Are you okay?"

"Actually, I'm a little worn out. I think I'll retire early tonight."

"I thought we might have a sleepover."

"I know, dear. But not tonight. I'm pretty tired." Her grandmother stood. "Do you know where my room is?"

"Yes. There's only one empty dorm in my hall. It must be the one Miss Carmen wants you to have. Did she already have your bags taken up?"

Grandma nodded.

"Okay. I'll walk with you," Mercy said. "We'll go slow."

Grandma K said her goodnights to the other children, and Mercy told them she would be back after she escorted her grandmother to her room. The empty room was three doors down from Mercy. She pushed open the unlocked door and let her grandma in. Happy to see the bunks lowered, Mercy checked the room to be certain all was in order and that her grandma's luggage was there. The room passed her assessment, and she gave her grandma a hug and kiss goodnight.

"I'm so happy you're here, Grandma. I'll check on you before I go to my room."

"There's no need. I'm going straight to bed. I'm sincerely sorry tonight isn't what you expected, but we'll have plenty of time over the weekend to visit and talk. I love you, Mercy."

"It's fine, Grandma. We have all day tomorrow and Sunday. And I love you too." Mercy closed the door behind her and reentered the dining hall in time for dessert.

"Is your grandma okay?" Tambora grabbed a handful of Greek almond crescents and put them on her plate.

"I think so, I think she just needs to rest." Mercy grabbed her own handful of the sweet cookies. She loved the flavor combination of ground almonds and orange blossom water used in the recipe.

"She's super nice, Mercy," Phin said. "I like her."

The twins agreed. They spent the next few minutes stuffing cookies in their mouths, taking turns to determine who made the best chipmunk cheeks. Tambora blew the others out of the contest by cramming in seven good-sized cookies. They stayed in the dining room until the kitchen staff chased them off, so they could clean and get ready for breakfast the next morning. No one wanted to split up, and they moved to the boys' room instead of going to their separate dorms. They sat on the floor in a circle and talked about their respective days. Phin and Mercy recounted the story of the birthing Mrs. Kishan read to them in class and her mention of Azrael before she passed out.

"You mean, Azrael, the first Metalicon?" Vesuvius asked.

"Yes. Do you know of him?" Mercy said.

"Of course. A guy at Fire Kids Camp told the birthing story last summer when we sat around telling ghost stories one night," Vesuvius said.

"I attended that camp, why didn't I hear this?" Tambora said.

"I don't know. Maybe you were too uptight to sneak out."

Tambora's nostrils flared, but she kept silent.

Vesuvius continued on. "Mrs. Kishan didn't finish the story with the part about the Metalicons, did she?"

Mercy shook her head.

"Okay. I'll tell you the rest, but we can only do this one way. Phin, flip off the light and I'll make a campfire." Vesuvius formed a glow bubble and placed his creation on the floor in the midst of their circle. The light eerily cast a blue sheen on their faces when Phin turned out the overhead lights.

"I suppose Mrs. Kishan left off where the Firsts watched the elements create more Ara'Jaeons, right?"

"Correct," Mercy said.

"Tambora, do I need to retell the first part of the story?" Vesuvius asked his sister.

"No. I know that part. Just go on about the Metalicons," Tambora said.

Vesuvius began his narration. "Well. The Ara'Jaeons were created, yada, yada." He hunched forward, his face illuminated by the glow. He softened his voice and spoke using the vocal fluctuations of a professional storyteller. "Excitement and anticipation filled the surrounding air. But under their feet, deep in the earth, something disturbing was happening. A hazy green light in an underground cave revealed the making of another, more sinister sect of Ara'Jaeons. Hot liquid metals of every kind gushed up from the cave's hard, rocky floor, combining to create its own ominous First. The metal became a solid figure, wearing a dark coat which dusted the floor. He sneered, his stormy purple-gray eyes were hard and cold. He threw his fist into the air." Vesuvius extended his own fist upward. "I am named Azrael. May this day be remembered as the day the Metalicons arose."

Mercy gasped. Phin leaned forward, his elbows on his knees, and Tambora clung to Mercy as they held on to every word Vesuvius said.

"A hundred more Metalicons, in dark clothing, came up from the ground and joined Azrael. They all raised their fists to the air and chanted his name." Vesuvius growled the chant. "Azrael. Azrael." He paused, stood, and tiptoed around the others. "Azrael slowly circled around his followers, his outstretched hands dripped with molten metal. He taunted the universe. 'Let the calamity begin.' Thus was the birthing of the Metalicons."

"That is truly terrifying," Mercy whispered. She and Tambora still clutched one another.

Phin grabbed Vesu's shoulder and gave it a squeeze. "Dude, you're a natural born storyteller."

"I've been practicing and memorizing this word-for-word straight from the writings of Onesiphorus, waiting for the right occasion to tell it," Vesuvius said.

Tambora yawned. "Sorry to spoil all the fun, but I think it's time for me to go to the safety of my bed. Vesu, walk me to my room? You've effectively scared me."

"Of course." Vesuvius puffed out his chest and escorted his sister.

"Well," Mercy said, her voice pitched about three levels higher than normal. "I guess I should go, too." She did not want to admit it, but she felt frightened to travel the empty halls on her own, especially given her history with Metalicons.

Phin stood. "Come on, I'll walk with you."

Mercy exhaled. "Thank you. I *am* kind of afraid."

"I could tell."

"What gave me away?"

"You sounding like a scared little girl was a good sign."

"I did not."

"You did."

Phin offered his arm to Mercy, and she gladly took hold, taking care to use a light touch. Exactly the way her mother instructed her the previous year, right before their neighbor's son escorted her down the aisle as junior attendants in a wedding. Mercy's stomach churned. She hoped she did not show how nervous she felt at walking so close to Phin. She kept her conversation short and concise so she would not babble on and on.

"Here we are. At my room," she said.

"Yep," replied Phin. "Goodnight. See you tomorrow."

"Not if I see you first."

"Why's that?"

Mercy gulped, hating to have to explain. "If I see you first, you won't see me because I'll run the other way."

"Why would you do that?"

"I—I wouldn't. It's just a joke." Mercy mentally kicked herself, feeling idiotic and embarrassed. "Goodnight, Phin." She entered her dorm room and sighed in relief to see CJ still gone, even though lights out had already passed. She hurried to undress and get into bed to avoid a confrontation. No sooner did she pull the covers over herself, when CJ blundered into the room and flicked on the lights. She wasn't quiet, but Mercy feigned sleep the entire time to not give CJ the satisfaction of thinking her commotion disrupted Mercy's slumber. She wondered again exactly what caused CJ's meltdown. She did not understand why CJ's parents experienced such an issue with her or why they turned CJ against her. She did not know how to resolve the situation without asking CJ about her parents. Getting fellow students to narc on their parents took a low position on her list of favorite activities. Mercy hoped if she kept her cool, the situation would return to normal in a day or two. Mercy fell asleep soon after CJ got into bed, content in the knowledge her grandmother slept down the hall.

Family and friends filled her dreams, her parents, both sets of her grandparents, and her friends at the Tray. She danced among them in a stunning meadow which was divided by a babbling brook and surrounded by mountains and a pine forest. She recognized the site, delighted to learn nothing changed since she first visited in the vision during her aptitude test. She twirled and spotted Miss Carmen, the Tray teachers, CJ, her Uncle Atticus, Telys, and his Metalicon buddies circling around them.

Each member of the surrounding ring beckoned her to them. But glee occupied her heart, and she declared no interest in involving herself in their drama. She frolicked and ignored them, happy and carefree, until the sight of a lone figure in the distance, standing in the shadows, grabbed her attention. She stopped dancing to scrutinize the tall, dark form and its opened, welcoming arms. A heavy weight tugged at her and she realized she carried a broken iron crown. All who gathered there stepped aside to make way for her to approach the mysterious individual. By no choice of her own, she drew close to the figure, her arms held out, offering a newly restored crown.

From a place deep inside her sleep, she heard a door creak open, and the sound woke her up. She opened her eyes to a shaft of light, coming from the direction of the door. A faint fluttering sound entered the room. She glanced over at CJ, whose motionless figure lay fast asleep. Mercy kept still and trembled on the inside. The soft noise occurred again, almost inaudible. She was certain someone, or something, lingered in the room. Her only thought was how Azrael terrorized her as a child. She held her breath, squeezed her eyes closed, and continued to play possum, hoping whomever wandered about the room would simply leave. A rustle sounded next to her bunk. She knew it waited for her acknowledgement. It frightened her to look, but the noise persisted. Taking great care to be slow and steady, she reopened one eye into a small squint. A Situation Clock hovered mere inches from her, its wings flapped frantically. The clock leaned in close to her and whispered, "It is 11:40, and all is treacherous down by the bay. Do you know? Is Grandma okay?"

CHAPTER 21

A DOODLE OF A MARK

More often than not, Mercy did not understand the vague insinuations of the Situation Clocks, but for once, the meaning was clear. Grandma was in trouble. She jumped from her bed, and her bare feet hit the floor in a dull thud. She threw on her slippers, put a robe on over her sleeping shorts and top, and dashed out of her room and down the hall to where she dropped off her grandmother earlier. She did not take the time to knock, but threw the door open with unceremonious haste. Undisturbed blankets covered the empty bed. Mercy struggled for breath and thought the vigorous pounding of her heart might cause an explosion in her chest.

The bay. The Situation Clock said there was trouble. No. It said treachery. Treachery was at the bay. Panic set in and without hesitation, Mercy broke out into a run. She did not care that she could not see a thing as she passed through the fifth floor. She did not care if she drew the attention of the Regulators. She did not care she was not allowed out of the building. She fled into the rain and made a run for the trails. Big raindrops, like liquid diamonds, plunged from the sky. They bounced off the ground up onto her bare legs, stinging them with every hit. By the time she arrived at the edge of the forest, she was drenched. Ahead of her, the gaps in the trees opened to the various meandering paths, snaking down the soft decline of the hill and to the bay. She did not know the easy trails from the more difficult. At random, she chose one in the middle. After all, she figured, they ended up at the same place. In that hour of darkness, the moon seized an opportunity to make a rare, rainy night appearance, and moonbeams filtered through the trees to guide Mercy's way down the trail. She looked to the sky, thankful for the light. Thick mud from the daylong deluge covered the ground. She stumbled several times on steeper passages or exposed roots and bloodied her knees and hands.

Muddy and bloody hands and knees. Any other time, Mercy would find literary inspiration from the phrase, but she pushed away the poetic muses, Calliope and her sister, Euterpe, before they interfered in her mission. She stopped for a moment to catch her breath. She hunched over and lost her dinner in the bushes. The wind picked up and whispered, "Hurry." She stood upright and used her grimy fingers trying to wipe the rain from her face before she took off again. Mercy did not know how much farther she needed to go, but she smelled the faint salty air of the ocean and heard the swell of the waves in the distance. Under normal circumstances, those sensations delighted her. Instead, she was overcome with trepidation at what she might discover. She fell again, losing her slippers. She jumped up and continued on, leaving the slippers behind.

In the distance, a man yelled, followed by a woman's scream.

"No! No, no!" Mercy cried out. She pushed on, frantic about what might have happened. Slipping and sliding with every step, she quickened her pace. Again, the wind whipped around her, urging her on.

The trees thinned out more and more the farther she traveled down the path, until at last, she caught a small glimpse of the ocean. The bay glimmered in the moonlight and summoned her to go closer. She bolted out from the forest trail onto the beach.

Frantic, disoriented, and weary, she searched for her grandmother. A rarity in nature, a moonbow appeared in the atmosphere. The arc ended on the sandy beach, right next to her beloved grandma, still dressed in the clothing she wore at dinner. Her form stretched out motionless in the sand and Telys squatted next to her. Panic and red-hot anger swept over Mercy and she dashed toward the scene. Sand clung to the wet mud on her feet, weighing her down, but she kept going. Then she discovered a knife buried in her grandmother's side.

"What did you do to her?" Mercy screamed and charged Telys, pummeling and kicking. "You killed her! You killed her!" She punched him again, until she dropped to her knees by her grandmother and whimpered, "You killed her."

Telys kneeled in front of Mercy and grasped her shoulders, addressing her with a surprising amount of kindness. "I've only just arrived. I didn't do this, and she's not dead. But we must get her up the hill to the Tray right away. She needs to be cared for."

As he bent over to pick up Mercy's grandmother, a loud yell sounded from a trail and shocked Mercy out of her stupor.

"ARGGGHHH!" A chorus of shouting voices rang through the midnight air.

The ruckus caused Mercy to spin around. The most welcome sight of her three friends, charging out of a portal and across the sand met her eyes. They jumped on Telys, attacking him in wild abandon. She did not know how they knew where to find her, but she was grateful they cared enough to be nosy.

Telys ducked and covered his head with his arms. He rose to his feet and in the mayhem, he grabbed an elbow of both of the boys. "Hey. Hey. Stop this right now. I'm not here to hurt anyone. We need to get Mrs. Kadarius to the Tray, and we don't have much time. We have to do this together. I'm going to carry her up the hill. Phin, use your Water skills to calm the rain."

"How do you know my name?" Phin wrenched his arm free from the Metalicon's grip and backed away.

The same thought ran through Mercy's mind when she first met Telys.

Telys let go of Vesuvius, who fell when the leverage gave way. "I am familiar with many things."

Mercy also received that exact explanation before.

"Then you know I've only just begun my training and I don't know how to do what you're telling me to do," Phin said.

"I'm aware, but it's okay, simply concentrate and do your best." Telys kneeled by Grandma K and felt her forehead. "Listen, I know you all have questions, but we're in a dire emergency here, and there's little time to waste."

"Phin," Tambora said. "Why don't we use one of your crystals?"

"Tambora, I'm so glad you thought of it," Mercy said. She was apprehensive to walk up the hill in its slippery condition, not to mention a portal would get her grandmother to the Tray more quickly.

Phin rummaged through his pockets and turned them inside out. "We were in such a rush to get here, I only brought one."

Mercy's heart dropped.

Telys said, "It was a good idea, but since it's not possible, we need to get going. Twins, you can light the way. Mercy, I know you're restrained, but it is essential, now more than ever, for you to focus and try to dry up the path ahead the best you can. I don't want to slip while I'm carrying her."

Mercy nodded.

"Can we all put aside our differences and work together to accomplish this?" Telys asked.

"Yes," the children answered.

Telys picked up Grandma's still form. "Mercy, you take the lead. Tambora, you go next and light the path in front of me and push aside any tree branches in the way. Vesuvius, you follow Tambora. And Phin, take the rear. Boys, be ready to help me if necessary."

Mercy ran to the front, stared at the muddy path, and willed the wet ground to dry up. She sensed panic creep up inside her. She could not fail her grandmother. But she feared she did not possess the capability to do what Telys asked. She kept a good pace ahead of the others, trying her hardest to give them dryer ground to hike on. But Phin's inability to slow down the rainfall did not help the situation.

"Mercy, I'm slipping on all of this mud," Telys called out from behind her.

"I'm trying," Mercy shouted, struggling to be heard over the rain.

"Try harder," he yelled.

She could not figure out what to do. Desperate to make the trek easier, she thought of all the times in training when Mr. Kishan's calm voice told her to focus and breathe. She needed to succeed. She did not have a choice. She stopped in her tracks and directed her attention inward. She envisioned the mud and pictured the muck drying to solid ground. Her breaths grew heavy from all the adrenaline, but soon, calmness came over her. She mustered up as much resolution as possible and focused on the path, and the mud hardened enough to ensure Telys a steadier foot hold. Mercy did her best to ignore her victory and keep her attention on her assignment and on the earth.

All the scrapes and scratches she accumulated on her hands and legs during her trek down made their presence known. She felt her concentration give way to the stinging, and she slowed down. Going downhill seemed endless to her, but going uphill took much, much longer. Somewhere along the trail, Mercy found her slippers full of mud. They were ruined, and she contemplated leaving them behind, but her ecological conscience got the better of her and she picked them up to throw them away later. Her desire to get to the top became unbearable.

The sudden slowdown of the heavy downpour lessened her anxiety, and she doubled her efforts to dry the ground.

"Yes!" Phin shouted.

"Good job, Phin. We're almost there," Telys yelled.

Several more minutes passed before Mercy emerged onto the lawn of the Tray. Soon after, Tambora appeared, followed by Telys and the boys. Everyone broke into a run to get inside. Once there, Mercy tossed her slippers aside, not caring where they landed. She glanced around, wondering if Telys needed help to get her grandma through the rotating red door. But he was agile and strong and required no assistance.

Telys instructed Tambora to find Miss Carmen straight away, and Tambora hastened up the stairs to Miss Carmen's personal quarters. He sent Phin to gather several clean towels and asked Vesuvius to run ahead to the visitor's lounge to clear a space for Grandma K.

Mercy's breath was ragged and her heart raced for fear of what might happen, but she felt oddly numb and robotic. She followed Telys into the lounge, stood by the door, and shivered. Her long curly hair matted onto her scalp and face. Her rain-soaked robe and pajamas dripped on the floor, forming a large grimy puddle under her muddy, bare feet. But it was the same for all of them. No one took advantage of the warm, forced air of the automatic dryers inside the entrance.

Tambora and Miss Carmen rushed into the room. The headmistress hurried to assist Telys with getting Grandma Kadarius settled on the sofa. Tambora placed her arm around Mercy, who could only observe as she peeked out over the interlaced hands she held over her eyes. Vesuvius stood on her other side, acting as a guard. Mercy was touched by their support.

Undistinguishable whispers between Telys and Miss Carmen made their way to her. Telys pointed to the blade which still protruded from her grandma's side. In the hazy distance, Mercy heard him mention the term *Blade of Betrayal*. Miss Carmen gasped and said, "Are you sure?"

Telys nodded.

Miss Carmen turned toward the girls, wringing her hands. "Tambora, please get Magister Pappas, and hurry."

Tambora patted Mercy's arm and ran out. By this time, Phin arrived, carrying several large, thick bath towels, which he and Vesuvius used to dry Grandma K's legs and arms, using care to not disturb the area of her wound.

"Mercy, I'm going to contact your parents. Would you care to come with me?" Miss Carmen asked.

"No. I want to stay here with my grandma."

"All right. I'll be back shortly." Miss Carmen touched Mercy's shoulder and gave a slight nod to Telys.

Telys beckoned to Mercy. "Hold her hand and talk to her. Keep talking, even though she doesn't respond. The topic doesn't matter, she needs to hear your voice. I'm going to step out into the hall to wait for the magister. Whatever you do, don't touch the blade. Boys, why don't you have a seat by the fire to dry off and allow Mercy some space."

Mercy studied Telys as he left the room, confused by his helpfulness. She knelt beside her grandma and put a soft, but cold hand between her own. "Hey, Grandma. It appears we won't have our sleepover at all while you're on the island. I'm so sorry you got caught up in whatever is happening here." Mercy's voice cracked. "Do you want for me to sing you a song? Any requests?" Mercy hesitated, hoping for an answer. "No? How about the song you taught me when I was little? The national anthem of your home country, The Star-Spangled Banner." Mercy sang, unsteady at first, but she became stronger and more confident as she went along. When she finished, she cried and the reverberation of the splashes of her teardrops on the hardwood floor ironically echoed the hollowness inside her. "Grandma, I love you. Don't leave me. Please fight this, and next year, when I'm thirteen, I can leave Ara'Ja and we can visit the United States together, the way we always talked about." Mercy rubbed the sleepiness from her eyes. She stroked her grandma's cheeks and prayed for her to wake up. Aware of a presence nearby, Mercy glanced up to find Tambora stood next to her.

"Hey." Tambora got down on her knees beside Mercy.

"Did you find Pappas?"

"Yes. He's out in the hall speaking to Miss Carmen and Telys."

Voices filtered into the room from the hallway through the partially opened door. Mercy strained to make out their words. "Shh," she whispered to the others. "Listen."

"She should stay here. She's better off here," Miss Carmen's authoritative voice came through loud and clear.

"No. We need to get her to a medical clinic," Telys responded.

Pappas, who sounded like the voice of reason, said, "It is safer for her to stay here. We cannot be sure he will not try again."

Telys raised his voice. "She was already staying here and look what happened."

"Telys, she departed the grounds of the Tray on her own accord," Pappas said. "This cannot be blamed on anyone here."

The children jumped at the sudden loud thud on the wall.

"Telys, putting a hole in the wall isn't helping the situation," Miss Carmen said. "She's not able to go anywhere tonight. She's not well enough. Besides, the portals to and from the island are closed down, and there aren't many physicians on Ara'Ja capable of treating humans."

"So, we're doing this on our own?" Telys sounded frantic.

"Yes," said Pappas.

"Have you ever performed anything like this before?" The tightness of Telys' voice gave away his anxious state of mind.

"No," Pappas replied.

From his admission, Mercy lost what little confidence she carried and, in a panic, looked to her friends hoping for reassurance.

Tambora put her arm around Mercy. "She'll be okay."

Miss Carmen spoke. "Telys, there is no one on Ara'Ja who is more capable than Pelagius. You know I'm right. She couldn't be in better hands."

"Okay. Then let's do it and get it over with," Telys snapped.

"This makes no sense. Why does Telys care so much?" Mercy murmured to Tambora.

Tambora shrugged. "I don't know. He probably feels responsible because he found her."

"This is all my fault." Mercy wrung her hands together. "She specifically asked me not to say she was coming here. She even mentioned an enemy."

"Mercy, it's not your fault. The blame belongs to one person. The person who attacked her," Tambora said. "I hope you know I didn't betray your confidence."

"I know. It was CJ. She told her parents. They must've talked. I know it."

The door swung fully open and the three adults entered the room, their somberness corroborated the seriousness of the situation. Miss Carmen spoke first. "Mercy, I attempted to call your parents, but apparently, all communication and portals coming in and going out of the island have been temporarily shut down. We're not able to contact them right now, and we also can't get your grandmother home to Crete for better medical treatment. We must take care of this ourselves. Please don't fret. Magister Pappas has the most extensive knowledge of anyone I've ever met. I am entirely comfortable leaving this in his hands."

"They're not coming?" Mercy sniffled.

"Not right now. I'm sorry, my dear," Miss Carmen said.

"Why are the portals shut down? When will they be up again?"

"I don't know. The shutdown appears to have happened suddenly a few hours ago. Only communications and travel between the island and elsewhere on earth are affected. I first learned about it when I tried to call your parents. Obviously, I couldn't get through, but I'll keep trying."

Mercy took in a deep breath to relax and wondered why the adults appeared fretful about how to extract the blade. In her mind, the solution should have been easy. "Why can't we just pull out the knife?"

"There are a few reasons," Pappas said. "One of which is withdrawing an object embedded this deeply into a human will cause massive bleeding. But this is a Blade of Betrayal, and it is infused with a potent, unnatural poison which will spread throughout the victim if allowed to remain too long. This poison is as dangerous to anyone who attempts to extract the blade. We must be cautious."

The new information caused Mercy more panic than ever. Her shoulders drooped under the weight of all her worry. "What is a Blade of Betrayal?" she asked.

Telys kneeled next to Mercy and took her hands between his own. "A Blade of Betrayal is a dagger forged by Metal and Fire skills for the sole purpose of using it on someone close to you."

Vesuvius gasped and plopped down next to Telys. "Whoa. That's low."

"How can you tell that's what this is?" Tambora asked.

Telys stood and addressed the children. "Some creations carry a branding caused by the intent of the element user." He pointed out a small marking on the handle of the knife.

"It doesn't look like anything. It's like a child's scribble. An accidental doodle," said Phin.

"It *is* accidental. This isn't done purposefully. It's caused by a link between the mindset of the maker and the creation. A byproduct, you could say. Few weapons can be created by this type of act, but a Blade of Betrayal is one."

"Does this mean someone betrayed my grandma?" Mercy's voice trembled.

"Unfortunately, it does," Pappas said.

Mercy's breath caught. Who would want to hurt her grandmother? The culprit could be anyone. Her grandmother told her she knew people on the island, but she did not identify them.

"Tambora," Pappas said. "Will you please retrieve a pair of silicone oven mitts and a pot of water from the kitchen?"

"Yes, sir." Tambora scurried away.

Miss Carmen pulled a large ring of keys from her pocket and chose one. "Phin, Vesuvius, here's a key to my office. There's a bottle of whiskey on a cart in my cupboard—"

"Oh, we know where you keep it." Vesuvius jumped to his feet.

Miss Carmen scowled. "Just go get it. We can use it as an antiseptic."

"Antiseptic?" Mercy asked.

"It's a product with cleansing properties humans use to reduce the risk of infection. Alcohol works." Miss Carmen pulled a single key from the ring.

Phin took the key and said, "You can count on us, ma'am."

The boys ran from the room, the sounds of their footsteps echoed into the lobby, leaving a silence to settle in the lounge. The few minutes her friends were gone felt equal to two lifetimes to Mercy. She continued to sit on the floor by the sofa and whispered words of encouragement into her grandmother's ear as she watched Telys pace. His actions confused her.

The first to return, Tambora set the pot of water down and handed the oven mitts to Pappas before she withdrew to stand close to the door.

Pappas patted Mercy on the shoulder and asked her to move over. He knelt down and studied the blade and the entry wound, then addressed the still unresponsive older woman. "Yvonne, I am Pelagius Pappas. You may remember me as a friend of Emzlie and Orion from years ago. In a few minutes, we will remove this blade from your side. I will not lie to you, this will probably hurt like the dickens, but I will do my best to keep you comfortable. Your granddaughter and s—" Pappas paused and cleared his throat. "Your granddaughter is here. She will be out in the hall during the procedure, but once we are finished, she will be back by your side."

"No," Mercy objected. "I'm staying here."

Pappas looked at Mercy straight on. His stare did not waver, and she knew hers flashed with challenge. "You *will* go into the hall," he insisted.

Mercy opened her mouth to protest, but Phin burst into the room, interrupting her. He carried a bottle, which he handed over to Miss Carmen.

Vesuvius followed Phin and gave back the key. "It's all locked up tight, Miss Carmen."

"Thank you, boys." Miss Carmen set the bottle down next to Pappas. "Kids, let's go out to the hall and let the men get to work." She shifted closer to the door, but stopped short of exiting. "And let's get this straight. We are not letting the men get to work because they are men. They are simply the most qualified." Miss Carmen straightened her posture and hustled Phin and the twins toward the door. She beckoned to Mercy. "Come, child."

"I can't. I need to stay here."

"Mercy, there's going to be some conversation in here you might find disturbing. It's really for the best to allow them to discuss their course of action without worrying about how you're affected. Understand?"

Mercy sighed, nodded, and followed Miss Carmen out.

Behind her, she overheard Pappas ask, "How did you get to this side of the island?"

"I used a portal crystal, of course," Telys replied.

"Why did you not use one to bring her to the Tray grounds instead of traipsing up the hill? You could have saved a lot of time in getting her here."

"I didn't have any more with me."

"Precisely how did you expect to leave without a second crystal?" said Pappas.

"My sources told me he would try something tonight and where they thought he was going. In my hurry to get there, I only grabbed one. And I obviously arrived too late."

Miss Carmen shut the door with a firm tug. This ruined any chance for Mercy to catch more of what went on inside. She changed tactics to concentrate on figuring out what happened to her grandmother.

According to Telys, a man attacked her grandma. Unless Telys lied to Pappas.

The lounge door opened and Pappas stepped out. The occupants of the hall paused their conversations, seeming to expect news, although only a minute passed since they departed the room themselves. He cleared his throat. "Um, Telys wanted a minute alone with Yvonne."

Mercy grimaced. What did Telys want with her grandmother? She was not quite ready to give him the benefit of a doubt. "Why? He's a Metalicon. Isn't he the enemy? Won't he try to hurt her more?" Mercy lunged toward the door.

Pappas caught her by the wrist. "You will need to speak to *him* on the subject. But, no. He will not hurt her. He is helping to save her, remember?" He let go of Mercy and crossed his arms.

Mercy could not argue his point. Telys was full of mystery. But yet, for unknown reasons, she was compelled to believe the magister. And, in her hour of need, she saw no other options except to trust, not only him, but the others as well. She sat down, closed her eyes, and rested her head against the wall. She remembered all the times Mr. Kishan told her to breathe, so she did. Mercy's muddled mind cleared, and she thought with coherence for the first time in what seemed like hours. She came to one conclusion. Someone, probably the Olivers, knew her grandma was visiting Ara'Ja and told the one person her grandma did not want to know. A wickedness was afoot. She resolved to bring the evil into the open. Mercy counted on one hand the number of people she told, CJ and Tambora. If anyone were to ask her, she would say, in all honesty, neither would be capable of betraying her—at least not intentionally—although, CJ said she told her parents. But they were deep underground at the Chomolhari Summit and almost unreachable. But then, not so unreachable that CJ could not contact them. And if CJ could call them, they surely could also call out. Additionally, CJ also told her they acted weird when she mentioned the visit. Mercy needed to think about the ramifications of those facts.

She drifted off to sleep while reflecting on CJ's parents, and fifteen minutes later, Mercy awoke to an empty, quiet hall. She tried to walk and realized her feet did not touch the ground. She called out for Tambora, but received no response. She tried to call for the others. No answer. She drifted toward the lounge, opened the door bit by bit, and peeked in. Her grandmother sat upright on the sofa, her legs stretched out on the seat cushions and her side toward Mercy. She stared straight ahead with her hands folded in her lap. Her lips quivered. "I know you had him killed."

"Who killed who, Grandma?" Mercy asked and proceeded closer.

Grandma slowly lifted her arm to point toward the end of the sofa. "He killed my Augustus."

Mercy gasped and followed her grandmother's gaze, eager to discover who cut short her grandfather's life. But before she learned who stood there, she was sucked through the door, plunked down, and returned to her sleeping position in the hall.

CHAPTER 22

THE ABANDONED PUPPET

Hushed whispers woke Mercy. She opened her eyes to a blurry head hovering mere inches from her own.

"Hey. You woke up." Vesu's face came into focus.

Mercy turned away, her voice shaky. "Who wouldn't with you breathing in their face like that. What's going on?"

"Pappas and Telys are in with Grandma K, discussing the procedure," Tambora said.

"So, nothing's been done yet?" Mercy stood.

"No. You've only been asleep for all of ten minutes," Phin said.

Pappas stuck his head out of the lounge door. "Carmen, can you come in? We need a third person after all."

Miss Carmen nodded toward Mercy. "I think Mercy is capable to assist. She wants to be with her grandmother."

Pappas glanced at Mercy and back to Miss Carmen. "I will take your word for it," he said, but his eyes betrayed his apprehension.

Mercy gulped. She wanted to be in there, but fearfulness consumed her. Fear that she might make a mistake. And fear she would witness her grandmother's suffering, or even worse, her death.

Mercy reached out to Tambora for comfort and guidance, and Tambora did not disappoint. She took hold of Mercy's hands and whispered, "You can do this. Pappas and Telys will be right there, doing the hard part. They only need you to assist them."

Mercy blinked away her tears and gave Tambora's hands a slight squeeze. "I'm coming," she told Pappas and followed him into the room.

Telys crouched in the corner, gathering plants with yellow flowers from a planter there. Pappas explained Telys used his Earth skills to grow more of the plant, called yarrow. They planned to grind the blooms and add hot water to make a poultice. Yarrow was a natural way to stop bleeds and draw out infection. Pappas held high hopes the properties would also work on poison in the same manner. Pappas instructed Mercy to cut several strips of gauze while Telys pulverized the yarrow into powder. As she worked, Mercy began a tentative conversation with Telys. "I didn't realize you have Earth skills. You obviously have Metal, and I know you have Fire because you made a glow bubble for me the other day. Do you have Water and Wind too?"

Pappas raised his brows, but wordlessly continued his task and Mercy realized he probably knew nothing of her previous dealings with the Metalicons.

"No. Just the two and Metal. It's very rare to have all four, as you know." Telys did not appear to notice Mercy's mouth drop open. It always surprised her to discover what people knew about her. Telys held his hands over the pot of water Tambora took in earlier and blasted the pan with heat until the water boiled. "Mercy, could you please grab one of those teacups from the tea set on the cabinet?"

Mercy retrieved the cup for Telys. He dipped it into the hot water and poured the liquid into the yarrow powder to make the poultice. He then soaked the strips of gauze with the poultice, while Pappas dipped a towel into the steamy water.

Pappas wadded a clean towel under her grandma where the blade protruded and poured Miss Carmen's whiskey over the wound. "Mercy, can you handle this? Once we get started here, we can not stop to attend to any other situation which might arise."

Mercy gulped. Although unsure of how she might react to the procedure, she did not want to leave the room. "I'm good."

"Telys, I am ready to begin. Mercy, can you step back a bit, please?" Pappas put on the silicone oven mitts and took hold of the blade handle.

Telys held a second towel, ready to wrap the dagger once it was out. Mercy stood against the wall, far enough away to not be in danger of exposure and close enough to help when the time came. Her job was to hand the gauze strips to Pappas one at a time the moment his hands were free. It seemed like it took an eternity for Pappas to get the knife out, and Mercy grew antsy. She put her weight on one leg, then switched to the other and back again. Grandma K moaned. Mercy was sickened to know her grandmother experienced pain.

"This knife does not want to budge," said Pappas. "I am going to have to pull harder. Be ready."

Pappas tugged at the blade with more intensity, until finally, the knife popped free. The sudden release of resistance loosened the magister's grip on the blade. It flew out of his hand, whizzing past Mercy's ear to lodge in the wall behind her. Mercy gasped at the close encounter, but remained helpless as she watched blood pouring out of Grandma's wound. She stood, unable to budge, and unable to pull her eyes away from her grandmother. Pappas took off the mitts and covered the gap left by the blade with the towel he soaked in the hot water.

"Mercy." She heard him call to her, but she still could not move. "Mercy, now!"

"I... uh..."

"Mercy," Telys whispered into Mercy's ear. "Give me the poultice and come away from the blade." With a gentle touch, he opened her hands. Taking the bowl from her, he steered her in the opposite direction of where the blade jutted out of the wall. In two steps, he reached Pappas and handed him strips of soaked gauze for packing into the wound.

Propped up against the opposite wall as though she were a marionette abandoned by her puppeteer, Mercy stayed immobile while they bandaged up her grandmother.

Pappas checked Grandma K's pulse and addressed Mercy. "Her pulse is strong. We have done all we can. Miss Carmen or I will have to change her packing every three to four hours. It may take a few days for the poison to work itself out of her system. Telys assured me there will be plenty of yarrow available to make the poultice. Did you take notice while he made it?"

Mercy nodded, too ashamed to speak.

"Can I count on you to keep a bowl of poultice and gauze made? We do not want to waste time whenever we come in to change the bandaging."

Mercy nodded again.

"Are you sure?" His voice was harsh.

"Pelagius, there's no need—" Telys said as he pulled the blade from the wall and wrapped it in a towel.

"Yes." Mercy was surprised at the meekness of her tone. She was deflated. She was not a hero. She was a failure. She could not even hand over a bowl of goop during a crisis.

She fled the room. Her loyal friends stood at the sight of her.

Tambora approached Mercy and hugged her. "How did it go?"

As always, Pappas's timing was perfect. He rushed from the lounge, carrying the towel-wrapped blade and gave a hardened glare in Mercy's direction before he walked away.

Mercy teared up. "I froze."

"Oh, sweetie." Tambora stroked Mercy's hair.

"It wasn't so bad." Telys emerged into the hall. "And it all worked out okay. Don't beat yourself up over it, Mercy."

Mercy's shoulders sagged. An expression of concern came over Telys and he made a step toward Mercy, but Miss Carmen's arm swung into his stomach, akin to a door slamming in the face of an unwanted visitor.

"Thank you for your help, Telys. I'm sure Mercy is grateful. But don't you have somewhere you need to be now?" Miss Carmen gave a nod toward the Tray exit.

Telys's nostrils flared. "Yes. I suppose I do. Mercy, I'll come by in a few days to check on you and your grandmother."

Mercy nodded, but Miss Carmen said, "I don't think that will be necessary, but the sentiment is appreciated. I'll see you out." Miss Carmen pulled a hanky from her skirt pocket and opened it up to reveal a crystal. "Take this crystal outside and portal back to wherever it is you call home."

Telys took the crystal and flipped it into the air, catching it in the palm of his hand. "Mighty kind of you. I'll be off now."

As Miss Carmen escorted Telys to the lobby, Mercy realized she forgot to thank him. She did not think about it for long, though. She knew her grandmother was alone and rushed to her side. She sat vigilant through the night, clutching her grandma's hand and singing the gentle songs they sang together when she was little. The procedure performed earlier was successful. But Grandma remained unresponsive except for a slight moan here and there. Mercy stared into the fireplace, getting lost in the flicker and crackle of the flames as they toiled to consume the pile of firewood. She tried to make sense of all the occurrences of that evening. She was concerned about giving up the care of her grandmother to people who could be untrustworthy. Although, she believed their caregiving was authentic. What puzzled her the most was the Metalicon. She was baffled by his interest in her and her grandmother. Her basic instinct was to be wary of Telys, but she found him irresistible and charming. Even though she did not understand what it was, there was something about him she suspected she could rely on. But then again, there were other traits about him she detested. He was a Metalicon who stole electricity from the Tray to retrieve the Fire orb. He was an enigma to her.

Light snores arose from the thick-cushioned easy chair placed next to the fireplace across the room, pulling Mercy out of her musings. Tambora insisted on staying with her. But she did not make it past three o'clock before she wrapped herself up in a warm chenille blanket and passed out, leaving Mercy alone to guard over her grandmother. Mercy did not mind. It meant she did not need to make small talk and also gave her private time to keep poultice on hand and be alone with her thoughts.

The hours which remained of the night passed slowly, as do most painful situations. The time was broken only by Pappas and Miss Carmen who arrived every hour to change the dressing. Mercy thought about the dream she experienced earlier. She wished she knew who her grandmother suspected of killing her grandfather. That disclosure would make an interesting ending to the story she wanted to write. She found paper and pencils inside a drawer of a writing desk by a window. She made use of the time by penning an outline of her grandparents' story as she sang quietly to her grandmother. Long after she ran out of songs to sing or uncertainties to probe, a single ray of sunlight streamed into the room. The beam carried the promise of a fresh new day after the lengthy stormy night.

There was a gentle rap on the door. It creaked open and the good-natured countenance of Miss Birdie poked around the corner. "Wonderful, you're up and about. Are you hungry? I have breakfast for you and Tambora," she said.

Mercy smiled at the older woman. "No, not really. But I might be soon."

"How about I just bring it in and leave it for you to have whenever you're ready?"

Mercy nodded. "Perfect. Thank you."

"And how's Grandma doing this morning?"

"I—" Mercy gave her frail grandmother a wistful glance. "I don't really know. She's still out. But I don't think she has a fever."

"Aye, that is a good sign, a very good sign." Miss Birdie, as usual, was compassionate and encouraging. She had her grumpy moments, as Mercy witnessed the day she called her parents. "Do you need me to bring you anything?"

"No, thank you, Miss Birdie."

"All right, dear, I'll leave you be." Miss Birdie headed for the door. "I'll check in on you later."

Mercy intended to wait for Tambora to wake up before she ate. She twiddled her thumbs as the sunlight advanced fully into the room, brightening every corner. Tambora slept on. The savory aroma drifted from the breakfast tray and made its way through her nose and down to her stomach, which growled at being ignored. Mercy crossed her legs, stared at her friend, and frowned. She checked the time on the old mantel clock over the fireplace and her heart dropped. Only fifteen minutes passed since Miss Birdie excused herself.

"That's it," Mercy said to herself. "I'm not waiting any longer." She lifted the lid on the breakfast tray, discovering the reason for the delicious smells. A good old-fashioned breakfast of bacon, eggs, and croissants with strawberries and cream greeted her. Mercy's stomach did a little happy dance in anticipation. She snatched a slice of bacon and guzzled down the deliciousness to dispel the literal illness which might get tossed up if she waited to eat.

"I was wondering how long it would take you to eat without me."

Mercy's hand, stuffed with more bacon, froze midway to her mouth. "You were awake this whole time, letting me famish?" Mercy asked Tambora.

Tambora sat up in the chair and folded the throw blanket. "Apparently, you're not too starved," she laughed. She grabbed a tray and sat on the floor next to Mercy. "Your grandma looks much better this morning. Has Pappas or Miss Carmen been here recently?"

"No. It's been a while. I imagine one of them will be by shortly," Mercy said, licking the bacon grease from her fingers.

"You seem better today, too. Did you get any sleep?" Tambora asked.

"No. But I feel better. I thought about what you said at dinner, about my wanting to be an author. You were right. I should be writing. That's what I did most of the night. I started working on my novel."

"That's wonderful, the one about your grandparents' meeting?" Tambora asked.

"Yes. I'm going to write a little each night. Hey. I wanted to ask you something last night, but didn't get a chance. How did you guys find out I was down at the beach? I was surprised to see you. Relieved, but surprised."

"A Situation Clock woke me up."

"That's how I learned about it, too."

Voices approached from the hall and the door whipped open. Miss Carmen and Pappas swept into the room, appearing peppy and bright-eyed. It was quite an achievement, considering they were up most of the night, rotating in and out of the lounge to clean and dress Grandma K's wounds.

"Harmony and balance, girls," Miss Carmen said.

"Good morning, Miss Carmen," Mercy and Tambora stated in unison.

"How is our patient this morning?" Pappas asked.

"I think she's doing well," Mercy said. "She still hasn't woken up though."

"That is to be expected. I notice her color is returning. A good sign she is not fighting infection," Pappas said.

Miss Carmen kneeled beside Grandma K. "Ladies, the magister and I are here to change the bandaging. You should finish eating elsewhere."

Tambora jumped up and held out her hands to Mercy to assist her. "Let's use this time to go to wash up."

"You always have the best ideas," Mercy laughed.

"You're laughing. It's a delightful sound," said Tambora.

Miss Carmen and Pappas were almost finished when Mercy and Tambora returned.

"Her progress is satisfactory," Pappas said. "We will continue to check in throughout the day, but try to keep things quiet in here. She needs her rest." Pappas cleared his throat. "Uh, Mercy, you did an outstanding job of caregiving during the night. Keep it up."

"I will," Mercy said. She knew the compliment was the magister's way of apologizing for his earlier behavior. Bit by bit, the heaviness on her shoulders lessened.

"Mercy," Miss Carmen said. "All communication and access portals to the island are still down. But I'll continue to try your parents."

"Thank you, Miss Carmen. Thank you both." Mercy fought back tears. She was touched by the help Miss Carmen and Pappas provided, but she needed her parents. Grandma needed her daughter.

Mercy and Tambora took their trays to sit on the window seat to finish breakfast. Heated by the autumn sun, the seat cushions comforted Mercy. She lifted her head to bask in the coziness. The warm rays wrapped around her, thawing out her bones. It felt heavenly after the cold, wet night. "I could sit here for hours," she said.

Tambora said. "When I grow up, my entire house is going to be made of windows with window seats, so I can sit in the sun and gaze out over the mountains and the ocean."

Mercy sighed. "I think I'll move in."

"Anytime." Tambora giggled.

"Hi, Mercy." A hesitant voice came from the doorway. "Can we talk alone for a minute?" CJ walked over to the window where Mercy and Tambora sat.

"I'll take these dishes to the kitchen," Tambora said. She gathered up the trays and left the room.

"Harmony and balance, CJ." Mercy stared out of the window, her palm resting on the glass and her lips pressed firmly together. She could think of nothing more to say to CJ.

"Mercy, I wanted to tell you how sorry I am about your grandma."

Mercy spied a flock of birds flying over the bay. She studied them to keep from addressing CJ. The lead bird played its part, sailing up and down amongst the clouds. The others followed suit, creating a dark, moving ripple across the sky. In that moment, her fascination for nature served as a distraction from the surrounding unpleasantness.

CJ continued. "I mean, it's just terrible, what happened to her. How could anyone attack an old lady?"

Mercy spun toward CJ, her face set as a stone. "I asked you not to talk about her visit. The wrong person found out she was here, and you're the only one who told someone."

"How did you reach that outcome? A whole cafeteria full of students and staff saw her here at dinner last night. It could've been any of them."

Mercy's mouth opened to speak and closed it again. That thought never occurred to her. She thought hard about how to keep her opinions intact while still conceding to CJ's point. In the end, she did not have the energy to continue the fight. "You're right. I jumped to conclusions. I'm sorry."

"That's okay. I hope your grandma gets better."

"Thank you." Mercy was not fully ready to surrender her theory and turned again to the window. The birds apparently made it across the harbor and were gone from sight.

"Do you need anything from the room?"

"No. Tambora's going to go up later and get me a change of clothes."

"Okay. Harmony and balance, Mercy." CJ sounded dejected.

"Bye."

"Oh. I almost forgot." CJ pulled something from her pocket and held it out to Mercy. "Tambora told me you buried these by the garden bench. I thought I would dig them up for you. I'll take them to the kitchen staff tonight at dinner, and hopefully, they can put him together."

A single sob escaped from Mercy's lips as she reached out and stroked the broken pieces in CJ's hand.

"I'll see you later, Mercy." CJ exited the room, leaving Mercy to wonder why she could not live up to her own name. She was hesitant to forget about the incident with CJ, and something still felt off. Her roommate was too quick to act like they were friends and that she did not just go berserk on Mercy the day before.

A few minutes later, Tambora reentered the room and Mercy wiped away all signs of weeping. She was weary of continual crying in front of her friend. Her genuine friend. "Hey. I have some good news," Mercy said.

Tambora lit up. "Did Grandma K wake up?"

Mercy heaved a sigh. "No. Not that good. But still good. CJ dug up the pieces of Loy-Roy and is taking them down to the kitchen staff."

Tambora's mouth dropped open. "Well. That explains that."

"Explains what?"

"Nothing, forget it. I'm happy for you and I hope they can get him fixed."

"So do I, but isn't there some kind of best friend code you're breaking by not telling me what you meant? You've played that card on me several times."

"Hmm. You got me there. Well. Earlier, CJ asked me about you and your grandma and I mentioned I was going to go out to the bench later today to dig up the pieces. Phin and Vesu just came in from outside. They were out by the garden and noticed a hole in the ground where we buried them."

"So, she was trying to get in my good graces, then," Mercy said

"Most likely," said Tambora.

"Looks like I'll just have to keep my wits about me," said Mercy.

———————————◆———————————

Phin and Vesuvius showed up to the lounge late that morning with board games in hand. "We thought we could help keep you occupied," Vesuvius said.

"Great idea. We need to keep it quiet, though," Mercy said.

"No problem." Phin put the games on a table across the room from where Mercy's grandmother lay. "We'll play over here to keep the noise down."

"At some point, I think we need to make a chart of everything we know, so maybe we can make sense out of it all," Mercy said as they set up for their first game of Clue. "But not here, not now. Later, when we're not in such a public place."

"It'll be like a real-life game of Clue," Tambora said. "I'll get a poster board and markers."

"And I'll get a big bag of M&M's from the commissary for us to share," Vesuvius said.

Tambora smirked. "I'll hang on to that for you when you get one or it'll be gone before the rest of us ever get the chance to have any."

Vesuvius grinned. "You're probably right."

They spent the rest of the morning playing games as hushed as they could. It was not too difficult to keep the noise level down. They were all in a somber mood. The kind you get when something dreadful has happened. But it's hopeful, because the worst was over and light filtered in from the end of the tunnel.

Tambora pulled Scrabble out of the pile of games. "Let's do this one next."

Everyone agreed, and they each selected their letter tiles for the first play.

"You guys, do you realize I haven't even been here four months? It feels as though it was such a long time ago when I arrived." Mercy played her first word. Singer.

"Hey. Check this out," Vesuvius said. "I can spell DeLuca."

He rotated his letter rack and showed the others. The letters slid off and spread out onto the table when he swung around the wooden holder around.

The edges of Mercy's vision blurred and blackness formed a faded-out frame around what she saw on the tabletop. To her surprise, the little tiles grew stick legs and arms and ran around. One waved at her. She smiled, returning the greeting. Mesmerized, Mercy observed their play until she grew tired of their antics and blew them down. When they fell, the letters were rearranged to spell C-A-U-D-E-L. Mercy blinked, and the display returned to normal with the tiles spilled out on the table in their original position.

Vesuvius swept the tiles toward himself and reached to pick them up.

"Wait," Mercy said.

"What is it?" Tambora asked.

"Look." Mercy pulled the letters to the center of the table and rearranged them in the sequence as shown to her in her vision.

Phin spelled out the letters. "C-A-U-D-E-L."

"Caudel? As in High Elder Nathaniel Caudel? The one who probably murdered High Elder Broomfield?" Vesuvius frowned. "I don't get it."

Mercy wore her patience thin, similar to a balloon stretched to its limit, straining to not burst. "Come on, guys. Look again." She switched the tiles to Vesu's original arrangement. "DeLuca. Caudel."

"It's an anagram," Phin said.

"Yes." Mercy knew Phin would be the first to catch on. "I wonder if there's a connection."

"You mean, Miss Carmen's real last name could be Caudel and not DeLuca? Why would she change it?" Phin asked.

"Obviously, she doesn't want to be associated with the Caudel rumors," Vesuvius said.

Mercy jumped up. "Vesu, you're a genius!"

"I am?" Vesu's cheeks grew red.

Mercy sat down and continued. "Remember Miss Carmen's wedding photo? Don't you think the man in her photo could be a young High Elder Caudel?"

Tambora's mouth fell open. "Oh no. No, no!"

"What is it, Tambora?" Vesu said.

"I'm pretty sure the guy in Miss Carmen's photo was an apprentice in the photo with your Uncle Atticus. High Elder Caudel was in that photo. She must've been married to him. She's not disassociating herself, she's working undercover for the Metalicons. It really could have been Caudel who killed Broomfield."

Mercy frowned and rubbed her forehead. "But Uncle Atticus told us it couldn't have been High Elder Caudel. His brother was Broomfield's assistant who was also killed. And brothers don't kill brothers. That's what my uncle said. He specifically emphasized that statement. I need to see him again. He's not even aware my grandma's here and has been injured. We need answers right away, especially since Miss Carmen is helping to take care of her. His early return is perfect timing. Phin, do you have a couple of portal crystals I can use?"

"Mercy, it's Saturday. The Assembly is probably closed," Tambora said.

"If he's not there, I'll go to his apartment. I have his address," Mercy said. "While I'm gone, one of you needs to stay with Grandma at all times. Promise me you will not leave her on her own for any reason. Allow no one but one of us to be alone with her."

"We've got this, Mercy, you won't need to worry." Phin stood and stepped toward the hallway. "I'll go get a couple of crystals for you."

"Thanks, Phin."

"What do we do if we're told to leave the room?" Vesuvius asked.

"Don't. Just ask them to wait for me. I shouldn't be gone long."

"Do you want me to come with you, Mercy?" Tambora asked.

"No. I really would feel better if you stayed here with my grandma, if that's okay."

"Of course, it is."

"Tambora, you're in charge," Mercy said. "Vesu, you're Tambora's assistant."

Vesuvius saluted. "Aye, aye, Captain, my captain."

"I'm counting on you guys." Mercy said as she hustled out and into the lobby to wait for Phin.

CHAPTER 23

THE EYES IN THE MIRROR

Mercy scampered to the maze, keeping the two portal crystals from Phin tucked safely in the pocket of her vintage houndstooth jacket. Once inside the maze and away from onlookers, she pulled one out, tossed it, declaring she wanted to go to the Assembly in Nikonea City. She knew the Assembly might be closed. To ward off intruders, portals did not function when entering a locked building. In fact, a portal would not materialize at all to anyone requesting to enter a locked building. But a waterfall portal appeared before her, so she could enter the Assembly. She dashed through and ended up in the empty Assembly lobby. She thought it was odd that the building was open with no one there. Mercy glimpsed a brightness in her peripheral vision. She turned to see the Emissary go around a corner and out of view. She ran after it but when she reached the corner, it was gone. She searched several corridors. However, the creature was nowhere in sight. Discouraged, she returned to the main lobby and tried the doors that led to the outside. They were locked. She was locked in. Mercy was perplexed by the fact she could portal into the locked building. But as the past few weeks taught her, normalcy sometimes took a hike when she was involved. She reasoned she most likely portaled into the building because the Emissary willed it to happen. In other circumstances, she might have panicked to not be able to leave, but she still held one crystal she could use to portal out of the building if she could not get out the usual way. Then she would walk to her uncle's apartment. The last time she went to his residence to visit him, she was with her Grandpa Kadarius. Uncle Atticus still lived in Athlenan, not too far from her own home, but he moved to an apartment in Nikonea City when he became High Elder. She saw his address on the business card he gave to her when she was in his office. She was happy it was a short walk. All the apartments in Nikonea City were known for their modernity and sophistication. And most residents of the city were people similar to the St. Clair family. Social, elegant, poised, and filled with self-assurance. Her uncle unquestionably made a successful transition from small town to high society.

Mercy hoped she could find an open exit when she was ready to leave, because if it was necessary to use her remaining crystal to get out, she would not have one to return to the Tray. But more important matters first, she thought. She needed to find out if her uncle was in his office. She stood at the lobby portal to the 117th floor where the High Elder's office was located. She waited, and the portal did not open. She unsuccessfully declared her destination. She could not figure out how to make it activate, then realized the inside portals must be deactivated when the Assembly was closed. She tugged at the doors of every audio communication booth she could find, but they were all locked up for the weekend. She scrutinized the grand staircase at the end of the lobby. She possessed no aspirations for trudging up 117 floors and she opted to explore for other exits. Mercy wandered the halls of the main floor and pulled at all the doors, but they were locked up tight. She came to a cross hall, but she grew tired and elected to backtrack before she portaled out. She thought she was alone in the building and jumped in surprise when voices sounded from around the corner. She recognized one as Telys.

"We have the Fire orb in our possession and we have solid leads on the others," said Telys.

"Excellent. I want them located and acquired within the next year."

Mercy was shocked to realize the second voice belonged to her Uncle Atticus. She was puzzled to discover him with Telys and she could not imagine how they were acquainted. But Telys seemed to know several people, which was likely the reason he was always aware of everyone's situations. She-moved to an alcove and made herself as small as she could to keep out of sight.

"Carmen is close to uncovering the truth about her husband's death," Telys said.

"No matter. We have control of the Fire orb, there is no longer a use for her. I'm sure you can think of a way to put an end to her theories of conspiracy," said Atticus.

Mercy's jaw dropped. Was Telys working with her uncle against Miss Carmen? Nothing added up. She was more confused than ever.

"I'll see what I can do. There are still those in Vatek who are scheming to get out. If they do, Mercy will be their first target."

Mercy perked up, surprised and alarmed at the mention of her name and even more alarmed to hear someone in Vatek was still after her. It could only be Azrael.

"I knew this would be a distinct possibility," Atticus said.

"We may still need Carmen to monitor Mercy."

"Yes, yes. I'm mindful of all of this, but I have others in place for that purpose. Carmen is redundant at this point."

"Maybe we should just tell Mercy the truth," Telys said.

Mercy's head jerked up. What was the truth? Why did all the adults have a problem with her?

"We don't want to involve her at this point if we don't have to," Atticus said.

"I agree, but you know it's inevitable. After all, Mercy was basically created for this precise purpose."

The voices and footsteps grew near to where Mercy hid, but stopped short of rounding the corner.

"Don't make the mistake of thinking I've forgotten. But it's not the right time," said Atticus.

Mercy struggled to keep from gasping out loud. Were they trying to protect her or hurt her? She looked for a hasty retreat. She did not want to hear any more. She did not want to find out what she was created for. She simply wanted to come from the love of her parents. Were they involved at all? She did not think such a possibility would even exist.

However, she realized several times over the past weeks, situations were not always as they seemed. She tiptoed back to the lobby, her heart and soul weighed down by what she overheard. She tossed the remaining portal crystal and gave the Tray as her destination. The portal opened just outside the red door of the Tray. Mercy darted into the building with no cares about who might see her. Her sobs and groans provided a feeble outlet for the brokenness she suffered. She proceeded straight to the staircase and sprinted up two steps at a time. Miss Carmen, who was in the lobby with a couple of students, jumped when Mercy dashed in and called after her to wait. Mercy ignored the command and kept climbing. She reached her quarters in record time and slammed the door behind her.

CJ looked up from the book on her lap. "What's wrong with you?"

"Out!" Mercy screamed.

"Why would you talk to me like that? I just did you a big favor with those pieces of that Petit Serveur you loved so much."

"Out!" Mercy yelled again and pointed toward the door. "And the only reason you dug up those pieces was because you overheard Tambora say she was going to do it and you wanted to get to it first."

"Okay, okay. I'm leaving. Don't get in such a snit about it." CJ hurried out and slammed the door with a passion equal to Mercy's.

Mercy threw herself to the ground, spread out on her stomach, and buried her nose in her elbow. She no longer wanted to be a pawn in anyone's convoluted war. Not for the Metalicons. Not for Telys. Not for the staff at the Tray. Not even for her parents or Atticus. She could not grasp who schemed with who anymore. The only ones who were faithful to her all along were her grandmother, Tambora, Vesuvius, and Phin. Mercy remained in her curled-up position for almost a half an hour until a soft rap sounded on the door.

"Go away," she moaned. "No one's here."

"Mercy, it's me, Tambora. Can I come in?"

"No."

"Please? Don't make me invoke best friend code number fifteen that states a best friend is required to be present during all personal crises."

Mercy knew to quibble with Tambora was useless. She gave in to save herself the hassle and energy it took to have an argument. "Okay. Just for a bit." She sat up when Tambora entered, aware of how she must look. Her eyelids were swollen and uncomfortable. She also knew, from previous bouts of prolonged weeping, her cheeks were splotchy and her nose and upper lip were enormous and red.

Tambora seemed stunned at Mercy's appearance, but she was quick to correct her expression. Mercy was grateful for the reprieve. She did not need to discuss matters as trivial as her snotty nose. "Miss Carmen told me you were upset and might need a friend. What happened?" Tambora dug into her pocket and pulled out a tissue. She handed it to Mercy. "Did you get to see your uncle to tell him Miss Carmen's real name?"

Mercy blew her nose. "Yes, well, no. I didn't get to actually see him. It's more that I overheard him. He was with Telys. And I couldn't ask about Miss Carmen because I couldn't let them discover I was there. They talked about how Miss Carmen wasn't needed, now that the Fire orb was found."

"Wait. They have the Fire orb?"

"Shoot. There's a whole Metalicon visit I haven't told you about. Well. The brief version is that they have the orb. But today at the Assembly, Telys asked about telling me the truth about something, but Uncle Atticus told him I shouldn't get involved yet. I wonder if they're trying to protect me from something. And they mentioned I was created especially for some kind of purpose, but they didn't say what it was. Do you think I'm an experiment?"

Tambora plunked herself down beside Mercy. "Oh, Mercy, no. No. You were created the normal way, like the rest of us, right? It's not doing you any good to worry about this. I have a way to get your mind on other issues. I've been thinking. Miss Carmen believes the attack on your grandma happened after the portals between the island and the rest of the world were shut down. Do you know what this means?"

"What?"

Tambora picked up Mercy's hand. "It means whoever attacked her didn't get away. He, or she, is still here on Ara'Ja."

"But that person could be anywhere on the island. It would take days just to search the Tray, let alone the rest of Ara'Ja, with all the cities and towns. And we don't know who we're searching for."

"I realize that. What I mean is, the chances of us being able to find the attacker just got a lot better, if we can identify the person before the portals open again."

"How do you suppose we could solve that mystery? The attacker could be anyone," Mercy said.

"While you were gone, I kind of had an idea." Tambora squinted and gave Mercy a wistful little smile, which normally meant she wanted to offer an epic suggestion.

Mercy was apprehensive. "What kind of idea?"

"I'm glad you asked." Tambora let go of Mercy's hand, stood, and paced the room. "You know how you're always seeing things? I thought maybe you could try to see something about the attack."

Mercy rose and followed Tambora's pacing. "Great idea. But, how? Every other time I've experienced one, the vision came out of nowhere. I didn't ask for it."

"True. What about that Emissary creature? It would probably help you do it."

"Possibly. But I've never tried to summon it before. No harm in trying though. No promises. And I'd prefer to be alone when I do this."

"Of course. I'll go down to sit with your grandma."

"How is she doing? I was in such a terrible state of mind when I arrived, I didn't check in on her. I'm a horrid, horrid granddaughter."

"No, you're not. She's doing all right. Her wound appears to be healing, but she's still not awake. Pappas says it's okay, though, because sleep helps with recovery."

"Thank you." Mercy took a big breath. "I guess I better try to call the Emissary."

"I'm going to leave you to it. Come down tell us what happens."

"I will," Mercy promised. "Could you please shut off the light on your way out?"

"Of course," Tambora said. "Good luck."

Mercy dropped to the floor, thankful for the semi darkened room. She performed a few of the breathing exercises she learned from Mr. Kishan. Where was Mr. Kishan, and what part did he have to play in what was happening? Mercy wondered. She chided herself for her paranoia as she realized he must have gone to his homeland when he disappeared to deal with his emergency. There was no way for him to return to Ara'Ja with the portals disabled. She put Mr. Kishan out of her mind and concentrated on summoning the Emissary. In silence, she pleaded, "Dear Emissary, I need your help." The room remained quiet. She was alone. Then it came to her the Emissary was probably not an omnipotent being and could not read her thoughts. Mercy repeated the words in a soft whisper. She held her head straight and still, moving only her eyes to glance around the room, but she was still alone. She felt silly and almost quit. She did not want to, but she knew she would have to try harder. She disliked attempting verbal conversations when by herself. She heaved a loud sigh and just short of yelling, she said, "Dear Emissary, I don't know if you can hear me. But if you can show up, I really need to ask for your advice. Please? Pretty please?" She waited. When again, nothing happened, she stood, ready to psyche herself up to get a vision on her own.

A dull glow emerged in the corner and grew until the Emissary appeared in all its regal splendor. Relieved, Mercy blurted out, "Whew, thank you."

"What would you have of me?" The glowing figure's faintly visible facial features radiated kindness.

"Over the past few months, I've had a couple of visions or maybe they were dreams. They happened spontaneously. I've never deliberately made them happen. But is there a way I can do it myself? Conjure up a vision?"

"As with all skills, it requires discipline and practice. But *your* mind is powerful enough to call up a vision. Unknown details are unnecessary. Simply picture what you know and the specifics will fill in for themselves. You are capable," the Emissary said.

"Thank you," Mercy said. "Hey. Are you a boy or a girl?" Mercy thought she detected a hint of a grin behind all of that glowiness.

"I am the breath of the wind, the cool drink of water, the hunger of the fire, the heartbeat of earth." The Emissary faded away, leaving a disappointed Mercy.

"What a beautiful concept, but that did not even come close to answering my question," Mercy said aloud. Although grateful for the starting point of a vision quest, she did not believe her efforts would work, but she thought it was worth an attempt. She closed her eyes, but her mind and focus were scattered. She scrunched her face to block out all thoughts, except for the night on the beach. After a couple of labor-intensive attempts, during which non related images flitted through her mind, she finally visualized the dark rainy night and her grandmother, standing on the beach, staring across the bay. Grandma stood, and she stood. She glanced at her wristwatch and continued to stand. In a show of unexpected impatience, she turned to Mercy and said, "This isn't working, try another way."

Startled, Mercy's eyes shot open. "I'm losing it," she muttered to herself. She put herself into the lotus yoga position, her legs crossed and her feet up on her thighs. She rested her hands on her knees with her palms up and touched her forefingers to her thumbs to form a circle with each hand to calm her mind and she began again. It did not take as long to bring up the beach scene that time, but Mercy was disturbed to see her grandmother still standing around with the specific goal of being assaulted.

Once again, her grandma addressed Mercy. "I'm not getting any younger here."

"I know, Grandma. I'm trying." Mercy heaved a sigh and climbed up the bunk to her bed. She sat on the edge and swung her legs in mid-air. She groaned, picked up her pillow, and crushed it over her face. She found delight in the changing colors and patterns she pictured each time she closed her eyes. She pressed the pillow closer to her eyes. Pressure always made the designs and colors dazzle more. She rested there for just a moment, in her seated position with her face covered by her pillow, and questioned whether she should quit or try again.

What came next occurred in such a quick manner, that at first, Mercy did not comprehend what happened. Flashes of images and sensations flooded at her through another person's viewpoint. The visions ran one into another at a seamless, blurred, and dizzying pace. She could not understand most of what anyone said. The voices were subdued, like cotton balls were stuffed in her ears, yet by instinct, she understood the essence of each conversation. Her thoughts were her own, but she was strangely imprisoned and mobile simultaneously. Mercy realized she must be lodged inside the memories of the body she occupied, and she was aware of every emotion and every action of that body as if she lived through it herself.

In the distance, Mercy heard her grandmother admonish her, or whomever the person was she inhabited. The person knew her grandmother as Yvonne. Mercy rocketed to the beach near the Tray where Yvonne addressed her in uncharacteristic anger. Mercy noticed her grandmother was dressed in the same outfit she wore for dinner at the Tray earlier that evening. Because Mercy embodied the attacker, she felt every bit of rage that individual held for Yvonne. Her hand lifted—the large hand of a male—and invoked a blade, hovering in a ring of fire. Yvonne gasped and turned to run when Mercy discharged the dagger and stabbed Yvonne in her side.

Horrified, Mercy yearned to scream and rush to help, yet she maintained no control over her movements. Yvonne crumbled to the ground, and blood rushed from the wound. Mercy's host bore no satisfaction from the deed, but knew the attack was essential for the plan to work. She abandoned the injured Yvonne and found herself in a dingy, dank cave. She sat across from a Metalicon who told her Nedim Kishan was there to beg for the lives of his five children, the children they held as collateral for his cooperation in keeping Mercy Markos under surveillance. Mercy and the Metalicon laughed at the pitiful man. Personally, Mercy did not find it funny at all. Why would she laugh?

Again, the vision shifted and her man hand opened a drawer. It was the drawer of her apothecary. She rummaged through the contents until she unearthed a paper covered in drawings of symbols. She pulled it out.

Her fingers touched the corner and created a small fire. She made sure the document burned. When the flame extinguished, her manly shoe kicked the ashes under the dresser to hide them.

She once again confronted a tearful Yvonne, whose hair looked a little darker than usual. She must be younger. Mercy told her she was required to leave Ara'Ja because her husband was dead. When Yvonne departed the island through a portal in Transport Plaza, Mercy experienced relief and felt safe from detection.

"Brother, come with me. You have metal too, don't deny it," she heard herself say in such a distorted voice, she barely recognized the words. She reasoned her brother would betray her, and she panicked. She tried to get a peek at who she spoke to, but the scene transformed once again into the same dark cave where she and the Metalicon ridiculed Mr. Kishan. This time, she and several Metalicons sat at a table and feasted. Though the voices were garbled, she understood they planned the murder of two men, High Elder Nathaniel Caudel and Augustus Kadarius, her grandfather. Mercy concluded the memories she received progressed in reverse, as the points in time seemed earlier and earlier.

Although shocked, there was little opportunity for Mercy to react to the murder plans because someone handed her a photo. The back was signed *Because of you*. Mercy, in her own reality, knew the photograph. An identical copy sat on the mantel above the fireplace in her home. The snapshot showed Mercy's parents cradling an infant with bright red curls. Mercy's grandfather took the photo soon after her birth. Scrutinizing the picture, she could feel the big, self-congratulatory smirk she wore for the success of a well-orchestrated plan.

She then stood in front of Telys, her hand extended to welcome him. She patted his shoulder, proud to be his hero and mentor. Telys faded away, and she was, again, in the presence of her murderous Metalicon co-conspirator. They discussed the Marokos and Kadius prophecy and how they needed the child of the prophecy to complete their plan. She mentioned Orion Markos was the last in his family line and Emzlie Kadarius was the last female of the Kadarius family. The singular hope to fulfill the prophecy was pinned on their union. An introduction of the two was imperative, but Orion was in the Ecclesia and stationed at the Belleza del Mar outpost, and Emzlie lived on Ara'Ja. Mercy's host made a call and urged the person on the other end to allow Emzlie to join the Ecclesia and to disregard her half human status. He succeeded in his bid to prove Emzlie was perfect for the open position at Belleza del Mer.

Mercy's surroundings changed again, and she walked down the hall of the Assembly toward the High Elder's office. The assistant sat at a desk outside the door, his head down, working with a ledger. Ms. Gochenour was nowhere to be seen. The assistant looked up as she walked toward him. The nameplate on the desk read *Solomon Caudel*. In her vision, she knew him. He wore his hair in short blond dreadlocks and looked just like the guy in Miss Carmen's wedding picture. He must be High Elder Caudel's brother, Mercy thought. Her Uncle Atticus mentioned he was Broomfield's assistant at the time of his death. Both of their deaths. Their voices were muffled, and she could not fully decipher every word they said. The assistant may have declared, "He's waiting in his office." Mercy walked toward the office door, but at the last second, she conjured a dagger, and directed the blade toward Solomon Caudel, killing him in an instant. Mercy was appalled at the murder, but she felt the murderer's self-justification that it needed to be done for the good of the cause. She tore out that day's page of the appointment book and touched her finger to the paper. Fire consumed the evidence of her visit and she blew away the ashes. She entered High Elder Broomfield's office. He regarded her with sad eyes and gave her a piece of a delicious dark fruit pie. He then turned away from her and she sent flaming blades into his spine.

The High Elder lay dead on an immaculate white floor, marred only by a red puddle, spreading out around him. She did not start the day with the intensions of killing, but she could not risk capture. She hurried to the door and spun around to point out a detail about a death in an old Shakespearian play. When she turned back, she caught a flash of herself in the mirror on the wall. She sported short, blond dreadlocks. Was the killer High Elder Nathaniel Caudel after all? But he would not have plotted his own murder with the Metalicon. And he certainly had no reason to attack her grandmother.

Curious, she looked directly into the mirror and gazed straight into the eyes of Broomfield's murderer. Her uncle, Atticus Kadarius. For a moment, time stood still, as they peered into each other's eyes.

Before her senses reacted, her vision gained speed and whipped in reverse through each event back to the present. Back to where her grandmother was injured and left for dead. Mercy dropped her pillow and fell from her bunk, landing hard on the floor. She did a quick mental inspection of all her facilities and appendages. She was not hurt, but she was shaky from the jolt of the tumble. Or perhaps her unsteadiness resulted from the shock in the revelation that Atticus—and she would call him Atticus, because she could no longer bear the thought of acknowledging the fiend as part of her family—Atticus not only murdered High Elder Broomfield and his assistant, Solomon Caudel, but he also plotted with the Metalicons to have his own brother—her grandfather—and High Elder Nathaniel Caudel killed in a Metalicon ambush. And the previous night, he attacked her grandmother and abandoned her to die.

Mercy came to realize Atticus supported her mother's appointment to the Ecclesia in order to set up an encounter between her parents. An encounter he hoped would facilitate her birth, which would begin the fulfillment of the prophecy that she would renew the iron crown. She rued the day she first learned about it. When Mrs. Kishan collapsed in class, the old voice in Mercy's mind called it the Iron Crown of Reward. The crown Azrael, the first Metalicon, needed. All the information pooled together and formed the basis of a cohesive plot. Mercy was created to benefit Azrael. Azrael, her childhood nemesis. The monster under her bed at night. Getting older, she assumed he was merely a fantasy, but the prophecy meant he was real. No doubt he used a type of astral projection to visit her from Vatek. She covered her face with her hands as old memories returned. She had forgotten a great deal. Azrael. He taunted her about a crown. She never fully understood why. She thought he played a game with her and it was his way of calling her an irrelevant and insipid little princess. She told him to leave, which he did. But he always returned the following night. After a few years, she ignored him, and his appearances became less frequent until the visits eventually ended.

Mercy had no willpower to pull herself up off the floor. But, she surmised, at least the fall from her bed saved her from the effort of the climb down. She curled up into a ball and held her stomach until she gained the strength to roll over and stretch out flat on her back. She stared at the ceiling and continued to work out the clues. She supposed her grandma held doubts about Atticus and he knew it, which was why he sent her away from Ara'Ja. Mercy grew certain her grandmother was suspicious. After all, she insisted Mercy not tell anyone about her spur-of-the-moment decision to visit. During their video call, she mentioned she would take care of Mercy's situation. But the question remained. Who told her grandma of the things which were currently happening? And who told Atticus she was coming? Maybe it was Telys who blabbed to Atticus. Telys, who knew everyone. And he seemed to know her grandmother. But he was livid with Pappas because her grandmother was attacked near the school. It would not be him. He did not want her grandmother hurt. Just what role did Telys play?

Mercy picked herself up to get to her friends and talk with them about her vision. Together, they could put the puzzle together. Together, they could do anything.

CHAPTER 24

THE DISHONOR
OF THE HONORABLE

Mercy sat across from Tambora and Phin at a table in a library private reading room. She was uncomfortable having the discussion in the lounge where the adults were in and out. She also did not want to leave her grandmother alone without herself or one of her friends. Vesuvius offered to stay behind with the stipulation he would be apprised of the complete story and would receive a large bag of M&M's for his very own as payment.

Mercy held her stomach to keep from getting ill while she told her friends about her vision. "After I killed High Elder Broomfield, I glimpsed myself in a mirror. But I wasn't me. I was Atticus."

"Your uncle, Atticus? The High Elder, Atticus?" Phin asked.

"Yes. Everything I witnessed was through his perspective. He attacked my grandma and left her to die. And he's responsible, directly or indirectly, for the deaths of at least four people. Do you remember when we asked him if High Elder Caudel killed Broomfield and Solomon Caudel? He told us a man would never murder his own brother. Right to our faces, he said it. But *he* murdered *his* own brother." Tears dripped from Mercy's chin onto her shirt. The room grew quiet when she finished and no one spoke for several minutes. The loud hum of the overhead lights was all that was audible. Shock and alarm thickened the air. In the heaviness, Mercy struggled to breathe. Her stomach churned in hopes her friends would believe her. She did not know what she would do if they had no faith in her. She may not believe herself if their positions were reversed.

Just when Mercy could no longer bear the hush, Phin asked, "You're absolutely sure about this?"

And there it was. The doubt. Hurt, but resolute, she said, "I'm more than sure."

"I believe you," Tambora said. "This is the only explanation that makes complete sense. Now you've found him out and we won't let him continue to get away with it."

"I believe you, too. I only wanted to know that you were one hundred percent sure," said Phin. "You know, attacking a human is a big offense against the Ara'Jaeon code of honor, and the Ecclesia is required to investigate an assault on a human."

Mercy almost cried in relief. They believed her.

"So, where are they?" Vesuvius asked.

The children jumped, startled at the intrusion.

"Vesu," Tambora said, "how long have you been there?"

"I've been here all along."

Mercy's heart almost stopped when she realized Vesuvius deserted her grandmother. "Why did you leave my grandma by herself?" She jumped to her feet.

"Miss Carmen and Pappas wanted to assess her wound and told me I had to leave the room, so I came here to find you."

"This is unacceptable. I need to go check on my grandma." Mercy ran toward the portal.

"Mercy." Tambora stood as Mercy spun around. "We're trying to help you here. You can't blame us if situations don't always go your way. We're doing the best we can. She's okay. Even if they're working alongside the Metalicons, both Miss Carmen and Pappas have proven they want to protect her, too. Come back and let's figure out what we need to do."

Her cheeks burned and Mercy bit her lip, embarrassed by the reprimand. She treated her friends as though they existed to serve her demands. Tambora did right to call her out. She hung her head and returned to the table. "I'm sorry, guys. I'm so worried, it's hard to not overreact."

"We understand, Mercy," Phin said. "We know you're in a weird situation and we're happy to help."

"So, where are they?" Vesuvius said again. "Where is the Ecclesia? Because a human has been assaulted."

"They probably can't get here while the portals are shut down," Tambora said.

Another revelation hit Mercy. "They can't get here. That's it! The reason the incoming and outgoing portals are shut down. Most Ecclesia members are stationed off the island, and Atticus closed the portals when he arrived to prevent them from getting here. Keeping the Ecclesia off the island would give him time to cover his tracks."

Phin rose to his feet and walked about the room, his hands clasped behind him. He stopped and raised his forefinger. "It's awfully convenient for him to return from his trip right after you learned about Grandma K's visit. Someone must have ratted to him about it."

"Who told him? Maybe it was a double agent," Vesuvius said, taking the typical spy pose with his hands and fingers simulating a gun. A sudden flash of fire discharged from his finger, almost hitting Mercy. She dodged at the last second. The shot whizzed past her and struck the calendar on the wall behind her, reducing it to ashes.

"Vesu, you've got to pay better attention to your abilities," Tambora said.

"I know, I know. I had a little lapse is all. Sorry, Mercy. I got carried away."

"It's okay. Believe me, it's of little consequence, compared to all the rest of what's happening right now. The prophecy, the murders, the attack, the Metalicons. You guys, there's more. The Metalicons have Mr. and Mrs. Kishan's children."

"No!" Tambora went white.

"Yes. They're extorting him. We need to figure out a plan quickly so we can get back to my grandma and hopefully save the Kishan children too."

"Of course, but there are still many questions we need to address. What is this crown you're supposed to fix, and why does Azrael need it?" Phin asked.

Mercy drummed her fingers on the table. "But of more present concern, who is working with who? Miss Carmen, Atticus, Telys, Pappas. They all seem to conspire with and against each other. And maybe there are even more people involved. Vesuvius, your spy theory is probably more accurate than any of us realize. CJ blabbed to Mr. and Mrs. Oliver about my grandmother's visit. And then Atticus attacked my grandma. The Olivers could have told multiple people. Who knows how many others knew, or who actually told Atticus?"

"But why would Atticus want to hurt Grandma K?" Tambora asked.

Mercy rested her elbow on the edge of the table, plopped her chin onto her fist, and thought for a moment. "I believe she suspected him and he wanted to keep her quiet. We need to take a chance and talk to Miss Carmen. She appears to have genuine concern for my grandma."

"Plus, if you remember, she griped about Atticus when we were in her office. It's not likely they're scheming together," said Tambora.

"That's true," said Phin. "And if she was in cahoots with him, she probably wouldn't have approved Grandma K's visit. Not to mention Atticus told Telys to get rid of her."

"Maybe we can get clarification if we ask Miss Carmen only about her husband and don't mention the Metalicons or the Fire orb at all," said Mercy.

"That's a great idea." Phin smiled at Mercy in a most dazzling way with twinkles in his neon eyes.

Her heart leaped and did a somersault. She reddened, lowering her head. She did not understand her reactions. Phin was one of her best friends. And they were far too young to get involved in a boy-girl relationship, according to her dad. The previous year, a classmate from her hometown tried to hold her hand. Her father told the boy she could not date until she was twenty-five. He said he was joking, but she was positive he meant it.

"I'll come with you," Phin said.

"Okay." Mercy sensed her blush deepen and hurried to change the subject. "But first, I need to stop and check on how my grandma is doing."

"Hey. Did you know the medallion is gone?" Vesuvius asked as they exited the library.

"No, I didn't. This is the first I've been to the library since we talked to Miss Carmen about it. Can you believe it was only two days ago? An entire lifetime's worth of events have occurred since then," Mercy said.

"I'll bet Miss Carmen got rid of it. I could see that decision in her eyes when we told her about it," said Phin.

As they approached the lounge, Miss Carmen stepped out.

"Miss Carmen, may we speak with you?" Mercy asked.

"Of course, do you want to talk here or would you prefer my office?"

Mercy looked to Phin for support. He flicked his eyes upward. "We should go to your office," Mercy said.

"All right, follow me."

"Actually, I want to see my grandma first."

"Of course. I'll go on up and wait for you there."

Mercy sat next to her grandmother and took her hand. "Grandma, I'm going to finish this. Your job is to concentrate on getting better." Mercy kissed her grandmother's pale cheek.

Phin crept up next to Mercy and knelt beside her. "Get better, Grandma K," he said. "Are you ready?" he asked Mercy, as Tambora and Vesuvius joined them by the sofa. "They'll sit with her."

"Yes. Let's do this."

———————◆———————

Miss Carmen's office door stood open. Mercy rapped on the door frame and peeked inside.

Miss Carmen sat at her desk. "Come on in, children, and have a seat. What can I do for you?"

Mercy cleared her throat, hoping she was correct. She glanced at the name plate on Miss Carmen's desk which read *Miss DeLuca*. "Miss Carmen, I don't know how to put this. But is your last name, DeLuca, an anagram for Caudel? Were you married to High Elder Nathaniel Caudel?"

Miss Carmen's face lost all color. "Where did you hear this?"

"I would prefer not to say just yet."

Miss Carmen leaned back in her chair, crossed her arms, and tapped a finger on her forearm. She bent forward, folding her hands on her desk. "No. I was married to his brother, Sol—"

"Solomon?" Mercy finished Miss Carmen's sentence, remembering the assistant in her vision who looked like Miss Carmen's photo. "He was murdered at the same time as High Elder Broomfield, right?"

Miss Carmen's eyes flooded with unshed tears. "Yes. He was the High Elder's assistant." She picked up the photo on her desk. "It hurts. Still. Even after all these years." She showed it to the children. "I should've been more careful to keep this photograph hidden. But I couldn't bear to not see him every day."

"He looks almost identical to High Elder Caudel. They could be twins," Mercy said.

"Yes. They looked very much alike and wore their hair the same way. They were incredibly close. Nathaniel was devastated at the double murder of my husband and High Elder Broomfield, but he stepped up and did his duty as the new High Elder all the same."

"Do you know who did it?" Phin asked.

"It wasn't Nathaniel, as alleged. He was a kind soul and would never harm anyone. He revered High Elder Broomfield and was devoted to Solomon. I want so badly to erase this stigma attached to his memory."

"Is that why you changed your name? You're trying to find the killer?"

"Yes. Partly. I was born on a small outpost between Russia and Alaska and didn't move here until 1945, early in my marriage. We were only here a few months when Solomon was murdered. I returned home after he died. When Nathaniel, along with your grandfather, were killed a few years ago in the Metalicon attack, his death took the restraint off the whispered rumors that built up over the years. Accusations ran rampant.

I returned to Ara'Ja to discover who killed my husband and to clear Nathaniel's name. No one really knew me, so I changed my name to Carmen DeLuca. I didn't want to draw attention to myself in order to be free to search around unnoticed."

"What would you do if you knew who murdered your husband?" Phin asked.

"I have a very high suspicion. I simply can't prove it." Her eyes narrowed. "Why?"

"First, I need to know what you and Telys are planning," Mercy said, forgetting she said she would not mention the Metalicons.

"Telys?"

"Metalicon, platinum hair, British accent," Phin said.

"Yes. I know who Telys is." Miss Carmen stood and paced the room, one hand placed on her waist and the other on her forehead. "What I don't know is why you say we are making plans together."

"Never mind, we already know you've been talking to him about more than my grandma. We overheard you once," Mercy said.

"What Telys and I speak about is of no concern to you."

Mercy felt close to losing control of the situation and could feel panic creep in, but she persevered as though she held all the cards. "I believe it is my concern. And as it's my destiny to fulfill the prophecy of restoring the Crown of Reward, I think I have the right to know."

"Where are you getting all of this? What prophecy?"

"Okay. We're finished here." Mercy stood, tired of the game. "Come on, Phin. We've got work to do." She pulled open the door to the hall. "Miss Carmen, if you're not doing anything wrong, I think we should work together. You can think about that."

Phin and Mercy stepped into the hall and Mercy closed the door. They were almost to the stairs, when they heard a door creak open behind them and Miss Carmen's voice call out, "You need to be careful. You don't know what you're getting yourself into."

Mercy spun around to answer the headmistress. "Thanks, but I think we do."

Miss Carmen threw her hands into the air and retreated into her office.

Mercy let out a big breath. "Whew. I can't believe I just stood up to her. Phin, we have to figure out a way to trap Atticus. We need everyone to know what he did. We can't merely tell them I experienced a vision. No one would believe us."

"Let's confront him and record a confession."

"It would be better for someone to hear it first-hand. What if we could get someone to hide and listen in?"

"Who?"

"It needs to be an adult." Mercy took her first step down the stairs. "It should be Miss Carmen."

"But she didn't want to cooperate."

"She's the only one we can be fairly sure isn't working with the murderer. And the more we talk to her, the more I think she would be on our side, especially regarding Atticus. You know, we've spent a lot of energy chasing both the prophecy and the murder and getting nowhere. We're closest to solving this murder. Let's finish this and worry about who is conspiring with the Metalicons later."

"That's probably the best idea I've heard so far. Should we go back up to ask her again to help us?"

"No. I don't think we should let her know what we're doing. She would only try to stop us. Let's figure out our strategy and then make sure she's around to overhear the confrontation."

Phin elbowed Mercy. "You're being a bit of a tough girl. I kind of dig it."

Mercy giggled. In horror, she realized in one brief, unguarded moment, she lost the entire tough girl cred she just earned.

As they neared the main floor, Atticus entered the school and scurried across the lobby into the visitor lounge. Mercy's stomach dropped. Grandma was in there. She felt Phin try to intensify his speed, but she held him back.

"Let me speak to him. I'll ask him to meet me privately somewhere away from the building so we can talk," she whispered. "Stand outside the door and listen until you hear our arrangements, then find help. Preferably, Miss Carmen. When you arrive, stay hidden until I get him to confess. He'll never admit to it if he knows others are there."

"Are you sure you will be safe with him until we get there?"

"I won't be alone with him for long. You'll be there, listening to it all." Mercy groaned inwardly at the sickly sweetness of her voice.

Phin cocked his head, an eyebrow raised.

Mercy bit her lip and turned away, unable to meet his gaze. She could not seem to stop herself from behaving like a school girl, experiencing her first crush. Although she knew she fit the description, she detested bringing the stereotype to life.

"I'll leave the door cracked open. Just stay out of sight," Mercy said, relieved to steer away from the awkward and flirty one-sided conversation she did not intend to start. Mercy stepped into the lounge. Tambora and Vesuvius stood between Atticus and Grandma. Tambora's hands were on her hips and Vesuvius positioned himself in the manner of a drill sergeant with his arms crossed and his feet apart. Mercy stayed near the door, delighted to know her friends were protective of her grandmother.

Atticus glanced toward Mercy. "Ah, Mercy. There you are. I thought I would stop by to check up on Yvonne. You've got good security set up here. They've refused to leave her side."

It took every ounce of effort Mercy could muster to be friendly and act as though nothing was wrong. "Hi, Unc—Uncle Atticus," she stammered, his name stuck like thick tahini butter in her throat. "Hey, guys. Can I have a few minutes alone with my uncle?"

"Are you sure?" Tambora asked.

"I'm sure," said Mercy.

Mercy held the door open for Tambora and Vesuvius, but was careful to not shut it all the way, so her friends could hear her conversation with Atticus. Mercy moved to stand by her grandma. "She still hasn't woken up. We don't know how long she'll be out, but once the portals reopen, someone will take her to Crete so she can get proper care."

"Yes. I'm working on that very situation, actually. Getting the portals up and running."

"Why were they closed?" she asked, wondering what kind of answer he would provide.

"That's classified information, Mercy. I could tell you, but then I'd have to kill you." Atticus laughed.

Mercy gasped and backed away.

"Only kidding, my dear. It's a joke in human society. Intended to deflect further questions."

"Ah, I see." Mercy forced herself to appear relieved. "That's pretty funny."

The door slammed shut, as if pressure from opening a door elsewhere sucked the air flow, pulling the lounge door closed. Mercy deflated, but it was too late to stop. A moment later, the door reopened and Phin popped his head in. "Do pigs wear striped or polka-dotted pajamas?"

"What?" Mercy asked, confused by the question.

"Never mind, we're having a silly discussion and wondered what you thought." Phin winked at Mercy and closed the door behind him, but not completely.

"Clever," Mercy thought and almost audibly sighed in relief. "Don't mind them. I have weird friends," she said. "Hey. Can I talk to you?"

"Of course, you can talk to me about anything."

A memory flashed before Mercy of a time, several years earlier, when she peered down at her uncle's laughing face as he tossed her in the air and caught her. She wondered if he was beyond redemption and how could he even return after the horrific deeds he committed. "It's kind of personal. Can we take a walk someplace where we can be alone?"

"We're alone now."

"Yes. But you know what they say, the walls have ears."

"What about the beach down by the bay?"

Mercy thought about the irony of meeting on the beach. The same location where he tried to kill her grandmother. "The beach is good. Can I meet you there in, say—20 minutes?"

"Perfect. It gives me time to check in on the portal situation. I'll meet you there."

Atticus left the room and Mercy hoped her friends found cover before they were noticed. She needn't have worried, though. A minute later, Phin and Tambora came into the room, sporting huge grins.

"That went a lot easier than expected," Phin said.

"I think so, too. Now you need to get Miss Carmen down to the beach. Give me a few minutes head start, though."

"Already done. Vesu has gone to find her. Tambora is staying here with Grandma K and I'm going with you to the beach. Don't worry, I'll stay out of sight."

The full weight of what she was about to do hit Mercy like a tidal wave, threatening to carry her out to sea and drown her. The contents of her stomach churned. She covered her mouth with her fist to prevent an accidental urping.

"Are you okay?" Phin put his arm around her.

"I will be. I just needed a minute."

Phin took hold of Mercy's hands. She felt confidence flow from his hands into her own. Mercy pulled away before she embarrassed herself. She took a big breath, stooped over her grandma, and kissed her forehead. "I love you, Grams." She looked toward the exit. "All right, Phin. Here we go."

Phin said. "I have a crystal in my pocket we can use to get to the beach."

"I prefer to walk down. It will give me time to figure out a plan." Mercy set off toward the door.

"Wait!" Tambora formed a ball of light and handed it to Mercy. "It's getting dark out. This will help you on the trail. It should last until you get to the bay."

Mercy nodded. "Thank you."

Mercy and Phin were quiet during their hike down the trail to the beach, thankful for the dry path from Phin's efforts the night before. She wanted to figure out how she would bring up the murder. Phin's presence calmed her and gave her strength. Vesuvius and Miss Carmen would also soon be there and her conversation with Atticus would be brief. All the same, a confrontation with a murderous criminal was a nerve-wracking situation for anyone, let alone for a twelve-year-old. The salty air and the sound of waves grew stronger as they descended. The stirrings of the ocean evoked memories of finding her grandma unconscious in the sand.

A few steps short of emerging onto the beach, Phin stopped and grabbed Mercy's elbow and whispered. "Mercy, why aren't you more afraid? You're confronting a killer."

"I *am* afraid." Mercy spoke softly, tossing Tambora's light into the air to dispel. "But he has plans for me. He can't jeopardize them by hurting me. At least not badly. The only way he'll try to get at me is to hurt someone I care about. And he won't know you're—I mean—" Mercy caught her gaffe. "I mean, he won't be aware anyone else is here except him and me until it's too late." She put her finger to her lips. "He's there. Shh—"

Phin ducked down behind a bush.

Atticus stood, facing the bay, his back to her. The night was already dark, but a vivid crescent moon and a sky void of clouds provided enough light to see. Across the water, the twinkling lights of Nikonea City sparkled and illuminated the skyline with just enough of a glow to appear enchanted. It was a lovely view of the peninsula, but her memories of recent events dampened any appreciation she could muster. She hoped she could get past it someday, as she loved the ocean.

As if sensing her presence, Atticus turned around, his white teeth glistened in the moonlight. It reminded her of the way a hyena might smile before it ripped into its dinner, and she hesitated.

"I wondered about you," Atticus said. "I was a bit late myself and you are later still. I solved the portal situation before I got here. All portals that were down are now up and running. We should be able to get Yvonne to Crete yet tonight." Atticus clasped his hands together. "So, to what do I owe this pleasure?"

"This will not be pleasurable." Mercy stepped forward.

Atticus eyed Mercy. "How so?"

Mercy needed to find a way to keep him talking for a few minutes before confronting him. Her mind raced, but came up blank, so she asked the obvious. "First, tell me about your trip. You were only gone for about a day, right?"

"Yes. Only a day. I needed to cancel my tour because Yvonne was attacked."

"No. That can't be. We were told you were returning even before she was hurt."

"No. No, I don't think so." Atticus brought his arm across his abdomen and placed his other elbow on it, his chin rested on his fist.

"I'm one hundred percent sure of it. She was with us at dinner when Miss Carmen announced it," said Mercy.

"Actually, now that I think about it, my team caught wind of a rumor of a planned attack on someone. Yes. That's why we returned."

"I want to believe you, I really do. But I don't."

"What is all of this about, Mercy? Have I offended you?" Atticus stepped forward, reaching for her.

Mercy recoiled, not wanting him to touch her. She thought she might vomit. "You could say that."

"Tell me. If you don't let me know, I can't make it right."

"It's too late. You could never make this right." Mercy thought her heart would break and bit her lip to control any tears.

Atticus set his hands on his hips. Mercy felt him scrutinize her.

"Mercy, honestly, you are talking in circles, and frankly, I don't have time for these shenanigans. If you need something from me, all you have to do is ask."

Mercy wondered if Vesuvius and Miss Carmen arrived yet. She dared a quick peek to the pathway. She supposed it would be helpful to keep the banter going a little while longer before she got his confession. "Do you ever wonder what you might do if High Elders Broomfield and Caudel hadn't been killed? I mean, either could've lived long enough to still be in office to this day." Mercy squatted down, pretending to study the wind patterns in the sand.

"I don't really know. Somehow, I always knew I would be the High Elder."

She lifted her head. "So, you would have explored opportunities elsewhere?"

"I suppose I would have come up with something. I would have probably created my own opportunities. I've always held the belief you sometimes have to make events happen for matters to go your way." Atticus rubbed his forehead. "Look, Mercy. Where are you headed with all these questions? What is going on?" His eyes narrowed.

Mercy got up from her crouched position. She put her hands behind her to hide her trembling. However, the move could not conceal her shaky voice. She hoped she did the right thing, but could devise no other way to get a confession. She took a sharp breath, anxious, yet distressed, to continue the discussion. "Create your own opportunities? Opportunities such as murder? Did you murder High Elder Broomfield and then arrange for High Elder Caudel to be killed, along with my grandfather, your own brother, so you could become the High Elder and help the Metalicons come to power?"

Atticus roared in laughter. "My, you have been busy creating stories, haven't you? Mercy, you've always possessed an active imagination, but this has gone far enough, don't you agree?"

"I didn't have to create any of this. I saw it with my own eyes," Mercy blurted out.

"Mercy, your parents weren't even born yet when High Elder Broomfield was killed. There's no way you could have witnessed it."

"I mean, I saw it with *your* own eyes. I had a vision, and when I saw it, I *was* you. He gave you fruit pie and talked about Shakespeare. When I caught sight of myself in the mirror, it was *your* reflection I saw."

Atticus froze. "Your eyes. I saw your eyes," he whispered. He shook his head. "No. What you say means naught. Merely the babblings of a young girl, eager for attention."

"You know that's not true. It's not my nature. You might as well admit it now." Mercy hoped she gave enough time for everyone to be in place to hear his confession.

"What good is an admission to you? No one will believe your word against mine."

"Maybe so, but at least I'll have made you confront your evil deeds."

"Oh, Mercy. I grow weary of this sport. Let's say, for the sake of argument, that what you believe is actually reality. What is the purpose behind your thirst for truth?"

"I—I just want to know. I feel I am connected."

Atticus stroked his chin and studied Mercy. "You're right. You are connected. Okay. You win. You will know all within the next few years, anyway. Might as well begin now. I'm an open book. What do you want to know?" He sat down on a nearby log and patted the space next to him.

Mercy declined the invitation to sit. Instead, she belted out, "You killed my grandpa."

"Is this a question?"

"Do you deny it?"

Atticus rolled his eyes. "Now my dear, he's so much better off, safe in Vatek in the company of others who have gone on before. He's happy there."

"You *robbed* me of him." Mercy fumed inside and questioned if she could stay calm throughout the interrogation.

"Mercy, my darling, have I not given of my time and my resources to tend to your every need? Have I not showered you with attention and love? Have I not shown up to every school function, birthday, holiday? What more would a grandfather do?"

"It's not about what he would do, but about who he was and what he meant to me and our family." Mercy's nostrils flared. "I believed you were part of the family. I was obviously duped."

"That is a dramatic statement, but next question."

"How did you find out my grandma was here on the island?"

"You realize, I am not alone in my dealings and my convictions. I have people who report to me about what goes on. Believe me, there are others who share my goals."

"Which are?" Mercy genuinely wanted to know. She needed to understand why anyone would hurt family.

Atticus stood and looked around before he spoke. He raised his arms at his sides, his palms up. "To have power beyond anything you've ever imagined."

"You already have power. You're the High Elder. There is nothing more powerful than that for an Ara'Jaeon."

Atticus stood taller and raised his chin high. "I'm only the High Elder because I seized it. I planned it. I created my opportunity, and I made it happen on behalf of Azrael. When he is resurrected, I'll be second only to him in all the world. Mercy, take what is yours. This kind of authority won't be handed to you. You must already realize you have Metal powers along with the other four."

Mercy swallowed hard. She suspected as much, but it was the first she heard it spoken aloud. She felt inappropriately elated to have it confirmed. She worried her friends might reject her, because if they were within earshot, they most surely noticed the proclamation.

Atticus walked toward Mercy, his hands outstretched. "Come with me and we can work together to find the rest of the element orbs. You could rule alongside Azrael and myself. We can teach you skills well beyond what you will learn at this dump." He seized Mercy's hands and sandwiched them between his own.

She compared the feeling to the warmth she sensed when Phin held her hands earlier. With Atticus, she felt cold and contaminated by his touch. Disgusted, Mercy withdrew from his grasp. "I will never work with you."

"Azrael will demand it. You might as well agree now, as a willing participant."

"Who is this Azrael, anyway?" Mercy knew the answer, of course, but she wanted to keep him embroiled in conversation.

"Azrael is the First of the Metalicons. When we retrieve all the orbs, we'll have control of Earth's natural resources and energies." Atticus put his hand over his heart. "Then, when we find and restore the Iron Crown, we will have the power to raise Azrael from Vatek and gift him with the orbs. He'll reign over Earth as he did once before, with us by his side."

Mercy frowned. "When did he rule before?"

"I see your Ara'Jaeon history is sorely lacking. It is not surprising. In the First Eon, when all Ara'Jaeons were still pure bloods, each group safeguarded an orb which housed the essence of their element. The Metalicons waged a war on the other Ara'Jaeons and acquired all the orbs, along with the Metal orb they already possessed. Azrael became the strongest Ara'Jaeon, having ultimate dominion on Earth. Eventually, the rest of the Ara'Jaeons grew stronger and banded together to defeat the Metalicons. Azrael was banished to the deepest depths of Vatek and all five of the orbs were scattered and hidden so no one ever again could wield so much power. Until he gets them back, of course. We now have the Fire orb, as you know, and we are close to finding the others."

Mercy was skeptical at what Atticus told her. His account was nothing like the history narratives she grew up hearing. "Why haven't I ever heard about this before?" she shouted.

Atticus smirked. "The Ara'Jaeons prefer to keep their history smelling sweet. You are already aware the Metalicons are only spoken of in the quietest of whispers, relegated to being an endangered subject. The aforementioned events were put out of sight, with no reminders they ever happened."

Mercy's abdomen gurgled. "You're working with Telys to get the orbs?"

"I am." Atticus stood, his tall adult stature towered over Mercy's diminutive adolescent height.

The situation was far worse than Mercy could have imagined. She hated to admit it, but Miss Carmen was right. She and her friends were clueless about the situation they were embroiled in. Holding her stomach for comfort, she said, "So what exactly does all this have to do with me?"

"My dear, surely by now you've worked out the prophecy. A daughter of a Markos and a Kadarius will help raise Azrael. That daughter is you."

All the pieces Mercy held snapped together inside her mind. She immediately understood how her vision wove together with what she already knew. She held all the pieces, but she no longer needed to seam them together. "You. You got my mother accepted into the Ecclesia, even though she's half human. Then arranged for her to meet my dad because they are the last of the Markos and the Kadarius families. If they didn't get together and have a daughter, the prophecy would never come true. And Azrael couldn't arise."

"One of my proudest accomplishments. Fate smiled on me the day you were born. So, this is what you were literally born to do." Atticus paced. Mercy sensed his rising frenzy.

Clouds covered the moon and stars, which were clear only a few minutes earlier. The wind became tumultuous, and the surf battered the shoreline. Mercy needed to yell to be heard. "No, never. I'll never do it." She held back her tears. She possessed two choices, and she chose not to help him.

"You think you will have options?" Atticus bellowed, as if he read her thoughts. "You will not. It's kismet, pre-destined. Join me now and control the world with us."

"I won't join your murderous schemes." Mercy buried her face in her hands, unable to look at Atticus.

"There is no way around it. It *will* happen. If you do not join me now, you will eventually be destroyed. Understand this, I made the invitation to join my quest to my brother, your grandfather. He refused. His fate may also be yours eventually, if you don't accept my offer."

Mercy knew what Atticus did, but his admission hit her hard. She sobbed. "I'll never betray my people. I will fight you. For my grandfather's sake, I'll fight you!"

"You think this family is so sanctimonious? You think I bring shame to the honorable Kadarius name? But I will not be the only one."

"Who else? Tell me!"

"Mercy, we've already discussed this. It is you. *You* will restore the crown which will bring Azrael back from his confines in Vatek. And in doing so, *you* will bring embarrassment and dishonor to those you love most."

"I won't do it," Mercy yelled, and under her breath, she muttered, "I wish the Emissary was here."

"Mercy." A voice called out from behind Mercy. A voice as soft as a gentle breeze, yet still audible over the crashing of the waves. Mercy jumped up and spun around. Her heart leapt at the sight.

CHAPTER 25

THE ONLY PATH TO VATEK

Mercy glanced toward Atticus. She wanted to see him when he realized his defeat. But he continued his rants without acknowledgement of the interruption.

"He cannot see me," the Emissary said.

The ocean breeze whipped the Emissary's robes around in a stunning, graceful way. Mercy embraced no fantastical notions that the gusty turbulence likewise enhanced her. She could not even keep her loose curls out of her face in the rising winds, and she clumsily spat stray hairs off of her lips several times a minute. "Dear Emissary, what can I do to defeat him?"

"Unfortunately, the only way to defeat him is to either discredit him or vanquish him to the Gates of Vatek, which would require you to mortally injure him."

"No other way at all? Killing him or getting him to confess are the only ways? Can't I just *make* him confess?"

"Hasn't he already?"

"No. He's not said the words. He's skirting around it."

"Mercy, you cannot compel him. Ara'Jaeons, in the same manner as humankind, must have free will to make their own decisions."

"But what about Mr. Kishan? It's not his will to be used by the Metalicons, they have his children."

"Regardless of the coercion in play, Nedim Kishan ultimately held the freedom to choose whether he would cooperate with the Metalicons."

"Can't you help me get Atticus to admit what he's done?"

"No. I must not. It is not my place. I am simply a messenger and content for you to name me as the Emissary."

"It's not fair," Mercy cried out.

"No. It is not." The Emissary faded away.

Mercy blinked. She still stood facing Atticus as he continued to brag about all they could do together.

He yelled, "Mercy. Are you paying attention? There is still time for you to join me. I will train you to become better than all the Ecclesia combined, and you will be at my side when we rule the world with Azrael. We'll be heroes."

Her actual hero lay unresponsive at the Tray, courtesy of the man before her, who challenged her to reign with him. "My grandma is the only hero I need. You caused her injuries. You and your murderous aspirations."

"To be fair, I've only killed those who were a direct threat to me."

Phin emerged from behind the bushes and ran to Mercy, whispering, "Hey. Tam and Vesu are here."

Without taking her eyes from Atticus, Mercy said to Phin, "I think we can speak freely. He's too far away to hear us if we aren't loud. I thought Tambora was with my grandma."

"Mrs. Kishan took over."

"Did Miss Carmen come too?"

"No. They couldn't find her."

"Then, did they bring Pappas?"

From his position by the shore, Atticus sang the song of the Ara'Jaeon Purpose Mercy and the choir performed at Parents' Day.

Mercy grimaced. "What a hypocrite."

Phin continued, ignoring Atticus. "Mercy, they couldn't find anyone except Miss Birdie and Mrs. Kishan."

"No one else?" Mercy's spirit dropped.

"No one who could help us. We think the teachers and staff were having an emergency meeting in the East Wing. Access to that area is blocked for students. They couldn't get in."

"What about sending Mrs. Kishan here instead of Tambora?"

"Mercy, sitting with your grandma is about all Mrs. Kishan can do. They didn't even have her go to the meeting. She doesn't seem quite recovered from when she fainted. I don't think she's strong enough right now for something like this."

"So, no one heard his confession?" She did not think she could sink any further. What was the point of her confrontation with Atticus if no one witnessed it?

"*We* heard him admit he murdered people," Vesuvius said as he and Tambora joined them on the beach.

"More interruptions?" Atticus shouted over the sounds of the crashing surf. He withdrew a hanky from his suit pocket and dusted off a nearby log, before he took a seat. "Don't worry about me. I'm only the High Elder. I'll just be over here, waiting until you and your little friends finish chatting."

"It doesn't count for much that we're the only ones who heard it. No one will believe us over him," Tambora said.

"Mercy, your time is running out. Finish up with your mates and let's come to an agreement," Atticus said.

"The only agreement we'll make is one where you surrender yourself to the authorities," Mercy yelled.

"Then I might as well leave right now, as I *am* the authority," Atticus said.

Mercy panicked. He could not leave, not yet. "No! We'll talk, we'll talk."

"What should we do now?" Phin asked.

"Try to keep him bragging until help gets here," said Tambora.

"But help isn't coming. You all said so yourself," Mercy said. "The Emissary was just here and told me the only ways I could defeat Atticus are to either uncover his crimes or send him to Vatek."

Tambora gasped with shock on her face. "No! Really? You know what that means."

"Yes, Tambora. I'm aware of what it means," Mercy said.

"What does it mean?" Vesuvius asked.

"Think about it Vesu. What has to happen for someone to go to Vatek?"

"They have to die?"

"Bingo!" Tambora took hold of Mercy's shoulders. "Mercy, don't do it. You'll never forgive yourself."

"I don't think sending him to Vatek will be necessary." Phin pivoted away from Atticus, pulled the crystal Mercy did not want to use earlier from his pocket and handed it to Vesuvius. "Take this out of sight so Atticus doesn't figure out what you're doing. Portal to the maze, scour the grounds, and find someone, *anyone* who is an adult, and get back here, pronto. Hopefully, the meeting is over."

"Got it." Vesuvius grabbed the crystal and took off into the cover of the trees.

"Mercy, if you can't keep Atticus talking, we'll have to find another way to keep him occupied until help arrives," Tambora said.

"Not we. Me," said Mercy as she straightened herself, her mind on one thought. Stopping Atticus.

"Mercy, no," said Phin. "If you're going to fight him, you'll need our help."

Tambora grabbed Mercy's shoulders again. They stared deep into each other's eyes. Mercy silently implored Tambora, who nodded and said, "Do it, but we're here if you need us. Phin, we have to trust he won't hurt her."

Mercy drew a deep breath. An image of Wonder Woman and her crossed arms came to her, and she thought maybe she could do something similarly. She lifted her face to the sky, her arms stretched out to her sides. She raised her arms above her, crossing her wrists and ripping them apart again. Lightning struck the binding cuffs, and they flew off. She squealed and brought her arms down.

Atticus laughed, motivating her to action. She held her arms out again, brought her breathing under control, and focused her attention on the betrayer. Her spirit broke away from her body and floated like a giant parade balloon, high over the bay. A brilliant light filled her essence, illuminating the night sky. Mercy glanced down at the beach and saw herself with raised arms. Her friends huddled nearby, staring up at her with incredulous eyes and gaping mouths. "Oh, man," she whispered, unable to comprehend how she accomplished the feat.

"Whoa! That's an eidolon," Phin said.

"What's an eidolon?" asked Tambora.

"A spirit image. I've read about them, but only in comic books," said Phin.

Atticus looked to the sky and smirked. "Ah, so this is how it's going to be? I must admit, I didn't expect you to be this advanced so quickly." He also lifted his arms and his spirit rose to meet Mercy's.

Mercy swallowed hard and cleared her throat, afraid her voice would crack and give away her uncertainty. "It's in the attitude, not the actions." Mercy quoted Mr. Kishan from one of her training classes, hoping she sounded empowered.

"That, it is," Atticus said. "But there is still the factor of experience. You're but a novice, calling out a seasoned veteran."

"I may be a rookie, but I'm determined."

Mercy and Atticus kept their physical feet planted on the ground, an unbroken stare between them. Frozen in place, they physically spoke no more. All the action took place high above them as their spirits grew to titanic proportions to challenge one another.

"I'll give you first shot," his spirit bellowed.

"I didn't come here to fight," Mercy said.

"Nothing risked, nothing achieved. It'll be good practice for you."

Mercy's apparition shouted, "This is for my grandparents and all the others you've killed or hurt." She clapped her hands. A crack of thunder and a ripple of wind radiated out from her and knocked her opponent's eidolon from his arrogant stance.

"Nice. But you'll have to do better." Atticus roared as his spirit recovered his balance. His image motioned at the forest and snapped its fingers. A rustling came from the direction of his gesture and a liana emerged from the bushy undergrowth of the trees. The long, woody vine slithered across the sand, looking very much like a serpent. It made its way to Mercy's feet on the ground. The gnarled plant slid its tentacles up her body and down her arms, wrapping itself around her wrists and binding them together. Similarly, her apparition's hands became bound and useless. The High Elder's specter opened his arms to the heavens. "Mercy, you are lacking in offensive *and* defensive moves. You're a child. A baby who drinks milk for sustenance. Aren't you ready to give up this nonsense? Accompany me and I'll teach you how to feast."

"I won't let you win. I can't." Mercy understood he toyed with her. But as her earthly body struggled to get free, the bushy shackles grew tighter with every move. She tried to raise her arms and break their hold on her as she did with the binding cuffs, but Atticus held his position to keep them secure.

"I've got this," Tambora said. "Phin, this way."

From her vantage point in the sky, Mercy watched her friends rush to the vine, still writhing on the beach. She continued to struggle, determined to keep her uncle's attention away from them.

Tambora motioned to Phin. "Try to hold it down." Phin sat on the twisted vine, using his hands to keep it secure. It thrashed and bucked like a wild horse as he tried to keep his grip. Tambora knelt on the sand and touched the thick, root appendage with her fingertip. Sparks flew where she made contact. The vine sizzled and smoked where she touched it until it burned through.

The wrapping around both Mercy's wrists and those of her spirit withered and died. She shook herself free, wiggling her fingers to show Atticus she was unbound. "Never underestimate the power of friendship," she said, as her spirit flung a water spout toward him.

Atticus stretched his palm out, transforming the water into a cloud of sand which fell to the ground in a big heap. "How sweet," he said. "But they can't help you with this." He opened his hand to reveal a small flame.

He tossed it and spun it around until it formed a ring of sparks and electricity. He flipped his hand and several metal daggers, all sparking with electrical energy, developed from within the center of the ring. "Mercy, I intend to show you I mean business. I don't care to hurt you, my girl, but if you give me no choice—"

Mercy inhaled deeply. Were those Blades of Betrayal? She closed her eyes and an image of a long steel rod popped up in her mind. She did not know if she really had Metal abilities, like Atticus said, but she felt the smooth, cold shaft in her hands. Unsure of what to do next, she concentrated on taking a defensive approach. She visualized herself hitting the daggers with the rod, diverting them away from herself. She opened her eyes in time to watch Atticus fling the fiery blades across the sky at her. She never imagined he would actually attack her. She knew it would sadden her later, but the need to protect herself kicked in, leaving her emotions on the shelf to be dealt with at another time. "I. Am. Not. Your. Girl," she said. Instinctively, she spun the rod in front of her. Faster and faster it went, like an out-of-control Ferris wheel. Mercy bit her lip and focused. She dared not stop to question it and risk faltering. Sounds of metal clinking against metal rang out. Her rod hit every flaming knife Atticus threw at her and they reversed course back to him. He ducked and eluded each return, but he kept up his barrage.

On the ground, Mercy walked toward Atticus. Her sky twin did the same. The blades were returned to Atticus at a speedy rate and the High Elder's reactions slowed. Mercy could tell he would soon tire, but she kept moving. Only two ways existed to defeat him. And since there were no adults around when Atticus confessed, there remained only one other option. Vatek.

"Mercy, remember what we talked about." Tambora's voice broke through the noisy gale. "You don't want to live with the same guilt as him."

Mercy paused and ducked to avoid the dagger coming toward her. Tam was right, as always. Her moral compass. The metal rod disappeared from her hands and Mercy brought her arms down, her spirit diminishing from the sky.

Atticus did the same and cast a portal crystal onto the beach. He stated he wanted to transport to his office at the Assembly Headquarters. He hesitated before he jumped in. "You know, I've taken out two High Elders, among others. But you have proved to be an admirable challenger, after all. Keep up the good work. We will meet again."

"But not as family." Mercy knelt in the sand, her shoulders drooped in defeat.

"Maybe you'll change your mind when you realize what we can do together. Harmony and balance, Mercy." Atticus leapt through the portal and disappeared.

Mercy wrapped her arms around herself and shivered. The sound of twigs breaking came from the edge of the forest. She looked up. Miss Carmen and Mr. Kishan ran out from the bushes to where Mercy stood. Behind them, Telys ducked behind a tree, but not quick enough to escape her notice.

Mr. Kishan knelt beside Mercy and held her shoulders. "Mercy, you did me proud tonight."

"Mr. Kishan, you're back," Mercy said, throwing her arms around his neck. She was weakened and his embrace gave her a sense of security.

"Yes. I was not on the island. I couldn't return while the portals were not operating."

Mercy pulled away. "Did you get your children from the Metalicons?"

"Sadly, I did not. How did you know?"

"I'm so sorry." Mercy looked down at her hands, ashamed to be the source of the Kishan children's kidnapping and unwilling to focus attention to her ability. "I—uh—overheard it in a conversation. What's going to happen to Atticus? He got away. Was it all for no purpose?"

Mr. Kishan lifted Mercy's chin. "No, Mercy. He had a surprise waiting for him at his office. When he threw his portal crystal and stated his destination, Magister Pappas and Mr. Romani took their own portal to get there first. Luckily, you kept Atticus ranting long enough to give them a few minutes lead so they could be ready to bind him when he stepped out of the portal. Now, they'll call in the Assembly members for an emergency hearing."

"Enough chit-chat." Miss Carmen wrapped her arm around Mercy. "My dear, you're trembling. Let's get you up to the school. It might help to know your grandmother has regained consciousness."

Mercy's body jerked to attention. Tambora squealed and clapped her hands and Phin patted Mercy's back, while Vesuvius made a victorious ninja move.

Mercy said, "She's awake? I need to get back."

"And so you shall. Come along, child," Miss Carmen said.

Mercy burst into tears. "I just need to see her."

CHAPTER 26

LOSE ONE, GAIN ONE

"Grandma, I'm relieved you're awake. I have so much to tell you. You don't know the excitement you've missed." Mercy sat on the sofa next to her grandmother, holding her hand. It was a full half an hour since she returned to the Tray after her run-in with Atticus.

Nightly curfew was in effect and the Tray was quiet and empty in the communal areas. No one was around except Miss Carmen, who sat straight and proper in a hardback chair at the end of the sofa. Pappas and Mr. Romani were still away. She trusted they put Atticus in custody. Phin and the twins were in the kitchen, eating the dinner they all missed. Tambora promised she would have someone bring a tray to Mercy.

"I think I have a good idea," Grandma said. "I heard a lot of what went on in this room while I was out. I overheard you and Atticus planning to meet at the beach. I was frantic, wishing I could stop you. I kept telling myself to wake up. Finally, I did, and I told that lovely Mrs. Kishan someone needed to get down to the beach immediately."

The mention of Mrs. Kishan brought the Kishan children to Mercy's thoughts. She hoped they would be found soon. "Grandma, how did you know to meet Atticus down by the bay last night, and why did he attack you?" Mercy asked.

"After your grandfather and High Elder Caudel were killed, I asked questions. The Metalicon attack was an ambush and no one could figure out how the Metalicons discovered their whereabouts. I just couldn't leave it alone. Then Atticus told me I was required to leave Ara'Ja. He said I was no longer married to an Ara'Jaeon, and I lost the right to live here. I didn't want to leave you or your mother and I begged him to let me stay. He refused. I was suspicious about him earlier, but by then, I was pretty sure he was involved." Grandma folded her hands in front of her. "When I was in my room after dinner, someone slipped a note under my door, asking me to meet him. I didn't see who it was. It probably wasn't very smart of me to go alone."

Miss Carmen said, "We've suspected for months Atticus was connected to the killings in 1945 of High Elder Broomfield and my husband, but we had no proof."

"We?" asked Mercy.

"Magister Pappas and I, plus a few others. We were having a meeting on that very topic while you were at the beach. When we finished, we stopped in to check on your grandmother and discovered she was awake. Mrs. Kishan filled us in on what was going on. We were just leaving to intervene when Vesuvius ran into the school. He told us you were getting a confession, but you needed us to witness it for ourselves. We realized he was being truthful when we stepped outside and saw the two figures beyond the trees battling in the sky over the harbor."

Miss Birdie poked her head in the room and asked if Mercy wanted her dinner. The aroma of seasoned meat caused Mercy's stomach to growl. She did not realize how hungry she was until she smelled the savory meal. Mercy hurried to the table where Miss Birdie left Mercy's tray and a mug of broth for her grandmother. Mercy took a bite of food as she sat. She closed her eyes to enjoy the flavorful chicken and vegetables roasted with Mediterranean herbs. She chewed an appropriate number of times, as her mother always taught her, and swallowed before she spoke. "Yum," she said and shoved another bite into her mouth while Miss Carmen and Grandma chatted.

A commotion in the hall interrupted the conversation. Familiar voices mingled with Pappas, the Kishans, and Mr. Romani. Mercy's heart flipped, and she dashed out the door. The teachers quietly left the lobby and went their various ways.

"Mom! Dad!" She hurried into their open arms. She was overjoyed to have a few minutes alone in the company of her parents.

Her father kissed her forehead. "Mercy, are you okay? I can't imagine what you've been through. We rushed to get here as soon as we discovered what was going on. Luckily, the portals were opened."

"Atticus told me he opened them. Probably to make a quick get-away." Mercy looked down. "Mom, I'm so sorry. He killed Grandpa, and he tried to kill Grandma. Why would he do that to his own family?" Tears slid down her face, onto her nose, and fell to the floor.

The corners of her mother's mouth curled up slightly in a wistful smile, and again, she pulled her daughter into her arms. "I don't know, sweetheart. Sometimes a desire for power is an addictive sensation. I'm sure it's what started this all those years ago."

"At least he's been captured," Mercy said.

"Captured because you got him to confess in front of witnesses," her father said. "You did a brave thing. Reckless, but brave. And we will discuss new rules about leaving the grounds unaccompanied."

"But I wasn't alone. Phin was with me."

"Mercy, you know what I mean."

Mercy sighed. "I know. But I've discovered so much these past few months. Did you know there's a prophecy about me? Atticus set you up to fall in love and get married. He needed you to have a daughter to help him resurrect Azrael, the first Metalicon. I can't do it."

Mercy's parents glanced at one another. "Mercy, until tonight, we didn't realize the full extent of why Atticus arranged for us to meet, but we are aware of the prophecy. We wanted a child despite it. We're not bound to any prediction," said Orion.

"And neither should you be," her mother said, skimming the tip of Mercy's wet nose with her finger.

A movement behind her mother caught Mercy's attention. She saw Telys slip into the lounge and kneel next to her grandmother.

Mercy's father lightly touched her mother's shoulder. "Emzlie, Telys is here. He's in with your mother."

Her mom stepped toward the lounge, sporting a rare expression of distaste. "Stay here, Mercy."

"I'm coming with you," Mercy's father said.

"No. I can do this. Stay out here with Mercy, she needs you more than I at this point." Mercy's mother walked into the lounge. "Get out," she said in a tone so crisp, Mercy was surprised.

"Emzlie," her grandmother said, "He has every right to—"

Someone firmly shut the door and Mercy was reduced to hearing only argumentative voices. She knew how Alice felt after she entered Wonderland, when she was shrunken and the world around her grew large and overbearing. What she just witnessed confounded her more than anything in her visions. She confronted her father for answers. "Dad, what is this about?"

"It's your mother's business, Mercy, and her story to tell, if she chooses."

Mercy plopped down on the floor outside the lounge door, hoping to overhear what was going on, but her father talked non-stop about the boring duties at SARA, obscuring any conversation coming from the inside.

The door opened and Mercy jumped up and moved out of the way as Telys walked out. He nodded at Mercy and her father. "Mercy. Orion. Harmony and balance."

"Telys." Her father acknowledged the Metalicon with his own head bob.

Mercy was stunned into silence as she watched Telys pass through the red revolving door and out of the Tray.

Mercy's mother came out. "Orion, we need to get my mother to Crete where she can get human medical help. I'll need you to carry her outside to where we can open a portal to Transport Plaza, and then take her off the island. Mercy, will you please quickly go pack up your grandmother's belongings."

"Yes, ma'am." Mercy walked the seven flights to her room, her shoulders hunched and head hung low, disappointed she and her grandma did not get to spend any time together except for dinner the night before.

Was it really only the night before? Many lifetimes ago seemed more accurate. She threw open the door to her grandmother's room. The suitcase sat on the floor, still closed and unpacked. Mercy grabbed it and hurried to her parents. She arrived in time to see her mother storm out of the building. Her father held her grandmother. He caught Mercy's attention, and he nodded toward the exit. Mercy followed him out to where her mother already tossed a portal crystal to the ground. The portal fissure was full of rose petals and the aroma wafted out from the gateway. Mercy did not realize there were scented portals. A whole new world of options opened up inside her imagination.

Mercy hugged her father as best she could as he carried her grandma.

"We'll return as soon as we get your grandmother settled," he said.

Mercy kissed her grandmother's cheek. "Grandma, I'm sorry we didn't get to spend more time together."

"As soon as I'm able, I'll return and we can take all the time we need. Tell all your friends goodbye for me. I love you, Mercy. You've been quite the warrior tonight," Grandma K said.

Mercy's father carried his mother-in-law through the portal, but Mercy stopped her mother to give her the luggage before she left. "Mom?"

"Yes?"

"Who is Telys?"

Her mother stared long and hard at her daughter. Mercy never knew her to be so undecided—or so icy. Her mother straightened her posture and said, "My brother," and proceeded through the portal without another word.

Mercy took a step back. She felt as though she received a punch in the stomach. And angry. She was angry her mother hit her with such life-altering news and then abruptly departed, giving no explanations. Mercy stayed outside for several minutes, paralyzed, as she tried to absorb the fact that Telys was her uncle. In the space of a few hours, she lost an uncle, and she gained an uncle. It was a dizzying moment for her. Telys was her uncle. How did she manage to have an uncle—make that *two* uncles—involved with the Metalicons? Something brushed against Mercy's shoulder, startling her, and she pulled away.

Tambora stood there, her eyes projected her concern. "Mercy, what's wrong? Did something happen with Grandma K?"

It took a significant amount of effort, but Mercy spoke. "No. She's going to be okay. My parents took her to Crete."

"That's a relief. You look like something terrible happened, and I was worried."

"No. Nothing too terrible. I don't think."

"Can you talk about it?"

Mercy shivered and rubbed her arms. In the past, she always wanted to retreat into herself before she discussed her feelings, but she felt strong enough to discuss her revelation. "Yes. I think so. I'd like to go inside, though. It's getting chilly out here."

"Let's go up to the student lounge and talk." Tambora took Mercy's hand and led her into the building. "The guys have gone to their room and we can be alone in there."

The news provided a slight relief to Mercy. Although grateful for their help, she was not eager to answer any questions the boys would ask. Neither girl spoke as Mercy followed Tambora up to the lounge.

Upon arriving, Tambora was the first to break the silence. "What happened out there?" she asked, getting straight to the point.

Mercy's eyes misted, remembering the shock. "My mother gave me some titanic news. And then she left without explaining herself."

"Parents," said Tambora in a tone matching the exasperation written on her face. "Tambora?" Mercy's throat tightened and her voice cracked. "My mom has a brother."

"What? No way."

"Yup."

"I can understand why you're upset. Your mom kept this information from you for twelve years. But think about it. It could end up being pretty amazing, too."

"Tambora, it's someone we know."

"Nuh-uh! Someone here? At the Tray?"

"Yes. I mean, no. But he's been here a few times."

Tambora leaned in. "And?"

Mercy bit her lip, trying to figure out how to tell her friend that a Metalicon was her uncle. She cleared her throat. "Uh, it's Telys."

"Telys? Telys the Metalicon, Telys?"

"Yes. Him."

Tambora stammered. "I... uh... oh... when... I don't know what to say."

Mercy widened her eyes. "That's a first."

Tambora giggled. "It is. But, wow. It's a lot to process. Are you okay?"

Mercy searched deep inside herself for an answer, then shook her head. "I don't know what to feel. He's never harmed me. He's actually been almost caring. But he's a Metalicon."

Tambora lifted a brow and considerably lightened the mood in the room when she said, "I think he's kind of cute."

It was Mercy's turn to giggle. "He is charming, for sure," said Mercy. "I wonder why he joined the Metalicons. He obviously wasn't born into it, but he has Metal talents. I knew Metal was in our family eons ago, but I only found out today several of us still have it. Atticus, Telys, me. And in my vision, Atticus and my grandfather discussed both of them having Metal abilities. So, my grandfather also had Metal. He must've kept it secret. Do you think when my mom found out Telys had Metal was when she started to hate him? Will she despise me, too, when she finds out about me?"

"No, Mercy. None of this will change your mom's feelings for you. Remember, Telys *chose* to join the Metalicons. That's most likely the reason she's upset with him. Face it, Mercy. Uncle Telys is on the dark side."

"Uncle Telys." Mercy reclined in her chair, twiddled her thumbs, and then leaned forward toward Tambora. "Don't let my mom hear you say that."

Tambora became serious, and she said in a voice full of innocence, "Mrs. Markos, can Mercy and her Uncle Telys come out to play?"

Mercy joined in the fun. "Mom, Uncle Telys asked me to spend the night in the Metalicon cave. Can I, please?"

Both girls erupted into cackling, the type of cackles attributed to chickens and old ladies.

Tambora went one further. "Hey, Mrs. Markos. Uncle Telys says Metalicons are good people, too."

Mercy laughed. "I've got another one. Hey, Mom. Uncle Telys says I can also become a Metalicon when I grow up." Mercy abruptly stopped her play-acting. "That's why. That's why she never told me. She knew I might have Metal and was trying to protect me."

Tambora reached across the table and covered Mercy's hands with her own. "Oh, Mercy."

"Tambora, why does life have to be so complicated?" She rose to her feet. "I think I need to go to bed now. I'm feeling exhausted."

"That's probably a good idea. Get some sleep, Mercy."

"Thank you. For everything." Mercy suspected she had never been more exhausted. "Good night, friend."

———————————◆———————————

Mercy was careful and slow to open the door to her room. She thought CJ might be asleep, and she did not want to cause a disturbance. But CJ sat up in her bunk as soon as Mercy stepped in. "I'm sorry," said Mercy. "I didn't mean to wake you."

"You didn't," CJ said and blew her nose. "I was waiting for you."

Mercy kicked her shoes off and unzipped her jeans. "Hey. Do you mind if I turn on the light?"

"I don't mind. Go ahead." CJ's voice was quiet, unlike her usual energetic tone.

Mercy found the light switch and flipped it on. CJ's eyes and nose were red and swollen and there were suitcases and clothes strewn about the room. "What's wrong?" Mercy made her way through the maze of items on the floor to her bunk.

"Mercy, I'm really sorry we didn't get to know each other better and I've been so rotten to you."

"And I'm sorry I screamed at you earlier today. I received some bad news, and I took it out on you. Please forgive me. But tomorrow is a new day and we can start fresh. Were you able to get Loy-Roy's pieces to the kitchen? What did they say?"

"Yes. They said they needed to send all the pieces to this guy who used to work at the factory where the Petit Serveurs were made. It might be months before they get it back. But they sounded hopeful."

"Oh." Mercy tried hard not to show her disappointment. "That's something, at least." She opened her dresser drawer and pulled out her most comfortable pajamas, hippie-style with a purple baby doll top and hip hugging blue and purple paisley bell bottoms, and glanced around the room. "Why is your stuff all over the floor?"

"I'm leaving the Tray early tomorrow morning."

"What? Why?"

CJ averted her gaze. "I can't stay here anymore because my parents have been banished from the Ecclesia. They were working for High Elder Atticus. Mercy, they asked me to call them every week to tell them about you and what you were doing."

Mercy's mouth hung open. "You what?" She was very close to losing the goodwill she and CJ just established.

"I'm so sorry. I didn't have any idea why they wanted to know. I thought they were interested in you because you're the High Elder's niece and because you have talents for all four elements. And I promise I didn't know he was going to attack your grandma when my parents told me to deliver a note to her, asking her to meet him. I just thought it was family business."

"*You* gave her the note?" Mercy could not bear to look at CJ and finished dressing for bed as she tried to calm the seething rage, looming just under the surface of her psyche. She reminded herself several times CJ was used by her parents. Mercy wondered what she would do if her own parents asked her to spy on her roommate. She supposed she would do it, thinking they must have a good reason. She flicked off the light, climbed into bed and tried to set aside her rising anger in favor of fairness. "I guess you didn't have a choice if your parents told you to do it. Where are you going to go when you leave here?"

"I'm going to stay with my aunt and uncle in Kiapoli on the far side of the island. My parents were taken to the Assembly where they'll be confined to a small studio apartment while they wait for their official inquiry. They haven't really done anything terrible or hurt anyone, only provided information for High Elder Atticus whenever he asked for it. Maybe they'll get to come home when the inquiry is finished."

"Not hurt anyone?" Mercy's eyes widened, taken aback by what she heard. "What about my grandma? She was hurt. She was hurt badly." A sharp intake of breath came from the other bunk.

"You're right. I wasn't thinking. I'm so sorry."

Mercy could not respond.

CJ spoke first. She sounded tired and defeated. "I really am sorry. Well. I better go to sleep. I have a big day tomorrow. Good night."

"Good night." Mercy thought she would have trouble falling asleep, but the minute she closed her eyes, she succumbed to deep, undisturbed slumber. When she awoke the next morning, CJ's bunk was empty and her belongings were gone. Although Mercy sympathized with CJ, there were many instances when she felt worn out by CJ's melodramatics, and relief was Mercy's dominant sentiment at CJ's departure, especially when Mercy considered she would probably have the room to herself for the remainder of the school year.

◆━━━━━━━━━━━━━━◆

Mercy sat across from her mother in the visitor's lounge, stone-faced with one leg crossed over the knee of the other, swinging her foot. Her arms were folded together and covered her abdomen, serving as a symbolic barrier to protect her from the unknowns in the pending conversation. Two days earlier, her parents took her grandmother to Crete, and, after making sure she would be okay, they returned to the Tray to discuss Telys with Mercy before they departed for SARA.

"Mercy, I understand this has been a shock to you. If I realized you were already in contact with Telys, we would have talked about this earlier," her mother said in their one-on-one meeting.

Mercy picked up the speed on her swinging foot. "It was a shocker, all right. But more than that, you were so cranky, and you just left me hanging. Like my feelings didn't matter."

"I understand your investment in this situation. Disregarding you wasn't my intention. I was outraged and surprised to find Telys here and back in our lives. I didn't trust myself to speak. I'm sorry I made you feel discounted."

"Why do you hate him so much?" Mercy struggled to keep her voice from shaking. Whether it was from a desire to not cry or from anger, she could not be sure.

"That's complicated. I always knew he had Metal. I have it too."

Mercy gasped, suddenly remembering the conversation between her mother and Pappas on Parents' Day. She realized they must have been talking about Mercy having Metal and that her mother knew from experience what Mercy would undergo. She felt an unexpected compassion for her mother and what she must have gone through.

Emzlie continued on. "A few months before you were born, Telys announced he was abandoning our family and joining the Metalicons. My parents pleaded with him to reconsider, but he insisted his destiny was there. The family disowned him and never spoke about him again. My father was heartbroken to lose his only son, and it haunted him until the day he died." Her mother's expression hardened and her nostrils flared. "The day he was killed by the Metalicons."

"Atticus," Mercy said. "He set it up. I don't think Telys was involved in that."

"Involved or not, he identifies himself as one of them, and I simply can't condone him becoming a part of your life."

"I think he and Grandma have kept in contact. I'm certain he was there when I had a video chat with her. She was on a portable comm."

"Yes. I've just learned about this. I don't approve and I plan on talking to my mother about it when she's feeling better."

"Surely, if Grandma stays in touch with him, it means she believes there's still good in him. Shouldn't we believe it, too?"

Mercy's mother studied her for so long, Mercy thought she was thinking up a punishment for insubordination.

"Mercy, you shouldn't be the mature one in this conversation. Of course, in theory, what you say is the right action to take." Her mother's eyes filled with tears. "But I've spent so many years being so—so *angry*. I don't think I can get over it this quickly." She raised her hands to cover her face.

Mercy pulled her mother's hands down and held them in her own. "Mom, he was a lot of help when Atticus attacked Grandma. I think he might even have been part of a plan to get evidence of it."

Mercy's mother smiled wryly and pulled out a portable comm. She dialed, and Mercy's father's voice sounded on the other end. "Orion, can you please meet me outside of the lounge? I've made a decision."

Mercy's mom stepped out and a few minutes later, both of her parents came in sat down. "Mercy." Her mom paused. "We're going to allow you to have contact with Telys, but only if he's here at the Tray and other adults are around. Under no circumstances are you to be alone with him."

Mercy's posture straightened, and she cocked her head. "Really?"

"Yes. Really." Her mother's mouth twisted as she reached for her husband's hand. "We trust your judgement and we have faith you won't be swayed to go against all we stand for. You should know your uncle and form your own opinions."

Mercy jumped up and threw her arms around her mother's neck. "Oh, Mom. Thank you." She noticed her mother tighten her hold on her father's hand. "You won't be sorry, I promise." Mercy sincerely hoped her oath would not end up on a short list called *Mercy's Unkept Promises*.

CHAPTER 27

A FATEFUL GIFT

The image in the mirror presented a wiser, more mature girl than the child who first entered the Tray four months earlier. The reflection was that of a young lady who faced a great deal about herself and the world around her. A girl who lost so much, but gained so much more.

Mercy scrutinized herself from head to toe. Loose tendrils hung in spontaneous, but striking, mayhem from her curly pinned-up hair, and tiny aqua pearls were scattered throughout her tresses. The only jewelry she wore was a pair of pearl drop earrings which once belonged to her paternal grandmother. She was dressed for the Christmas Dance that night in the first full-length gown she ever owned. Most of the students knew ahead about the dance and arrived at the beginning of the Fall term with their outfits in tow. Others were sent by their parents. Unaware of the dance when she first arrived, Mercy and her mother took a trip to a fancy shop in Nikonea City to purchase the gown after their heart-to-heart chat before her mother rejoined the Ecclesia. The white sleeveless bodice was covered in white Venetian lace with a wide aqua satin ribbon at the waist. Mercy twirled around. She loved to watch the full ball gown billow out. The sheerest of white chiffon overlaid the aqua satin skirt. Earlier in the day, she spent an hour admiring the scrolling vines of lacy flowers and paisley leaves of the hemline applique which matched the lace of the bodice. Mercy gathered the skirt into her hands and lifted it to view her shoes. Aqua velveteen ballerina flats with wide satin ribbons laced around her ankles. Mercy never thought of herself as much of a princess, but she admitted she felt spectacular.

There was an understanding among the group that they would all attend the ball solo. The no-date situation was ideal, in Mercy's opinion. It created the perfect scenario for her and Phin to spend time together in a boy-girl situation without the embarrassment of going on an actual date. She hoped he would think she was pretty and ask her to dance.

A knock sounded on her door. She opened it to find a Situation Clock hovering there. It chimed, "It is 6:00, and almost time for Cinderella to leave for the ball."

Mercy grinned and reached out to pet the clock. They were ornery, for sure, but after one woke her and prompted her to search for her grandma, she called a truce with them. "I'll be down in two minutes," she said. She checked herself in the mirror once more and dashed from the room. She slowed down when she reached the second floor to give herself time to catch her breath. She intended to make a grand entrance down the stairs into the lobby. Her breathing was normal when she reached the top of the final staircase, but her heart pounded. She stood still and observed her friends by the water garden, whispering.

Vesuvius sported a smart black tuxedo with satin lapels, a white shirt, and black bow tie. His normally tousled hair was combed down in a sleek side part. Tambora wore a chic full-length midnight blue silk A-line gown. Topped with a velvet off-shoulder band, the fitted bodice ended with a thin, simple velvet belt at her waist. Mercy beamed at Tambora when their eyes met and Tambora ran toward the stairs, her skirt rippling behind her.

Mercy began her descent, holding onto the railing for her coy entrance. She caught sight of Phin embroiled in a conversation with Beau. After Conrad's expulsion, Beau became a somewhat more tolerable version of himself, and the group attempted to be civil to their former tormentor.

Mercy almost swooned at the image of Phin, dressed in all black, and she gripped the rail tighter to keep from losing her balance. His tuxedo jacket with the mandarin collar was casually open, revealing a tailored black vest and black shirt. He completed the ensemble with a narrow black tie. With his long dreads tied in a ponytail and one hand in his trouser pocket, he appeared every inch like the bad boy she knew would one day upend her heart. She took a few more steps down the stairs, eager to join him in the lobby.

Phin caught sight of Mercy and his periwinkle eyes grew large and round. He moved to the stairway and stood with one foot on the bottom step. "Whoa. Mercy, you look fabulous."

Mercy offered a timid smile and her cheeks grew hot. She glanced down to take the last few steps. She lifted her eyes, ready to connect with Phin. Instead, she witnessed Adele Grayson, with her perfect blonde curls and pretty rose gold frock, sidle up to Phin and slip her hand through his arm.

Adele tugged at him. "Come on, Phin, I'm thirsty."

Phin grinned at Mercy and said, "Adele is my date tonight," as he was dragged away.

Mercy raised her brows and her voice went up an octave. "Oh," she said with a plastic smile glued onto her face. What was he doing on a date, she wondered. Hadn't they all said they were going stag? She was sure they did.

Vesuvius followed Phin, but glanced back briefly before he sprinted to catch up to Phin. "You really look great, Mercy."

"Thank you." Mercy whispered in a barely audible tone. Phin's date caught her off guard. She no longer enjoyed any anticipation for the dance and spun around to flee to her room, wishing fairytales would tell girls what to do if Prince Charming chose someone else.

"Mercy, wait." Tambora hiked up her skirt and sprinted up the steps. "I understand how you must feel right now. Don't think I haven't noticed how you look at Phin."

"You know I like him?"

"I do. But I kept quiet because *you* kept quiet. Best friend code four point five. 'Thou shalt not say any—' "

"If you knew how I felt, why didn't you warn me about Adele?" Mercy interrupted, not in the mood to listen to a recitation of codes.

"If I knew Phin was bringing a date, I would have told you." Tambora grabbed Mercy's hand. "Hey. Don't let them keep you from our biggest party of the year. We deserve—YOU deserve—to have some fun. Come on down. The dining hall looks so lovely with the cream and gold decor. And there are massive portals open on each end of the room, making it three times as large. We can stay on the opposite side from them and we don't even need to see them at all during the evening. Please? I have no one to dance with. We'll have loads of fun. And when it's over, we'll swipe some popcorn from the kitchen and take it up to your room and trash talk boys."

Mercy attempted a smile. She did not want to be responsible for Tambora being alone at the ball. She knew Vesuvius would hang out with Phin all night. She allowed Tambora to walk her down into the lobby. When they strolled past the floral arrangements sprinkled throughout the lobby, the flowers stood straighter and their blooms opened wider, tugging at Mercy's heart. She reached out her hand to stroke their petals as she passed them.

Voices came from the stairwell. Tambora tugged on Mercy's arm. "Mercy, look," she whispered. "I think Mr. and Mrs. Kishan are bringing down all their luggage."

Mercy moved to the base of the stairs as her teachers approached. "Mr. Kishan, aren't you coming to the dance?"

Mr. Kishan put a hand on Mercy's shoulder. His eyes misted over. "No, Mercy. We're leaving the Tray. The Assembly has pardoned us for our part in the High Elder's scheme, but they've ruled we've been compromised. It is no longer appropriate for us to stay here."

"I don't understand."

"We cooperated with Atticus because he seized our children. The perception of the Assembly is that we've shown ourselves to have a weakness and we are no longer considered completely trustworthy to not yield to it again. And they are correct to assume this. I would do the same in their position."

"But it was me Atticus had you observing and I'm not complaining. I'll tell them I don't care. Who can I talk to?"

"You may talk to me." Magister Pappas strode into the lobby, wearing the black and gold brocade jacket Mercy loved so much. "I have been named as the interim High Elder, but I am afraid it will do you no good to petition me. This was the decision of the Assembly as a whole."

"And we completely agree, High Elder." Mr. Kishan pressed his hands together under his chin and bent into a slight bow.

"We are okay with this decision," Mrs. Kishan said, repeating her husband's movement. "This will free us to work full time on getting our children out of the hands of the Metalicons."

Mercy was not ready to give up. "I can help get them back. I'll talk to Telys. He's my uncle, you know."

"No, Mercy. Leave Telys out of this." High Elder Pappas cleared his throat. "He can be of no help here. I ask for you to keep your distance from him."

"Why? My mom said I could visit with him," she demanded. He was her family and therefore, it was her right to know.

Pappas burrowed his brows. "For reasons that jeopardize the safety of many members of the Ecclesia and Assembly, including your own parents, not to mention the students at the Tray."

Mercy opened her mouth to argue, but Mr. Kishan interrupted her. "Mercy, we appreciate your concern and willingness to help, but this really is what is best for all involved."

Mercy longed to voice her disapproval, but integrity informed her impulses the world did not revolve around her desires. The reminder kept her quiet.

The red revolving door spun and Mr. Romani entered, followed by a burst of children of various ages. Each resembled miniature versions of Mr. or Mrs. Kishan. With cries of thaath-tha and am-ma, which Mercy assumed meant father and mother, they ran to Mr. and Mrs. Kishan, who dropped their luggage and rushed forward to greet the children with hugs and kisses.

Mr. Romani spoke. "Atticus finally talked and told us where the Kishan children were being held. The Assembly deployed a rescue team.

Sorry, Pelagius. We had no time to fill you in. The Metalicons were getting ready to move the children to an undisclosed location."

"Understood," the High Elder said. "Casualties?"

"None."

"Then, all is well," Pappas said as Mr. Romani headed toward the makeshift ballroom.

Mrs. Kishan put a hand on her husband's arm. "Nedim, we really must be going." She embraced Mercy and Tambora. "Girls, it's been an honor to have taught you. Harmony and balance to you both."

"Harmony and balance, Mrs. Kishan." Mercy and Tambora said in unison, their voices dejected.

Mr. Kishan clasped Mercy's shoulder. "You have come so far, but you still have far to go. I believe in you. Just remember to breathe. Remember to focus. I do not fear for you, as you have proven your ability to rise above your disappointments and disillusionments."

"Thank you, Mr. Kishan. I wish you all the best in the world." Mercy wiped her eyes. "Harmony and balance."

"Harmony and balance, Mercy. Take care." With that word of farewell, the Kishans left through the red revolving door of the Tray, disappearing into the night.

"Magist—um, High Elder, may I ask what happened when you and Mr. Romani confronted Atticus in his office that night?" Mercy asked. Peering into the acting High Elder's eyes, Mercy's vision shifted, and she and Mr. Romani entered the High Elder's office at the Assembly.

"It is over, Atticus," Mercy said. "There is no point to continued insurgence. Come peacefully with us and we can make sure you are treated fairly and humanely." It took a moment, but she realized she, once again, experienced the scene through the eyes of someone else. This time, she viewed through the magister's eyes.

"I will do no such thing," Atticus spat.

"Then you leave us with no choice." Mercy raised her hand, but Atticus was faster and threw a series of fireballs at her. Mr. Romani, however, was even quicker and put up a wall of water to douse the flames. With the former High Elder's attention diverted, she stepped out from behind the water and created a whirlwind around Atticus to hold him captive while she, from the viewpoint of Pappas, chanted an abbreviated version of the same restraining narrative he used at her own restraining ceremony.

Atticus struggled to free himself, screaming curses to both Pappas and Romani, dooming them to eternal agony deep within the bowels of Vatek.

She addressed Mr. Romani. "Rogelio, would you care to do the honors?"

"With pleasure," Mr. Romani said and threw a small capsule to the floor which became a large standing glass box, similar to what Mercy saw in the Metalicon cave. "Atticus Kadarius, I confine you to the Assembly containment chamber until such time as the Ara'Jaeon Assembly sees fit." He grabbed the older man's arm and shoved him through the door of the box, closing it behind Atticus, and leaving him enclosed within. Mr. Romani then tossed a small crystal and named the Assembly as his destination. A portal developed and she and Mr. Romani carefully pushed the glass box through the portal, then jumped through themselves.

Mercy blinked, breaking eye contact with her teacher. She stood in the Tray lobby, shocked at what she experienced and unsure why the visions happened again. Pappas addressed her, answering her question about his confrontation with Atticus as if no time passed since she asked him. "There was a bit of a struggle, but nothing we could not handle. Atticus is now in the Assembly containment chambers, awaiting his trial."

High Elder Pappas offered his arms to both girls. "Ladies, will you allow me to escort you into the dance?" Mercy swallowed hard and took hold of the High Elder's elbow. Tambora chatted animatedly during the short stroll, but Mercy kept her eyes downcast, wishing the night was over.

Gold fairy lights were strung throughout the darkened dining room. The extra-large open portals on both sides of the room created a space so big, Mercy felt small and invisible. White drapery disguised the transition between the dining hall and the portal rooms. It was beautiful and Mercy hoped the evening would not be as horrible as she expected.

The dance band was not set up yet and Mr. Romani was in a corner directing several Wind and Water students as they performed Christmas music with their talents. Bamboo pan flutes began the airy musical introduction to Dance of the Sugarplum Fairy. Students with Water skills manipulated drinking glasses, filled with water at various levels, and picked up the resonating main melody while the pan flutes continued to play in the background. It was a pleasant cover of the traditional orchestral version of Tchaikovsky's popular composition.

Against her better judgement, Mercy scanned the room for Phin and Adele. She located them standing by the punch table. Adele said something and touched Phin's arm. Phin laughed, firing a bullet straight into Mercy's heart. She turned away and focused on Miss Carmen, who ambled around, fiddling with the decor. Mercy rubbed her wrists where the binding cuffs once rested. After the confrontation with Atticus, Pappas took over Mercy's training. He told her it was pointless for her to wear them because of her capability to break their hold. Instead, he worked with her on how to control her gifts. Mercy wondered if he would have time to continue with her training and his duties at the Tray once he officially took over as interim High Elder. She worried he might be named the next High Elder and he would quit the Tray entirely. She hoped not. The past few months taught her she needed practice—and lots of it—if she were to do battle with Azrael someday. Pappas was her best shot at honing her skills.

The dance band finished setting up. The drummer played a few measures of a driving disco beat and the keyboard came in with the intro bars of the old 1980s tune, *I'm So Excited*, by the Pointer Sisters.

"I love this song," Tambora yelled above the music. "Let's dance."

Mercy abandoned her desire to be alone, deciding she would attempt to forget her frustrations for at least one night. "I'm trying to be a good sport here, but I'm not a hundred percent sure I'm ready for this much excitement right away. I need to ease into it," Mercy said.

"Come on, you promised."

"I didn't." Mercy pretended to laugh.

"You came with your best friend to a dance. That signifies a promise, according to the best friend code number 27."

Mercy rolled her eyes. "You'll never run out of codes, will you?"

"Nope." Tambora bounced in place, acting impatient to get her groove on. "Admit it. This song was made for dancing."

"Okay. You win," Mercy said.

Tambora grooved onto the dance floor, raised her arms in the air and jumped around in a circle. Mercy danced with her, wishing the exuberance of the animated music resonated with her, as well. But the lyrics only reminded her of her earlier excitement for the evening when she planned to get closer to Phin and later on when his date with Adele gutted her. The band finished the first song and went into another dance number, *Happy*, by Pharrell Williams. Mercy noted a theme in the music and blamed the universe for sarcastically aiming the message directly at her. Vesuvius joined her and Tambora, performing his own version of the twist, a dance from the 1960s. His goofy moves compelled Mercy to dance freely. Her heart lightened as she and Tambora squealed over Vesu's antics until she glimpsed Phin and Adele. Amid the wild dancing, they alone performed a slow dance. Adele gazed up at Phin. Her forearms rested on his shoulders and her hands were placed behind his head. He held her waist and his head was down, their foreheads almost touching. Mercy stood still and stared at them. The music faded to a distant hum and everything around her blurred except for Phin and Adele. She heard her heart beat in her ears as she bid farewell to her hopes. The song ended, and the room became noisy again to Mercy's ears, but she still felt disconnected and disoriented.

She leaned into Tambora and yelled, "I'm going to go get some punch."

"Okay. I'll join you in a minute."

Mercy nodded and hurried away toward the food and drink area, but once she was out of Tambora's sight, she made a run for the door and fled. She ran up the entire seven floors to her room. She wanted to get out of her gown. She would never be a princess and possessed no business pretending otherwise. She stopped when she realized the door to her room stood ajar. She thought she shut it earlier when she left for the dance, but she admitted to herself, she might not have closed it hard enough in her haste to leave. She hesitated before she nudged it open, bit by bit. She peeked around the door and gazed into the dark room, trying to scan for any movement. She sensed nothing suspicious, so she reached for the light switch on the wall and turned it on. The room was as she left it, except for a gift-wrapped package on the floor. She picked it up to glance at the tag. *Merry Christmas, Mercy*, was written on the card. She did not recognize the handwriting and there was no signature. She wondered who sent it, but she wanted to prolong the anticipation. She set the package on her desk to open after she changed into her pajamas. She arranged her princess clothing and accessories in a box and packed them away inside her trunk to take home at the end of the school year.

She sat at her desk, examining the wrapped gift. She allowed the warm feeling of knowing someone thought of her to wash over and soothe the brokenness of her heart. It was a night filled with highs and lows, like the bouncing of a rubber ball, and she just wanted peace for the rest of the evening. She picked up the present and studied the wrapping and bow. The gift wrap was metallic gold, and the bow was made from metallic silver ribbon with randomly printed gold stars. It looked elegant, like something Tambora would send. But she was with Tambora from the time Mercy arrived in the lobby until she left the ball. At no time could Tambora have slipped out to put a gift in Mercy's room. She put the gift down and paced the room to prolong the excitement, all the while, keeping one eye on her prize.

A light tap on the door grabbed Mercy's attention. "Just a minute," she called out. She did not feel like sharing the surprise of her gift, so she hid it in one of CJ's empty drawers. Just as Mercy closed the drawer, her door opened.

Tambora peeked in. "Hey. I just wanted to make sure you're okay. You weren't at the punch table when I went to find you. You've changed out of your gown. Did something happen?"

"No… I… uh… well, yes. I saw Phin and Adele dancing, looking googly eyed at each other. I needed to get away."

"Oh. I'm sorry. I'll go change and we can spend the evening together. Maybe we could go out for a walk."

Mercy's eyes darted toward the drawer which held her gift. "I think I would just rather be alone. Maybe I'll do some writing. You go back to the party and have fun." Mercy grabbed Tambora's hand and led her to the door. "There are a lot of boys who I'm sure would love to dance with you. Go make yourself available. We have plenty of time we can talk. Christmas break starts tomorrow and we have two entire weeks, Remember? All of us students will be here over Christmas."

"Right. Because something is going on with the Ecclesia and none of our parents are coming home for the holiday."

Mercy inched toward the door, hoping Tambora would follow. "And we know what that is, don't we? The Metalicons have gotten the Fire orb and are searching for the others."

"I hope the Ecclesia can stop them."

"They will. They're brilliant at what they do." Mercy opened the door.

Tambora stepped into the hall. "Are you certain you don't want me to stick around?"

"I'm sure. Go have fun. You can tell me all about it tomorrow."

"Good night, Mercy."

"G'nite, Tam." Mercy closed the door. Unable to bear the suspense any longer, she grabbed the gift from the dresser drawer and tore the paper off. Inside was a simple cardboard box which was taped closed. She opened her desk drawer and pulled out a pair of scissors to cut the tape. Once the tape was cut, she took a deep breath. Behind her slightly parted lips, a genuine smile lurked, waiting for the opportunity to break free. With careful movements, she opened the box flaps. Inside was an object covered in black tissue paper and a note on top. Not very festive, she thought, but who can fault the wrapping on a gift? She opened the note. It read, *You know what needs to be done.* Mercy pulled back the tissue and gasped. She recoiled and jumped to her feet, shocked by the contents of the box. She waited across the room, her back pressed against the door as she came to terms with the contents of the box. Who would give her such a thing? Was it done purposely or was it simply a matter of fate? Her heart pounded hard, pulsating up to her throat. She tiptoed back to her desk and stood over the gift, peering in, but not touching anything. It was ancient and primitive, nothing special about it at all. No ornamentation, no engravings. Just pieces of a humble broken circlet with a few crude spikes poking out of the top. Not like what she would expect from something attached to so much destiny. Her thoughts were in turmoil. Should she get rid of it? If she did, would it fall into the wrong hands? That occurrence could bring about disaster. What would happen if she kept it? She would need to keep it hidden. She did not want anyone to discover it was in her possession. Would she live in fear of it being detected? But someone knew she had it. The someone who gave it to her. Mercy summoned all the courage she could muster and quickly reached out, throwing the tissue paper over it. She tossed the box top back on, trying to not touch anything, then flung it into her trunk to disappear along with the despised ballgown. She contemplated asking for help, but her emotional state was not prepared to deal with it. For the first time, she locked the trunk. With the broken crown out of sight, she controlled its future. When the time came, she intended to refuse to fix it.

Mercy tossed and turned all night, only falling asleep just before dawn. A voice called from the hall and awakened her early. "Mail," it said from the other side. She sat up in bed and saw an envelope slide under her door. She climbed down her bunk ladder, reluctant to open it, but her mother's handwriting dispelled her fears. She snatched up the letter from the floor and ripped it open. Inside was a Christmas card from her parents, accompanied by a note and a gift card to an electronics store in Nikonea City. The letter stated she would soon be thirteen, so she could use the gift card to get the messaging and translation device they previously said she needed to wait for. She fidgeted to keep from screaming, because she wanted to finish reading the letter. Her mother explained their assignment would not soon be over. They would not be home over the summer to care for her. When school let out for summer break, she would leave the island to stay with her grandmother in Crete for the entire summer.

Her thirteenth birthday was soon. She would have the device she wanted, but even more thrilling, she would be old enough to leave the island, away from all the troubles, the prophecy, and worry over who in Vatek was trying to get free and influence her. She was going to experience the world outside of Ara'Ja for the entire summer with her beloved grandma.

She threw on a robe and slippers and ran out to celebrate with Tambora. The memories of the previous evening—the disappointment over Phin and the shock of receiving the crown she would repair—erased from her mind. Only excitement remained. The future did not look so bleak, after all.

———————◆———————

The Situation Clock zoomed to Mercy's room on a mission. The door stood ajar, and the clock slipped in, ready to give the time and state of affairs. But Mercy was nowhere to be seen. It pondered whether to go ahead with the announcement as the intended receiver was not there to hear it, but the duty of a Situation Clock was an unalterable compulsion, and it chimed the message it was compelled to give.

"It is 8:35, and that which is forgotten will be returned to remembrance in unforgettable ways."

THE END

ABOUT THE AUTHOR

Sally Gratz Garcia was born and raised in Battle Creek, Michigan, where she spent her early years with her nose firmly entrenched into countless books, singing in school choirs, and practicing piano for her dad's listening pleasure. She currently resides in Warsaw, Indiana. She has two grown sons and five grandchildren. Sally enjoys listening and singing along to most genres of music, playing keyboard, cooking, crafting, and being with family. *Mercy Markos and the Blades of Betrayal* is Sally's first novel. She is presently writing a sequel.

NOTE FROM THE AUTHOR

Word-of-mouth is crucial for any author to succeed. If you enjoyed *Mercy Markos and the Blades of Betrayal*, please leave a review online—anywhere you are able. Even if it's just a sentence or two. It would make all the difference and would be very much appreciated.

Thanks!
Sally Gratz Garcia

We hope you enjoyed reading this title from:

BLACK ROSE
writing™

www.blackrosewriting.com

Subscribe to our mailing list – *The Rosevine* – and receive **FREE** books, daily deals, and stay current with news about upcoming releases and our hottest authors.
Scan the QR code below to sign up.

Already a subscriber? Please accept a sincere thank you for being a fan of Black Rose Writing authors.

View other Black Rose Writing titles at www.blackrosewriting.com/books and use promo code **PRINT** to receive a **20% discount** when purchasing.